Praise for Annette Christie's

THE REHEARSALS

"Funny, romantic, and surprisingly thought-provoking, *The Rehearsals* is both a highly enjoyable romp and a poignant meditation on love and second chances."　　　　　　　　*—Shelf Awareness*

"Romantic escapism with an irresistible *Groundhog Day* twist. You will be charmed by Megan and Tom as they relive the worst day of their lives...until they get it right. Annette Christie has written a fun yet thought-provoking rom-com."
　　　　　　　　　—Elin Hilderbrand, *Marie Claire*

"A funny, clever, enchanting story about finding our way back to ourselves and to those we truly love. *The Rehearsals* is refreshingly honest about the ups and downs of long-term relationships, whether romantic or family, handling its themes with wit and zest. Terrific fun from beginning to end!"
　　　　　　　　—Sarah Haywood, author of *The Cactus*

"A delightful debut...Christie's clever time-loop plot allows for great depth of emotion as her protagonists explore different paths and come to terms with what they can and can't change about themselves and each other. This charming story delivers equal amounts of honesty and hope and is bound to win the hearts of rom-com fans."　　　　　　　　*—Publishers Weekly*

"The only thing worse than living the same day over and over, à la *Groundhog Day*? Doing so with your fiancé after calling off your wedding, which is exactly what happens in Christie's debut about the power of second chances."   —*E! Online*

"This story delivers, one hundred percent, on the promise of its intriguing premise. Christie grabbed me on the first page and didn't let me go…A touching novel by a wonderfully talented author."   —Mary Simses, author of *The Wedding Thief*

"A deeply special book, warm and wise and filled with undeniable tenderness."   —Rachel Lynn Solomon, author of *The Ex Talk*

"A compelling, clever look at the hard work of growing up in our relationships—with friends, family, lovers, and ourselves."   —Rosie Danan, author of *The Roommate*

"A whip-smart *Groundhog Day* reincarnation that will have you laughing and cringing in equal measure. *The Rehearsals* not only takes you on a wild ride; it forces you to ask if you're living your best life. Hilarious, heartfelt, and stay-up-all-night addictive."   —Kelly Siskind, author of *The Knockout Rule*

"Christie keeps the tone light…There's a feeling of resolution at the end, which isn't what the characters expected, but it's what they needed. Fans of Christina Lauren and Meg Cabot will savor this charming relationship comedy."   —*Booklist*

"Sparkling and witty…Through Tom and Megan, we discover the importance of second or more chances, and how learning to listen (to others and yourself) is the key to love and happiness."   —Roselle Lim, author of *Natalie Tan's Book of Luck and Fortune*

"Christie is a master of creating characters that feel like friends, where you hate to turn that last page and say goodbye."

—Jen DeLuca, author of *Well Met*

"A humorous, honest look at the complexities of relationships and the sacrifices we make to maintain them."

—Suzanne Park, author of *So We Meet Again*

"Utterly delightful...Christie beautifully weaves wedding angst with secrets, betrayals, confrontation, and what it really means to choose someone else, and yourself."

—Laurie Elizabeth Flynn,
author of *The Girls Are All So Nice Here*

"A clever and engrossing story...I loved the whole backdrop to the *Groundhog Day*–style predicament: the picturesque wedding venue, the clashing families, and the way the recurring day developed layers and surprises."

—Helen Cooper, author of *The Downstairs Neighbor*

"Utterly captivating, charming, and brilliant. With a compelling plot and relatable characters, *The Rehearsals* explores the raw emotions behind the question of 'what if' and the true meaning of second chances."   —Sonia Hartl, author of *Heartbreak for Hire*

"Megan's and Tom's betrayals are explored compassionately and honestly...A compelling story about the power of second chances and forgiveness that's sure to spark conversation."

—*Kirkus Reviews*

THE REHEARSALS

ANNETTE CHRISTIE

BACK BAY BOOKS
Little, Brown and Company
New York   Boston   London

Copyright © 2021 by Alloy Entertainment, LLC
Reading Group Guide copyright © 2022 by Annette Christie and Little, Brown and Company
Excerpt from *For Twice in My Life* copyright © 2022 by Annette Christie

Back Bay Books / Little, Brown and Company
Hachette Book Group
1290 Avenue of the Americas, New York, NY 10104
littlebrown.com

Originally published in hardcover by Little, Brown, July 2021
First Back Bay paperback edition, July 2022

Back Bay Books is an imprint of Little, Brown and Company, a division of Hachette Book Group, Inc. The Back Bay Books name and logo are trademarks of Hachette Book Group, Inc.

The publisher is not responsible for websites (or their content) that are not owned by the publisher.

The Hachette Speakers Bureau provides a wide range of authors for speaking events. To find out more, go to hachettespeakersbureau.com or call (866) 376-6591.

ISBN 9780316592994 (hc) / 9780316592970 (pb)
LCCN 2020945528

Printing 2, 2022

LSC-C

Printed in the United States of America

For MLC—
I'd choose you over and over and over again

DAY

1

CHAPTER ONE

MEGAN

BEGIN AS YOU *mean to go on.*

These were the words Tom and Megan spoke to each other every New Year's Eve after kissing at midnight and before running like hell from whatever social event they'd agreed to attend while the rest of the party guests mumble-sang their way through "Auld Lang Syne." Because every new year all Megan and Tom really wanted to do was hole up in their cozy apartment and spend the night feasting on cheese platters, champagne, and each other.

Begin as you mean to go on.

It was fitting, then, that these were the first words in Megan's mind as she opened her eyes the day before her wedding. The thought was followed swiftly by a mental checklist she swatted away as she remembered that, at this point, all the details fell on the shoulders of the resort's very capable wedding planner. He was responsible for five weddings this long weekend alone, the September holiday being a popular time for big events, so he could certainly handle the Givens/Prescott affair.

Megan luxuriated in the hotel linens for a moment more before swinging her legs around and padding across the chilly hardwood floor. The tile in the bathroom was heated. She made a beeline for it. When her toes got cold, they took forever to warm up again.

The complimentary fluffy white robe hung on the back of the bathroom door. She pulled it around her, put her slightly warmer feet into the accompanying slippers, and drew the curtains back on the expansive bay window, blinking in the bright light. Staying in the suite came with a myriad of perks; the view of Roche Harbor was her favorite.

It was early and yet there was movement outside already. Young children, still clad in pajamas, clutched towels and travel-size shampoos as they walked with their grown-ups across the wooden docks of the marina to the public showers.

From the window Megan could even see her grandparents' rickety sailboat, *Happy Accident*, featuring an emerald-green hull in need of a paint job and rotting wood trim. The summers she'd spent here on that boat enveloped her, warming her more than the heated floor had, because sailing trips were a time of ultimate freedom. They were the rare moments when Megan's secret sense of adventure could be indulged and she could give up being "the responsible one" for a while, knowing her gran was in charge.

That's why she was here, back on the island she'd escaped to every summer with her family. While she'd grown up in Montana, somehow San Juan Island had felt more like home, and she'd always hoped it would be the place she'd get married.

Being here was perfect. She had everything she needed to throw the wedding she'd dreamed about for years. Save for her fiancé.

Megan checked her phone and felt a tingle of anticipation when she saw Tom had sent a message while she was still sleeping.

Plane landed. On my way to the ferry.

She smiled instinctively. Once they were on the same landmass again she'd feel even better. She sent him a text that read Tell that ferry driver to step on it along with a selfie, knowing he'd laugh at the way her bedhead made her look like a troll doll ("Only cuter," he'd always add).

The faint beep of a key card carried through the door. *That conniver*, she thought with glee. He was here already, throwing her off with his "plane landed" texts. Megan dropped the curtain and was just about to drop her robe to surprise Tom with a little tasteful pre-wedding nudity when her mother burst into the suite. Megan quickly tightened her belt.

"I've heard Amazon can deliver same day, but every dress I've looked at says it ships in one to two weeks." One hand on the small of her back, the other pressed against her chest, Donna Givens was living up to her reputation for overreacting.

Megan adopted the soothing tone she reserved for this woman who, despite birthing her, played the role of the child in their relationship. "Mom. What are you doing with a key to my room?"

"They gave you two at check-in, dear, really. I grabbed the second one." She opened the curtains wider, blinding herself—and Megan—with the abrasive morning sunlight.

"The second one is for Tom."

"Yes, well, Tom isn't here, is he?" Donna took a seat on the chaise longue beside the fireplace. Her blazing hair could easily be mistaken for flames.

"He couldn't miss his client dinner last night." Megan's tone was inching on defensive. She wasn't happy about Tom's delayed arrival either, but they both had demanding jobs and long ago had made a pact to allow work to come first when necessary. Having Tom hop on a red-eye and get here a little later was an easy compromise.

Donna sniffed, fiddling with the scarf around her neck. "Choosing work over wife. That's Husband Number Three behavior."

Megan bristled. And not just because it was behavior more reminiscent of Donna's fourth husband (the workaholic who now had a picture-perfect family the next county over) than her third (the belligerent drunk she threw out after two weeks and often forgot she'd even married). She bristled because Tom wasn't *anything* like the husbands and boyfriends cycling through Donna's revolving door of paramours. Because, and this was more to the point, Megan wasn't anything like Donna.

Megan toyed with her engagement ring, rubbing at it absentmindedly with her thumb. Tom worked a lot, but he wasn't a workaholic. He'd simply had a dinner he couldn't miss. She wasn't sure why, and, truthfully, it'd felt as though Tom was skirting the issue when she'd inquired. Regardless, she trusted him. If he said the meeting was nonnegotiable, it was. "What were you saying about dresses and Amazon?"

"I need something to wear to the rehearsal dinner tonight." Donna gazed out the window. "You can see Gran and Granddad's boat from here."

"I know. I saw." Keeping her mother focused on her crisis long enough to solve it wasn't a new battle for Megan, who quickly sorted through her long-accrued arsenal. She sat down beside her mother on the chaise, took both her hands, and waited for Donna's attention to return.

Donna looked back.

"You have a dress," Megan gently reminded her mother.

"I have an uninspired frock." Donna reclaimed her hands and stood to pace the room. "It isn't posh enough."

"Why are you being British this morning?"

It was the wrong thing to say. Donna's face reddened. When Megan's mother fell into one of her erratic moods, it was best to put a stop to the spiral while it was nice and slow. Since Donna could rarely resist flattery, that was where Megan would start. "Mom, the dress is beautiful. You look beautiful in it. Wrap dresses make everyone look ten years younger."

"I tried it on this morning and Gran…"

"What did Gran do?"

"She called me a floozy."

"Gran once called Brianna and me floozies because we went to Seven-Eleven while wearing pajamas. *Flannel* pajamas," Megan pointed out. Her grandmother was always butting heads with Donna, but Megan and her sister had long ago learned to laugh at the elderly woman's stodgy sass. Besides, what Gran lacked in tact, she more than made up for in hugs and home-cooked meals, two things Donna didn't excel at, and two things the girls had always craved.

For as long as Megan could remember, she'd been the emotional thermostat of the family. Her mother ran too hot, ricocheting between men who likewise boiled or were too cool, filling their home with fevers and chills. With both Megan's siblings equally unreliable, it became her job to maintain the balance. Some days this was a more difficult task than others.

"Have you heard from Alistair yet?" Megan had two motives for asking about her brother. First, it would distract Donna, and second, Megan needed to let the restaurant know exactly how many people were attending the dinner that night.

Donna waved away the question. Her mother no longer bothered trying to keep tabs on Alistair. Instead, she chose to be demonstrably elated when she did see him and all but forgot his existence when she didn't.

"He's taking after his father more and more every day." Donna inhaled deeply, as though she were the heroine of a story filled with unredeemable villains.

Donna had met Husband Number One, Alistair's father, at a bonfire in high school. They fell in love when they were drunk, fell out of love when they sobered up, and had been repeating this pattern ever since. He was the one husband who kept returning, but as soon as Donna got attached, he'd make a break for I-15 and ride it out of Montana. Megan's and Brianna's father, also known as Husband Number Two, had been Donna's rebound. Their marriage lasted long enough to bring the two girls into the world but ended shortly thereafter. Although their dad lived in Great Falls, Megan and Brianna never saw him. His lack of interest had inspired Megan's own. She thought of him as rarely as he, apparently, thought of her.

Megan crossed the room to her mother and stroked her drugstore-dyed ginger hair. "Gran's old-fashioned. I'm sure you look stunning in your dress."

"Her criticisms are just one more thing on my plate this weekend." Donna pouted as though *she* were the one getting married. This self-pitying face was usually accompanied by the line "Cheer me up, Moopy." Megan beat her to it, pulling out more tools.

She hugged her mother. "You're exquisite. The dress is perfection. I guarantee Tom's mother will be jealous of how fabulous you look."

Donna brightened, straightening up. "That's it!"

"What?"

"You can go by and see Tom's parents, just to check in because you're such a thoughtful future daughter-in-law, and then you can ask Carol what she's wearing tonight so I can follow suit."

"I'm not—"

"I love you, Moopy." Donna kissed Megan's temple and dashed out the door, wiggling a goodbye with her fingers.

"I love you too, Mom."

Feeling drained already, Megan shut the door behind her mother and glanced at the hotel's alarm clock. At least Tom's ferry was due to arrive soon. Showering could wait. She settled for spraying in some dry shampoo, arranging her hair into an artful topknot, and putting on a casual jersey-knit dress. Megan smiled as she added the final touch: the delicate filigree chain and heart pendant she'd laid on the dresser the night before. It was the first gift Tom had ever given her, back when they were eighteen. It'd been a bit on the nose for Valentine's Day, but Tom had picked it out all by himself, hoping and believing he had achieved the height of romance.

And he had.

The vulnerable, earnest look on his face when she'd opened the box caused her chest to ache with an overwhelming need to make him as happy as he'd just made her.

Later he'd admitted it was the first present he'd ever given to a girl. Megan was a first for him in a lot of ways.

She hadn't worn the necklace in years but she'd pulled it out for this weekend to remind them both of how they'd fallen for each other in a beautifully clumsy and all-encompassing way. Looking at it gleaming against her collarbones, Megan was surprised by how quickly it carried her back in time.

She'd met Tom their freshman year in Natural Disasters, a science class they'd each chosen because it was an easy A. From day one, she'd found herself stealing glances at the guy with a sexy sensible haircut and strong jaw who smiled and laughed readily. Yes, he was objectively good-looking—*very* good-looking— but there was something more, something intrinsically gentle and endearing about him; when she looked at him, she'd felt as if an invisible thread connected them.

The second week, she'd forgone her usual spot in the back and deliberately sat five rows down. Right beside him.

He'd smiled shyly.

She'd joked that, if given a noogie and some red lipstick, their professor would be the spitting image of Robert Smith from the Cure. He immediately got the reference, and they spent the remaining half hour writing their favorite lyrics from "Just Like Heaven" and "Pictures of You" in the margins of each other's notebooks, and her life had never been the same.

From that day on, Megan and Tom were practically inseparable. They went to lunch together every day and picked food off each other's plates. They played Frisbee on the quad. They took the long route to their classes, fall leaves sweeping around them. Megan soon felt Tom's permanence in her life. It seemed as though he'd been there forever, even when he hadn't; as though he would continue to be there forever now that he was.

While they'd come a long way from those carefree early days, they'd felt married for as long as they'd been together, so they'd never been in any rush to corral their two divisive families into one overhyped weekend. But now, after twelve years together, they were making it official. Something about turning thirty felt right, a next step to mark all that they'd shared—and perhaps for once to bring their two worlds together.

Rubbing the pendant affectionately between her thumb and index finger, Megan grabbed the keys to the rental car and headed out to meet her fiancé.

But first, she would swing by the Prescott suite to do some dress reconnaissance. When she knocked and no one answered, Megan felt a bit relieved and decided she'd grab breakfast while half-heartedly looking for Carol. The resort was small enough that locating her future mother-in-law wouldn't be a challenge.

On summer weekends, local artisans and vendors flocked to Roche Harbor for an elegant market held just outside the hotel. It was one of Megan's favorite things about the island, a way to connect to the people who lived here and to memories of summers past. Today, the salt air was invigorating and there was just a hint left over of the morning chill. Megan stopped at two booths to pick up some scones and coffee, and, sure enough, she spotted Tom's mother doing the same.

"Good morning, Carol." Megan had been with Tom for years, but somehow every conversation with John and Carol made her feel like Bambi struggling to his feet for the first time. She carefully plastered on an easygoing grin.

Carol, who was carrying a small bag bearing the distinct butter stains of pastries, responded with a pinched smile. "Megan, darling, I just got word that the wedding rehearsal isn't going to be held this afternoon. When do you intend to have it? After dinner? That sounds terribly inconvenient."

Of course the first words out of her mouth were a complaint. Megan smiled tightly. "There was a scheduling conflict with the hotel, but the wedding planner said we could just skip the rehearsal—he'll make sure we're all in the right places at the right time."

"Mmm." Carol clearly didn't approve. "Anyway, what are you doing here? I'm sure you have a thousand details you should be checking on." Somehow Carol could sound simultaneously curt and gracious. It threw Megan off even more. Carol was petite and dainty, from the tiny jut of her chin to her size 5 shoes, but Megan knew a formidable giant slumbered underneath.

"There's always time for freshly made scones!" Megan immediately knew she was being too effusive. The Prescotts did not respond well to effusive. In a more restrained tone, she said, "I was just on my way to meet Tom's ferry."

"How lovely. Though I believe he has a golf game scheduled with the boys this morning?"

"The boys" were Tom's dad and brother. Both decades too old to be referred to as such.

"I know. I promise I won't interfere. I just wanted to see him before we're both in the thick of it today." When Carol made no move to respond, Megan found herself babbling to fill the millisecond of silence. "Isn't this place gorgeous?"

"It is. Shame it takes two planes and a ferry to get here." Carol gave Megan the once-over. "What's on your feet, dear? Are those the hotel slippers?"

They weren't, in fact. "No, these are just some sandals I brought."

"Mmm." Carol's nose wrinkled as though Megan had broken wind. "Anyway, I won't keep you, but before you run off, did you remember to rearrange the seating at tonight's dinner so my tennis friends could sit a bit closer to John and me?"

"Yes. I took care of it." It'd meant moving Megan's aunt and uncle, whom she adored, farther away, but she'd done it. "I'll double-check just to make sure."

"Good girl." Carol air-kissed Megan on each cheek as she said goodbye.

Once Megan was safely in the rental car, flushed from the humiliation she always seemed to feel in Carol's company, she realized she'd forgotten to ask Carol what she would be wearing that night. She made an educated guess and sent a text off to her mother:

Muted color. Not interesting. You'll look so much more sensational.

With the fire of her mother's dress drama extinguished, she could relax. A slow smile crawled across her face. She was marrying her perfect man in the seaside town she loved. Everything would only get better from here.

CHAPTER TWO

TOM

TOM WOKE UP to the bloated belch of the ferry's foghorn and an announcement welcoming passengers to Friday Harbor. This was followed by a cheerful "Good morning, sunshine" from the man sitting next to him, who bore a striking resemblance to Henry Winkler.

"Morning," Tom replied, his voice scratchy, and nodded. A searing pain shot from the base of his head through the muscles under his shoulder blades.

He was accustomed to waking up to music; without it, he felt a bit lost. Every night he and Megs agreed on a new song to use as an alarm for the next morning. Music had always been a piece of their relationship, from the first day they'd met. He still remembered the way her face had lit up when she'd written down lines from her favorite song by the Cure and said, "A good lyric simultaneously tells a story and makes you feel as though someone's drop-kicked your heart into your throat."

He was still a bit proud to remember his smooth reply: "So does a good conversation."

Megs told him later *that* was the moment she'd fallen for him, which he'd loved. That charged moment between them was when he'd fallen for her too.

Waking up alone on a boat with a crick in his neck was not how he wanted to start their wedding weekend. Neither was flying in the middle of the night just so he could make his tee time with his father and Brody. But as his old man liked to say, "Choose your sacrifices, son."

This usually preceded him telling Tom precisely which sacrifices to make. Case in point: he'd put Tom on the dinner with the stiffs from Prescott and Prescott's latest Big Pharma pet, telling Tom it was time to prove his commitment to being a mergers and acquisitions man, even though Tom was getting married less than forty-eight hours later.

Tom's exhaustion was so overwhelming, he barely even remembered landing in Seattle before dawn and catching the shuttle to the ferry.

He rubbed a hand over his stubble and his tongue over his teeth. He needed a shower and a toothbrush. A gallon of potent coffee was also in order. Rolling his head from side to side in an attempt to soothe his neck pain, Tom calmed himself down the best way he knew: by thinking of Megs. With hectic work schedules and the wedding planning, they'd struggled to see much of each other lately and had resorted to leaving little notes around their apartment. Before Tom left for the airport, he'd found a charmingly cheesy one in his underwear drawer: *This underwear will look great...on the floor of our hotel room.* He couldn't wait to show her just how much he agreed.

But thoughts of Megs also brought a rising wave of anxiety. Because there was more he needed to tell her today than "I love you." After the client dinner last night, he knew putting it off was no longer an option.

He moved to loosen the tie he'd forgotten he'd long ago removed and tried to convince himself that talking to her now, today, *wasn't* too little too late. She was Megs. Supportive, warm, rational.

And, really, this was good news.

She'd probably even be happy. He'd tell her first thing and they could celebrate this afternoon, well before the rehearsal dinner was under way.

His thoughts were interrupted by a small lurch forward indicating they'd arrived. Tom squirted drops into his bloodshot eyes (free sample a spouse of one of the Big Pharma execs had passed under the table the night before, whispering, "You look tired").

But once he was off the ferry, every annoyance and pain melted away. The sun was bright above him, the ocean below a magnificent indigo. He'd been to San Juan Island only a handful of times before. With every visit, he understood more and more why the place meant so much to Megs. It was painted with a palette of greens. It seemed alive. Magical. It was a place of solitude, within arm's reach of the real world, yet free from it. Everything breathed a little easier here, including Tom himself, who often struggled to relax.

He inhaled a great healthy gust of sea air and spotted Megs waving to him unabashedly with one hand, holding a tray of coffee in the other. He dropped his luggage and, careful not to spill the drinks, hugged her as though he hadn't seen her in months. When he smelled the familiar scent of her shampoo, his stomach dipped in a pleasant way. Somehow, even after twelve years, he still had such a crush on her. Megs was quick-witted and kind. Ambitious and gorgeous. She loved to watch terrible movies because they made her laugh, and she listened to songs for the poetry of their lyrics, not just for their melodies. Who wouldn't have a crush on her?

With her body close, he felt something press up against his clavicle. He released her, and his eyes went straight to the heart pendant.

At the time he'd bought it, he'd convinced himself it was the perfect sophisticated gift to show her how he felt. Seeing it now years later, he realized it wasn't quite as elegant as his

eighteen-year-old self had thought. But for Megs to wear it anyway made his heart twist in his chest.

"I like your necklace." He tilted her chin up for a quick kiss.

"I like your face." She kissed him back.

Still holding their coffee, she managed to grab the garment bag
he'd abandoned on the wooden planks of the docks. Now that
their reunion was over, an uneasiness crept into Tom. He tried
hard to pretend it didn't exist.

Just as they reached the sidewalk, a pedicab pulled up at the
curb. The driver was a woman with long, silvery hair and leg
muscles that were more impressive than his own.

"Fancy a ride, you two? Where are you heading?"

"We're good, thanks." Megs jingled her car keys.

Tom took out his phone, which had been struggling to locate a
signal, and found it lit up with texts and missed calls. Megan took
hers out too, likely to ensure she hadn't received any time-sensitive
e-mails from work. She was supposed to have the next two weeks
off, like Tom, but her job was as relentless as his own.

Tom pressed the icon for his voice mail and was greeted by his
brother's voice.

"It's Brody. We're already at the tee, Spare Parts. Get here now.
Get here five minutes ago."

"Spare Parts." The nickname that wouldn't die. Tom didn't
know who'd first coined it, who'd first claimed that was why his
parents had him—just in case their golden first child needed a
kidney or something—but it had stuck.

"Is it just me or is that baby unusually hairy?" Megs tugged at
his sleeve to get his attention, tucking her phone back into her
bag. Tom turned his head, cursing under his breath at the stiffness
in his neck, just in time to see a man wearing an enormous fishing
hat and a baby carrier pass by.

Inside the carrier was a cat.

Megs was pursing her mouth so tightly to stop from laughing, her lips turned white. They shared his favorite kind of look; a *The world is insane but at least we have each other* kind of look, which gave way to laughter as soon as the cat man was out of earshot.

"Let's go to Roche and get you checked in," Megs said. "Your mom seemed adamant that I not interfere with your golf game this morning."

He smothered the nagging feeling of guilt at leaving her to deal with both their families on her own. Megs could handle it. And she'd handle it efficiently. He and Megs had long ago made a silent pact not to criticize each other's families, and he continued to adhere to that promise—regardless of how badly he often wanted to tell Donna off for the way she treated Megs.

"Sounds good." He put a hand on the small of her back as they walked to the car. "I'm desperate for a shower."

The drive from Friday Harbor to Roche was short. Megs talked about her mom's morning freak-out (par for the course), which she had clearly handled with grace (also par for the course). Tom uncomfortably shrugged off her subsequent questions about the client dinner. He tried to figure out how to broach his news— should he give it to her with the tried-and-true *I've got good news and bad news*, or should he just come out with it?

With Megs already parking the car, he began to panic and decided on option B. He had to just say it already.

"Megs, I—" he began at the same time her phone started chirping relentlessly. She didn't even hear him as she scrolled through a series of texts.

"*Damn it*. I have to go deal with my sister. I'm supposed to meet her in the lobby." Her topknot was already losing shape, tendrils crawling out to frame her face.

"Do I even want to know?" Tom asked as they got out of the car, ashamed at how relieved he was that Brianna was taking the spotlight off him. It would be insensitive to say anything now, when Megs appeared to have the makings of a crisis on her hands. He and Megs would talk later. When she was more relaxed.

She shook her head and tossed him the extra key card she'd gotten from the front desk and the keys to the rental so he could get to the golf course. She scrutinized him, her forehead creasing with concern. "Are you okay?"

"Yeah, I'm just bagged from the dinner and traveling last night. I'm going to run up to the room and take a quick shower— that'll help."

"You sure it was a client meeting and not a secret bachelor party?" she asked wickedly.

"You got me. Last night was a real showcase in debauchery. Years of Leo's attempts to get me to let loose finally paid off."

She laughed at the absurdity of that notion. Tom and Megan had decided to forgo bachelor/bachelorette parties altogether. Instead, they'd worked several weekends in a row to secure a longer honeymoon. Besides, Tom had never engaged in a day of debauchery in his life—despite the best efforts of Leo, his wildest and very best friend.

In fact, he'd never slept with a woman other than Megan. He'd never even entered a strip club. He'd watched his friends chase shallow encounters with pretty people, but that sort of life had never appealed to Tom. There were plenty of pretty people. There was only one Megs, who could make him laugh until his eyes watered and whose heart had more capacity for generosity and patience than anyone else's. Who knew him better than anyone else and loved him still.

She gave him one more kiss and wished him luck on the golf course.

"There's the man of the hour!" Brody greeted Tom with his patented one-armed half-hug. "You look like shit."

"Thanks." Tom self-consciously raked his fingers through his hair, still damp from his rushed shower.

"Hello, son." His father greeted him with a handshake just as he'd done his entire adult life. The Prescotts weren't huggers. Brody's attempt was the most Tom ever got from his family. "How did things go last night?"

"Pretty straightforward. They seemed happy." The weekend of his wedding, and Tom worried his father was going to dwell on the upcoming merger the entire time.

"Can you believe this place?" John continued, ignoring Tom's response.

"Beautiful, right?" Tom replied gratefully, taking in the lushness of the island.

"Not even a proper eighteen-hole course." John spoke over Tom again. "They say it is with this 'two sets of tees' nonsense, but this is a nine-hole course. I don't know how people live like this."

With that, John Prescott strode toward the first tee, leaving Tom and his brother to catch up.

"Hey." Brody adjusted his sun visor, adopting an impish grin. "Guess how many times Mom has said, 'Can you believe it takes two planes and a ferry to get here?' "

"I don't want to know." Tom rubbed his eyes.

"I'm turning it into a drinking game." Brody revealed a flask in the pocket of his Kjus chinos.

"Perfect." Tom grabbed it and took a swig.

Brody squeezed Tom's shoulders affectionately. "Ease up, Spare Parts. This is supposed to be the best weekend of your life." The squeeze shifted into an annoying ruffle of Tom's hair.

His brother was right. Tom was giving these small gibes about the island too much weight.

"And hey, you survived another flight. I'm so proud of you."

Accustomed to his brother's teasing about his fear of heights, Tom took the jab good-naturedly and grabbed the flask again. "You mean two flights and a ferry."

"You're getting to be such a brave little boy."

The remainder of the morning passed with more tipsy badgering from Brody and very little nonwork talk from his dad. This game was supposed to be more than that. It was Tom's wedding weekend, after all. He decided to take things into his own hands.

"So, Dad." Tom busied himself reorganizing his already organized clubs so as not to draw too much attention to his question, one he hoped might make them feel closer even though the Prescotts didn't do camaraderie and they definitely didn't do emotions. He'd held on to a tiny bit of hope that this might be the day. "Any words of wisdom before I walk down the aisle?"

"Isn't the bride the one who does that?" Brody asked. "You're supposed to be standing there waiting for her."

"Words of wisdom…" John scratched at the chin he shaved not once, but twice a day. "Megan's a smart choice for a partner. You've done well on that."

Heat traveled to Tom's cheeks. This was the most praise he'd ever received from his father. "Yeah?"

"Indeed. She's driven. Works hard. Good-looking enough to be arm candy, smart enough to hold a conversation." The hairs on the back of Tom's neck stood up. His dad wasn't done. "But my advice hasn't changed since you two started this little relationship."

A foreboding feeling told Tom to stop, not to press. He ignored that feeling. "What do you mean?"

"Even when you select a partner who makes sense on paper, there are always variables that are unaccounted for." He raised his eyebrows at Tom's brother. "Broderick knows what I'm talking about."

"To my wife, Emmeline," Brody mumbled, raising the flask before taking another swig. This one lasted longer. There were times when his brother resembled their father so acutely, Tom could imagine he was seeing John thirty years ago.

"In Megan's case," John continued, "it's her disastrous, infestive family. So, my advice? Marriage doesn't always have to mean compromise."

"I'm not sure I'm following, Dad." Tom had looked forward to this moment. A milestone as meaningful as getting married was sure to bridge some of that gap he always seemed to feel with his father, give them a new way to bond. But now he was torn between wanting to know what his dad was getting at and wanting to stop what was turning into an uncomfortable conversation. It suddenly seemed ridiculous to think a wedding might make Tom seem more worthy, more mature in his father's eyes, like someone who'd finally caught up to Brody. In the end, Tom opted for his long-standing coping mechanism: biting his tongue to keep the peace.

"Look, when something's important, like where you and Megan spend your holidays or how much influence her washout of a mother has over your eventual children, you lay down the law. You get what you want."

Tom wished he'd pumped the brakes. This was *not* the advice he'd hoped for.

"And if Megan ever complains…" his father continued, lining up his putt. "There's always golf."

With that, John tapped his ball into the last hole.

CHAPTER THREE

MEGAN

MEGAN'S YOUNGER SISTER entered the lobby, bringing a gust of wind and an air of ennui with her. "Megan, where have you been? I've texted you like thirty times." Brianna tossed her bleached-blond hair behind her shoulder to accentuate her accusation. Megan experienced her usual clash of emotions at seeing her sister: deep-seated fondness born of silly childhood memories coupled with frustration at the deliberately irritating woman she'd grown into. Brianna was a loud and proud shit-disturber.

"Sorry, Bree. I got your messages when I was picking Tom up from the ferry."

"Well, get ready to head back to Friday Harbor because Mom wants us to go shopping with her. And you have to drive."

"But she rented a car the same time I did, and Tom's got my car. Didn't you rent one?"

"I forgot to renew my driver's license." She rolled her eyes. "Actually, I cheated on a guy who works at the DMV. It's a whole thing."

"Ah. And why does she need to go shopping?" It was a scenic drive to Friday Harbor, but Megan's instincts told her she was getting roped into more Donna shenanigans.

"She needs a new dress. Plus she overheard your future mother-in-law calling the hotel dark and now she wants to pick up candles and fresh-cut flowers to perk the place up."

"Why does she need a new dress? I already solved that problem."

"You obviously didn't." Brianna produced a Snickers bar from her purse and noisily unwrapped it. "She tried it on for me this morning and I told her it wasn't necessarily mother-of-the-bride appropriate."

No matter how old the two of them got, conversations with her little sister always left Megan silently counting to ten in an attempt to keep her cool.

"What exactly did you say to Mom, Bree?"

Brianna snorted. "I believe my exact words were 'Whoa, Mama. That dress really shows off your bazongas.' Anyway, she's meeting us down here. I'll tell her she has to drive."

Of course it had taken Bree less than a minute to reignite the fire Megan had worked so hard to put out.

"Should we invite Gran to come with us?" Brianna turned the hand not holding the Snickers bar into a finger gun. "Could be entertaining..."

"Let's keep Gran and Mom separate for as long as possible today."

"You have a distinct lack of fun about you." Brianna briefly scowled before brightening. "So did you give any more thought to me staying with you and Tom?"

While Megan always opted for the most direct path from A to B, her sister usually took a route that resembled her tangled mop of hair. She'd dropped out of one state college and three community colleges, quit at least two jobs, and been fired from five—all in the past eight years. Brianna's latest venture was enrolling in a New York film school, a vocation that particularly stung because Megan had long ago given up on her dream of making documentaries for the sake of a reliable income.

"I told you already, you can stay with us until you find your own place," Megan said. "A week or two will give you plenty of time."

"Wow. A whole week. Lucky me," Brianna muttered under her breath.

"Pardon me?"

"It's not like you don't have the space. You guys have a two-bedroom in SoHo. You know how expensive it is to live in New York, plus I'm already in debt."

"That's not my fault, Bree," Megan said, futilely attempting to reason with her.

"No, and it isn't my fault I haven't fallen in love with a lawyer from a stupid rich family."

"Oh, please. You think I'm sitting at home eating bonbons and watching daytime television? I work hard to pay my portion of the bills." She didn't need to defend herself to her chronically unemployed sister, and yet she *really* needed to defend herself to her chronically unemployed sister.

"At your pretend job?" Brianna batted her fake eyelashes.

"I'm a senior visuals editor at *GQ*."

"Yeah, but no one knows what that is."

"*Everyone* knows what *GQ* is."

Before their conversation could combust any further, Donna swept into the lobby looking far more confident and put together than she had an hour prior.

"Oh, girls, you aren't fighting, are you?" she said with a tinkle of fake laughter. Then she leaned in and hissed, "People are watching. Do *not* embarrass me."

Megan's heart felt as though it could power a nuclear plant. She took several deep breaths, felt her cheeks flaming with silent rage. What had she expected? It wasn't as though she and Brianna had ever stood a chance of getting along.

There were four years between them. When they were little,

Megan enjoyed mothering her. Brianna thrived on the attention, since Donna's maternal instincts were spotty at best.

But whenever Donna was between boyfriends, she'd while away the time by pitting her daughters against each other. She'd gossip with them separately as though they were gal pals caught in a power struggle, not a mother and her two daughters. "God, your sister is moody," Donna would murmur to Megan while making dinner and then she'd launch into some tale about Brianna. It wasn't long before Megan sensed the distance stretching between herself and her sister, realizing Donna was whispering into Brianna's ear too. As long as Megan and Brianna were at odds, they'd both love Donna best.

Megan got in the front passenger seat of their mother's rental car, leaving Brianna to climb in the back. Once they were en route to Friday Harbor, Brianna launched into the conversation Megan had tried to sidestep.

"It's not like I'd be moving in with you guys forever. Just for the first year. At most." She leaned forward, squashing herself between Donna and Megan so she could flip through radio stations as she spoke.

"Put on your seat belt, Bree." Megan hated that she still had to be the maternal one even though her mother was sitting right there.

"You two *have* been shacked up now for, what? Almost ten years?" Donna unhelpfully offered. "Why can't you let your sister and Dan stay with you?"

Megan kept calm, staring straight ahead. "Sorry, Bree. Tom and I aren't ready to have kids yet. And who's Dan?"

"Which Dan?" Brianna asked, seemingly uninterested.

"The Dan who's apparently moving to New York with you? What happened to Jonah?"

"Jonah and I had a fight."

"About what?" Megan had always had a difficult time keeping

up with Brianna's so-called serious boyfriends. It was a definite apple-not-far-from-tree situation, considering Donna's history.

Donna raised her eyebrows meaningfully. "Jonah and Brianna fought about Brianna's inability to pay rent because of how much money she spent at Sephora."

"You and Jonah broke up over makeup?" This was harder to follow than a soap opera.

"It was a *lot* of makeup." A fact Brianna didn't seem to be sorry about.

Luckily, as soon as they parked and she set foot on the rolling hill of Friday Harbor's main street, memories of days spent chewing watermelon bubble gum with worn *Archie* comics tucked under her arm buoyed Megan. She saw the stone stage at the small public park where Donna and her sister, Paulina, would listen to local jazz bands as Megan and Brianna scoured the docks, catching buckets of shrimp with nets as tall as they were.

"We'll try there first." Donna pointed to an inviting little shop.

While their mother tried on the only three dress options in the store, Brianna doused Donna in negative commentary ("That makes you look like you're going to a PTA meeting") that Megan aggressively attempted to counteract ("I think it makes you look sophisticated").

When they finally left, it was with tea lights and tiny vases (which Donna was planning on filling with fresh-cut flowers from the Roche market) and a reasonably priced shawl. Megan promised herself a long bubble bath as a reward for talking her mother into buying the shawl to wear over her wrap dress.

On the drive back, Brianna became so involved in her phone, she eased up on the drama. Donna rolled down the windows, allowing a cross breeze of ocean air to whip through their hair as they sang along to a radio station that cut out whenever they went around a corner. Megan started to feel lighter than she had all morning.

By the time they returned to the hotel, Megan's lightness had graduated to elation. Regardless—and in spite—of her family, she was going to have a fabulous weekend. She couldn't wait to commit herself to the person she loved most in the place she loved best.

She glided through the lobby doors and stopped dead. Even from a distance, she recognized the broad shoulders of the man leaning casually against the check-in desk, one hand raking through his messy hair.

In the chaos of the morning, she'd blocked out the fact that Leo would be arriving today. Her stomach plummeted and she eyed the elevator. Did she have time to make a run for it?

Before she could act, Leo was in front of her. Standing close. And then closer.

Leo's hair was longer than the last time she'd seen him, two years ago. Streaks of honey wove through his natural waves, no doubt due to his days spent in the sun. Her eyes skipped over his piercing gaze and went straight to his full mouth, which was saying, "Can we talk?"

Well, now it was *really* too late to make a run for it, even though every part of her was screaming loudly that she should.

Megan's list of regrets was small yet mighty. And she was staring at regret number one. Try as she might, she couldn't squash a flash of fondness for their past. At Harvard, Leo and Tom had been randomly assigned to be roommates, yet they quickly became more like brothers. Megan loved watching their symbiotic friendship, seeing how Tom kept Leo grounded and Leo kept Tom light, despite the fact that Leo's second year was short-lived. When academic probation grabbed hold of him, instead of rolling up his sleeves and getting to work, Leo took off his shirt, quit school, and spent his days exploring the natural wonders of New England, his Nikon camera around his neck and an army of lenses strapped to his back. Leo had an eye for beauty in seemingly mundane places and a lust for an extraordinary life.

She didn't know whether it was viewing Leo through Tom's

rose-colored glasses or Leo's natural charisma that first endeared him to her, but over those years, the three of them had become almost inseparable.

College began with the three of them watching terrible B movies and laughing at *Mystery Science Theater 3000*, carried on with them spending restless nights in borrowed sleeping bags under the stars as Leo led them along nonexistent trails, and ended in an unmitigated disaster that still sent Megan into a cold and constricting panic whenever she thought of it.

And now, the day before Megan's wedding, Leo was in front of her, looking at her with expectations she desperately tried to believe she was imagining.

She thought of the last time she'd seen him. She'd come home from a late-night photo shoot to find him crashing on the couch in their SoHo apartment. Even then, it'd been years since they'd been face-to-face. Tom was already asleep.

Leo'd cracked an eye open. Without saying a word, he reached into the pocket of the worn jeans he'd left lying on the floor and pulled out a folded piece of paper. He passed her the note as though they were in middle school. She opened it carefully, as though the teacher might catch them.

It said: *I miss you.*

The words were bruising even in their simplicity.

The truth was, she missed him too. She had been missing him ever since their colossal mistake and she would continue missing him until it didn't hurt anymore. Because denying herself that friendship was the only way Megan could think to punish herself. And she deserved the pain.

She'd tossed his bruising note into the garbage and told him not to make trouble before heading off to her bedroom, where Tom lay.

The couch was empty before dawn.

Now she had to face him again, and Tom was nowhere to be seen.

"Is there somewhere we could go?" The years had definitely been kind to Leo despite the hard, unruly way in which he lived—off the grid and without expectations for himself or anyone else.

"Sure…" Megan remembered the resort's pool, located away from the rest of the grounds. Not only was it populated with children and families, there was something decidedly unsexy about the scent of chlorine. "We can talk by the pool."

When they arrived, Leo sat atop a picnic table instead of on its bench. If she weren't so nervous, she would've laughed in his face and exclaimed, *Can't you do one orthodox thing?* Instead, she sat beside him. On top of the table.

"It's nice to see you," Megan finally said, her wedding-weekend manners kicking in.

"It's nice to see *you*," he replied, jovially mocking her civility. And then the facade dropped and so did his head. "Is it actually nice to see me? Because it feels like you hate me."

"I don't hate you." *I hate myself for thinking about you.* Even her silent honesty filled her with self-loathing. She clung to false cheer, admitting, "You're one of my favorite people on the planet, Leo. You always have been."

The encouragement was enough for him to lift his head.

The silence between them was a crashing meteorite. The sensation of missing someone who was so close she could toss her hair and have the strands brush his shoulder was both delicious and distressing.

She had to break the tension. Just as she said, "Leo, I—" he countered with, "Givens, I've thought about you so much since—"

They both stopped, and their thoughts trailed away, disappearing into the sea. Guilt ravaged her conscience. The pendant around her neck conducted heat from the sun, burning her skin.

"I just have to know. Do you ever think about what happened between us?" he asked finally.

"No." The force of her refusal surprised even her.

Of course she was lying. She often revisited it. On nights when insomnia took her from her place in bed next to Tom and into their guest room/office. On days when her commitment to a job she knew she should be grateful for made her feel agitated, because she couldn't stop thinking about the dreams she'd given up for it.

The weekend she and Tom graduated from Harvard, they'd introduced Donna to John and Carol for the first time. Megan had spent the entire graduation weekend quietly fuming at the Prescotts' superiority complexes and silently embarrassed her mother was trying so hard—and failing—to impress them. At dinner the night before graduation, Donna and Tom's parents finally found common ground in deciding Megan's future. They determined that Megan would stay in Cambridge while Tom did law school, maybe get her own graduate degree, after which she'd follow him to New York City, where he'd begin his ascent at Prescott and Prescott. Never mind that she'd already been considering going to grad school and then New York, independent of Tom; the assumption that she'd just do what he needed watered a seed of resentment of not being totally seen. Of feeling like little more than an adornment to Tom's bright future.

Before they all went their separate ways, John delivered his parting shot: "Quite a surprise this little relationship stuck after all the young women Carol's been parading in front of Tom." He laughed at his own fond memories. "But Tom couldn't be dissuaded by country-club girls over catered meals, so here we are."

To which Tom said nothing.

Megan had been floored. *Humiliated.* Why hadn't Tom told her his parents were trying to set him up? And why, in all this time, had he never told them to stop?

Later, after they'd celebrated their final night as college kids, Tom had fallen asleep on the floor of his and Leo's apartment.

Still reeling from what John said at dinner, Megan had sneaked out and climbed the fire escape to the roof to watch the sunrise, Leo at her side.

And then Megan had made the first decision of her life that wasn't carefully planned, one that muted the echoes of that awful conversation. She kissed Leo. Or, more accurately, Leo kissed her, his strong hand on her jaw, and she'd kissed him back, inviting his warm tongue into her mouth with her own.

Her fingers had traced the ridges of his muscles, the smoothness of his skin, while his hands grabbed at her ass in a way that didn't feel cheap; it felt as though he was worshipping her curves. She pulled at his shirt; he pulled at hers. He hiked up her skirt; she unzipped his fly. Every movement was one of desperation, an attempt to capture and hold emotions that neither could pretend were fleeting.

Making love to Leo was just that: love. Because didn't she love him? As a friend, yes. But as more?

Leo, she'd thought, would never have let someone belittle her family and judge her upbringing. Leo wouldn't have let his parents try to set him up with other women to dissuade him from loving her.

In fact, Megan *had* met Leo's parents, and each of them had pulled her in for a tight hug and showered her with compliments.

Every story of lust and love has a postscript. Megan's was that when they were spent, skin slick with sweat and gleaming in the sunrise, she'd said nothing, had instead followed a thread away from Leo.

It was the same thread that had led her from her high school in Montana to Harvard.

From the back of that Natural Disasters class to a seat five rows down.

It was the thread that always brought her away from destructive behavior fit for Donna Givens and back to a life with Tom.

Since that night, everything she knew about Leo, she gleaned from Tom, social media, and Leo's infamous blog. She learned about him guiding tours of twenty-somethings through Thailand, taking them to bucket parties on the beach and sneaking the more adventurous travelers to clandestine drug-filled shacks. She saw him tagged in photos of women who fell hard for him only to watch him fly away to the next adventure. She studied the avant-garde books he raved about online when she delightedly discovered he had a Goodreads account. And after each search she wiped her browser history in a ritual designed to cleanse herself of this what-if shame.

The ritual was never truly cleansing. And each time she succumbed to her late-night Leo curiosity, she hated herself more. As punishment, she didn't let herself see or talk to him if she could help it.

Tom never once questioned the way Megan had drifted away from Leo, as Megan made clear her efforts to forge new friend-ships at work.

Now, confronted by Leo for the first time in years, she told herself she wasn't afraid. That those feelings had been squashed and she wasn't some monster who still longed for another man.

However, the snappishness in her response said otherwise. "What do you want, Leo? What could you possibly hope to get from me here? Today?"

Instead of growing defensive, Leo covered the flicker of a smile with his hands as he looked up at the sun, then back at her. He brought his hands down to his lap, taking his time with his response. "I haven't even had the chance to say anything—how are you already annoyed with me? You know what? It doesn't matter. Because it's *still* good to be next to you. It feels like I haven't heard your voice since the dawn of time."

He was hitting all the buttons she'd kept hidden—including her weakness for his disarming honesty. It only made her hackles go higher.

"Stop being hyperbolic. I've said hello when you've been on the phone with Tom."

"From the kitchen or the living room." He was teasing her, immune to her cold rebuttals. The conversation was already bringing to the surface bittersweet nostalgia. "You've successfully avoided me for, what? Eight years now?"

"I haven't been avoiding you. You've crashed on my couch at least a dozen times."

"Five times."

"Six." Correcting him was an error. He'd know she'd been keeping track.

"But every time I've come for the weekend you've had to work late, and we haven't even talked." He shrugged in a self-deprecating manner. "You really have a way of making a guy feel like he's not wanted."

"We haven't needed to talk. You passed me notes."

"*One* note. Which you threw away."

Yes, she'd thrown it away. Just as she'd deleted drafts of e-mails and filed away her remorse—about things she'd done as much as about things she *hadn't*.

Leo's voice dropped. "So you didn't try to talk Tom out of making me his best man."

"Of course not." The accusation (was that what it was?) snapped her acutely into the present. "What would I have said? 'Please, love of my life, not him. I secretly slept with him the day we graduated.'"

A breeze smelling of salt and chlorine ruffled their hair. She sensed the shift in Leo before he spoke. His smile faltered, his courage slipping. He rested a hand on the table between their bodies and leaned on it with his full weight.

"So Tom is most definitely the love of your life?" His voice was so low, she almost could've imagined the question. And yet he was waiting for an answer.

How could he ask her that on the weekend of her wedding? The day before he was to stand up beside Tom? And how could she sit here and let him do it? She had to end this. *Now.*

She waved him away in a gesture that reminded her of her mother (making her inwardly cringe), lightly laughing. "Who else would it be? *You?*"

"Is it so absurd that it would be me? Am I that unlovable? Come on, Givens." Leo scratched his scalp, standing up and turning to her, his face full of every word they hadn't uttered. In his eyes, she saw glimmers of the college boy who'd reached out a hand when she was sadder and more uncertain than she'd thought possible.

"You know what? It should be me. *Me*," Leo insisted, gaining momentum. "The guy who really sees you, who has never once asked you to be anyone but *yourself*. The one who's had to watch all the bullshit John and Carol have put you through, knowing you deserve so much more. The one who sent you encouraging letters all through your master's in visual arts that you *should've* put to use filming documentaries instead of staging pretty pictures for a men's magazine."

She opened her mouth to defend herself, but Leo didn't let her speak. "Who only once *got* to love you on that roof the day of your and Tom's graduation. And has wanted to again for eight years."

His volume was reasonable, but it felt as though he were shouting at her and sucking the air from the atmosphere all at once.

"I know telling you all this is a long shot. I'm not so cocky that I expect to sweep you off your feet with one conversation." He laughed bitterly. "And I know it's your wedding weekend and the worst possible time to come to you with this, and it makes me a pretty terrible person...but I know I'd feel worse if I said nothing. For so many years I thought Tom would do right by you, but every time I talk to him, it's obvious he's still bending over backward for his parents."

"He's not bending over backward for them," Megan said defensively.

She weakly added, "The Prescotts are demanding, yes. But we make it work."

The line between Leo's brows deepened. "Even now, it's written all over your face. You think I'm not paying attention? We may be in your favorite vacation spot, but this wedding has *John and Carol* stamped all over it. Admit it—Tom's still putting them in the driver's seat of your relationship, isn't he?"

Megan's throat was dry. She tried to swallow in order to speak and found she had nothing to say.

"I can't forgive him for that," Leo finished. "For not putting you first all the time. *Every* time."

Megan's heart was pounding out a warning to her. There had been good times and bad times with Tom, of course, and during the bad spells, she'd be lying if she said she hadn't imagined someone, somewhere, sticking up for her. But she had certainly never imagined it happening now. What was she supposed to do with this information? This conversation?

Leo's voice dropped along with his head. "If you tell me you're happy, you're sure, I'll stand beside Tom tomorrow and wish you both the best."

Happy. What did that word even mean?

She loved Tom. When she'd woken up this morning, she'd been nothing but excited. But when you repeat a word too many times, it starts to sound like gibberish, and that's what was happening to the word *happy* as it rolled around in her mind. She thought of Carol, of Donna. Of all the times she'd held her tongue. Still, she knew what her response should be.

"I'm happy." The words didn't ring true, not even to her own ears, and she couldn't figure out why.

"*Givens.*"

"*Leo,*" she retorted, as though they were still kids and this was a game.

"Are you seriously going to set up house and give *John* and

Carol grandbabies?" Leo said their names with such disdain, she wondered if Tom knew how much Leo hated his family. "Megan?" He waited until her eyes were on him. "Are you going to close up shop on everything you've ever wanted and, at the age of thirty, let Tom's family decide not only who you are but what you do? Your entire future? A future so predictable and derivative of John and Carol's, I know you'll be miserable?"

"Why is this any of your business?" she snapped, his words hitting too close to home. Her phone rang and she silenced it without looking at the call display. "What do you care if I become a Prescott and have little Prescott babies? You don't know me anymore."

"Yes, Megan, I do." It came out as a prayer. "We used to see each other every single day. You're still that same person, the one who's always looking for the opportunity to do good. Who never lets the world see how exhausted she is from holding everyone else together. Of course I know you."

The table was growing increasingly uncomfortable and Megan shifted, trying to find a better position. She'd been so confident, so secure before Leo had shown up. Hadn't she? Resentment at the way he was blindsiding her, pushing her off balance grew. She was ready to push back. "Not anymore, you don't." It felt like her lungs were in her throat as she tried to take a deep breath. "You can't possibly know who I am now."

"Yes. I really do. You think I haven't noticed you climbing your way up in one of the most competitive industries in one of the most competitive cities in the world and kicking all that ass with grace? And I bet you've been doing all that while still running your family and arranging this wedding on your own."

Megan tried not to flinch.

"I've watched you continue to put everyone else first, including Tom—*especially* Tom—but haven't you ever thought about being with someone who won't make you do that? Someone who'll support *your* dreams instead of asking you to compromise?" Leo sat beside her again, careful not to touch her, though it was clear in the twitch of his hands that he wanted to. "I love Tom, but he's taken the wrong road, and I'm sick of watching him wreck your life. These eight years have changed nothing. I'm still in love with you. It's become increasingly clear I always will be."

How many times had she imagined him saying those words and then hated herself for it? But Leo could barely stay in one city, never mind one relationship. Tom...Tom was steady. He committed to everything. She'd long ago made her choice.

"Well," Megan began, trying to cut the tension. "Your timing is impeccable, Leonardo. I wonder if anyone had *Best Man Tries to Steal Bride* on their wedding bingo card."

He pulled his eyebrows together, his lips parting ever so softly. He stared into her eyes so deeply, she felt like he could put a hole right through her. "My timing's shit. But this is my last chance to save you—to give you the chance to save yourself from what could be an enormous mistake. I'm asking you to choose me. To choose *you*. Leave with me."

He was serious. And more than that, he was the only other person who knew what Tom was like with his family—and he was telling her to leave. She was suddenly too hot and too thirsty to think straight. When had the sun gotten so high?

Megan's attention was grabbed by someone waving from the distance with one hand, holding her pregnant belly with the other. Her aunt Paulina. The voice of reason and Megan's favorite family member. Her aunt was flanked by Gran, squinting from under a Roche Harbor hat; Brianna, who was looking at her phone; and Donna, who was looking at Leo as though she knew all his secrets. Never had Megan been so grateful to see her family. "I've got to go," she told Leo and left him without looking back.

CHAPTER FOUR

TOM

CAN YOU BELIEVE this place doesn't have a proper club-house?" John said for the third time since they'd returned to the course after consuming burgers and pilsners at a nearby restaurant. "It's one man and a cash register. Where's the pro shop? Where's the restaurant? I feel like I'm golfing in someone's backyard."

"I also can't believe it takes two planes and a ferry to get here." Brody offered Tom another sip from his almost empty flask.

"It doesn't count if *you* say it," Tom muttered under his breath, although he still took a sip. "The drinking game is *Mom* has to say it."

"Mom's not here, Spare Parts."

Tom didn't feel like drinking. He also didn't feel like golfing anymore. Why hadn't Megs answered his call? He felt a desperate need to make sure she'd be free when he got back so they could talk. Properly. However, when it came to making decisions, his father and his brother were always a quorum, and they'd decided to do the same nine holes with the different tees.

He wished again that Leo had accepted the invitation to join them for the game, but Leo had said he couldn't get there in time. Leo often felt more like a brother to Tom than Brody did.

Tom was sure the day would've been better with him around. Leo could talk Tom down from anything. If he had joined them, he'd be cracking jokes right now and helping Tom figure out how to tell Megs about the move.

"Start us out, Broderick." John patted Brody on the shoulder, then gave him a gentle push. His Ulysse Nardin watch reflected the sun, briefly blinding Tom.

"Aww, let's let the second fiddle go first this time."

Brody often joked about being his parents' favorite. Tom wasn't sure whether he joked because he believed John and Carol loved them both equally or because he was amused by their obvious bias. Because, when it came down to it, Brody didn't seem to have to work for their approval. Having a pulse seemed to be enough. John and Carol had attended every one of Brody's tennis matches throughout his adolescence; they'd sent out engraved announcements anytime he graduated from anything. When Brody started dating, John and Carol basically courted each girl's parents. Brody got married right out of college, and to this day, John and Carol had a long-standing weekly brunch date with his in-laws. By contrast, this weekend was only the third time John and Carol had met Megan's mom.

Tom wasn't truly sure whether this marathon he'd been running all his life was to catch up to his older brother or surpass him. He just wanted to finally gain some recognition in the family.

There had been times when Tom had tried not running the marathon. In high school, after a brief period of hanging out with Brody and his posturing buddies, Tom traded in bravado for some friends his own age from the junior volleyball team. They even formed a short-lived and completely ill-conceived garage band. This Lilliputian act of independence went largely ignored. Tom had tried again when he'd applied to be an associate at a smaller firm, one with a more humanitarian business model. But his mother found out and accused Tom of betraying his family name—an indictment that filled Tom with unmeasurable guilt. How could he refuse to work at Prescott and Prescott when his father had invested so much in his schooling and when it would allow him to spend more time connecting with his dad—not to mention his brother?

Neither one of them told either John or Brody about his rogue act, and he entered the doors of Prescott and Prescott without looking back.

"Tom, you're choking up on the club like it's a baseball bat," John called as Tom was readying his stance to take a swing.

"He hasn't so much as made par on a single hole today, Dad. Maybe he thinks his chances of getting a home run are better."

Tom pulled back the club while the two men laughed and then swung with a force that—even he could admit—compromised his stance.

"Would you like some ice cream with that slice?" Brody jogged up to the tee and snapped his glove against Tom's ass.

Brody, of course, walloped the ball beautifully over the fairway, then took a cheeky bow. Their father's shot was like an instant replay of Brody's.

"How's Megan feeling about the move?" John asked suddenly after watching his ball land.

"I haven't told her yet." The golf game was doing nothing to help the crick in Tom's neck, and at the mention of his impending relocation, his chest constricted. For a while, waiting to tell her until the move became official had been a kindness, a way to avoid adding to her daily stress; he'd never imagined it would take so long. Now, telling her in a rushed moment before they said "I do" seemed grossly insensitive. What had he been thinking?

Brody let out a full belly laugh. "You're getting married tomorrow and you haven't even told your future wife she's moving to Missouri? Tom, sometimes you're the stupidest smart guy I know."

Maybe Tom was having a heart attack. A copper taste was spreading across his tongue. Of course, it was also possible he'd just bitten it and that was the taste of blood.

John went very still. Intimidatingly so. The more still his father got, the more Tom wanted to move. Go for a jog. Do a tap dance.

"Is there something you're not telling *me?*" John scrolled through his phone. "Ian said the meeting went well last night. That he's glad you're on board as their in-house counsel and that you're willing to relocate closer to headquarters." It was a little unorthodox, but it wasn't the first time a high-maintenance client had made such a demand. One of Tom's old friends from law school had moved to Texas last year at the behest of an oil company.

"I'm going to tell her," Tom said. And he was. He had a plan. A plan that kept getting derailed—and one he couldn't proceed with if he never got out of this golf game. But something of this magnitude needed to be handled delicately. Tom wasn't going to spring it on her until they had time to talk.

Really, Tom tried to convince himself, it was exciting that this had become a wedding surprise for her—he could picture just how she'd laugh when she heard what his raise would be. Good news and bad news. That's how she'd see it. And hopefully, like Tom, she'd understand that the scales were tipping in the good-news direction.

John adjusted his visor. "There are things you can control in this life and things you can't. You can always, *always* control how hard you work. There's pride in that, in a man pushing himself to see who he really is. If you're not up for this job, Thomas, if you aren't serious about it…" John's voice carried a warning. A challenge.

"I'm up for it," Tom insisted. "Like you said, last night's dinner was a success, wasn't it? And they started talking about moving me out there months ago. None of us are changing our minds."

Not even Tom. He knew saying no wasn't an option, so he'd

never entertained the idea, had allowed himself to think only of the positive: more money in a place with a lower cost of living. It really was an incredible opportunity that would probably mean better hours than he was clocking in New York. He'd have more time to spend with Megs. Plus, they could have a house and an actual yard. He knew there were things she missed about Montana, and a lot of those things she could have in Missouri. She wouldn't even be giving up that much, because she could switch departments at *GQ* and work remotely. She'd be excited when the shock wore off, he knew it. He knew *her*. He just didn't want her to have to work through that shock during their rehearsal dinner. Why wouldn't this golf game end?

John's phone rang. He stepped away from Tom and Brody, plugging one ear with his finger. Tom recognized the sound of his work voice; his father had an uncanny way of making clients feel as though they were the top priority but that John was still the most important person in the room.

"If you don't want her to leave you at the altar, you'd better tell her quick," Brody said. "Someone's bound to slip up and say something. Everyone on our side knows about this and they're all at the hotel with Megan while *you're here*."

Suddenly, Tom was perspiring and parched. And a little tipsy. Taking swigs from Brody's flask after a red-eye and no breakfast was proving to be a bad idea.

Brody was right.

Why hadn't he thought about that? Everyone from their side of the guest list knew about the relocation. If Megs heard about the move from anyone other than Tom, he could kiss that good news/bad news conversation goodbye. Tom wasn't sure if he was going to be sick. Maybe he was going to pass out? In either case, he didn't have any time left. This revelation was a ticking time bomb. Tom couldn't risk it detonating.

While John and Brody took their next shots, Tom ran for the

car, fumbling for the keys with one hand and calling the woman he loved most in this world with the other. The person he'd chosen as his family. The only person he worried more about disappointing than his father. She didn't answer. He sent Leo a text asking if he'd seen Megs. Leo didn't respond either. Maybe it was the patchy cell service. Maybe Leo's flight had been delayed.

Once he was in the car, he couldn't get back to the other side of the island quickly enough; he drove well over the speed limit and parked haphazardly alongside the crowded gravel lot. He didn't care if he got a ticket at this point. He had to get to Megs.

He couldn't stop picturing his mom running into Megs and offering to help her pack for Missouri (although that might require a personality transplant) or someone from the firm congratulating her on Tom landing the in-house counsel job (something Tom had hinted at but not outright admitted because that particular conversational path led to the Midwest). There were myriad ways Megan could find out about Tom's deception and he wanted to kick himself for staying in denial for so long.

Brody was right. For someone who'd gone to Harvard and Harvard Law, Tom had to admit he could be a colossal dumbass.

He scanned the hotel lobby, ran up the stairs to their suite and back down again, walked along the docks, all the while getting sweatier and more frantic. He had just finished searching the aisles of the market when he saw her through the window of the hotel salon, surrounded by her gran, Paulina, Donna, and Brianna.

His shoulders slumped. Now was not the time. He'd have to wait until she was done.

He found an unoccupied bench overlooking the water and composed various texts to Megs...

We need to talk

Can we meet up before the dinner?

There's something I need to tell you

Each one he erased before pressing Send. They seemed too

melodramatic. She'd assume the worst—that he'd had an affair or was calling off the wedding. And anyway, this was good news. *More money, more responsibility*, he reminded himself. *More time together. A fresh start.*

At least, that was the mantra he'd been repeating to himself for nearly two months now. But why? Why hadn't he just said something earlier? Shame coiled around him and squeezed.

He should've been discussing this with Megs the whole way along.

The more these thoughts gnawed at him, the more Tom realized that he and Megs had gotten into an undeniable rut; rarely would they talk about anything beyond the minutiae of their days. He couldn't pinpoint when they'd stopped talking about anything that actually mattered. How had their conversations become little more than snippets of domesticity? He really had tried to search for the right moment, but broaching a big topic between dropping his keys in the dish by the door and asking her which takeout place she wanted to order from didn't feel right. And by the time they'd eaten and caught up on their respective days, they were both mentally exhausted and wanted only to park themselves in front of an addicting show to unwind.

This routine had been going on for days, weeks, months.

If he couldn't tell Megs, Tom really needed someone else to talk to. Had Leo arrived yet? A glance at his phone revealed his service had flickered out again.

There was a dearth of people Tom could confide in these days. Between Megs and work, he'd let so many friends from law school slip away. Getting beyond the superficial with his colleagues at Prescott and Prescott had proved futile, since he shared a name with the firm.

He scrolled through the contacts on his reception-less phone. It seemed he was on his own.

Tom squinted in the sun and watched as boats docked and

departed, racking his brain for clues Megs might have left—a trail of bread crumbs—indicating how she'd react to his news or if she had any idea it was coming.

They didn't argue. Never had. Megan was a master of emotional control. It wasn't that she was robotic, because she was the warmest person he knew. She hugged people like she meant it and asked "How are you?" because she genuinely wanted to hear the answer. There were times when she'd come home from work and speak sharply about a vendor who'd refused to respect her, and then, instead of blowing up, she would take several deep breaths and come up with a plan. She'd get off the phone after a particularly aggravating discussion with Donna, and, rather than break down or throw something, she'd go from consternation to resignation, then offer to watch Tom cook (they'd discovered early on that she was much more adept at ogling him than being his sous-chef).

As for Tom, he'd learned almost from the moment he was born into the Prescott legacy that tantrums were not tolerated. If you had feelings—a notion so gauche, Tom's mother wouldn't even say words like *depression*, *anxiety*, or even *hurt*—you were to bottle them up, use them as fuel to shoot yourself to the moon. Or, in Tom's case, the firm of Prescott and Prescott.

He rubbed at his stinging eyes. His entire body felt bloodshot.

Because, at the bottom of his stress and avoidance, he felt like an asshole for not talking through what worried him and what excited him about moving to Missouri even before it all became final. Yes, Megs was overworked, but he still should've confided in her. Somewhere along the way they'd stopped doing that and he didn't know why. Tomorrow they were going to commit to each other for the rest of their existence. He knew she would support him through this. Yes, she might be upset, but she'd definitely understand. And somehow he'd make it up to her. No more surprises. From now on, Tom was going to try his hardest to open up to her more. He'd never let something like this happen again.

CHAPTER FIVE

MEGAN

EVEN THOUGH SHE knew the lead-up to the rehearsal dinner would involve tolerating Donna and Brianna, Megan had still romanticized it all: reminiscing with Paulina about her and Hamza's wedding, having her hair and makeup professionally done, seeing all the details she'd been coordinating for the last eighteen months come to life. Like the sign hanging by the entrance to their private dining room that said BETTER TOGETHER (a reference to the one song Tom knew how to play on his much-neglected ukulele) and the centerpieces on each table that included anemones (the flower Tom had given her on their first date). All around the room were nuanced nods to who they were, to the warm permanence of their relationship.

After all, Carol may have dictated the size, scope, and season of the wedding, but Megan had made damn sure the rest was her and Tom. She wanted a guarantee they'd be able to relish the weekend no matter the baggage that came with it, so she'd infused little touches where she could: music curated from their college playlists and artfully placed photographs of their adventures, like the sailing lessons they'd taken on the island and the road trips that had carried them far from their careers over long weekends.

But here she was, in the cordoned-off private section of the hotel's restaurant with friends and relatives who wanted to wish Tom and Megan well, and she was unable to banish the conversation with Leo from her mind.

Really, Megan reasoned, she just missed connecting with Tom. He was her touchstone. They'd meant to meet up before dinner, but things at the salon ran long and then Paulina begged for an impromptu photo shoot. Not seeing Tom coupled with what had happened with Leo left her feeling untethered. Uneasy.

She shook off the lingering guilt and tried to enjoy her surroundings, how she felt in her champagne midlength dress with subtle metallic threads in the lace overlay that glittered tastefully as she made her way through the room.

The tables were covered in white linen, polished silverware, and sparkling china. Through the big bay window, Megan could see the first stars of the night. They were faint in the early-evening sky, yet still twinkling, reminding her of the night she and Tom had decided to officially get engaged.

The evening before, they'd celebrated her twenty-eighth birthday with friends at a Korean restaurant in the East Village, and for some reason, the night ended with her crying at home on the couch, Tom holding her as she struggled to find words for what she was feeling. Something about the milestone of another birthday, one bringing her closer and closer to thirty, made her question where she was, *who* she was, how she'd gotten there. She wondered when or if her long work hours would ever abate, when she'd feel like the life she was living was one she'd deliberately made, not one she'd just stumbled on or been pushed into. There were days when she wasn't sure she recognized herself anymore. Was this the sink-or-swim moment people had warned her about when she and Tom moved to New York?

Megan tried to explain to Tom the homesickness she was feeling for a time when she wasn't overwhelmed and exhausted; for her family, whom she loved, even though they drove her crazy. She admitted that she missed Montana. She wanted to go outside and see a sky filled with stars, not just a sky of big-city light pollution, because something about being under endless stars anchored her. The galaxy made her feel small in a way that reminded her to keep things in perspective, not to allow herself to be overwhelmed by daily life.

The following night, after a long photo shoot and an even longer *GQ* team meeting, Megan had come home to a candlelit dinner. After they ate, Tom told her he had a surprise for her. He turned out all the lights in the apartment, and the ceiling lit up with glow-in-the-dark constellation stickers.

"I thought a lot about what you said last night. I can't give you everything you miss, but here's your starry sky," he'd said, his voice soft. "And there's something else I want to give you…" There was a crack of a jewelry box opening as he dropped to one knee. She'd dropped with him, overcome by the gesture.

The proposal came out as declarations of love from Megan as much as Tom. He might have bought the ring, but the question and the answer came from them both.

At the rehearsal dinner, Megan stopped first at her gran and granddad's table to kiss their cheeks, soft as tissue paper. Her gran was a busybody, but her strong will and dedication to her family had always inspired Megan. Unlike Gran, Megan's granddad was a gentle soul who spoke only when he felt he had something to say and who was always there to offer his cardigan if he saw you shiver or give you a dollar for the candy store. Megan loved him with a fierceness that only grew as they both aged. She'd seen a similar sweetness in Tom from the very beginning.

Tom entered, looking as handsome as ever if just a tad scattered. She gave him a quick hug and kiss that was interrupted by her grandparents, who wanted to hug him too. He looked like he was about to say something to her when he was steered away by Carol, who wanted him to make the rounds.

"I'm so glad you decided to have the festivities here, Meggy."

Gran patted her cheek as though she were still a child. Meg relished the tiny moment of feeling taken care of.

"Everything's just so nice," added her granddad.

Talking to her grandparents, Megan reclaimed the peace and nostalgia that had drawn her to the island, anchoring her before the inevitable storm of toasts and food and chatter.

Dinner was to begin at seven o'clock. Tom had been too wrapped up in his billable hours to give her more than a cursory "Sounds good" when she'd asked what he thought about the menu she'd selected: a house salad served with wild salmon crostini followed by stuffed prawns with saffron cream and bacon-wrapped chicken breast with wildflower honey. For dessert, hand-dipped chocolate truffles and an assortment of almond macarons.

"Should we mix the families up a bit?" Donna asked as she made her way to the head table. She tossed her shawl over her shoulder and hovered behind the chairs. "So we're sitting Prescott, Givens, Prescott, Givens?" (Although she'd been married four times, Donna had kept her maiden name, and she'd vehemently insisted her children carry the Givens name too.)

"Such a nice idea," Carol replied, sitting down right next to John. "But I'd hate for you to end up between John and Brody and have them talk shop over your head the entire time."

Donna managed to look only mildly put out as she took her place next to Brianna, who was already elbow-deep in the bread-basket. The empty chair to her left waited for Alistair, should he choose to show up.

Megan and Tom had planned to begin the evening by presenting their wedding party (Paulina and Brianna on the bride's side; Leo and Brody on the groom's) with gifts. Megan's smile at her fiancé wavered as she tapped an invisible watch on her wrist to indicate they needed to get started. He nodded and stood with her, staying surprisingly silent. His fingers tapped against his legs, a nervous tic she quickly recognized. It seemed they were both ill at ease. But what was wrong with Tom? She pushed the query from her mind—there was no time to worry about that now—and focused on the evening's itinerary.

"Tom and I would like to thank everyone for their support and for making an effort to be here to celebrate with us." Megan despised public speaking. The words felt clumsy in her mouth, her mind jumbled as to what she actually wanted to say. She picked at a scab of resentment that this was yet another thing Tom was making her take the reins on even though he didn't mind talking to a large crowd. "We'd especially like to thank our wedding party and give them a little token of our appreciation."

From a bag under the table, Megan produced four professionally wrapped gifts: intricately engraved cuff bracelets for the brides-maids and sets of unimaginative cuff links for the groomsmen, since Tom had left the gift buying to the last minute. The room broke into applause as they handed out the trinkets.

Overwhelmed, Megan stammered, "And n-now... get ready to eat!" She gave a nod to the waitstaff to start serving, desperate to escape the spotlight.

Finally, Tom spoke. "But if any of you would like to make a speech, feel free!" To Megan he whispered, "That was the plan, wasn't it?"

He was right. Since the reception was when the parents, her matron of honor (Paulina), and Tom's best man (Leo—oh God) would be making their toasts, they'd agreed to leave the floor open during the rehearsal dinner for anyone else to say a few words.

Her smile was tight as she nodded. How could he make her feel bad when she'd been the one to go over the plan repeatedly with him?

Wine flowed. Platters of seafood and salads were circulating family-style, much to Carol's ongoing horror. She'd let Megan know more than once over the past year that she believed all the guests should get their own plates and serving the food family-style was almost as inelegant as a *buffet*.

One by one, well-wishers chimed in. Though Donna kept trying to get up and speak her mother-of-the-bride mind, Carol stopped her every time she began to stand with some inane question about Montana ("What did you say the population of Great Falls was?").

Megan tried to listen to Tom's great-aunt Florence's speech, a seemingly endless drone of platitudes ("May you laugh often and cling to each other when times are tough"), instead of letting her eyes search the room of fifty people to find one: Leo, who was seated with some close family friends of the Prescotts. Whenever she looked over, she found him looking back at her, and her stomach twisted. She moved to angle her chair away from him and talk to Tom, but Tom seemed to be focusing intently on his salad, his leg shaking under the table.

"Am I late for the party?" Alistair's voice not only interrupted Great-Aunt Florence's speech but snapped Megan out of her Leo trance. The room quieted.

Both Alistair and Leo eschewed conformist lifestyles and were allergic to growing roots, but while Leo had used his wanderlust to develop a successful business, Alistair hopped from couch to couch, draining the bank account of any woman who would have him.

And tonight, her brother had shown up to her rehearsal dinner wearing cargo shorts, a distressed T-shirt, and sunglasses perched on the bridge of his nose.

"I heard there was something rad going on in Roche Harbor, so I hopped on the road to see my little sister hitch her wagon to this guy."

Carol's face was ashen, John's stern. They'd never met her brother before, and this first impression was not going to reflect well on her. Megan flushed with embarrassment, but when she glanced at Leo, she saw him grinning with amusement, not even a hint of judgment on his face.

However, Megan could see the distaste of all the guests on Tom's side (65 percent of the total, to be exact. She'd had to cut some extended family and a few friends to make room for more Prescott VIPs). She wanted to grab a bottle of wine and a straw, tell everyone to get fucked, and run for her grandparents' boat. She settled for standing and hugging her long-lost brother. Tom good-naturedly shook Alistair's hand.

Alistair's arrival unofficially marked the end of the speeches. The music was turned up as entrées made their way around the room.

"Where've you been?" Donna asked Alistair, her shawl slipping farther down her shoulders the more wine she consumed.

"I was dating this girl in Brazil and things got serious. But then it turned out she had a husband and things got more serious, but in a *Am I seriously gonna die?* kind of way, you know. So I hitchhiked for a bit and then somehow ended up getting back to America, where a guy paid me to be a roofer. Do you know how hard it is to be a roofer?" No one answered. "*I* didn't think being a roofer was hard, but then I nailed my hand to the roof, and I was like, no, thank you."

"Are you currently unemployed, then?" Carol asked, a melody of judgments in her tone.

"*Currently?*" Brianna scoffed. "Try *perpetually.*"

"You're one to talk," Alistair shot back.

"*Children, please,*" Donna hissed while John and Carol exchanged heavy looks and Brody laughed into his wineglass.

Megan wanted to crawl under the table and perish.

Although he was usually good at segueing to more acceptable topics of conversation to keep the peace, Tom was being uncharacteristically quiet. In fact, he'd been a little jumpy all evening. Not that Megan could talk, with Leo looming across the way.

"Well, welcome back, Al," Megan said a little too loudly in an attempt to shut everyone up. She pushed the food on her plate around with her fork. "Glad you could make it."

"How are you liking San Juan Island?" Donna asked the Prescotts, performatively changing the subject.

"Have you noticed the sand has the distinct consistency of dog poop?" Brianna asked, clearly thinking she was hilarious.

John openly ignored Megan's family while Carol wrinkled her expensive little nose and said, "It's so quaint."

"Quaint?" Donna pressed.

"Lovely," Carol went on. "Shame it takes two planes and a ferry to get here."

Brody guffawed so hard, he nearly sprayed wine over his dinner plate. He grabbed his napkin, apologizing to the table. "Must've gone down the wrong pipe."

If things between her and Tom weren't so inexplicably off right now, Megan would've been keeping a mental tally of items they could gossip about once they were safely in bed. Instead, she let every exchange slip through her fingers. She didn't care to remember any of this—which wasn't how she'd thought she'd feel the day before her wedding.

"Hey, Tom. Has Megan talked to you about me moving to New York?" Brianna was breaking off bits of a dinner roll and tossing them in her mouth. Megan didn't miss Carol calculating just how many crumbs were speckling the tablecloth. Instead of answering, Tom choked on a bite of his own roll.

Typically, when Tom and Megan were at a function, be it family or professional, where they had to be their most polite selves, they'd give each other a small signal of their alliance: two taps on the side of the nose with an index finger. It was a gesture that appeared inconsequential to anyone else and yet contained multitudes of meanings for them.

I know you think this function is absurd/dull/a disaster too.

Me and you against the world.

They don't get it, but we do.

I love you.

Tonight, when she thought they'd be reaching for each other in that small way, Tom was avoiding her eyes. Or maybe Megan was avoiding his. Neither lifted an index finger from a wine-glass stem.

"I know, I know. I'm supposed to save my words of wisdom for the main event," John said after abruptly rising to his feet. Someone turned the music down. "But this seems as good a time as any."

Beside Megan, Tom blanched. Before she could run the gamut of possibilities Tom could be worried about, John dove into his impromptu speech. Instinctively, Megan reached for Tom's hand under the table. Tom's skin was clammy. He did not squeeze her hand back.

"Turning thirty seems to be agreeing with Thomas." John's confident baritone soared through the room. "He's finally making an honest woman of his college girlfriend here..." There was a light dusting of appreciative laughter. "And he won over one of Prescott and Prescott's newest and most important new clients—no, no, don't ask for details on the merger. I'm not engaging in insider trading at my son's wedding."

More laughter. Megan couldn't figure out where John was going with this.

"Well, that client asked specifically for Thomas to be the point man for the account."

The crowd applauded politely while Megan racked her brain for any knowledge of this. She knew he'd been working hard on the pharma acquisition, but Tom hadn't mentioned he'd been put in charge. Squeezing his hand again, she tried to catch his eye. Tom's hand felt like granite; his face was growing paler.

"Now, as most of you know," John continued, "this means a big move to Missouri, so as part of our wedding gift to the happy couple, Carol and I have purchased a rather large home for them in the beautiful community of Kirkwood."

Everything blurred as though Megan had just been plunged underwater. The crowd gasped and clapped. Megan let Tom's hand drop and tried to swim back up to the surface. *Kirkwood?*

"Don't worry, kids." John winked. "It's got four bedrooms. Plenty of space to give us some grandchildren."

Megan was going to be sick. This had to be a joke. A mistake. A dream. How could they be moving to Missouri? How could Tom not tell her?

And how was she finding out about this in the middle of her own rehearsal dinner?

"Megan..." Tom's whisper wasn't what she wanted. She couldn't even look at him right now.

The bodice of her dress pressed against her rib cage; the spaghetti straps dug into her shoulders. She scanned the room, looking for a life preserver, for a sign, for—she didn't know what. Someone who looked as shocked as she felt. Someone to validate her rising panic.

Her thoughts were interrupted by forks tapping on glasses, a tradition that meant she and Tom had to kiss. Which was the last thing she wanted to do. Still, she tilted her chin up to his face and he planted a chaste kiss on her lips, his eyes begging her for answers she couldn't begin to give.

Unable to help herself, she risked another glance in Leo's direction and found his eyes were on her. He was draining his wineglass with fervor, his Adam's apple bobbing.

For the first time, Megan wondered: *Is Leo right? Do I need to save myself from this?*

This was not a sea of joyful faces—this was a pond of accommodated Prescotts and along-for-the-ride Givenses. She was stuck with her family's dysfunctions, but did she really want to add a lifetime of placating her in-laws? Of watching Tom make his father's expectations a priority over her own? Did she really want to leave everything behind for a man who didn't at least *talk* to her about one of the single biggest developments of his career? Not to mention *their lives?*

Her engagement ring felt tight, her dress increasingly constricting. She had to leave, find a place to breathe. To think. Alone.

"I'm just going to make sure the kitchen remembered some vegan dessert options," she announced as she stood. But no one was looking at her. Except for Tom, but *fuck that guy.*

Megan had made it all the way down the stone steps of the restaurant when she felt someone touch her arm. She spun around, expecting to be face-to-face with Tom, only to find Leo looming over her.

He was two stairs above her. His cheeks were flushed, his eyes rimmed with the red of having too much to drink or being jet-lagged or maybe both.

"*Givens.*" Those two syllables said more to her than was fair. The hold she had on her temper exploded.

"Now?" Megan yanked him down the two stairs and then flung his hand away. "*Now?* This is when you're going to corner me? After I just found out—surprise!—that I'm moving to someplace called Kirkwood, Missouri. In fact, I already have a house there for my brood of inevitable Prescott children!"

"Did you really not know all that?" He looked shocked.

"Please, Leo. I'm not up for this. I really don't want to talk to anyone right now."

"I get it, but, look—this is my last chance before everything changes." He was persistent, pleading. He was also drunk. "I gave you some time to think it over."

"You gave me, what, four hours to consider calling off my wedding and running away with you?"

Leo's breath hitched. "So you are considering it."

"Of course I'm not. And I don't need one more thing pushing down on me today," Megan said, her chest heaving with panic, her head pounding with pressure. "I just need some fucking air."

Her high heels would only slow her down, so she slipped them off, scooped her fingers under their straps, and headed for the docks, leaving a crestfallen Leo and a restaurant full of guests behind. Overhead, clouds fused together, covering the stars.

CHAPTER SIX

TOM

TOM REMOVED HIS napkin from his lap, folded it, placed it on the table, and stood.

"Excuse me," he said to everyone at the table before going off in search of his bride. Shame heated his cheeks. Why had he let this happen? This Missouri news hadn't been a speeding locomotive; he'd had time to warn her. What an idiot he'd been. And now, the night before their wedding, Megs was furious at him.

Fair. He was furious at himself too.

At the bottom of the steps of the restaurant, he ran into Leo. "Are you a sight for sore eyes." He pulled Leo into a hug. Finally, Tom had a friend in all this. Leo knew Megs almost as well as Tom did. He might be able to offer some advice on how to get through the mess Tom had made. "I'm sorry I haven't been able to talk to you properly since you got in. It's been a day."

"It's okay, brother." Leo hugged him back, reeking of booze. "It's been a day for me too."

They walked down to the rock stub wall beside the path and took a seat. The clinking of glasses and murmurs from various celebrations danced around them. The sky suddenly cleared, stage curtains opening to the bright stars twinkling in the night.

"I'm so glad you're here. I swear, I feel as though I'm standing in the middle of a movie set and everyone has different scripts and I'm so stuck in my head..." Tom knew he wasn't making sense. He also knew Leo would get it. Leo had always been empathetic to the immense pressures Tom felt from his family.

More than anything in this moment, Tom missed the days when they were Harvard freshmen, Tom a history major, Leo permanently undeclared, sharing a suite in one of the dorms. Things were easier back then.

"Weddings are bullshit, Tommy boy," Leo said. Tom noticed how beaten down his friend seemed. Not Leo-like.

"First of all," Tom said, irritated he wasn't getting the pep talk he needed, "thanks for coming to my wedding to tell me weddings are bullshit." He knew he should ask Leo what was wrong, but Tom had a crisis of his own. "Second, have you seen Megs?"

Leo ran his hand through his hair and looked up at the moon. "Yeah."

"You gonna tell me where she is?" Tom prodded.

"Nah."

Instincts kicked in. Had she left? Tom jumped to his feet, ready to run after her. "Where is she, Leo?"

He looked away from the moon and met Tom's eyes, his gaze sad. His best friend looked like a stranger, Tom thought. He was beginning to panic.

"I slept with her."

Tom's whole body went cold. "You slept with who?"

"Megan." Leo covered his mouth as though even he couldn't believe what he was saying. Then he took that hand and rubbed his face with it. "The morning you two graduated from Harvard."

The shock tipped Tom from one side to the other until his fury emerged, burning white-hot. It grew and rose until he felt he could scorch the earth just by taking a step.

The morning they'd graduated. How could that be true?

Megs's eyes had sparkled with tears at graduation and he'd assumed they were from nostalgia and a reasonable reticence about what was to come.

He couldn't believe it, couldn't picture it. They'd just introduced their parents to each other for the first time the night before. They'd made plans for the next steps in their lives together at a restaurant that was classy enough for the Prescotts but not so upscale as to make Donna uncomfortable. He could still feel Megs's hand clutching his under the table as John looked everywhere except at Donna, and Carol wrinkled her nose delicately and ordered Bloody Mary after Bloody Mary.

It was the type of meeting that was a quiet disaster. Unsettling in its refusal to explode.

Tom and Megs had laughed nervously about it later, when they were alone. He'd felt even more bonded with her; it was them against their parents. And the world.

And then she'd turned around and slept with Leo.

The thought sickened him to the point of dizziness. He needed it not to be true. "You had sex with Megs?" Tom wanted this to be a joke, for Leo to burst into laughter, cutting the tension, extinguishing his rage.

Leo raised his hands in a half-hearted apology. "There was always something between us and I tried to stay away because of what you two had, but I couldn't. I can't."

Tom's vision was blurring. He vibrated with a sudden jarring enmity for Leo. "You *can't* stay away from my *fiancée?*"

"I'm sorry, man. I love her."

Tom wanted to shove him off the rock wall. Off the edge of the world.

"We both love her, Leo," he spat. "But you don't get to love her like I do."

"I don't *get* to? Who's supposed to give me permission? You?" Leo's lazy confidence formed a barrier as he crossed his arms.

"Yeah, me. Your best friend. The guy who's known you for twelve years. The one who introduced you to Megs in the first place. *As my girlfriend.*"

Leo raked his fingers through his douchebag beach hair and over his asshole face. Tom turned away. He had never despised anyone as much as he despised Leo in this moment, someone who'd never been pressured to do anything or be anyone. Leo's parents had never once said *You need to go to a good school.* In fact, Leo openly admitted he'd applied to Harvard as a lark.

Before they hung up after every phone call in college, Leo's parents gushed about how proud they were of him, how much they loved him, and how they admired his (heavy on the air quotes) "unique bravery."

Now Leo was using that bullshit bravery to blow into Tom's wedding and claim he loved his fiancée.

Megs.

The love of Tom's life.

Tom turned around and decked his best friend.

He'd never punched anyone before and it hurt like hell. Leo cursed, a hand cradling his jaw. He was saying something, but it wasn't anything Tom wanted to hear, and he opted to walk away before he did more than just punch Leo once.

Tom kept going even as his surroundings blurred in his peripheral vision.

Megs.

Leo.

Missouri was beside the point now. It didn't matter. Not when every good memory he'd had of his best friend and the love of his life was rotting. He watched his life as he'd known it for the past ten years burn.

Tom had never been enough for anyone—not his father, not his mother. Not even Brody. But Megs had always looked at him as though he were enough. More than enough.

But now—

Now he knew he'd been wrong this whole time. Because she'd run to the guy who was his polar opposite, free and wild.

The weight of this revelation pulled him down and he crouched on the gravel path, hidden from the restaurant—from his rehearsal dinner—by a copse of trees. He was trying to regain his balance before standing up again, but the ground beneath him kept moving.

He wasn't just losing Megs, he was losing Leo. The other person Tom loved more than anyone.

He couldn't stop torturing himself by looking at every old memory through a new lens.

The first time Megs came to his dorm to watch a movie and she sat between him and Leo.

When Leo found out he was on academic probation and took his shirt off, threw it at her, and yelled, *"Anarchy reigns supreme!"*

Curled up with Megs in that college dorm room, Leo on the other side of the wall.

Their final night of freedom, when they were supposed to stay up all night together but Tom had fallen asleep.

All the ways Megs had avoided Leo since . . . saying she had to be on set when she knew Leo was in town. Claiming she had errands to run when Leo called.

But how could Leo possibly believe he was in love with Megs if he had barely seen her in the past eight years? Hadn't properly spoken to her in that time?

Unless Tom was wrong about that too.

He shook his head; he clearly didn't know what had been going on the past eight years. All he knew was that Megs wasn't who he'd thought she was.

She was a liar.

CHAPTER SEVEN

MEGAN

SHE'D NEVER FELT so betrayed by Tom. But with Leo's proclamations fresh in her ears, Megan felt as though she had no right to the anger burning within her. It wasn't fair. How many times had she bitten her tongue rather than speak up about something because of the guilt that had been eating away at her for eight years?

But this. This was too much.

Returning to her suite, the only safe place she could think to go, Megan had to walk past the intimate outdoor wedding reception of two women slow-dancing to the Beatles' "And I Love Her" while their guests clutched tissues and one another. Megan could barely look.

That was what Megan and Tom had wanted. Despite Leo and before she knew about Missouri. It was what they'd wanted this weekend to be.

Megan got to the suite and closed the door behind her. She sat down but she couldn't stay still. She had to stand, she had to pace, she had to somehow make her mind slow down.

But she kept thinking of Tom taking a job in another state without telling her. Assuming she'd just give up her own career, her own friends, and follow him. That she'd continue being a marionette, the Prescotts pulling the strings, that he didn't even need to ask. Like his parents years ago when they'd mapped out Tom's New York future, he'd just *assumed* she'd go along with it.

She heard the beep of the key card, saw the door open, and was suddenly, finally, alone with Tom.

Only now she wasn't sure she wanted to be. Inexplicably, his eyes were blazing, his chest heaving. What did Tom have to be so upset about?

Before Megan could start yelling, Tom took off his suit jacket and threw it at the wall. She'd never seen him throw anything. Something was wrong. More wrong than Missouri. "Tom, are you—"

He stared at his jacket, now on the floor. When he finally raised his chin, he did it so slowly, Megan stopped breathing. She felt it before he said it.

He knew.

"You and Leo."

Megan nodded, terrified this was finally happening and furious she hadn't had the guts to make it happen before now.

"For how long?" His voice was low, a growl rumbling underneath, as though he were trying not to cry or had just been screaming.

She swallowed hard, unable to meet his eye as she gathered her thoughts, trying to guess how Tom had found out. What had she missed when she left the dinner? "Just the one time, Tom, I swear. It was eight years ago and I am so, so sorry I didn't—"

"You expect me to believe it was *one time* when he *just* told me he's in love with you?"

He rubbed his right hand, which appeared red and swollen. Oh God. He'd punched Leo. "All those times you begged out of hanging out with us when he was in town, all those times you hollered 'Hello' rather than talk to him on the phone, it was because you two were secretly messaging and meeting and whispering, disregarding my—"

"*No.*" Missouri aside, Megan felt a desperation to make things right that pushed her across the room. She needed Tom to know she was telling the truth. She took his hands in hers, searched his eyes for some fragment of *them*.

The very first time Tom and Megan had kissed was on their first official date. After weeks of hanging out, trying not to let their casual touches linger—trying to keep things between them breezy, featherweight, even though everything inside of each of them said, *This is the one*—Tom had invited her out for dinner. A proper dinner at a charming Mexican restaurant with a margarita menu longer than the entrée options. Megan knew she was already falling in love with him. They'd drunk enough tequila to feel bold (the server hadn't even bothered to ask for ID) and took a meandering walk through the streets of Cambridge. They stopped on a little bridge that looked like something Monet might paint if he had attended an Ivy League school. Megan touched Tom's chest because she couldn't keep *not* touching his chest. He touched her cheek so softly because she knew he was tired of *not* touching her cheek. And then he'd said, "Please, may I?" and she'd said, "What are you waiting for?" and the kiss that she felt like she'd traveled every mile between Montana and Massachusetts to experience finally happened.

Megan's eyes welled at the memory.

"I swear to you. I *swear* it was a stupid mistake that happened once. I had no idea he was trotting the globe while still having feelings for me—or believing he did. I'm sorry I didn't tell you, but the reason I didn't tell you was that it didn't matter. *It didn't matter.*" Tom refused to meet her eye. "I didn't see the point in hurting you unnecessarily for something that happened when we were twenty-two and would never happen again."

For a split second, he seemed to be softening, but then he threw off her hands and strode to the window. She could see the rigidity in his shoulders. He whipped around with a tremble in his jaw. "It's bad enough that you cheated, but why did it have to be with *him?* And if I wasn't good enough—if I'm *not* good enough, then why are we even doing this?"

His fury ignited her own.

"Hold on there. I'm not the only one who's made mistakes. What about this move to Missouri? I can't believe you went behind my back, Tom. When were you going to tell me? When the moving truck arrived? I'm so sick of not getting a say in anything. Like you think I can't be trusted to make decisions about my own life."

"You *can't* be trusted," Tom spat. "You and Leo proved that."

Her rage braided itself with her shame, with the fear he was right. Wasn't that why she hadn't ever voiced her frustrations about John and Carol? She'd given up the right to demand anything from Tom when she'd slept with his best friend. Her guilt about Leo had made just as many of her choices for her as Tom's parents had.

"That's low and you know it," Megan whispered. "You can weaponize my mistake or you can own up to the fact that when it comes to your family, you just roll over. We're leaving New York City and you didn't have the decency to even consult me. How dare you."

"I..." Tom had no response. Whether it was out of the pain of facing the truth or because he didn't want to waste his breath continuing this argument, Megan didn't know.

The faint clanking of ancient pipes broke the silence. It carried on until Megan's adrenaline drained away, replaced with a fatigue so deep, she thought she'd drown in it. She'd almost forgotten there was still a rehearsal dinner going on just outside their window.

"I didn't know how to tell you," he finally said.

"You weren't supposed to *tell* me! You were supposed to ask. To talk to me about it. What about my life in New York? My work? My friends? Did that even occur to you?"

"I thought you could switch departments and work remotely for a while," he mumbled. And then his eyes grew vicious again. "But all that is irrelevant, isn't it? Because I might have taken a job without consulting you, but you slept with my best friend."

Lightning flashed and thunder cracked outside. She waited for the accompanying rain to start hitting the windowpanes but heard nothing. The thunderstorm passed as quickly as it had started.

The silence that followed became a planet between them, with its own gravity and atmosphere. It expanded into a galaxy until fear and weariness, fury and despair, gave way to the numbness of practical matters.

"The guests," she began quietly, too tired to formulate more than fragmented thoughts. "Our families. The rehearsal dinner. The wedding."

Tom paused for so long, Megan thought he might come and hold her. Might try to make things better. But when the pause was over, it ended with a terrible blow.

"This isn't a wedding." Tom's eyes flickered with bottomless anger and hurt. "This is a fucking funeral."

His words took the wind out of her. "Are you saying..."

"I'm calling it off." Tom spoke the words with more finality than she'd ever heard before.

The first time Tom kissed Megan was on an enchanted bridge during a time when magic felt real. Possible. They'd reached for each other because every molecule within them needed to.

And now, in a dimly lit suite overlooking the ocean and her grandparents' boat, *Happy Accident*, Megan realized Tom would never kiss her again. She didn't touch his chest because she couldn't. He didn't touch her cheek because he didn't seem to want to. He grabbed the suit jacket he'd thrown in his fury and walked out the door.

Gone.

She clutched her stomach, winded from the brutal exchange. Corrosive tears burned down her cheeks, marking every hurt she'd kept to herself for the past twelve years. Every time Tom'd aligned himself with his parents rather than her. Every time he'd kept his mouth shut when they'd insulted her family. Because if she could only admit it, sleeping with Leo had felt less like a betrayal and more like payback. A betrayal for a betrayal.

She crawled into bed and pushed her face into the pillow, her professionally applied makeup staining the white hotel linens; sleep eventually overtook her. There was a part of Megan's subconscious that wished morning would never come.

DAY

2

CHAPTER EIGHT

MEGAN

BEGIN AS YOU *mean to go on.*

The words came to mind before Megan could stop them. Before she could block memories of New Year's Eves and a future that was over before it had begun.

The only thing worse than a hangover from too much drinking was a hangover from a life-changing fight. Her head pounded. Her heart was shattered.

She must've fallen asleep in the midst of her tears, and if she didn't get a hold of herself, she knew they'd start again.

This had been the second night in a row she'd gone to bed without Tom. It occurred to Megan that every night from now on, she'd be going to bed without him.

The first time Megan and Tom had slept together was a couple of weeks after their first kiss. He'd invited her to one of his family's properties. He'd called it a beach house, but it felt like a palace. That was when she'd first realized Tom came from money, a bit of trivia that seemed so irrelevant. What drew her to Tom was his kindness, the way he felt rooted. He was intellectually sharp but didn't lord it over anyone. He had a great sense of humor but never tried to grab the spotlight. He seemed to see everything she liked about herself and brush away everything she hated. She felt like the enhanced version of Megan when she was with him.

That first night at the beach house, they'd cooked dinner; he learned just how hopeless she was in the kitchen and put her in charge of pouring the wine and objectifying him. For dessert, they dipped cream puffs in melted Belgian chocolate. A few bites in and they could no longer keep their hands off each other.

The first time with Tom had been sensual but also peppered with soft laughter and a bit of fumbling. They were both eighteen, neither of them terribly experienced; she'd been his first, and he'd been her first-*ish*.

To her, it was perfect. After he ensured she climaxed, they stayed wrapped up in each other and she thought, *This is someone I can tell all my secrets to.*

But then she'd kept a secret. And now, because of it, this morning she'd have to tell everyone the wedding was off—her family, the guests, the wedding planner. Humiliation and devastation roiled through her.

Above all else, this was the first day in twelve years she'd have to face without knowing Tom was hers. He'd ripped himself from her so suddenly, it felt like a violent act.

She couldn't do it. Couldn't face everything. She was just pulling the pillow over her head when she heard that faint beep of the key card.

Tom.

She sat bolt upright in bed, surprised to note that at some point last night, she'd put on her pajamas, a pair of striped shorts and a tank top.

Instead of Tom, Donna Givens burst into the room. If Tom had told her the news, she seemed to be taking it rather well.

"I've heard Amazon can deliver same day, but every dress I've looked at says it ships in one to two weeks." Donna placed one hand on the small of her back and pressed the other against her chest.

Megan froze. "Didn't we…"

Donna's demeanor indicated she hadn't heard about Megan and Tom's fight the night before. If she had, she'd be throwing things by now, accusing Megan of ruining both her own and Donna's futures.

"Didn't we *what?*" Donna snapped. "Are you listening? I need a new dress."

It took Megan a minute to connect the dots. She was talking about a new dress for *today*. That was it. Because of course her mother suddenly wanted to get another new dress for the wedding. Odd that she'd brought up Amazon again, though.

Except…

Megan looked back down at her pajamas. There was no way she'd put them on last night. She rubbed at her eyelashes. No mascara. There was also no way she'd washed her face before bed. Maybe she'd cried the mascara off?

She gave her mother the once-over. She was in the same dramatic pose as yesterday, wearing the same blue blouse with the same scarf around her neck. And there was definitely no way she'd repeat an outfit in front of Carol. None of this made any sense. And if it didn't make any sense…

"It was a dream," Megan mumbled, her heart speeding up. That was the only logical explanation. She tried to remember the previous night…not the rehearsal dinner and awful fight, but the actual night before, when she'd arrived at the island and unpacked her suitcase and happily gone to bed. It felt far away.

She shook off the feeling, because if the rehearsal dinner and the whole day leading up to it *had* been a dream, that meant there'd been no fight and there'd be no surprise move to Missouri.

Most important, that meant the wedding was still on.

A grin broke out across her face. Megan felt she could cry from relief. Tom still loved her. They would still have their life together. Imperfect though it was, they'd gotten through a dozen years together. That was longer than almost all of her mother's relationships combined.

She knew Tom's heart perhaps better than she knew her own. He would always try to do the right thing, always cherish her and try to make her laugh when she got bogged down. Their relationship had its complications, but there was so much good in it. Looking back on what she and Tom had built together, starting when they were only kids, filled Megan with pride.

Sure, there had been mistakes...

Swatting away guilty, insoluble thoughts of Leo and the dream version of her that he had asked to run away with him, Megan embraced the chance to make her rehearsal-dinner day the one she'd actually wanted. Her subconscious had kindly created a worst-case scenario, preparing her better than all her spreadsheets and to-do lists combined. She knew now that if Tom learned about Leo, it wouldn't alleviate her guilt. It would soil everything, steal her future with him. She wouldn't let that happen.

"*What* was a dream?" Donna asked.

"Nothing. Don't worry about it." Megan got out of bed, shoved her cold toes into the hotel slippers, went into the bathroom, and closed the door behind her.

While she got ready, Donna yelled at her through the door in a vaguely British accent, "I see Tom hasn't even arrived yet from his *oh so crucial* client dinner?"

"You're being English again," Megan said through a mouthful of toothbrush.

"I need something to wear to the rehearsal dinner tonight," Donna told her, then paused. "You can see Gran and Granddad's boat from here."

"*I know.*" Her subconscious had done an impeccable job.

"Cheer me up, Moopy," Donna prodded, tapping lightly on the bathroom door.

Megan swung it open, digging deep for the patience required to parent her own mother. "If you don't feel comfortable with your dress, why don't we go to Friday Harbor and see if we can find something you like better?"

"That's a splendid idea." Donna kissed Megan's forehead. "I'm going to dash off and invite your sister to go with us."

In her dream, she'd put on the heart pendant and met Tom at the ferry dock. But she didn't want to do things the same way; it seemed like bad luck.

If she were being truly honest, the dream made her a bit afraid to see Tom. The fight they'd had might not have been real, but it still contained truths she didn't want to face. Not right now. Not during what should be one of the best weekends of her life.

Instead, she sent Tom a text telling him she'd leave the rental-car keys in their hotel room and that she couldn't wait to see him later.

Since she'd dug it out specifically for this weekend, she still put on the necklace, then set out to grab breakfast at the market before meeting her mom and sister. At least this time she had no reason to seek out Carol.

It was a beautiful morning, warm with a hint of crispness. Megan inhaled the sea air as she took in the sights of the morning: the children in pajamas holding hands with their grown-ups walking across the docks to the showers. Oddly enough, the coffee vendor looked familiar, as did the woman who sold her the scone. Or perhaps her dream was getting fuzzier the more awake she felt.

She took her time, weaving through the booths, sipping slowly as she watched boaters wake and cook breakfast on their stern grills. This was her happy place. For the hundredth time, she was filled with a sweet serenity that, despite all the wedding details the Prescotts pushed for—and offered to pay for—they'd at least agreed to hold everything in the place closest to her heart.

As much as she wanted to spend the morning cloaked in this quiet comfort, she knew it was time to head up to the hotel lobby.

"Megan, darling, I just got word that the wedding rehearsal isn't going to be held this afternoon. When do you intend to have it? After dinner? That sounds terribly inconvenient."

The voice was coming from behind her. Megan turned to see Carol's pinched face. Again. *No, not again,* she told herself. *That was a dream.*

"Good morning, Carol!" Megan smiled tightly, her heart pounding. "Yes, there was a scheduling conflict with the hotel, but the wedding planner said we could skip the rehearsal—he'll make sure we're all in the right places at the right time."

"Mmm. Anyway, what are you doing here? I'm sure you have a thousand details you should be checking on."

"I was just enjoying a bit of quiet time before diving into all those details." Megan tamped down her effusiveness. "This place is so gorgeous."

"It is lovely," Carol agreed. "Shame it takes two planes and a ferry to get here."

A prickling crawled up the back of Megan's neck as Carol's gaze traveled down. "What's on your feet, dear? Are those the hotel slippers?"

This was déjà vu, that was all. Wasn't that what déjà vu really was? Something you'd experienced in a dream that coincidentally occurred in real life? "No, these are just some sandals I brought." Her voice sounded hollow to her own ears.

"Mmm." Carol wrinkled her nose as though Megan had broken wind, just as she had in the dream. "Anyway, I won't keep you. I just wanted to make sure you'd rearranged the seating at tonight's dinner so my tennis friends could sit a bit closer to John and me."

"Yes. I took care of it." Megan's heart beat erratically. This was wedding jitters, that was all. Though the explanation didn't quite make sense, she tried to convince herself it did.

"Good girl." Carol air-kissed Megan on each cheek as she said goodbye.

CHAPTER NINE

TOM

TOM PRESCOTT WAS sleeping so deeply, he was as good as dead. The startling bellow of a foghorn blaring directly into his ear brought him back to life.

He jolted awake, clamping one hand over his pounding heart. The garbled noise of a vaguely familiar voice was welcoming him to Friday Harbor. Tom's eyes felt like sandpaper when they were closed and even worse when he opened them. He instinctively reached for his eye drops and found them in a plastic baggie— the same one he'd put them in for airport security—in the pocket of a suit he knew he hadn't been wearing at the end of yesterday.

He was sitting on a kelly-green perforated metal seat.

On the ferry.

In the same clothes he'd worn to dinner with the pharma clients two days ago.

Two days ago. That had to be right. Yesterday had been dedicated to the catastrophic tragedy he wished he could erase from his memory forever.

But why was he back on the ferry pulling into Friday Harbor?

Instead of slowing down, his heart beat faster and with such fervor, Tom was positive it'd burst out of his chest if he removed his hand.

"Good morning, sunshine."

Tom turned, knowing who the voice belonged to and also knowing that it was impossible. A pain shot from the nape of his neck down to his shoulder blades. The Henry Winkler look-alike gave him a friendly smile.

"Good morning?" Tom questioned with a nervous nod.

Beneath his hand, his heart was slowing. Stopping, perhaps. This was what was happening. He was hallucinating. Did that happen when someone experienced cardiac arrest?

His lips were as dry as his throat. He ran his tongue over his fuzzy teeth, wanting a toothbrush almost as much as he wanted to figure out what the hell was going on.

The last thing he remembered was the fight.

Jealousy and embarrassment pulsed as he replayed the night before.

The rehearsal dinner. His father's speech. Megan's flight. And then—Leo saying he was in love with Megs. Tom's fist twitched in muscle memory.

He'd confronted Megs; they'd had the first real fight of their entire relationship.

And Tom had chosen to hit the detonator on the wedding and run.

He remembered thinking he couldn't go to his parents' suite. It would have been priceless fodder for his dad's disappointment. Nor could Tom go to Brody's hotel room. Hanging out with Brody and Emmeline even when Tom *wasn't* in crisis was awkward enough. They were either so polite to each other they seemed like strangers or so passive-aggressive he wanted to bolt for the nearest exit.

So Tom had dragged his feet into the hotel's market, bought a bottle of Jack, and took refuge in the rental car. Sleeping in the back seat had aggravated the persistent ache in his neck, but he'd had to choose between facing his family and sleeping in the rental car, and the car was the lesser of the evils.

He remembered sleep had been eluding him, not because he'd been origami'd into the back seat of a midsize luxury vehicle but because the foundation he'd built his whole world on had shifted. He'd counteracted his insomniac thoughts with long swigs from his bottle of whiskey as he'd tried to imagine a future without Megs. All he saw were blank pages, empty scenes, and heartache.

And now he was back on the ferry, docking at the island he didn't remember leaving.

He pulled out his phone, cursed the lack of cell service, and settled for pressing the calendar icon. It reminded him that today was the day of his rehearsal dinner in Roche Harbor.

The familiar aches and griminess he felt indicated he wasn't hallucinating. This was real.

So there had to be a rational explanation for why he couldn't remember getting on this boat. And why he was wearing his work suit.

Or maybe, if this morning wasn't a hallucination, yesterday had been a dream. *That was it.* He'd just experienced a dream so vivid it'd felt like reality. A couple of weeks ago Megs had dreamed Tom ate the wedge of smoked Gouda she'd bought to reward herself for getting through a tough week and she woke up mad at him...until she saw the cheese was still in the fridge. Dreams could feel that real.

Yes. That had to be it. Yesterday had been a dream. Definitely a dream.

And if yesterday had been a dream, that meant Leo and Megs had never...

He rubbed at the fist he'd used to punch Leo—which showed no sign of having hit anything—then let it drop. He could have burst out laughing from relief. His life, his relationships were all still intact. The world as he'd known it still existed.

As soon as his best friend arrived today, Tom would tell him about the dream and they'd have a good laugh.

A change in time zones and too many hours at the office. This was where his confusion was coming from. Whenever Tom pulled an all-nighter at work, he would come home and bellyflop into a three-hour sleep. And every time he woke up, it took him several minutes to figure out where he was. Megs loved teasing him about his coma naps.

He put his eye drops back in his pocket and tried to shake off the nightmare. He was sure Megs would be there when he got off the ferry, and his world would shift back into place.

Except when he got off the ferry, Megs wasn't there. He carried his luggage up the ramp and looked around, hoping she was running late. He stood motionless by the curb, staring at the incline of the road and the restaurants and shops he could've sworn he'd seen just yesterday.

"Fancy a ride? Where are you heading?" A pedicab appeared in front of him. The driver was a woman with long, silvery hair and leg muscles more impressive than his own.

Wordlessly, Tom shook his head. His heart started pounding again as the pedicab soared off in search of other customers. Tom squinted in the sun and spotted a giant fishing hat across the street. His eyes traveled in slow motion down from the hat, and he saw a man wearing a baby carrier…holding a contented tabby cat.

This wasn't just déjà vu. This was déjà vu on speedballs.

A taxi was idling near the ice cream shop. Tom awkwardly jogged over, luggage in tow, and climbed in. After asking the driver to take him to the resort at Roche Harbor, he pulled out his phone and saw that he had a text from Megs and a voice mail. When he listened to his brother's familiar yet somehow new message ("It's Brody. We're already at the tee, Spare Parts. Get here now. Get here five minutes ago"), a chill ran through his body.

He didn't know what was going on—couldn't even fathom it. But whatever it was had eclipsed the enormity of the terrible day before.

So it was a new day…and yet it was going very much the same way Tom had known it would. Brody was sipping from his flask, making jokes about Tom's longtime fear of flying and their mother's "two planes and a ferry" complaints. John was slapping Brody on the back and taking little jabs at Tom, launching questions about the previous night's client meeting.

The whole morning, Tom barely spoke except to answer his dad as best he could. This clearly irritated Brody, who liked to get a rise out of him. They'd had this dynamic their entire lives: Tom seeking attention from his older brother, and his older brother delivering only teasing. It was a hamster wheel Tom couldn't seem to dismount.

"What's your deal, Spare Parts? Getting cold feet? In a fugue state? Or is this one of those things where it turns out you've been dead this whole time?"

"Are you asking me if I'm Bruce Willis in *The Sixth Sense*?"

"I was thinking more like *Weekend at Bernie's*."

Tom tried to laugh but it came out strangled. Even he could feel the quiet mania he was projecting.

"Are you on drugs or something?" When Tom ignored this, Brody tapped him on the forehead the way he used to when he'd pinned his little brother and wouldn't let up until Tom named ten candy bars. *Tap, tap, tap.* "And if you *are* on drugs, young Thomas, will you please be a good little brother and share?"

Tom shook his head, afraid of what he was disrupting in the space-time continuum. Maybe if he went through the motions of participating in this golf game, everything would go back to normal.

Although…

Tom wasn't sure he wanted things to go back to normal.

Yesterday's "normal" was the worst of his life. He needed answers. Understanding. *Something*. Not knowing what else to do, whenever his dad and Brody got involved enough in the game, Tom turned away and tried to call Megs. She'd always been his touchstone, and even after the fight they may or may not have had the night before, somehow the prospect of hearing her voice seemed like the right next step. A way to start fitting the pieces of this puzzle together.

But Megs didn't answer. Unease continued crawling up and settling over him like a second skin.

When it came to the point in the game—the ninth hole—where Tom had previously asked his father for advice, Tom realized he didn't want to hear that speech again. Today he was staying silent and following a different trajectory.

He nearly laughed at himself. All he could think was that this day was repeating. But that didn't make any sense. The idea was so absurd, he nearly leaned over the water hazard to splash his face, wake himself up.

So Tom silently lined up his putt. He was about to gently guide the ball into the ninth hole when John interrupted him.

"You know, Tom, I'd say you're doing all right this weekend."

Tom froze, praying his father was referring to his golf game. "Thanks?" he tentatively ventured.

"Megan's a smart choice for a partner. You've done well on that. She's driven. Works hard. Good-looking enough to be arm candy, yet smart enough to hold a conversation. But even when you select a partner who makes sense on paper, there are always variables that are unaccounted for." He raised his eyebrows at Tom's brother. "Broderick knows what I'm talking about."

"To my wife, Emmeline." The vaguely amused look that had been on Brody's face all morning vanished as he raised the flask in a toast, then took that long swig. Tom tried to block his father out. He tried a gentle swing and overdid it. His ball rolled farther away.

He walked toward it, pressing his lips together so he wouldn't say a word.

"In Megan's case," John continued, "it's her disastrous, infestive family. But look—marriage doesn't have to mean compromise. We've already set the precedent of the two of you spending the holidays with our side of the family. When you start having kids, you don't want that Donna woman influencing them. So you've got to be tough about that. You get what you want, you lay down the law, and if Megan ever complains about it..." He lined up his putt. "There's always golf."

Just like he had the first time, John tapped his ball into the last hole.

There was absolutely no way Tom could have dreamed so many minute details of a day that hadn't happened yet. Which meant...

No. That didn't make sense either.

Still, Tom could think of no other explanation.

Could it be possible? Was this really happening?

He thought of everything he'd seen and heard and felt *twice* now: Henry Winkler on the ferry. The crick in his neck. Brody's drinking game. His father's "advice" that couldn't be stopped.

Adding it all together could mean only one unthinkable thing: *Tom was reliving this day.*

A prickle settled over his skin as the world seemed to wobble. How was something like this possible? Should he go to a hospital? To a psychic?

He very nearly sat down right on the green, but he didn't want to attract attention to himself and the inner panic rising like a flood inside him. This was an inexplicable situation and his best course of action, he supposed, was to keep moving forward. Pretend he was fine.

Even though he was most definitely *not* fine.

Because whatever was happening was impossible.

And if yesterday wasn't a dream…then what he'd learned was true.

Megs and Leo really *had* slept together.

Tom's throat went dry; his stomach churned. His knuckles ached with the phantom pain of a punch that hadn't happened. His anger felt as fresh as it had the night before.

He'd been betrayed by the two people he'd thought would always love him, be loyal to him. Who'd chosen him. By his best friend and the woman he'd trusted more than anyone.

He'd never felt so alone in all of his life.

As quickly as he crumbled, he snapped out of it. Megan had betrayed him, so Tom was wasting his time here. He didn't need to stay for the burger and pilsner at the restaurant his dad didn't think was good enough; he didn't need to witness his brother's day-drinking or endure his dad's reminder that he was an idiot for not telling his fiancée about Missouri yet. He considered leaving without a word, but he needed Megs to know that *he knew* what she'd done.

And so the only thing Tom had to do was find Megs and call off the wedding again—this time before the sham of the rehearsal dinner celebrating their sham of a relationship even began.

CHAPTER TEN

MEGAN

WHETHER IT WAS out of morbid curiosity or because she was moving in some sort of trance, Megan continued on through the day as she already had once before. Although, by skipping the part where she'd met Tom at the ferry, Megan found herself in the hotel lobby at the same time Paulina arrived. She held on to that small change in her day like a precious heirloom. Proof she wasn't losing her grip on reality.

There were the family members you were born with and the family members you chose; Paulina Tate-Shahid was both to Megan. Despite being the much younger sister of Megan's erratic mother, Paulina had a calming presence—and a wicked wit.

While nervously sipping her extra-large coffee and waiting for Donna, Megan saw her aunt. Paulina's husband, Hamza, was beside her, hauling their luggage. Megan ran to them. "Paulina!"

Her aunt embraced her fully, her pregnant belly wedged between them. "Hi, my darling girl. Hamza and I are so excited to be here."

"So excited she may piddle on the floor," Hamza added, a twinkle in his warm maple-syrup eyes.

Paulina spun on him, her endless auburn locks twirling with

her. She held up an index finger. "Once. That happened *once*. And in my defense, this kid of ours seems to have set up camp on my bladder."

"You look gorgeous," Megan said as Hamza kissed Paulina's forehead sweetly.

"I look like I swallowed another person. Who's *also* pregnant."

Megan laughed despite her unease at the inexplicable day she was having. "I can't tell you how relieved I am to have some voices of reason here."

Paulina and Hamza exchanged a knowing look.

For the first fourteen years of Megan's life, Paulina had lived down the street, babysitting her and her siblings whenever Donna would abruptly leave, claiming she had a job interview, only to return smelling of cigarette smoke and perfume samples.

Megan had been crushed when Paulina left to do her undergraduate degree at Boston University, which felt light-years away from Great Falls. But it was one of their first long-distance conversations that had clarified her own path. Megan had told Paulina about a photography class she was taking in which she was documenting how a recent drought had affected Montana, and Paulina said, "Oh, Megan, that's amazing. I can definitely see you spending your days telling stories. Artists aren't created, you know. They're born. That's who you've been since day one."

Her words had flipped a switch in Megan. She began watching documentaries, admiring how filmmakers brought focus to overlooked stories, infused them with atmosphere and context. Paulina went on to pursue a graduate degree in England, where she fell in love with Hamza and decided to stay permanently, so Megan's horizons expanded even further.

Applying to Ivy League schools was Megan's version of making a wish and blowing dandelion seeds into the wind. She didn't expect her wish to come true. And yet the acceptances rolled in, so she chased the legacy of her aunt, the only role model she'd ever had, to Massachusetts, believing she had two options: become Donna or emulate Paulina.

At Harvard she'd found purpose. And Tom.

"How are you holding up?" Paulina tucked some stray hairs behind Megan's ear. "Where's everyone else?"

As though on cue, Brianna breezed into the lobby, already halfway through a monologue about how she'd exacerbated Donna's self-consciousness with one "innocent" comment about her bazongas.

Paulina gave Megan a quick squeeze and took Hamza by the hand. "We're going to get checked in and settled. Good luck."

The day took a familiar shape from there. Megan rode to Friday Harbor for an impromptu and wholly unnecessary shopping trip with Brianna and Donna. When Brianna brought up staying with her and Tom in New York, Megan stopped herself from saying that she was apparently moving to Missouri, because with any luck, that part would stay in her dream. A small relief amid all the confusion.

"Has anyone heard from Alistair?" Brianna asked out of the blue as they drove back to Roche. Brianna had never been comfortable with silence.

Donna openly ignored the question. Megan shook her head, both an answer and a *Don't go down this road* gesture. Donna was very sensitive about matters concerning her firstborn, and Megan wasn't sure she could take any more of her mother's antics this morning.

"Well," Donna huffed, "if you hear from him, remind him he still has a mother, should he ever want to speak to her."

"I'd text him, but he told me not to," Brianna continued, oblivious to the emotional temperature shift. "He said he doesn't always have international plans on his phone and my messages were costing him too much money."

This time Megan ignored Brianna too.

Despite a few variations here and there, Megan was experiencing everything she had the day before and the repetition left her feeling more and more disoriented. As the details added up, she was finding it increasingly difficult to believe it had all just been a dream.

She was so thrown, she ignored every call and message from Tom. She couldn't trust herself to have a normal conversation with him, was terrified she'd blurt out echoes of their fight from the night before or let something slip about Leo. Until she could fully understand what was happening, she needed to keep her head down.

And she did. Right up until she realized she was approaching her potential run-in with Leo. That, she definitely could not handle a second time. She'd barely survived the first.

The only mature response to this was to hide.

As Donna parked the car back at the hotel, Megan could only assume Leo was in the lobby. "I'm going to go for a walk," she told her mother and Brianna.

"Maybe she's making a run for it," Brianna stage-whispered to Donna. "I wouldn't blame her. Tom's the exception. The rest of the Prescotts are real pieces of work."

As Megan weaved up the steep driveway toward the island's private residences, she heard her mother say, "Oh, Brianna. Watch your mouth. Wouldn't you put up with a little snobbery for that lifestyle?"

Her sandals kept slipping on the gravel path. A trail of sweat was making its way from underneath her thick hair down the length of her spine. Most distressing, she had no solid game plan. Megan's only strategy was to stay away from Leo. It was shortsighted, considering he was the best man at her wedding, but it was all she had.

Once she dead-ended at a wealthy private home, one designed by a real-life Disney architect who'd created some iconic sets (a fact Megan had been thrilled to learn in her youth), she was trapped. If she lurked nearby and there were people in the house, they'd likely call security. *Damn it*. Where could she go?

She started pushing her way through the dense forest and brush, her legs getting scraped, spiderwebs snagging her body, her hair increasing in size with the mugginess. By the time she popped out the other side, she was in shambles—thin streaks of blood on her legs from thistles, the topknot she'd put her hair in earlier totally wild. Her eyes felt as though they could leap from her head at any moment.

Megan found herself near the back employee parking lot of the hotel. Relieved, she sat in the shade of a maple tree. She dabbed at the sweat on her forehead and was attempting to arrange her hair into a bun when she heard her name.

"Megan?"

She could weep; she could run. But suddenly this meeting felt inevitable. The only way out was through. "Hi, Leo."

"Hey!" He jogged toward her, clearly expecting her to stand and give him a hug. When she stayed put, he knelt down beside her. It was hardly fair of him to catch her in this state. Especially since Leo always looked so comfortable in his skin—not to mention his clothes. On Leo, a T-shirt that cost five dollars looked like it cost five *hundred*. Something about how he carried himself made casual seem couture.

"I've been searching for you," he said. "You look—"

"Like Bigfoot's bride?"

"I was going to say beautiful. Although…" He carefully picked a few twigs and a small leaf from her hair and handed them to her like peace offerings.

But there was no peace where Leo was concerned. She knew that now, although she still couldn't decipher how or why.

"Can I talk to you? Please?" His voice was tentative, but he had a spark in his eye. A look that dared her to say yes, to love him. Leo, with his lazy smile and easy charm, was meant to be adored. And Megan *had* adored him. But that adoration was self-destructive. More than she'd let herself realize in her late-night fantasies. Because Leo was the type of guy Donna would choose—unpredictable and wild.

A pang of nostalgia, so sharp it made her short of breath, came on suddenly. She remembered the first time she and Leo had hung out, just the two of them. Tom had strep throat and they'd decided to go to CVS to find things to cheer him up. They'd bought a yo-yo, a packet of baseball cards, Popsicles the color of nuclear waste, and teen magazines with quizzes like "What Shade of Lip Stain Best Represents *Your* Personality?" and "Are You Ready to Tell Him How You Feel?" They'd laughed so hard in the incontinence aisle, Megan nearly peed. Leo, oversize brat that he was, offered to buy Megan a package of Depends.

She briefly indulged one of her favorite forbidden daydreams of living out of a tent with Leo, him scouting locations for new tours while she pursued the subject of her documentary, the one that would sweep the awards at international film festivals. They'd have no family members for miles and miles. And she wouldn't have to work at a job she'd taken because it was convenient for *his* career.

Because that's exactly what she'd done for Tom. While he went to law school, she'd stayed in Cambridge with him and got her master's. When he moved to New York to be an associate at his dad's law firm, she'd gotten a job at *GQ* so they'd be together. Every decision she'd made was to stay in step with him. What would things look like now if she hadn't?

In another life she could've chosen the path that would take her through the brambles with Leo. She could've dropped the idea of security and pursued passion instead. Together they could've spent months off the grid, making love in shabby tents, pretending everyone else had evaporated from the earth.

In another life.

Or this one.

Her skin prickled. The thought was a betrayal of everything she believed. So Megan did what she always did when her resentments grew too loud. She plucked a Tom memory from the drawer in her mind that she kept locked up and safe just for moments like this. The memory was of the first note Tom had ever written her (not including the Cure lyrics in her notebook). She recited the note's contents to herself, just as she did whenever her doubts about Tom loomed too large.

"Come on, Megan." Leo picked a few blades of grass and playfully tossed them at her nose to get her attention. "You've been avoiding me for years—don't think I haven't noticed. You can give me ten minutes now."

"I'll give you two," she said, against her better judgment.

Leo chuckled. "Remember when you used to time me to see how fast I could get to the liquor store and back with more beer?"

"You'd always show up with these weird craft-brewery samples that had flavors like Fruity Pebbles and Bull Testicle." She shook her head at the memory. "You now have one minute."

"You're killing me, Givens." Leo rubbed at his eyes in frustration. "We have this unspoken conversation between us that's been steeping for eight years and I don't know where to even start."

"Thirty seconds, Leo."

"*Givens*. Please. Just hear me out?" While Leo waited for her to respond, he continued to pick nervously at the grass, an alluring smile on his face but fear in his eyes. "Aren't you afraid of what you're signing up for? Of what you're signing away? I care about you, Givens. I'm worried about you. I just...your happiness means a lot. To me. And it should mean a lot to you too. I just have to know. Are you happy?"

She risked a look at her former best friend, a hundred different scenarios playing out in her mind, underscored by the sound of her own voice chanting, *What do you want? What will make you happy?*

Megan thought of the gifts Leo had sent her and Tom over the years. When they'd moved to SoHo, Leo sent them a sculpture by an artist she loved as a housewarming gift. Two Christmases prior, they'd received a rare copy of Megan's favorite episode of *Mystery Science Theater*. Leo sent gifts they'd both enjoy but that were particularly meaningful to Megan. She didn't know whether to be flattered or appalled.

Before she could decide just what to say to him, what magical combination of words would make everything right, a shadow loomed over their heads. She looked up, expecting for a moment to see Tom. It was merely a cloud passing over the sun.

This was why everything was happening again.

Maybe Megan was psychic and whatever she had experienced the day before was a warning. Was she supposed to choose a different path? Megan absorbed that...if so, this was her second chance. She was getting a do-over. An opportunity *not* to get caught up in reliving a decade-old mistake that shouldn't matter. *Didn't* matter.

She had friends who subscribed to the theory that the universe gave them signs, that there was some sort of—not necessarily a God, but a divine tapestry of energy guiding people toward their destinies.

Rebooting an entire day was a hell of a sign. And Megan was not going to ignore it.

Today was about leaving Leo in her past, about keeping her one error in judgment in the shadows so she could embrace her trajectory with Tom. Above everything else, Tom was her future. He had to be.

Because why else would they have stayed together for twelve years? And even though things weren't perfect, and it could some-times feel like they were stuck in a rut, they still had so much good between them. When their demanding jobs and even more demanding families didn't get in the way, when she didn't let herself resent him for being the sole decision-maker, she knew what they had was special. He could still give her butterflies with his sexy smile, make her laugh with an inside joke. And she never felt safer or more secure than when she was with him. Everything with Leo was unstable. Unpredictable. Unwritten. But Tom, *Megan's* Tom—he was safe.

"I don't have time for this today, Leo." Megan stood, brushing stray strands of grass off her jersey dress. "What happened between us happened when we were kids. It has nothing to do with Tom and me now."

As she left Leo behind, Megan could feel the phantom *I miss you* note in her hand, so she mentally cradled the first note Tom had ever written her in her other palm. She squeezed her fists tight, running off toward the salon, wanting to proceed with her appointments, with the festivities of the weekend and the plans that had been set long ago. No more distractions.

She was getting a do-over, and this time, when she showed up to the rehearsal dinner in her beautiful dress to sit with her beautiful fiancé, the evening would end with a kiss.

CHAPTER ELEVEN

TOM

THE LOCK SCREEN on Tom's phone still offered nothing more than the background photograph of him and Megs at the botanical gardens in Montreal. They'd driven up to Canada during a rare long weekend and spent three days filling up on poutine and crepes, trying desperately to learn French through immersion.

What a relief that pretty much everyone in Montreal spoke English.

In the photo, Megs was midlaugh, her nose wrinkling adorably. His face was in profile because he couldn't take his eyes off her. The photo had been taken by another tourist, a woman who was there with her husband to celebrate their fiftieth anniversary.

"We've already been together for over a decade," Megs had said while they chatted amiably. "Getting to fifty years will be no problem."

Tom had kept the photo front and center as a reminder of that day. Of how easily they could see an entire lifetime together.

Now the photo made him want to chuck his phone against a brick wall.

He shrugged into his suit jacket. It felt too tight around the shoulders.

He'd been calling and texting Megs intermittently for hours but there had been no response. At first he wondered if something had happened to her. He'd considered texting her family to make sure she was okay and then, like a flood, he thought about her with Leo. She was probably avoiding Tom to sneak off with his best friend and didn't even have the courtesy to answer her damn phone.

He was pissed. Telling her just how pissed was all he wanted—it would quench his anger like a cold beer on a hot day. There was no way in hell he was going to sit through that rehearsal dinner; he was calling off the wedding the moment he found her.

But he was in their hotel room and she was God knew where.

He remembered when she'd first started out at *GQ*, not long after they'd moved to New York together; she'd gotten the opportunity to sit in on an interview with the legendary Kenneth Birch, one of the few men in Hollywood with a truly successful and long-lasting relationship. When Tom asked if Megs had heard any good celebrity gossip, Megs laughed and told him that Kenneth's juiciest stuff had been about his own life. He'd talked about how couples tended to have the same fight over and over again, that while the words sounded different in each, the meanings were the same. The insight had been interesting, if a little disappointing; Kenneth had starred in dozens of movies over the course of at least three decades, and Tom had been hoping to find out which of Kenneth's costars threw tantrums on set.

But for some reason, that story had stayed with Tom. Even though it didn't seem to apply, because he and Megs never fought—with the exception of Megs tossing a pillow at his face and telling him to cut his toenails because they were scratching her calves in bed or Tom telling Megs to wear her nasal strips to clamp down on her snoring. But even when they'd first moved to New York and everyone told them over and over again that they'd sink or swim in the city, they'd never felt as overwhelmed as they should've, and they'd certainly never taken it out on each other.

That was their secret drinking game, regardless of whether or not alcohol was present. If someone responded to Tom and Megan's "take over New York" plan with the phrase *sink or swim*, they'd share a look and mime taking a shot.

They didn't even fight when John and Carol kept offering to foot the bill to get them out of their dodgy neighborhood and their even dodgier apartment and when all they could afford to eat was peanut butter and whatever carb was on day-old sale at a nearby bakery. Tom and Megan were more than content making love on the stained futon they'd bought off Craigslist to the sounds of their upstairs neighbors trying to train their dog. Their relationship felt untouchable.

He knew now it'd already been touched. Defiled. Because the Megs who'd moved to New York with him and who'd mimed taking shots and who'd eaten peanut butter on stale dinner rolls was also the one who'd slept with his best friend and never told him.

His anger, the hurt he felt, was as fresh as it had been when Leo made the confession during *yesterday's* today. How could she avoid him all day and leave him to stew alone in his misery?

He rolled that word around in his mind: *alone*. Because he had to be alone in this. Everyone else seemed to be going through the day for the first time. And if Megs were experiencing this loop thing too, she would've answered one of his calls—or tried to call him.

He gave up on trying to reach her. They'd see each other at some point during this day. His stomach clenched at the thought.

As much as he wanted to confront her, to call everything off as soon as he could, he also *didn't*. Because living through the ensuing fight again was beyond cruel.

Tom couldn't stay in this hotel room one more minute waiting for Megs to show up. With only an hour until the dreaded rehearsal dinner, he decided to get himself some courage in a glass to deal with what lay ahead.

There was a casual restaurant close to the pier and then there was the one higher up, offering better views and a pricier menu, where their rehearsal dinner would take place. Luckily, the former also had a bar.

He walked up the stone steps and shook his head at the hostess who wanted to put him on the patio with the rest of the polo-wearing guests dining on charcuterie platters and crab cakes. He didn't want a stunning view or to be surrounded by happy families making memories in the last days of summer. He didn't want to look at *Happy Accident* in the marina. He wanted to lurk in a dark corner and try to make sense of this day. Of his life.

He perched on a bar stool, not caring whether he was wrinkling his suit, and stared at the menu.

"Oh, man, you look like a goomba," said a sultry voice from behind the bar. Tom glanced up from the happy-hour menu.

Her name tag said CASEY. She wore her jet-black hair in a high ponytail that hung straight down to her waist. The azure ends appeared to have been dipped in a blue-raspberry Slurpee. She had a tiny stud in her nose. Her eyes were lined in a way that flicked at the end. It occurred to Tom that *this* was what Megs had meant all those times she'd talked about trying and failing to do a cat-eye.

"A goomba," he said.

Her lips, a surprisingly appealing orangey red, broke into an easy, sardonic smile. "Yeah. You know, those little mushroom guys from Super Mario who have angry eyebrows and perma-frowns."

"I know what a goomba is."

"Then you shouldn't have said 'A goomba' like you didn't."

Tom had thought that if he couldn't talk to Megs, he wanted to be alone. Yet he was enjoying this. Here was someone he owed absolutely nothing to. Someone who could distract him from the storm ahead, if only for a minute. "You're saying I look like an angry little mushroom man."

"You *do* get it." Casey leaned on the bar. "What can I get you? Something to cheer you up, perhaps?"

"Yeah. I'm thinking a scotch."

She leaned in closer and stage-whispered, "I don't know if you know this, but alcohol is a depressant." She turned around, made his drink, gave him one more smile as she placed it in front of him, and left him to brood.

He replayed yesterday in his mind. He replayed today. He searched for some sort of answers as to why it was happening—*how* it was happening—and came up empty. When he started replaying the fight he'd already had with Megs and had to have again, he needed distraction more than scotch. So he caught the bartender's eye and raised his glass in her direction as a miniature cheers.

"How's that scotch going down? Like liquid sunshine?" Casey sauntered over, her smile crooked. Inviting.

"About what you'd expect." Tom's voice sounded troubled, even to himself.

"Bartenders are supposedly unlicensed therapists, right?" She rested her elbows on the bar.

"So I've heard."

"Then may I offer you some unsolicited advice?" She tilted her head. "I've heard that people *love* receiving unsolicited advice."

He laughed despite himself. Despite everything. "Be my guest."

"Whatever's making you look like an angry mushroom isn't worth it."

"Oh yeah?" Tom sat up straighter, crossing his arms, his body language transmitting full skepticism. And perhaps a little intrigue. "What makes you so sure?"

"Life's too short, man. Too damn short. Especially for someone like you—handsome, together. You can spend your days tying yourself in knots for the things that ultimately make you miserable, or you can chase the great unknown."

"The great unknown?" Tom scoffed. It sounded like something Leo would say.

This woman, objectively beautiful, had never been a Prescott. She'd probably never had the surest thing in her life blow up in her face, only to have to confront the explosion again the next day. The great unknown actually existed for the Leos and the Caseys of the world. Tom wanted it to exist for him too.

Instead, he was neck-deep in known miseries.

As much as he dreaded calling off the wedding (again), he was also dreading the fallout—his parents' disappointment in his failed relationship, their embarrassment at becoming fodder for country-club gossip, the inevitable moments he'd forget and want to text Leo something funny. He dreaded missing the way Megs would try to distract him while he cooked by shimmying to music around him. Above all, he dreaded the nights he'd now spend alone, without Megs's cold feet and the soft sounds of her breath beside him.

The person who caught him when he felt like he was falling had always been Megs, and this time she'd been the one to push him off the cliff.

"Oh yeah. The great unknown." Casey's voice brought Tom back to the bar. She nodded as though this were scientific fact. "If you ask me—and you didn't, but we've already established you live for unsolicited advice—the great unknown is the whole point."

"Thanks for the advice," he said. He raised his glass to her again, swallowed its contents, and said, "And thanks for the liquid sunshine. I feel so much better." But he didn't. He felt categorically worse, unable to get the phrase *the great unknown* to stop spinning in his head.

It was dawning on Tom, as the so-called liquid sunshine loosened him up, that all those years, the fact that they *weren't* fighting was so much worse than actually fighting. Because what they *hadn't* been fighting about was Megan screwing around on him. With his best friend.

They'd never fought about the fact that it had happened or *why* it had happened. They'd never fought about how it was or if Leo was better or how she'd felt afterward, keeping it from Tom.

He'd never been given the chance to yell or process what had happened. He'd been cast as the ignorant fool in Megs's betrayal, and, yes, that was much worse than having the same fight over and over again.

Megan had looked at him mere hours later from under the brim of her black graduation cap, the tassel bouncing when she laughed, her eyes reflecting the sun.

And now she wasn't even returning his calls. What had happened to her today to stop her from meeting him at the ferry dock? To make her avoid him? There was no way for her to know his intention was to break things off, so why was she ghosting him?

He straightened his tie and left the bar. He was still frustrated their paths hadn't crossed, and now he had to endure another dinner of subtle horrors just so he could end things afterward. Because there was no way he was making a scene in front of all their guests. In front of his dad. No, Tom would grin and bear it until the dinner was over. He could do that.

In the private room of the upscale restaurant, she finally walked through the door; stunning in a champagne dress that caught the light whenever she moved, her expression bright and questioning. He couldn't help but look at her mouth, the one he'd been kissing for his entire adult life. The one that had kissed his best friend.

He crossed the room and gave her a cursory brush of his cheek against hers for their audience's sake.

"Hi?" The syllable sounded like a question, one he ignored.

"Hi." He'd meant for the reply to come out clipped, but a small shard of his anger, his broken heart, slipped out too.

Her eyebrows furrowed. "What's wrong? And why do you smell like scotch?"

He turned away from her, ignoring both her questions. "We should do the rounds."

Before she could protest, he crossed the room to the first guests he recognized from his parents' list, tennis friends of his mother's. Out of the corner of his eye, he saw Megan hesitate before making her way to her grandparents' table.

Somehow he survived a parade of small talk, of accepting best wishes and congratulations he no longer wanted. When they sat down at their table, he immediately turned away from Megs to engage Brody and Emmeline in a conversation about New York politics. If anyone noticed the chilly air between himself and his fiancée, no one said a word. Prescotts and Givenses kept to themselves as guests found their seats and appetizers rolled out.

Minutes, gestures, words. Sips, bites, swallows. He was passing through the evening as though surrounded by a fog, punctuated only by meaningless sounds and movements.

"We have to give out the gifts," Megan whispered to him as he mindlessly munched on a crostini.

"Be my guest." Tom took another bite. He felt a small satisfaction in the way his dismissal made her shoulders tense. Let her be angry at the way he was ignoring her. He had more to be angry at her about.

He watched her stand, her jaw clenched, and then forcibly relax her face into a smile. "Thanks for coming, everyone. We really appreciate all of you. Now we have some gifts we'd like to hand out to our wedding party."

The speech was surprisingly curt—particularly when compared to the speech she'd given the first time he'd experienced this dinner. He helped her hand out the cuff links and whatever was in the wrapped boxes she was giving to Paulina and Brianna (he couldn't quite recall what she'd settled on, had only vague memories of discussing it over rushed breakfasts of toasted bagels and coffee in to-go cups).

"Now we'll open up the floor to guests who would like to say a few words. Or, if you'd prefer, feel free to just eat and enjoy the company of family and friends." The way Megan had said this, it was clear she didn't want any speeches. He couldn't blame her. Listening to Great-Aunt Florence drone on had been difficult the first time. Although, he reminded himself, Megan hadn't experienced that yet. *He* shouldn't even remember it.

He looked over to where Leo was seated and found him looking at Megs intently. All this time, Tom had thought he was the only one to share secret looks with her. Tom's fists clenched under the table as he tried to steady his breathing. He couldn't believe he'd never seen what was going on between them...that he'd trusted them both so implicitly.

Sitting at a table with Megs beside him, in the shadow of John's and Carol's looming presence, Donna's ridiculousness, and Brianna's entitlement, Tom was on the verge of cracking. Of yelling, *Surprise! This whole weekend is a sham! Let's all find the nearest exit and get the hell out.*

He tried to tune out Great-Aunt Florence, who'd been undeterred by Megan's suggestion of forgoing speeches to eat. He couldn't listen as she implored him and Megs to "cling to each other" and "laugh often."

Alistair showed up, predictably unpredictable, in his cargo shorts, with his absurd stories of precarious travels locked and loaded. Food made its way around the tables; conversations became more uproarious as wine bottles were drained. His mother was asking Donna inane statistical questions about the state of Montana. The whole affair felt much longer than it had the first time.

Before Tom could remember what happened next, his father stood and commanded the room's attention like a general leading his troops into battle. "I know, I know. I'm supposed to save my words of wisdom for the main event, but this seems as good a time as any."

The sound of cutlery against plates stilled. The music quieted.

The first time his father had said a version of these words, Megs had taken his hand under the table. Tom folded his arms across his chest, not giving her the opportunity. Yes, taking this job without consulting her was a dick move. But his self-righteousness over-shadowed his guilt. What Tom had done wasn't a betrayal. No, he'd been trying to *protect* her. To avoid overwhelming her.

What Megs had done was cheat and lie and *lie and lie*...

John kept speaking, and Tom waited for the moment he knew his father would throw the Missouri grenade. The first time, he'd been too craven to see Megan's reaction. Now, morbid curiosity took over and he turned his face just enough to gauge her expression.

"Now, as most of you know," John was saying, "this means a big move to Missouri, so as part of our wedding gift to the happy couple, Carol and I have purchased a rather large home for them in the beautiful community of Kirkwood."

He waited for Megs's eyes to flash. For her to clutch her stomach or rub at her ring.

But she was eating. Taking a bite of prawn. She didn't seem thrilled...but neither was she acting like someone who'd just learned her life was being upended.

Had she not heard John?

"You're moving to Missouri?" Donna hissed at Megs.

Now Tom turned his whole body toward his fiancée.

But Megs only shrugged. "Yep."

"When were you going to tell me?" Donna tossed her napkin onto the table, clearly relishing an opportunity to get riled up.

"Oh, I only found out yesterday."

Megs's response sent a current through him.

She...

He hadn't...

Every noise faded out and then crescendoed when he heard a

guest at a nearby table say, "The bride and groom seem to be a little distracted, don't they? Shall we get them focused again?" This was followed by dozens of forks clanging against dozens of wineglasses.

The entire room wanted to see Tom and Megan kiss.

They turned to each other, a challenge in her eyes, fury in his own, and gave each other a kiss that shocked their audience into silence. This was passion fueled not by love, but by spite.

Not caring that he was being rude or abrupt, as soon as the kiss ended, Tom said to Meg, "Let's go talk," and stormed out, sparing one moment to glare at Leo as he left. He felt Megan follow. Leo made a move to get up from his chair and Tom leveled him with a look. Leo slowly sat back down and averted his eyes.

The last thing they heard as they exited was Brianna's crass "Who wants to bet they're going up to the suite for a pre-wedding boom-boom?" and Alistair laughing.

"Where are we going?" Megan asked as they rushed away from the restaurant. She took off her heels and ran to keep up with his long strides.

"We've got a few things to discuss."

"Okay."

He couldn't read anything in the way she'd said those two syllables or in the way she continued to follow him along the winding cobblestone path without any more questions. He couldn't read Megs at all anymore.

Above them, clouds moved and expanded, bloated from the weight of unshed rain.

They burst into the hotel lobby, walked past the elevators, and took the stairs two at a time. When they arrived at their suite, Tom couldn't get the key card to work for a minute because his hands were shaking.

He was ready to fight. But he needed to know something first.

"Who told you about Missouri?"

She had the gall to smirk as the tension between them rose and dropped and rose again. "Well, we both know it wasn't you."

There was something in her posture, her aura, the way she wasn't backing down. It was like she knew what was coming next.

If the answer to what he was about to ask was no, she would definitely think he was insane. Still, he braced himself and said, "This day. Have you already been through it before too?"

Tom heard her sharp intake of breath. He realized she knew. *She knew.*

"Too?" she asked. She swallowed hard and he nodded in response. They froze, thieves caught in the night.

"What's happening to us?" she whispered, her eyes locked on his.

"I don't know. I thought it was just me, but…"

The oxygen was sucked out of their inevitable fight. Tom tried to reconcile his feeling of relief at not having to go through this senseless experience alone with the pain of having to go through it with the one person he didn't ever want to see again.

And yet here they were. Trapped together.

The magnetic force of habitually being close brought them both to the bed—though tension kept them on opposite sides—and the weight of living this surreal experience brought them down. Tom didn't know how long they'd been sitting on that sinking mattress, their backs to each other. He would've believed ten seconds; he would've believed ten days.

"You and Leo," he eventually said gruffly, because he couldn't help himself. There was still a minuscule part of him that thought, *hoped*, that part could've been a dream.

"You and Missouri," she shot back, though the rebuttal lacked any real oomph.

It was true. Real. Messed up beyond belief. But Tom didn't want to fight. What was happening felt too big, too loaded. He felt as though his equilibrium was off and it was taking every ounce of his strength just to sit upright. All he wanted to do was fix whatever was broken in this day. *Then* he could worry about Leo and Missouri and…the rest of his life. He tried to strategize a next step and came up empty. Megs was always better in a crisis than he was. She'd take action where he'd freeze.

"What do we do?" he asked, cutting through the thick wedge of silence. Despite himself and the pot of anger boiling in him, he still believed Megs could handle almost anything.

She shrugged with great effort, as though her shoulders were encased in concrete. "Maybe we should sleep on it. Figure everything out in the morning. Pray this is all some vivid fever dream."

"You don't pray," Tom reminded her, surprised to note the kindness in his voice.

"I could start." She let out a breathy laugh. "I'm willing to do anything to return order to the universe again."

"Should we go back down there?" He absolutely did *not* want to return to the rehearsal dinner, but abandoning it altogether didn't sit right either. He was a pleaser, even in moments of despair.

"Pass," Megs said wryly. "I've already lived through it twice. I'm good."

Another silence stretched out between them. Uncertainty loomed as the graceful notes of "And I Love Her" played outside their window. The heavy clouds he remembered from the night before seemed to be gathering more lazily tonight. He saw only a small flicker of lightning.

Tom cleared his throat, stood up with feigned renewed energy, and said, "Okay. We'll sleep on it. What else can we do?"

It was just after ten o'clock, too early to go to bed, but Tom felt as though he'd been awake for days. The last time he'd felt this tired was when he was studying to pass the bar and Megs had just gotten her first promotion at *GQ*. She'd come home late each night to find him half asleep with his books open, the television turned to something quiet and palliative, like a baseball game.

They'd shovel cold cereal into their mouths and talk about their days before collapsing into bed, their arms reaching for each other while they slept.

Now she pulled down the covers on the bed and looked at him expectantly. But there was no way he was going to crawl under the sheets with her, even just to sleep. The world might be upside down and oblong, but this wasn't the Megs he thought he knew, and they were long past those days of exhaustion.

He turned his back and walked to the door. When he reached out for the doorknob, she spoke up.

"Where are you going?"

"I can't sleep here."

Always focusing first on the practical matters, she didn't let it go at that. "Where are you going to sleep?"

Tom rubbed at his fist, the one he'd hit Leo with yesterday. Then at his eyes, to fight the prickle of tears behind them. "I'll figure it out. Probably the same place I slept the first time we lived through this. In the car."

If he stayed any longer, he'd lead her into another high-octane fight. And he didn't have it in him to confront her betrayal, to ask the question whose answer he feared most.

Are you still in love with Leo?

DAY

3

CHAPTER TWELVE

MEGAN

SLEEP SEEMED IMPOSSIBLE. And yet she must have slept because she woke up in her striped sleeping shorts and tank top, the mascara she hadn't washed off the night before gone from her lashes.

Before Megan could even look at the clock, she heard the beep of the key card as Donna burst into the room.

This was the third time she was going to have to go through the day of her rehearsal dinner.

The. Third. Time.

Her jaw clenched so hard, she could've cracked a tooth. Megan threw the covers off her body. *"No."*

The force of that one syllable surprised both her and her mother. Donna's mouth opened and a squeak came out. "Wh—what?"

As though she were powered by a dozen espressos, Megan tossed the covers onto the floor, swung her legs around, and marched toward her mother. Pointing an index finger at Donna, she said, "I know you're worried about your dress and I'm sorry Gran called you a floozy, but she tends to do that, doesn't she?"

Megan's mind was racing. There had to be a way to get off this carousel from hell. She took a breath to stop herself before she did something rash, like throw her mother out the hotel window. *Okay, okay, okay.* The universe wanted something, and it clearly wasn't for her to hide the Leo slip-up, since Tom was going through this time loop with her and already knew. So it had to be something else. Something that affected both Tom and Megan.

She pictured Tom last night. Tie askew, face pained and bewildered. His reaction when she'd pulled the covers down on what was supposed to be *their* bed.

He'd turned his back on her.

They hadn't fought the way they had the first night, yet somehow *not* fighting with Tom felt just as bad.

Regardless of how they'd gotten there, two nights in a row, they'd ended up apart. And each morning she woke up on the same day.

That was it.

If she wanted tomorrow to be different, *today had to end differently*.

Her shoulders relaxed as she began to feel some semblance of control. She had to break the cycle. And to do that, she needed Tom. Since they were stuck together, it only made sense that they'd have to break out together.

She took a deep breath and started getting ready. Not caring about changing in front of Donna, Megan stripped off her shorts and tank top and put on her jersey dress, empowered by at least knowing where to start: with the person she'd never *ended* this day with. "Here's the plan: I'm going to go meet Tom at the ferry. I'll run into my future mother-in-law on the way and figure out what she's wearing, which, in the end, won't make a difference, because Brianna will inevitably mess with your head. Then I'll meet you both in the lobby and we can all go shopping in Friday Harbor to buy, I don't know, I'm just spitballing here, but maybe a shawl to go with your dress."

Donna was gaping. Megan was almost enjoying this. She grabbed the heart pendant off the dresser and fastened it around her neck. "We should probably pick up some tiny vases to fill with flowers and a few tea lights to jazz this place up a little. I hear Carol thinks it's too dark, and even though it'll brighten up as the sun gets higher, we don't want her saying this place isn't good enough, do we? That *we* aren't good enough?"

If Megan weren't in such a hurry, she would've allowed herself to fully relish the shock on her mother's face. She'd done it. She'd rendered Donna speechless.

In the bathroom, Megan said, "Deal?" through toothpaste foam as she furiously brushed her teeth. She spat into the sink, rinsed her mouth, and decided to make the topknot she was about to put her hair into more secure with bobby pins and some hairspray. Heaven knew this day could get barbaric.

When Donna still couldn't formulate a response, Megan gave her a hug. "I'll take that as a 'Yes, Moopy.'"

Even though Megan wanted to arrive early to meet Tom, she made sure to grab coffees and pastries. Driving from Roche to Friday Harbor, she felt jittery and yet, for the first time since this all began, optimistic. The feeling continued when she parked the rental and walked down the wooden docks to wait for the man she still hoped would be her future. That was what the universe wanted for her, and, deep down, she wanted that too. How could she be with anyone other than Tom? As much as she dreaded holidays with the Prescotts, she couldn't imagine Thanksgivings and birthdays and Christmases without Tom.

Sipping coffee, she bounced on her heels a little to expend some of her restless energy. She'd thought she'd feel calm when the ferry arrived. Instead, her restlessness came to a crescendo as the foghorn blew and the ferry docked.

Even from a distance, she'd recognize him anywhere. It was as though her body were tuned specifically to his. She'd long ago fallen for the way his broad shoulders and strong arms could wrap around her like a cocoon, the way his height allowed him to rest his chin on the top of her head. His body was firm without being sculpted, and he was handsome without being cocky about it. Her optimism entwined with her nerves. *We can do this together,* she told herself. Of course they could. There was so much they'd already experienced, had already had to work through. Besides, Tom was the One. The universe had basically said as much.

As Tom got closer, she took in his rumpled appearance, and her stomach twisted. For a moment, her resolve wavered as she thought of all of the hoops he'd quietly jumped through without her. Taking point with the pharma client. Discussing the move with the client, with his parents, but not with Megan. Saying yes. Staying silent about it for so long.

Tom could pinpoint Megan's exact betrayal and hold it over her head. What she had was a series of hurts. Really, his choices were all part of an ongoing issue. There were all the times Tom stayed silent rather than defend her family. How they'd spent every holiday with the Prescotts. Her job was the result of Carol's pushing. Tom's job had been decided by John. She could hold up each one of these afflictions and implore Tom to understand why she had a right to be angry too, how each issue had led to a crack in their relationship. She could bundle them in her arms and tell him she was tired of carrying this load. But maybe it could balance the scale when placed beside the fact that she'd slept with Tom's best friend and never told him.

Begin as you mean to go on.

The phrase haunted her. All those cracks and fissures needed to be filled with forgiveness. She needed to be able to move past his betrayals, and he needed to move past hers. Because if they didn't, the universe might very well hold them hostage forever.

Megan's eyes connected with Tom's as he drew closer, and a surge of understanding rose between them. Yes, the loop was happening again, and yes, they were in it together. It was so strange, feeling relief at a time of so much uncertainty. But there was a comfort in knowing she wasn't trapped alone. And that the person with her was Tom.

They'd already been through so much together: college, law school and her master's degree, a move to New York, hangovers, illnesses, and family events. If they could survive all that, surely they could handle this. At least, she hoped they could.

He moved to hug her, then pulled away awkwardly, seemingly thinking better of it. "How are you?" she asked.

"It's so strange. With the exception of that first day, I never remember getting on the ferry. And yet that's where I wake up. Every morning."

"At least you're not waking up on a plane," Megan said, trying to break the tension. She knew, despite all the traveling he'd done in his life, Tom hated flying.

"There is that. What if I woke up departing JFK? I'd be reliving two planes."

"I think that's an exposure-therapy tool called flooding."

Their banter was casual and fueled by a nervous energy that Megan wanted to extinguish completely. She handed him his coffee, he thanked her, and they began the walk up to the rental car. Before they could step off the curb, a pedicab pulled up.

"Fancy a ride, you two? Where are you heading?"

"We're good, thanks." Megan jingled her car keys at the woman. As the pedicab pulled away, she elbowed Tom in the ribs. "Cat in a baby carrier, three o'clock."

"If we never get out of this day, I just might befriend that guy," he replied.

It was meant to be a joke, clearly, but the notion of them being trapped in this day forever settled a sober silence over them. Trapped in this day forever…but Megan wasn't going to let that happen. They continued walking. "I have a plan," she said simply.

The side of his mouth quirked up. His tone nostalgic, he said, "Of course you do."

"The universe obviously wants us together." She paused to gauge his expression. Neither one of them had ever subscribed to any sort of spirituality. "Otherwise it wouldn't keep repeating this day when we call the wedding off. It's giving us another chance to fix it."

"It's not an unreasonable conclusion, considering these completely unreasonable circumstances," he agreed. It was a start. A baby step in the right direction.

"So if we want this day, this whole loop, to stop—" She didn't want to finish this thought for fear of igniting another fight. Getting to the destination she had in mind was more of a precarious leap than a step. They reached the car but he made no move for the passenger door. His eyes were on her, waiting for her to finish.

This is Tom, she reminded herself. *The guy who held my hair back when I got food poisoning and threw up all night. I can say anything to him.* Megan searched for a delicate way to put it. "We need to—we should think about…getting back together."

The longer he took to respond, the more the anxious buzzing inside her spiked.

"You're saying the wedding needs to be back on." He crossed his arms over his chest.

She nodded and swallowed the lump in her throat. She unlocked the car and got in to give him a few minutes to put his luggage in the trunk and process what she was proposing. When they were both inside, buckling their seat belts, she continued. "But I don't think it's as simple as deciding to get married tomorrow. We need to do things right today."

"What do you mean, *right?*" Tom's skepticism was bleeding in and she needed him to stay with her.

"I mean that you and I have made a lot of choices over the past two days, both inconsequential and *highly* consequential, and they all led to the same outcome. Today we need to make a pact to stay together and extinguish the fires along the way." She gripped her cooling coffee cup with one hand, gesticulated emphatically with the other. "No matter what it takes, whatever happens, we need to do each thing *right*."

"The wedding needs to be back on," he said, massaging his neck as though it was stiff. Two days ago, she would've reached over and helped him.

"The wedding needs to be back on," she agreed, pressing the car's ignition start button.

He put a hand on hers. "Is that what you want, though?"

Her stomach dropped as she relived the past two days. And then Megan gathered any doubts she had about their relationship and pushed them down as far as she could, because that was the only way they were going to get out of this. Brushing a strand of hair out of her face, she said, "Of course it is."

Tom turned away to fiddle with the adjustments for his seat.

"Tom?"

He stopped, looking back up at her slowly. Mouth tight.

"We need to find a way to move past this. It isn't just a matter of plastering smiles on our faces and saying, *Wedding's on!* We have to actually forgive each other."

He nodded, though Megan could tell his heart wasn't in it. The coffee soured in her stomach. She wasn't sure she wanted to hear the truth...still, she asked, "Do you think you can forgive me?"

He took a long time to answer, so long her hand trembled on the ignition button. Eventually he said, "Yeah. I can do that."

They filled the ride to Roche Harbor with small talk about the scenery as though she were a ride-share driver and he a passenger, both in search of a five-star rating. She parked the car at the hotel and took his garment bag so he could roll his suitcase more easily.

She stood beside him as he got a room key. In a few minutes, they'd have to go deal with their respective obligations. Although they were facing this day together, they still needed to split up. Doing things right meant appeasing their families. This was a divide-and-conquer situation; Tom needed to get to his golf game, and at any minute, Donna and Brianna would appear to go shopping.

"Let's meet before the dinner tonight," Megan said, twisting the filigree chain around her neck just a little.

"Sure. I'll text you." He held his arms out to finally give her the hug he'd withheld at the ferry docks, but the brief embrace could've been between acquaintances.

The intimacy would return, Megan told herself. They had enough history—enough good memories together—to ensure that it would.

She was going to make this work. She willed Tom to look at her one more time, wishing his eyes held the same affection they had days ago when she was kissing him goodbye at home just before she'd left for the island. Instead, he released her and walked away.

CHAPTER THIRTEEN

TOM

TOM HAD DISCOVERED the secret to his golf game, and it was that he needed to be coiled so tightly, worrying about righting the chronology of his life, that he *couldn't* think about his form or his dad's commentary. His score on the golf course was at an all-time low.

He was absolutely killing it today.

Often on the green, the unspoken rule was not to outplay the person you're trying to ingratiate yourself with, usually a client. Tom had never considered whether that rule applied to playing with his dad because, before today, Tom had never been able to beat him.

As it turned out, John was responding positively to Tom kicking his ass.

"The Pacific Northwest seems to be agreeing with you, son," John said in his baritone rumble as Tom's ball soared straight and high over the brush.

Tom nodded. "I'm just working hard. You know how important hard work is."

The comment came out more acerbic than he'd intended, a tone he didn't usually take with his dad, but he was rattled. Why was his dad so obsessed with hard work, anyway? What about other virtues? Like supporting your family emotionally instead of just financially? Or being more accepting of people outside the approved Prescott Circle of Influence?

When John had outlined what Tom's extracurricular activities at private school would be (fencing, basketball, volleyball), Tom didn't even wonder if they were things he was interested in or enjoyed. Likewise, when John set Tom up for Harvard interviews and dictated the majority of his coursework to prepare him for law school, Tom didn't argue; he just did his best to ace every class. It was lucky Tom actually had a love for history, as that was one of a handful of John-approved majors.

Tom took a breath. Cleared his mind. Because, according to Megs, they had to do everything "right" today. Whatever that meant. He'd spent his entire existence trying to do everything right without reaping most of the desired benefits. Still, however muddled his feelings for Megs had recently become, she was more insightful than most people. And so he decided to try. At this point, it couldn't possibly make things worse.

"Of course the Pacific Northwest agrees with him. I've always suspected he was a hippie at his core." Brody raised his flask, clearly too tipsy to try to hide his blatant day-drinking from other golfers, though they were few and far between.

Tom forced a good-natured grin. "Having a good golf game hardly makes me a hippie, Brody." Truth be told, Tom thought he could stand to have a little more of a Damn the Man attitude. But why make waves when falling into line had already been hard enough?

As a child, Tom had tried speaking up when Brody was a dirtbag to him. Each time, he'd been met with a reproving comment from his father. "Are you going to tattle on your brother or are you going to be a man?"

Brody's teasing had never been laced with intentional cruelty, so Tom had learned to quietly absorb it. His interactions with Brody were usually warmer than the ones with anyone else in his family.

If there was one thing Tom knew about himself, it was that he would take what he could get.

"What do these island hippies have against progress?" John snatched the gloves hanging from his back pocket and pulled them over his hands. "They're obsessed with homeopathic remedies and can't figure out how to get a solid Wi-Fi signal. They probably think a proper eighteen-hole course causes cancer."

Tom's jaw clenched behind his mandatory smile. He couldn't manage another laugh at his father's gross generalizations, but that didn't mean he had to argue with him. In this family of lawyers, Tom would avoid the debate. For eternity, if he had to.

He tried not to linger on the idea of playing this golf game for eternity. The universe was sure being an asshole. *Shit*. He probably shouldn't think that. The universe was obviously already pissed off at him.

John lined up his shot, then strategized with Brody before he took a swing. Mulling over how to do this day more "right" than he had before, Tom had an idea. Asking his father for advice wasn't the best way to bond; he needed an opportunity for them to *really* talk. Maybe he could try to convince his dad to delay the relocation as a peace offering to Megs. But if he was going to push for that, he'd prefer to do it in a place where they could order alcohol. There was one nearby restaurant that Tom knew for sure had tablecloths—a must for John Prescott. John didn't do rustic.

Tom pulled out his phone to put the next part of his plan into action.

"Hey, Dad," he said, tapping on his phone, "since there's not a proper clubhouse here, do you want to do lunch in Friday Harbor? I just made us reservations."

"Why would you make reservations *before* asking me if I wanted to go?" John challenged.

Tom's jaw was beginning to ache. Between that and the crick in his neck, his body was a wreck. His mind wasn't faring much better. "I thought I'd get a jump on it and reserve us a good table. One overlooking the water."

"How romantic," Brody deadpanned. "A date with Dad."

"Isn't Brody invited?" John leaned on his club, adjusting his visor. "What's going on here, son?"

Tackling his move to Missouri was not something Tom was keen on doing with Brody inserting slurred wisecracks. But today was about compromise. With a few swipes on his phone, Tom changed the reservation from two people to three. "Of course Brody's invited."

"Let's go now. This course is garbage." Brody threw his clubs in the back of the cart.

"Agreed." John got in behind the wheel.

Tom noted this was the first incarnation of this day in which Brody and his dad suggested quitting in the middle of the game. It didn't seem like a coincidence that this was also the first day Tom had been winning.

The gap between wanting to forgive someone and having the emotional capacity to do so seemed insurmountable. And yet Tom worked at closing that gap inch by inch as he sat across the table from his father, who was sipping slowly at an expensive scotch, and Brody, who was quickly draining the beer glistening in his pint glass.

He thought about the time he and Megs had been on their way to his grandmother's home in Connecticut in a blizzard when their rental car broke down. He'd raised the hood and stared blankly at an engine he didn't understand while she put on their four-way flashers and made all the phone calls. And then they'd waited, huddled in the car, to be rescued. Later, when he admitted he'd been embarrassed at his inaction, she'd kissed his nose and reminded him that keeping a cool head wasn't the same thing as freezing up. That his positive outlook was worth more to her than his knowing how to fix an engine. And he'd kept her laughing while they waited in that cold car by trying to remember all the verses to "The Twelve Days of Christmas."

Fixing a day that wouldn't end was much more complicated than dealing with a broken-down car. Still, he was willing to put his faith in Megs right now because she had to be right. The only explanation for the repetition of this day was that they had done something wrong. Several things wrong, more likely. If they were being pushed together, he needed to find a way to get over what had happened between her and Leo. And he wanted to. He really did. Getting over it was far preferable to what he currently felt: the chronic, dull throb of jealousy and foolishness.

He flipped through more memories of Megs to help bridge the forgiveness gap and landed on one of his favorites.

One morning, not long after he'd passed the bar and made it through his first year as an associate at Prescott and Prescott, he was inexplicably edgy as he knotted his tie in the bathroom mirror. Sensing his nerves, Megs hopped up and sat on the counter so he was looking at her face instead of his reflection. She put her arms around him and pulled him close. "You're the best person I know—not to mention the best-looking. And you're going to do great things over there as *you*. Not as the boss's son."

Megs's pep talks were better than the meditation app on his phone and he'd immediately felt his breathing regulate, his heart slow. The tremble of his hands stilled.

But he couldn't wrap his head around *that* Megs being the same one who'd slept with Leo. And every time he tried to come to grips with her deception, he'd see it from a painful new angle.

"You seem pensive. Looking for words of advice, Spare Parts?" Brody asked, interrupting his thoughts.

What he wanted was to talk to John about the move to Missouri, but he was nervous that doing something right for Megs meant doing something wrong for his dad, and regardless of how he handled this situation, he wasn't going to make *anyone* happy—

which wouldn't get him and Megs out of this time trap. "Looking to give any?" Tom asked his brother, mostly to stall for time while he tried to figure out what to do about Missouri.

"God, no." Brody leaned back and snorted. "Remember how I used to solve Rubik's Cubes by coloring the squares in with a Sharpie so they all matched? That savvy logic doesn't apply to marital problems."

The ice cubes in John's scotch clinked together as he set down his tumbler. "Well, if it's advice you're looking for—"

"Actually, Dad," Tom said, quickly cutting him off. He didn't want to hear the speech; it grew more offensive with each listen. "I'm good."

"You sure?" John asked. "Because Megan may be a great catch, but all the other fish that come with her are not."

"We've been together for twelve years, Dad. I'm already well acquainted with her family. They aren't all bad, in fact—"

It was clear John wasn't listening. Which didn't matter, because at that point a server came to take their order.

Once the waiter retreated, John miraculously steered the conversation just where Tom wanted it to go. "How'd Megan handle the news about Missouri?"

Tom took a long pull from his water glass, still not knowing if he was doing the right thing. "Surprisingly well." This was his moment to ask. Surely they could postpone the move until Megs was ready. Tom gathered as much courage as he could and was about to open his mouth when Brody spoke up.

"You're going to be missed around the New York office." Brody took his napkin off the table and spread it over his lap.

"I'm touched, brother."

"Oh, not missed by me." He leaned back, mischief radiating off him like heat.

John's phone rang. He took the call outside, leaving Tom and Brody alone.

"Then by who?" Tom didn't know where Brody was going with this, but he had a feeling the punch line would be directed down, straight at him, just as it always was. The bright side about moving out of state was there wouldn't be anyone around to call him Spare Parts.

"By Gina." Brody gave Tom a knowing look.

"Gina?"

She'd started as an associate at Prescott and Prescott the same time Tom had. Gina was incredibly bright and definitely too sweet for the cutthroat environment, and having her as a confidante at work was part of what got Tom through those first few years. In the end, she took a job at a firm that focused on environmental law, and Tom had been sad to see her go. They'd mostly lost contact after that, save for bumping into each other at a midtown deli they both occasionally grabbed lunch from.

"She just left whatever firm she was at and interviewed for a position at Prescott," Brody went on.

"That's great," Tom said, taking another sip of water. "I hope you offered her the job. She's really talented. She'll be a great asset."

Brody smirked, his eyebrows raised, and pointed at Tom. "She told me she thinks you have pretty good assets too."

Tom coughed, choking on his water. "What are you talking about?"

"Let's just say as soon as the interview was over and we basically offered her the position, she spent the next several minutes interviewing *me* about *you*. She seemed pretty disappointed when I told her you were getting married this weekend."

Tom felt his heart speed up to a canter. He and Megs had gotten together at a young age, but it wasn't as though he'd stopped noticing other women. He'd just had no desire to act on anything. Sure, he and Gina had been close. Her upbringing had been so similar to Tom's that when they'd met, they'd almost immediately developed their own shorthand. Of course he'd kept their relationship professional, smothering any attraction he felt for her. He'd never seriously entertained being with anyone other than Megs, because why would he?

Still, it was always flattering to hear someone was interested in you. So Tom let himself be flattered. Gina hadn't changed the way Tom felt about Megs then, and even now, in light of everything...

The now-familiar humiliation of her infidelity pressed against him. But he knew what he had to do.

Keep the peace. Do this right. Don't rock the boat.

"Yeah, well, I'm obviously off the market." Tom nodded as though he were one of those bobblehead dogs people put on the dashboards of their cars. "So thanks for letting me know, but it's moot."

"What's moot?" John asked, sitting back down just as their meals arrived.

"Tom's girlfriend," Brody sang as though he were a first-grader.

"Your mother told me she didn't think Megan knew about Missouri. Thought you'd forgotten to tell her."

"'Forgotten,'" Brody scoffed, complete with air quotes. "Just like Emmeline 'forgot' to tell me she's going to Newport Beach next weekend."

"What?" Tom turned to his brother, tired of his confusing interruptions. How drunk was he?

"Nothing." Brody took an oversize bite of his crab sandwich.

"No, Megs knows about the move," Tom assured his dad, mentally adding, *Thanks to your enlightening speech that we're about to hear for the third time.*

"Good. Because I have a surprise for both of you. You'll just have to wait until later to find out what it is."

Stifling an internal groan—and a more distant flicker of curiosity about Gina's own record with fidelity—Tom realized he couldn't ask his father to postpone the move. Instead, he dutifully sat forward and feigned interest while his father monologued about Missouri, silently hoping that the relocation was the universe's idea of doing things right.

CHAPTER FOURTEEN

MEGAN

NOT ALL OF Megan's interventions were going as planned. Leaping too quickly with Donna first thing that morning had in fact knocked down a series of flammable dominoes. Most upsetting, it had cast Megan as the villain, taking the spotlight off her gran. Megan spent countless minutes on a sofa with her mother in the hotel lobby trying to convince her she loved the dress she already had but simply wanted to ensure *Donna* felt her best. Brianna, ever the contrarian, had stomped into the lobby, a Snickers bar in hand, and declared, "I don't see why we have to buy a new dress for Mom. *I* think her bazongas look resplendent in the one she has." Somehow, in this version of the day, Brianna got to be the hero.

"Don't get too excited, we're just going to buy her a shawl to cover up her cleavage." Patience waning, Megan realized her answer hadn't passed through her normal filter; she'd been too busy trying to remember what time Leo arrived so she could coordinate her return from Friday Harbor.

"I don't know why you're turning Mom's outfit into such a plot point," Brianna said wickedly. "Mom has a banging body and should show it off if she wishes. God, Megan, you're such an ageist."

"I—"

"*And* a sexist," Brianna added, gleefully clocking that she was getting under Megan's skin.

The actual shopping trip didn't fare much better. Donna was so upset over being called a floozy by Gran and by Megan's outburst, her mood was all over the place. A British accent came and went, and she didn't seem to have any idea what she wanted. She kept moaning about Husbands Number One and Four. To top it all off, Donna hadn't yet heard Carol refer to the hotel as dark, so Megan's early-morning insistence that they buy the vases and candles was ramping up her insecurities to new heights.

Megan regrouped and got a handle on her next orders of business:

Calm Donna down by continuing to build her up.

Encourage good behavior from Brianna.

Find Leo before he found her.

She felt like she was using every ounce of energy she had placating Donna and Brianna as they made their way through the shops of Friday Harbor. It was working well on her mother; however, her sister was growing increasingly suspicious.

"Why are you being so nice?" Brianna asked after Megan pointed out a retro-chic duvet cover she thought Brianna should buy for her New York bed.

"Because I care about you." What Megan really wanted to say was *Because I need to get out of this day before I give up and lobotomize myself.*

Brianna scoffed. Sure, Megan hadn't delivered that line with much emotion. She worried she wasn't making enough headway with Brianna.

There was an ace up Megan's sleeve for her enfant terrible of a grown sister, but she didn't want to use it unless she really had to. If by tonight, Megan sensed she still wasn't doing things right with Brianna and was angering the universe somehow, she'd take a more concrete approach to helping her sister move to New York.

But *only* if she felt it was totally necessary.

The car ride home was full of loud music and singing, though Megan's voice strained with the force of convincing everyone she was having a great time.

Once back in Roche Harbor, Megan practically ran to the lobby, knowing Leo would be there at any moment. Her heart both soared and plummeted when she saw his back, the muscles pulling his shirt taut across his shoulders.

"Hey!" The word escaped louder and faster than she'd expected, her voice echoing through the hotel. An elderly couple looked up in alarm, as did a bellhop.

Leo seemed to turn around in slow motion. He operated at a different pace than the rest of the world. His smile rattled her resolve.

But this was the day to do things right.

"Megan." He pulled her into a hug, the warmth of his body and his scent familiar—not just from the other versions of this day but from lifetimes past.

"Can we talk?" Her voice wobbled only slightly, as did her ankles.

"You took the words right out of my mouth."

Leo slipped his hotel key card into the pocket of his worn jeans and offered the crook of his elbow for her hand. She pretended she didn't see it. Forgoing a long walk over to the pool, she stopped him just outside the hotel.

To the uninformed, Leo's smile might have appeared easy. But Megan saw the worry creeping into the small creases at his eyes, the faint lines between his brows. If the uneven cobblestone didn't bring her down, knowing what was in his heart and what she had to say might.

Just as she opened her mouth to speak, Leo said, "*Wait*. Before you say anything, can I have a minute? I've missed you for so long, I just want to enjoy *not* missing you."

The interruption was throwing off the speech she'd been mentally preparing.

"I'm sorry, maybe that was the wrong thing to say," Leo continued when she didn't respond. "It's just...I think about us a lot. About what happened. And I couldn't come here without checking to make sure...is this what you want?"

You mean reliving the same day three times? Megan was tempted to say. *Having my life blow up in my face, only to wake up at the beginning of the war every day still wounded from a battle that doesn't appear to have occurred?*

Instead, what came out was an impatient "Is *what* what I want?"

Megan was tired and thrown. Her brain wasn't working as it should. It was Leo's fault. He was going off script. She should've anticipated that changing her approach would have an impact on how he behaved. She'd never been good at improvising. Megan was a planner. And now they were having an intimate conversation out in the open.

She pulled him off to the side of the entrance, where they'd at least have a pocket of privacy.

Leo didn't miss a beat. "This. Is *this* what you want? The Prescotts. Their life." He took a deep breath, scuffing at the ground with his shoe like a lost little boy, then squinting in the sun. "I wasn't planning on being this blunt, but you're looking at me and you don't seem to be the blushing bride-to-be. I care about you. I want you to be happy. Is Tom what you want? Because—"

Everything snapped into place. She couldn't let herself fall into the philosophical loop of wondering who she'd be happier with, which life she wanted. She couldn't believe she'd let that happen the first time he'd shown up on the island. Right now what Megan wanted was normalcy. She wanted emotions that operated within reasonable parameters and for the weekend she'd been planning for years to actually move forward. The universe had made it clear where she was supposed to be, and she had to trust that.

And so Megan replied, "Of course Tom's who I want."

"But—"

"Leo. This wedding is happening. My life with Tom has *already* happened. You have to move on."

"Givens," Leo pleaded, "come on, just hear me out. It might have been eight years ago, but I remember every detail of that night—that morning—we had together."

"Like you just said, that was eight years ago."

"So you think all my feelings have just shut down?" Leo ran his fingers through his wavy hair. "Do you know I buy a copy of *GQ* every time I'm at the airport? I thumb through the pages and try to figure out which ones you worked on—so I can feel closer to you."

Megan's breath hitched. It'd been a while since Tom had taken an interest in her work. He was so buried in his own, he simply didn't have the bandwidth. And vice versa. Their conversations tended to revolve around what they were going to eat and watch and which of their college friends or coworkers had a baby shower coming up. This was what a decade of domesticity looked like…right? She was starting to wonder if there was more to why she and Tom didn't feel as close as they once had. Or at least to why this one day, and its new revelations, could've exploded their relationship so disastrously. But this wasn't doing things right. Everything here was wrong. Leo was wrong. She had to get rid of him.

"That's all very sweet, Leonardo." She regretted using his full first name the second it escaped her mouth because it contained just enough warmth to make him smile. "It's also ridiculous. We've hardly spoken in years."

"That may be true, Givens, and yet you can't tell me there's nothing between us." His words, his tone, grew more serious.

He seemed to believe he was gaining ground. She had to shut him down.

She spoke with the conviction she'd had to use on many men in the media world. "I know you've come here thinking you have these highly romantic lingering feelings for me, but you love the thrill of the chase and I love Tom. So."

That last syllable didn't have the weight of finality she'd tried to infuse it with.

His laugh was timid. Bitter. She'd taken him by surprise. "Okay."

"Okay?" Her eyes whipped up. She took inventory of Leo's every atom and the way they formed and chilled to exude casual indifference. *If you don't choose me, I'll go back to my life of beautiful people and even more beautiful places,* the atoms seemed to say. And then his cold expression crumbled, just a little.

"I mean, I can't talk you into loving me. I just thought...I hoped, I guess..."

The tears in his eyes weren't fair. She had to look away. She couldn't say she was sorry or tell him he hadn't imagined their chemistry. She wasn't allowed to share all those nights she'd googled his name just to feel closer to him. Those confessions would make Leo feel better and Tom, if he ever found out, feel worse. If she indulged those feelings even a little, she really would be single-handedly responsible for ruining Tom's future, and hers. "You should go, Leo."

"You seem to be forgetting that I'm the best man."

"Tom will understand, trust me." She muttered the last part under her breath.

They looked at each other, him waiting for her to crack. It wasn't going to happen. Not today.

"I promise I'll go if that's what you really want. I just..." He widened his stance enough to indicate he was staying put. "Look, I know Tom's the lawyer, but humor me for a minute. Let's have a little debate about this whole thing."

"You want to debate our feelings?" Irritation coiled alongside the thrill of potential banter. Part of Megan wanted to prolong their talk, to wander down this road. But she couldn't.

"Okay, maybe not a debate. But definitely a discussion. And then...look, I'm not going to stick around if it really is him."

"Then I'll see you later." Megan still couldn't move, despite her farewell, so she added, "Don't forget the duffel bag you dumped in the lobby."

"But…" He moved to brush the hair that had come loose from her topknot out of her eyes before seemingly thinking better of it. "I can't leave knowing you're unhappy. That you might have regrets. Can you answer one question for me?"

Megan nodded. The other versions of this day hadn't prepared her for this. Those were feeling more and more like dress rehearsals for a different play.

A family hauling endless luggage accidentally knocked into her as they tried to get to the hotel's front entrance. She motioned for Leo to follow her toward the docks.

"How do you know it's him? That he's the one?"

Thankfully, he'd asked her an easy question. And so, as she always did, Megan relished the memory of Tom's first note to her. "Do you remember the first time I came over to watch *Mystery Science Theater* with the two of you?"

"I mean, we watched it a lot. I don't know if I remember the *first*—"

"I basically had a meltdown on your couch."

His face softened. "Yeah. I remember."

Megan had been hiding so much about who she was with Tom and, by extension, with Leo. She hadn't confessed her mother's lack of maternal skills, her emotional manipulations. She certainly hadn't told them about the parade of subpar husbands and boyfriends Donna marched through their home. She didn't say how alone she felt when she wasn't with them. How much she missed Paulina. The depth of her resentment toward her brother and sister.

But that night, she'd just gotten off the phone with her mother. Donna had been in rare form, accusing Megan of abandoning the family, of being as bad as all the men who'd left her. She'd wailed as Megan stood in the middle of her dorm room, phone pressed to her cheek, clad in flannel pajama pants and a sweatshirt, a partially written essay about the globalization of contemporary art on her computer screen, and took it. Every jab, every unfair accusation. She let herself be the scapegoat for her mother's misery.

Megan didn't fight back, and once Donna had exhausted herself, she hung up. Megan sat down in the middle of her floor and silently began to bandage her psychological wounds.

Then she stood up, brushed her hair, got dressed, and held it all in until she got to Tom and Leo's place.

They'd greeted her with such easy joy. When they offered her a beer and a package of licorice, knowing it was her favorite candy, their unmotivated kindness was too much. She cried on their couch and let everything out. It wasn't until after she'd composed herself that the horror of her moment of unbridled vulnerability overcame her.

They would look at her differently now.

Tom would see her as weak. High-maintenance. Someone with baggage.

The rest of the night was fine, but she'd cried herself to sleep when she got back to her dorm. The next morning, she'd overslept, then had to run to her car to retrieve a textbook. On her windshield, tucked under one of the wipers, was a note. A note that was so small and yet meant everything to her.

Megan floated out of the memory and back to Leo. "It was the note," she said.

"Tom wrote you a note." Leo's voice was skeptical. "Tom texts and e-mails. He doesn't write notes."

"He left it on the windshield of my car back when we were freshmen. Remember that old Nissan I'd inherited from Paulina?"

A dark cloud was passing over Leo's face. He must know he was beaten. He'd have to turn around and leave the island now.

"After I was a mess in front of you both and told Tom about my family, I was convinced he'd start pulling away. Instead he wrote me a note that said, 'I don't know why people call it falling when I feel like I'm soaring.'"

Even now the words gripped her. A salve, a salvation.

"Anytime I get frustrated with his family—or with him—I remember that he decided to love me unconditionally years ago. And then I vow to love him unconditionally back."

Leo swallowed hard and nodded. "That's great, Megan. I totally get it."

She'd done it. Closed this chapter. *Finally.*

She reached out to give him one last hug. Any lingering feelings, she squashed with her resolve. She knew what she had to do.

As they embraced, he said into her ear, "Except *I* wrote that note."

CHAPTER FIFTEEN

TOM

THEY'D DECIDED TO meet at the ice cream shop on the pier before the rehearsal dinner. This seemed like a safe spot where they could talk uninterrupted. Brody was lactose-intolerant and Tom's parents were intolerant of the frivolity of a shop that served only brightly colored desserts. Megs had assured Tom her side of the family wouldn't show up unexpectedly; she'd rushed through an impromptu photo shoot with them (not that anything was impromptu by now) and suggested they go have a predinner cocktail on *Happy Accident* while she allegedly checked on some last-minute details.

Besides, Donna believed ice cream was more of an "afternoon delight."

The route Tom took to the shop wasn't exactly direct. He needed time to think. Process. And so he meandered through the evergreen trees and down to the beach and tried very hard to process forgiveness. Commitment.

For twelve years he'd dedicated himself to Megs. To their relationship. It wasn't that other romantic opportunities, like Gina, hadn't presented themselves; he simply knew what he wanted. *Who* he wanted. Getting to know someone new on that intimate level he already shared with Megs had held little appeal because he was with a woman who made him feel safe. Adored. Someone he could cry with as easily as laugh with; someone who gave killer pep talks and had long ago accepted him for exactly who he was.

And up until three days ago, Tom had been convinced he knew exactly who Megs was too: a whip-smart, funny, loyal, secretly goofy, gorgeous person. Someone he thought would never hurt him.

How was he supposed to make the decision to stay with Megs when she seemed so different to him now? It was as though she'd been wearing a costume since graduation. How was he supposed to just forgive her when he wasn't even sure he trusted her anymore?

Eight years was a very long time to lie to someone. Even if that lie was a lie of omission.

By the time he arrived, Megs was sitting at a wooden picnic table, in full makeup and wearing her shimmering dress, illuminated by the lights of the shop. She held an untouched mint chocolate chip waffle cone in one hand and was partway through the ice cream cone in her other hand.

"You better hurry. Yours is melting." She offered him the waffle cone.

He took a lick, relishing the freshness of the mint and the crunchy subtle sweetness of the dark chips. Her familiarity; her features, her scent. The facial expressions he'd long ago memorized. They'd been a source of comfort for him for so long. Maybe they could be again.

He might just have to fake it for a while.

They took a few minutes to eat their ice cream in silence. It seemed oddly appropriate. After all, the first time they'd told each other "I love you" had been over ice cream. It was the end of their freshman year and the compacted stress of finals meant they hadn't seen each other all week, the longest they'd gone except for winter and spring breaks.

After Megs had stayed up all night reading, she'd taken her *final* final exam and collapsed on Tom's couch immediately afterward.

"I'm already breaking out from stress and forgetting to shower, but is it wrong that all I want for breakfast is candy?"

Seeing an opportunity to make her happy, he'd said, "Give me five minutes," strapped on his Nikes, and quite literally run two blocks to the nearest convenience store. He returned shortly after carrying grocery bags bursting with ice cream, miniature candy bars, licorice, and something he thought was sprinkles but had the added benefit of coming in the plastic casing of a tiny toy cell phone.

As worried as Tom had been about his exams, he'd been more worried about the semester ending. Despite he and Megs seeing each other exclusively, neither of them had "dropped the L-bomb," as Leo had sarcastically put it. The words had nearly fallen out of Tom's mouth hundreds of times, but fear of rejection had muted him.

Because what if Megs was just having fun? What if Tom was a placeholder to her? Spare parts until she found someone she really loved?

Megs had fallen asleep in those few minutes he'd taken to go to the store. Her hair was in a matted ponytail, her forehead showing a handful of those stress blemishes she'd complained about. He thought his heart would break free from his chest right then and there.

She opened her eyes, took one look at the spread of pure sugar on his desk, and said, "Hey, Tom. You know I love you, right?"

He'd immediately told her he loved her too, so much, and they'd spent the rest of the day on a sugar and love high.

The memory was one of his favorites. It seemed almost quaint now in its innocence. How could he be sure she hadn't been thinking about Leo then too?

He crunched on a shard of dark chocolate, mentally renewing his vow to do things right today. "What flavor did *you* get?"

"Rocky road." She winked at him and he almost gave in to the moment of dark comedy and laughed. Or maybe he wanted to cry.

"I thought you opted for ice cream with some sort of caramel or no ice cream at all. Isn't that your dairy war cry?"

She took a bite of marshmallow. "That *was* my cry, yes. But then I thought that if I'm going to repeat the same day over and over again, perhaps I should start eating themed ice cream. Or perhaps I should try a new flavor every day."

The smile disappeared from her lips at the same time his did.

They could be stuck in this day forever.

Trapped in a loop of the same conversations, the same stifling intentions, the same fight.

Tom couldn't live like that, in the worst day of his life, regardless of how much ice cream he ate. No, they'd do what Megs had suggested that morning: they'd get things right today.

As though she sensed the change in his mood, her eyes dropped. He could see her professionally applied eye shadow shimmering, the thickness of her fake lashes.

To an onlooker, he thought, they were two lovers dressed in their finest, enjoying the innocent levity of an ice cream date. But reality could be coy; it could be cruel. And there was no escaping what had to be done.

They needed to plaster smiles on their faces, pretend they were the same people who'd proposed to each other under a ceiling of plastic glow-in-the-dark stars, and make it through the rest of the evening on their best behavior.

Megs looked serene sitting there on the pier, wearing the champagne dress she'd been so excited to show him, licking ice cream as though she didn't have a care in the world. God, she was beautiful. He'd thought so from the very first day she sat beside him in Natural Disasters.

Of course, he'd encountered beautiful women all his life. Wealth offered a myriad of ways to make someone aesthetically appealing. But something about Megs had been different. It was as though there were a lamp inside her, permanently flicked on. Everything shone. Her eyes danced when she spoke. Her mouth broke into easy grins. She laughed unselfconsciously. And there was something else there...a kindness at her core. One that drew him to her. Megs was a lighthouse.

More than anything in this moment, he wanted to love her freely again, with all the stresses of adulthood yet to come.

"I sent Leo packing." The words had come out with difficulty, even though he could tell she was trying to pass it off as something as simple as mailing a letter.

An unnameable feeling contorted in his chest. She hadn't wanted to do it. It was in her voice, the rigidness of her posture. The idea that Tom would always be her second choice chilled him.

He couldn't think about that. Not now. They had to do things right. And so he said, "Okay," and nodded. Too many times. He was still making things complicated. So he followed it up with a simple "Thanks," begging his mind to stop the side-by-side comparisons. Of Megs and Leo. Of Megs and him.

She polished off her ice cream and stood up to throw away her napkin. Tom wasn't hungry anymore. He discreetly threw his cone in the garbage behind them, not wanting to hurt her feelings by not finishing it.

"Hey, so you know how when we were freshmen and I thanked you for writing me that note? The morning after I broke down in front of you for the first time?"

He squinted, staring off into the middle distance, as though attempting to recall a vague memory.

"Remember?" she prodded. "That note that said it didn't feel like you were falling, it felt like you were soaring?"

Of course he remembered. Because when she'd brought it up, covering him with kisses and thanks, he'd put two and two together; after all, the quote was a rip-off of an Edward Albee line Leo liked.

"Yeah. I remember."

"*You* didn't write it."

Tom shook his head. "No."

What she didn't understand, might never understand, was how badly he'd *wanted* to be the person who'd written her that note. It was why he hadn't corrected her years ago. It was why it stung to admit it now.

He'd been in second place his whole life. Trying to keep up in that race for his father's approval. Trying to get his mother's attention.

"You let me believe you did." Megs's accusation was pointed but not angry.

And then, when he'd found someone he cared about more than anyone else, his best friend had tried to undermine that. But back then, Leo had temporarily fallen in love with every woman—and most reciprocated. Tom figured if he left it, didn't cause a stir, Leo would move on to someone else. Someone who wasn't Megs. As far as Tom knew, that's what had happened, because he could still remember the impressive parade of girls walking in and out of Leo's room the rest of the year.

"I did let you believe that," Tom agreed. There was no point denying it. He hated lying. He was terrible at it.

"Well?" She was waiting for an explanation he didn't have.

"I'm sorry," he said. Because those two words felt like the least complicated path.

"Okay." She nodded. "I'm sorry too."

What was her apology for? Sleeping with Leo? Not loving Tom best? Some yet-to-be-unearthed indiscretion?

At that point, on his third journey through this day, it didn't matter. What mattered was that they were doing everything right.

He took a breath, took her hand, and made himself smile as they walked to their rehearsal dinner.

CHAPTER SIXTEEN

MEGAN

MEGAN THOUGHT ABOUT the note. About the words that had comforted her time and time again. A strand of the rope anchoring her to Tom.

She let herself get angry. It was another thing Tom had lied about. In some ways, a much smaller crime than lying about the move. Yet somehow, this lie felt so much more weighted. Because it meant that a piece was now missing from their twelve-year relationship.

And then, because there was nothing else she could do, she let it all go.

Or at least, she tried to.

They walked into the rehearsal dinner together, hands loosely clasped in a sign of reticent unification. In the other two versions of this day, they'd been too busy or too angry or too scared to connect before. Today the effort was made.

Sticking so close they were practically upright spooning, Tom and Megan made the rounds.

"Aunt Florence," Tom said, stopping to squeeze the elderly woman's hand. "I hope you're planning on giving a speech tonight."

"Oh, I don't know if I have anything to say," she coyly replied, adjusting the index cards up her sleeve.

They moved over to Megan's grandparents.

"We're so happy you kids decided to get married here," her granddad said, his milky blue eyes glistening. "It's been such a special place for the family."

"Oh, don't blubber," Gran said with an affectionate sigh as Megan and Tom took turns kissing her cheek.

Apart from Paulina and Hamza, Megan didn't have a lot of examples of enduring love in her life. She was grateful to look at her grandparents and see a version of what she was working toward. What she ultimately wanted. As difficult as her gran could be, she and Megan's granddad loved each other, and their weaknesses complemented each other just as much as their strengths did. While her granddad was soft edges and a kind heart, Gran was stoic and brash. While Gran could be insensitive, Granddad could be overly emotional.

Megan reminded herself now that this could be her. If her grandparents could find a way to make things work, so could she and Tom.

Minus Gran's tendency to call everyone a floozy.

With each exuberant wish of a lifetime of love from each new guest they greeted, Megan and Tom took turns feigning adoring looks at each other.

See us, universe? their entwined fingers seemed to say. *We're negotiating. We're doing what you require.*

"Oh, look. It's the happy couple." Brody raised his glass of pinot noir as they found their way to the head table.

Tom put his arm around Megan's shoulders and gave her a squeeze while she greeted Brody's wife, Emmeline, whose poise was undermined only by the way her body continually shifted away from her husband, leaving a kink in the circle of seats.

Megan remembered the first time she'd met Emmeline. It was

at Harvard, during homecoming, when Brody decided to relive his college glory days. He'd brought his new bride along. Megan had been so excited to meet her, sure she'd be an ally in the Prescott family. Within seconds, she could tell Emmeline had taken in Megan's discount clothes and split ends and written her off.

Since then, Megan hadn't put much effort into befriending her soon-to-be sister-in-law. At every Thanksgiving dinner and Christmas party, Megan would attempt conversation and Emmeline would respond with clipped answers before disappearing. Megan had long harbored the belief that Emmeline spent most holidays hiding in one of the bathrooms of Grandmother Prescott's sprawling estate. She'd tried to talk about this theory with Tom, but each time he'd laughed it off and claimed he sometimes wanted to hide from Brody too.

Dinner began promptly at seven o'clock. When her future mother-in-law cringed at the family-style service, Megan let it roll off her back. It was good for Carol to have to share salad tongs with the Givenses. Family-style would be the great equalizer. Even if Carol was squirting hand sanitizer into her palms under the table every time she touched something.

"These wild salmon crostini are *delectable*." Donna stretched out the word, creeping dangerously toward her fake British accent. "Aren't they delectable, Carol?"

Knowing her mother was desperate for attention and Carol was the least likely candidate to give it to her, Megan lunged for one, stuffed it in her mouth, and nodded enthusiastically. "*Delectable*."

Brianna, on brand as always, had her eyes glued to her phone.

"What's going on?" Megan asked, nudging her sister kindly as Tom relived his golf game with John and Brody.

"I'm texting Alistair."

"I thought you weren't supposed to text him."

When Brianna scowled, Megan realized she wasn't supposed to know about Alistair's long-distance complaints. That was something Brianna had revealed only on the second version of this day.

"I know *I'm* not supposed to," Megan lied. "He's always complaining about his cell phone bill like it's my fault he's couch-hopping all over the world."

Brianna brightened. "*Right?* I mean, if you don't want people to contact you, just don't give out your number."

Megan rolled her eyes. "Exactly."

"Well, buckle up, because our dirtbag brother should be here any minute."

She feigned surprise. "Oh, really? Great."

And he'll show up in cargo shorts and tell a sketchy story about his latest girlfriend followed by a cringeworthy anecdote about why he isn't smart enough to be a roofer, and it'll turn this dinner into a free-for-all of silent judgment and humiliation.

"I was just wondering if maybe telling Megs and me about any surprises now instead of in a speech in front of everyone might be better," she heard Tom saying.

"Who said anything about a speech?" John replied as Donna butted in and asked, "What surprise?" and Carol chided him for being disrespectful to his father.

Damn it, Tom.

At least when John had first made the house-in-Missouri announcement in his speech, it hadn't caused this full-table fracas.

Megan needed to act now because Alistair was about to make this situation worse. She had to divert the table's attention, and fast.

She grabbed Tom's hand, turned toward Brianna, and finally took that unwanted ace out of her sleeve. "Hey, Bree. Tom and I were talking and we think you should live with us when you move to New York."

"We do?" Tom's voice cracked.

"And Dan too?" Brianna asked, brightening.

"Who's Dan?"

"Dan too. It just makes sense." Megan kicked Tom's ankle under the table, ignoring his questions. "It's a big move and we want to make sure you're happy. We might be relocating with Tom's job, but you can stay in our apartment for free for as long as you want. Until you're feeling financially ready to move on."

"As long as she wants?" Tom muttered under his breath, kicking her back.

Megan couldn't believe he had the nerve to fight her on this when she'd just publicly gotten on board with the move to Missouri.

Brianna squealed. "Oh my God, you guys. You won't regret this."

As the waitstaff cleared away the appetizers and salad plates and brought in the main courses, Megan took the opportunity to whisper into Tom's ear, "Let's just make everyone happy tonight, okay?"

"I know. You're right." Tom took a swig of water. He turned to her and whispered, "We haven't handed out the gifts yet. And shouldn't Alistair be strolling in here any minute? What's our game plan there?"

Megan stood up, a bolt of inspiration hitting her. She tapped her fork against her glass. The room quieted down. "Thank you so much, all of you, for coming. My heart is full. First we'd like to hand out gifts to our wedding party."

Tom was right. They were late on this, and Alistair was going to show up at any minute. But if the festivities were in full swing, he might just slink in quietly. Alistair wouldn't hesitate to interrupt a casual speech, but surely he wouldn't take the focus from the bride. As such, Megan was prepared to filibuster, because if he didn't tell his story, the Prescotts would have one less thing to complain about. Maybe it would ease the tension in the room.

As they handed out gifts, Megan kept one eye on the wall clock. "Tom and I are grateful...eternally grateful...*deeply* and eternally grateful to have you all here with us. I know San Juan Island isn't the easiest destination to get to, especially for you East Coasters."

There was an appreciative titter across the room.

"It does take two planes and a ferry to get here," Carol said, loudly enough for Donna to redden and Brody to choke on his stuffed prawn before raising his glass in a toast.

But Megan wasn't done. She ignored them all, letting her voice carry, elongating syllables where she could.

"To have you here to celebrate our love, and love in general, for what is life with no love?" Oh no; she was pretty sure she was paraphrasing dialogue from a sitcom she'd seen a dozen times, and Alistair still hadn't arrived. "It's a lonely life. A dark life. And I am so grateful—"

"You said that already," Brianna cut in.

Why wasn't Tom joining her? He was letting her flail.

"I did. Yes," Megan agreed. She needed to change tack. "Tom and I have been together for years. When I first met him—"

"When Megan first met Tom—" A voice cut through her speech. Alistair was standing at the door, his sunglasses still on even though the sun was going down, his frayed cargo shorts a beacon for fifty stares. "She was a goner."

Damn. Her rambling wasn't dissuading him from making himself the center of attention. He was a real piece of work, her brother. Megan had grown up with Alistair and yet she still couldn't fathom where all this baseless confidence came from.

"She came home for Christmas her freshman year of college and was like, 'I met the cutest guy.'"

To her horror, Alistair was adopting a high-pitched, girlish—not to mention vaguely sexist—squeal that was apparently supposed to be Megan. She suddenly missed the versions of this day where her brother only told a ridiculous story about himself.

Taking the murmurs of the guests as encouragement, Alistair waved his arms around comically, continuing his roast. "'His name's Tom Richie Rich and he's a dreamboat!'"

"Tom is definitely a dreamboat," Megan cut in, pretending to laugh. "Welcome to the rehearsal dinner, Alistair, prodigal son of the Givens family."

She knew the biblical reference would be caught by the East Coast Protestants while likely going over Alistair's head; her brother's religion was primetime television and hunting.

Even though she didn't want to hear Great-Aunt Florence give another speech full of platitudes, it was better than letting Alistair get one more word in.

"And now we'd like to open the floor to the rest of our guests." Megan raised her glass. "Aunt Florence, Tom has always told me you have the soul of a poet. Won't you start us off?"

Aunt Florence fanned herself, blushing from the effective flattery, and began droning on about love. It was only slightly worse than Megan's own speech.

"Nice save," Tom whispered when she was once again seated beside him.

Mentally, she chided him for leaving her alone up there. On the surface, she kissed his cheek and thanked him.

"I'd love to give a speech," Donna said prissily. "But I can't seem to get a word in edgewise."

Carol let out a passive-aggressive little hum.

Tired of putting out every fire herself, Meg poked Tom in the ribs. He was extremely ticklish and flinched. But the motion caught Leo's eye, several tables away, and she felt his gaze keenly. Hadn't she told him to leave?

Something locked between them, strong enough to require great effort for Megan to pull her focus back to her own table.

"We'd love it if you'd give a speech tomorrow," Tom said to Donna smoothly. "When all the guests are here."

This time Carol clucked her tongue as Donna beamed.

Megan chewed her lip, silently counting all the promises they'd made to family members thus far; if their plan worked and tomorrow actually arrived, the fallout would be brutal.

"You too, of course, Carol," Megan added, because if she had to bear the humiliation of her mother up there, so did Tom.

Carol put her fork down. She'd been pushing her food around rather than eating. "I'm sure your mother will say it all."

Digging to the bottom of her quickly depleting supply of compassion, Megan tried desperately to find any way to connect to her future mother-in-law. Someone she wasn't hardwired to love. Someone she was struggling even to like. Because the universe wasn't likely to be pacified with lip service alone and Megan was getting concerned that that was all she and Tom were doing. Megan needed to offer up a true kindness, one that wasn't motivated by selfishness alone.

She watched Carol squeeze another dollop of sanitizer into her palm and scrub it into her skin.

Perhaps Carol's actions were less about her thinking she was too good to share food with the Givenses (although she likely believed that was true) and more about a deeply rooted neurosis.

Carol was a germaphobe.

Carol was anxious.

Carol covered both these very real and sympathetic struggles by being a withholding and raging snob.

"I'll be right back," Megan said to the table. At Tom's questioning look, she patted him on the shoulder. "It's fine. Trust me."

She ran to the kitchen and found a senior-looking employee. "Excuse me? I know we asked for family-style and I don't want to make things more difficult for you, but do you think we could have a separate plate made up for the mother of the groom?"

Instead of heading back to her own table, Megan lingered in the kitchen doorway, watching over the guests. She willed herself to relish this moment, to take in every detail, but her eyes kept traveling to one person. Megan felt an itch in her palm. The phantom note, giving her paper cuts. All her efforts today had been about doing things right, making everyone happy, ensuring she and Tom would be together in the end.

But she couldn't help wondering: What if being with Tom *wasn't* right?

Later, they walked back to the hotel quietly, past the couple dancing to "And I Love Her."

"Great song," Tom said, so low she almost missed it.

"Great song," Megan agreed just as quietly.

The sky was too cloudy for stargazing. She thought again of those plastic stars Tom had stuck to their ceiling, of their engagement, and wondered how long it would take for them to feel that free to love each other again.

By the time Megan and Tom were in their suite, Megan was more exhausted than she'd thought possible. Outside, thunder rumbled, threatening another storm that simply wouldn't materialize. She found herself wishing she could crack those clouds open like coconuts and let the rain out herself. There was something cleansing about a good downpour.

Megan's eyes hurt from looking bright and agreeable. Her stomach hurt from pushing down irritation, stress, and fury. Her heart hurt from the effort of trying to love every person in the right way when she wasn't confident she knew what any of those ways were.

Tom and Meg collapsed on the bed still in their formal wear and kicked off their shoes one by one, letting them thump to the floor, not caring if the noise annoyed the guests in the room below.

"We did it." Megan inexplicably wanted to cry.

"We did it." Tom sounded choked up too. "We did everything right."

She rolled to look at the face she'd stared at almost every night for over a decade. He followed suit. Gazing at each other in that familiar way was a small comfort at the end of any difficult day. Normally, it was something she looked forward to, because regardless of what happened at work or how many frenzied voice-mail messages she received from her mom, Tom was a constant. There was worth in even their smallest traditions. Like lying side by side and sharing a kiss before rolling over and going to sleep.

Megan had made her choice and she wasn't going to let herself be weighed down by endless what-ifs.

They each leaned in, meeting halfway, to share a perfunctory kiss.

"See you tomorrow," Tom said.

"I really hope so."

DAY

4

CHAPTER SEVENTEEN

MEGAN

WHEN MEGAN OPENED her eyes, she oriented herself by remembering how the night had ended. If Tom was beside her, it meant they'd moved on. If he wasn't...

She turned her head slowly to his side of the bed.

Empty.

She lifted the covers to confirm what she already knew: she was wearing her striped shorts and a tank top. This day was never going to end.

The lock on the door beeped. Oh no. There was absolutely no way Megan was going to go through this song and dance again. Instinctively, she rolled off the bed and onto the floor, cursing quietly when her knee bumped against the frame. As the door opened, she scooted underneath the bed to hide from her mother.

There was a pause. Could Donna see her from where she was standing? More important, it was surprisingly clean under the hotel bed. Not a dust bunny or forgotten candy wrapper in sight. If she ever broke out of this loop, Megan was filling out a comment card and leaving a tip for the cleaning staff.

"Moopy?" Her mother padded around the room. There was a small squeak as she cracked the bathroom door open and then

Megan felt the mattress sink just a little as her mother sat down, her ankles so close to Megan's face she could've bitten them.

Her mother gave a great exaggerated sigh (as it turned out, Donna's dramatics weren't reserved for an audience). Megan felt the mattress spring up again and watched her mother's feet walking out of the room. She didn't roll out from under the bed until the door had clicked shut and she'd counted to ten in case Donna was coming back.

Rubbing at the knots forming in her neck, Megan deliberated over what had gone wrong the day before. Yes, she'd had some doubts, an aching moment or two of weakness. But she'd pushed those doubts aside. She'd committed herself to Tom.

Which meant the mistake hadn't happened on her end. Her temper flared. Whatever was keeping her in this day must be Tom's fault. She needed to find out what the hell he'd done to keep her imprisoned in this nightmare.

Every action was an eruption, an act of exasperation. She pulled her dress over her head in a rage. Brushed her teeth as though she were scraping mildew off shower tiles. Didn't bother with the dry shampoo because oily hair didn't matter. Nothing mattered.

Nothing except figuring out just how Tom had screwed her over.

She drove the rental car with abandon, gritting her teeth when rocks bounced up from the highway and left pockmarks in the windshield. No need to bother with the parking lot; Megan slammed on the brakes, making the tires squeal, at the curb close to the ferry docks. *That* would block the stupid pedicab driver from offering them a ride.

Today, she would keep everything that was supposed to happen from happening, down to the most minute detail. Maybe she'd steal that baby carrier and walk around with the cat.

The ferry was slowly making its way through the pass toward Friday Harbor. Every second that ticked by added fuel to Megan's fury. When Tom set foot on land, she was going to explode.

CHAPTER EIGHTEEN

TOM

THE FOGHORN THAT Tom swore got louder every morning.

The sharp pain piercing through his neck.

The ferociously perky "Good morning, sunshine!" from the poor man's Henry Winkler as Tom's eyes squeezed shut, then fluttered open.

Tom was going to die in this never-ending day.

In every other version, Tom had responded to Henry Winkler. He didn't have it in him today. He stared straight ahead, jaw clenched.

This apparently only persuaded the man to try again, because Henry Winkler leaned in and tapped the green perforated metal between them. "I can never sleep on this ferry, so I envy you. I just caffeinate and caffeinate until I have the jitters. And then do you know what I do?"

Since not responding hadn't shut down the conversation, Tom relented. "I don't know," he said through gritted teeth.

Henry Winkler chortled. "Caffeinate some more!"

Tom couldn't take it anymore. He couldn't summon the energy to be even remotely polite. "*No.*" The word came out before Tom had even decided what to say.

"I beg your pardon?"

He took the eye drops out of the plastic bag in his pocket and squirted them into his eyes with abandon. The liquid dripped down his cheeks. He must've looked like a maniac. He didn't care. "I said *no*."

"No what?" Henry Winkler adjusted his glasses. There was dog or cat hair all over his sweater vest.

"No to this day, no to small talk with you, no to all of it." Tom had never been so blatantly rude in his life. He didn't hate it.

But to his horror, Henry Winkler's eyes grew watery, and guilt kicked Tom in the nuts. "I'm sorry," he said sincerely. "I'm having a bad morning."

"It's okay." Henry waved him off. "It happens to the best of us. But think of it this way: It'll get better. And if it doesn't, tomorrow is another day."

If only Henry Winkler knew.

While the ferry docked at a glacial pace, Tom's list of regrets sped through his mind at breakneck speed. He wasn't just thinking about the mistakes he'd made recently; he was going back further. Since misery loved company and Tom was all alone, he decided to drag himself down as far as he could.

He remembered how, as a first-year associate, he'd been expected to do a lot of the grunt work at Prescott and Prescott. On one particularly grueling occasion, the firm had been preparing for a high-profile antitrust case. A team that included both Tom and Brody was assembled and essentially locked in a war room for weeks. They combed through thousands of documents, knowing there was a good chance that the case would settle out of court and their efforts would be for naught.

One of the other lawyers assigned to the war room was a woman who'd been at the firm for a couple of years, Mayumi. She and Tom had been working side by side for a few days, finding small ways to keep up morale. She had a particularly dry sense of humor that he liked. One late afternoon, she invited Tom for lunch.

Tom politely declined. He enjoyed Mayumi's company and figured the invitation was platonic, but Tom avoided even the faint aroma of infidelity. He didn't want to spur any office gossip, nor did he ever want to give Megs a reason to worry.

The memory snagged on his sense of irony as he stomped off the ferry. He'd done everything right yesterday, just as he'd tried to do everything right his whole life, and he was *still* spinning his wheels in this pit.

Now he was wondering if he'd done himself a disservice. His devotion to Megs was appearing less romantic and more and more misguided. Maybe he would've been happier with Gina or Mayumi or...someone else.

His memory conjured the second part of that anecdote; unsurprisingly, upon hearing his little brother politely refuse Mayumi's lunch invitation, Brody'd offered to take her to his favorite deli.

Tom was fairly certain Brody had never cheated on Emmeline. His brother did, however, openly embrace any opportunity to chat up an attractive colleague; it was almost as though he *hoped* the gossip would get back to Emmeline. Whether Brody's behavior was a reaction to or the cause of the state of his listless marriage, Tom wasn't sure. The relationship Brody and Emmeline had wasn't what Tom would ever want for himself, but who was he to judge? You never really knew what relationships were like from the inside. And Tom and Brody didn't tend to talk about anything below the surface of the frozen pond their family skated on.

But Tom didn't want to skate. Today, all Tom wanted to do was find a dark room to hide in. Maybe with a bottle of Jack.

With his garment bag slung over his shoulder and his suitcase bumping along the docks, Tom grew angrier. And then he spotted Megs standing at the top of the ramp, her arms crossed. He didn't want to hear one more of her well-intentioned plans. Her stubborn belief in her own logic made him *really* want that bottle of Jack.

Why had he trusted someone so morally murky?

Megs didn't know any better than he did. Nobody did. Everyone was just ricocheting through life, trying to get through with as few bruises as possible.

And this morning Tom had woken up black-and-blue.

He picked up speed, his suitcase bouncing until it flipped onto its side, no longer rolling on its little wheels. Tom picked it up and awkwardly carried it by the still-extended handle, his garment bag dragging along the ground.

He hadn't even reached the top of the ramp when she spat out, "What did you do?"

"What did *I* do?" Oh no. This little blame-shifter wasn't going to put this whole space-time clusterfuck on him. "What did *you* do? Did you really send Leo away? Because for some reason, he was still at the rehearsal dinner last night. Did you really end it with him? Or did you decide to sleep with him once more for old times' sake?"

"No, I didn't sleep with him again. And how could I have ended something that didn't even exist?" Her hair blew wildly in the breeze off the ocean. "It happened years ago and I keep apologizing. Will you hold that against me forever?"

He shrugged like a sullen teenager. "Maybe. I mean, I didn't do anything wrong yesterday."

"Actually, Tom." She tucked her hair behind her ears and glowered at him. "You didn't do *anything*. Full stop."

"What do you mean?"

"You left me to flail up there during our speech. You didn't talk to my family at all. I mean, we're well past this, but how much of this wedding did you actually plan with me?" She pointed her finger at him. "And how dare you get too comfortable on the moral high ground when we still haven't properly discussed your plan to hijack my life and take me to Missouri."

The pedicab rolled up, coming in at an awkward angle to account for the rental car inexplicably in the middle of the road.

"Fancy a ride, you two? Where are you heading?" the silvery-haired strong woman asked. For the fourth time.

"*Go away!*" Tom and Megan yelled at her in unison.

"What do you mean, I didn't do anything last night? Which last night?" Tom asked, getting them back to their fight. He had no idea what she was talking about or why she was angry with him. Aside from the Missouri thing, which he was the first to admit had been shitty.

"*Last* last night! When I was trying to stop Alistair from embarrassing me in front of your parents and so I just kept talking."

Ferry passengers were trickling around them, not even trying to hide that they were eavesdropping. Tom didn't care.

"What did you expect me to do, *Megan?*" He was still holding his suitcase, his garment bag draped over the top, and his biceps were starting to burn, so he tossed it to the ground. "Interrupt you and say something coherent?"

"Yes!" Her arms flew out. "That would've been great! I was clearly dying up there! But you never say anything! Ever!"

She was making less sense as she went on. Tom was torn between wanting to dissect where this particular tirade was coming from and wanting to jump into the freezing ocean just to feel something other than hopeless frustration. Instead of asking her to clarify, he just stared at her. He knew it was a dick move. Something his dad would do.

"You've never defended me to your family," she said. "They treat me like I'm trash—"

"They approve of *you*, they're polite to *you*," Tom said.

"In a passive-aggressive way that lets me know I'm with you by their grace. You know as well as I do they wish you were with someone who came from better stock because they hate my family—"

"*You* hate your family."

"I'm allowed! They're mine!" She threw her head back and let out a guttural yell, alarming several passersby. Then she seared Tom with a gimlet eye. "You're a coward, Tom. A fucking *coward!* You've never stood up to your family. Not for me, not for yourself. And if you want to live your life letting them bulldoze their way across you, be my guest. I want no part of it."

He nearly doubled over. They'd never spoken to each other like this. How long had Megs been holding that all in?

You're a coward, Tom. A fucking coward.

Pain gave way to anger, which he tamped down with feigned apathy. Let her think he was a coward. He knew better. He'd spent his whole life keeping the peace. Every day trying to both impress his parents and love Megs. That wasn't cowardice, it was a relentless, exhausting act of bravery.

Fine. If the day was going to reset every morning, then there were no consequences. And if there were no consequences, then Tom definitely wasn't going to waste today getting obliterated by his (former?) fiancée.

The man with the giant fishing hat approached them with trepidation, his bright-eyed tabby twitching its whiskers with interest. "Excuse me. Sorry to interrupt, but I just wanted to make sure everything was okay."

"Not now, cat man," Megs snapped. The man scurried off.

"All right. I'm a coward." Feeling wild, Tom tossed his garment bag off the ramp. He'd wanted it to drift out to sea in a dramatic fashion, but instead it sort of rolled down the small cliff onto a short rocky beach. Oh, well. The tide would come in and take it away. "You want to know what this coward's going to do today?"

"*What?*" The word came out as a small blast of disdain from that mouth he'd kissed a million times.

"Whatever the hell I want."

Tom kicked his suitcase, still lying on the ground, off the small cliff too. This time the momentum took it right out to the murky, seaweed-infested water with a satisfying splash.

CHAPTER NINETEEN

MEGAN

THE LIQUOR STORE offered Megan three types of gin: botanical, citrus, and peppercorn. When the cashier asked her preference, she said, "Surprise me. And throw in one of those two-liter plastic bottles of club soda."

She didn't know what Tom was going to do today and she didn't care. But Megan was going to get drunk in the bathtub.

While adding more hot water by turning the faucet with her toes, causing the bubbles to rise up to her ears, she tried to let the gin and soda iron out her thoughts until her mind was wrinkle-free. A place of refuge.

She didn't want to think about how much Tom was to blame—for everything. For his invertebrate way of letting his family dictate his entire life and *their* entire life together. For the way he thought he was remaining a neutral party when what she really needed him to do was stick up for her family. Even once would've been nice. Donna might be a head case, but she'd always treated Tom well. And Brianna could be a pain, but she had her moments. Megan's family wasn't all bad, because, if they were, what did that make her?

Maybe if Tom had shown more respect for the Givenses, it might've been contagious and rubbed off on John and Carol.

The first time she'd met them was Thanksgiving of their sophomore year. They were babies, only nineteen, but their love felt bigger than their age, bigger than their experience (or lack thereof). Driving with Tom to his paternal grandmother's house in Connecticut rather than flying home to be with her own family had felt brazen.

It hadn't occurred to Megan to worry about what she wore to dinner—until she took in Carol's and Emmeline's pointed once-over. It also hadn't occurred to her to refresh her mental résumé before sitting down to converse with John, not realizing that impressing the Prescotts was a full-time job.

Everyone had been polite to her in the most cursory way. She wondered if she'd imagined their disapproval. If her breeding had been East Coast wealth, for example, would they still have insisted she and Tom stay in separate rooms?

Tom did manage to sneak into her room every night. They slept together only once, worrying about the creaky bed, but spooning with Tom until the sun came up made the daytime hours more bearable.

Until the morning they were scheduled to drive back to Cambridge.

Megan had showered and blown out her hair and was coming down the stairs for breakfast when she overheard Tom talking to his parents in the library.

"You aren't really serious about that girl, are you?" John asked. "She's smart, but I'm afraid her background is too different. You know how important it is for children to have a father figure in the home."

"What does Thomas know about serious relationships? He's still a teenager," Carol had scoffed.

"Well, son? Tell us if this is something we need to worry about."

And then Megan heard Tom speak in a voice that didn't even sound like his own. The Tom she knew was compassionate, optimistic. Jovial. This one sounded meek. "It's not a big deal," she heard the man she loved say. "We're just having fun."

But Tom was the first guy Megan had taken seriously. Every other boy she'd kissed had been a quick and playful diversion.

She knew Tom had never felt about anyone the way he felt about her. He'd told her that the first time they'd slept together and often ever since.

Why didn't Tom's parents approve of her? She wasn't high-maintenance like her mother. She wasn't a deserter like her father.

Sure, she didn't have traditional parental role models, but she could rattle off countless names of successful, incredible people who'd grown up in homes that didn't look like the Prescotts'. What kind of monster believed there was only one right way to be raised? One way to be worth something?

Of course, what kind of person spied on her boyfriend's family from the hallway?

As much as she wanted to put John in his place, she'd swallowed the argument. Instead, she'd cleared her throat loudly enough to announce herself, plastered on a bright smile, and thanked the Prescotts profusely for their hospitality. They might have found fault with plenty of aspects of Megan's life, but her manners were impeccable.

While she and Tom drove back to campus, they laughed about the stiffness of the weekend, full of relief to be back to a life where they could be themselves. She'd never mentioned the conversation she'd overheard or any of the other disparaging comments that followed over the years.

Every family was complicated. It didn't seem fair to openly pick on Tom's when her own was equally problematic.

She and Tom both put up with a lot. She supposed they'd had

a tacit agreement—Tom trusted Megan to take point on dealing with Donna's (and Brianna's and Alistair's) antics, and in turn, she'd let him deal with his family in his own way.

She sank further into the bathtub, sipping from a plastic cup she'd found by the sink. The ratio of gin to club soda was rapidly increasing. She chewed on the rim, her bottom lip flexing to tip more into her mouth, letting the cool gin swirl between her bottom teeth and onto her tongue. She was well on her way to full-fledged inebriation when she heard the beep of the key card unlocking the door.

"Megan Rose Givens," Donna called. "Where in the fresh hell are you? I've been looking for you all morning."

"In the bath." Megan's words were garbled as she still had the plastic cup between her teeth. She opted to ignore her mother's sudden and inexplicable Southern drawl.

"I don't want to see her naked," she heard Brianna state matter-of-factly.

Megan arranged the bubbles over the bottom half of her body, then snatched a washcloth off the edge of the tub and placed it over her breasts.

In an instant, Donna was looming in the doorway, Brianna's face peeking over her shoulder.

"This is a fine time for *you* to be luxuriating," Donna snapped. "When I am in crisis."

"Mom's in crisis," Brianna echoed dryly. "Why haven't you been answering your phone? Why does no one in this family answer my texts?"

"Because you don't seem to like any of us." Megan topped up a cocktail that was basically straight gin at this point. She was glad the liquor-store employee had given her the botanical flavor. It was indeed refreshing.

"I like you sometimes." Brianna glared at her before recoiling. "Ugh, rearrange your bubbles. I don't need to know your preferred bikini-wax shape."

"I don't wax. I trim." Megan was enjoying giving very few fucks. Maybe she'd give them all away. Or not have any left. Her ability to be coherent was getting blurry.

"Would you two stop bickering?" Donna bellowed. "You're always making everything about the two of you when I have a very real and very disturbing problem."

"Mom's dress is too boobalicious," Brianna said, popping two sticks of gum in her mouth at once. "And I reminded her there are minors at this establishment."

"Mom's dress is moot."

"My dress is *what?*" Donna seemed to feel she'd been offended, though she wasn't quite sure how. She was teetering from Southern to British.

"Moot." Megan sat up, sloshing water over the sides of the clawfoot bathtub, her washcloth still sticking to her chest like a terrycloth bathing suit. "Irrelevant. There's no wedding, ergo there's no wedding rehearsal dinner."

Donna spun toward Brianna. "I can't talk to her when she's drunk. She's acting just like Husband Number Three. *You* deal with her."

She marched out of the bathroom and, from the sounds of things, proceeded to flump herself onto Megan's bed.

Brianna was grinning wickedly. She snapped her gum. "You and Mr. Perfect have a fight?"

"Several, actually. Over the course of many days. Or one day, if you want to get technical."

"I can't talk to her either. *She's bonkers,*" Brianna hollered at their mother over her shoulder.

"Tell her to get her act together and help me find something to wear tonight," Donna yelled back.

"You're supposed to get your act together and help Mom," Brianna unhelpfully repeated. "She also said you're her least favorite child and she's bequeathing everything in her will to me. You may not have heard her say that last bit. It was quiet."

The last of the gin coupled with the unwelcome arrival of Donna and Brianna had turned Megan's mildly bemused misery to anger. It happened so quickly, she almost didn't register it.

"You know what?" She stood up, grabbed a towel, and wrapped it around herself as her washcloth top fell and she accidentally flashed her sister. "I don't have to put up with *you*, I don't have to solve Mom's imagined crises, I don't have to marry Tom, I don't have to do a damn thing. Not today, not ever."

Brianna took a step back. "Whoa. Bridezilla is rearing her freaky head."

Brianna's sass was covering up real unease. Even through her gin-soaked haze, Megan could see it. Megan had dedicated her entire existence to making everyone else comfortable, including her sister, whom she'd basically raised. Megan had been a pleaser since birth because she'd had to be. If she wasn't actively trying to make everyone happy, her critics grew raucous. She'd always believed the world needed pleasers.

However, today was different. Today, making her sister feel uncomfortable was making Megan feel powerful. She pushed past Brianna, dripping wet and wondering vaguely if she'd grabbed a hand towel instead of a bath towel by mistake.

"Get the hell out of my room! Both of you. Today is about *me* and no one else."

To Megan's great pleasure, Brianna and Donna both scurried away. The door slammed behind them.

As she toweled off, she caught a glimpse of herself in the mirror.

Her face was flushed, her eyes wild.

She was unabashedly naked.

Suddenly, there was only one thing she wanted to do today.

CHAPTER TWENTY

TOM

COWARD.

Ever since Megs had launched that particular grenade, he'd tried to scrub the word from his brain.

Tom repeated his long-believed mantra: *I'm not a coward, I'm a peacekeeper.*

He hadn't spoken up during Megs's speech because he knew she could handle herself. Furthermore, he'd had no idea what she'd been trying to accomplish and therefore couldn't see what he was supposed to do to help her.

After throwing his tantrum, and his luggage, by the docks, Tom started walking. Friday Harbor was downhill from everything else and the incline was making his quads burn in a way he actually enjoyed. So he kept on. There was enough of a shoulder on the road to keep the walk from being too dicey. Part of him wished the security of the shoulder away.

Coward.

She thought he was a coward. And for how long?

Megs didn't have the faintest idea what it was like being a full-time Prescott.

When Tom was eight, he'd begged his father to teach him to

play chess, a bid for his attention. John directed Tom on how to set up the board, then told Tom he could go first. After pestering his father with questions about how every piece moved, Tom had tentatively nudged a pawn forward.

John beat him in three moves.

When Tom asked John to teach him how, his father replied, "Ask your brother," and left the room. Tom ran after Brody and wore his brother down until he agreed to play. They set up the board, but this time Tom demanded to go second, thinking that was part of the secret.

Every move Brody made, Tom mirrored it. Brody's pawn moved ahead two spaces; Tom met it in the middle of the board. Brody moved a knight; Tom's knight galloped out. Tom hoped his father would walk back into the room and see that Tom had survived, that he hadn't been beaten yet.

But John never materialized, and Brody became so irritated with Tom's inability to make his own moves, he tipped over the board and went to a friend's house.

Tom braced himself as a pickup truck whizzed past him. He moved farther into the trees, his thoughts meandering to his mother.

As a child, he'd never placed a kiss on Carol's cheek without seeing her delicately wipe it off with a handkerchief afterward. She'd never been affectionate. And she never would be. Her interest in Tom seemed to be based solely on John's moods, because if Tom irritated his father, Carol would scowl at him from across the room.

And so he'd learned to move carefully when instructed to... or not to move at all.

Maybe that did make him a coward.

Megs didn't get it. She couldn't possibly. If you were a Givens, you knew what you were dealing with. The dangers weren't disguised. Alistair's inability to be a productive member of society was out in the open. Brianna almost always said whatever was on her mind. Donna's mania was on display. The Givenses' potholes were clearly marked.

Being a Prescott, on the other hand, was like walking through a funhouse of expectations—every time you thought you'd figured it out, you realized the mirror was warped. Mistakes were made quietly and judged equally as quietly. Every encounter within the Prescott bubble was therefore accompanied by a low-grade terror.

Tom had thought that by the age of thirty, he'd feel like his own person rather than John and Carol's son. Now it seemed he'd forever be the kid begging for their attention and then regretting it when he got it.

That was ending here. Today. On this endless day.

Today, he'd take a jackhammer to the prescribed path he'd been on. He wasn't going to try to please anyone but himself.

He just had to figure out how to do that.

The farther he walked, the less he noticed the crick in his neck. Instead, he felt the burning in his legs, the trickle of sweat trailing down his chest and in the matching canal down his back. It was getting hot. Tom tossed his suit jacket into the trees. He unbuttoned the top two buttons of his dress shirt and rolled the sleeves up to his forearms. He was feeling better already.

Until he realized where he'd subconsciously walked to.

The golf course.

Before he could turn around and run in his Italian loafers, he heard his brother call out, "Spare Parts! You made it! But what the hell are you wearing?"

The notion of playing golf with Brody and his father while he was sticky with sweat and indulging his angst filled him with dread.

Until.

Tom remembered something paramount: not a damn thing he did today mattered.

Leo and Tom had an expression they'd come up with in college, one they'd use whenever they were burned out from studying or tired of telling their self-aggrandizing roommates, who referred to themselves as the Philosophy Kings, to clean their moldy tofu out of the fridge. It came from deep within their guts, where their basest instincts lay. They'd look at each other and they'd yell, *"Anarchy reigns supreme!"*

And then they'd do something stupid. To take the edge off.

They'd never grown out of it. The last time Leo was in New York, he'd talked a very stressed-out Tom, who'd just learned about his potential relocation to Missouri, into going to a piano bar intended for Broadway fans. Megs had gone upstate for the weekend with a few friends from work, a detail Tom now understood with new clarity, and Leo persuaded Tom to stay out all night. Alongside dozens of strangers, they belted out songs Tom only sort of knew, and he got drunker than he'd been since the last time Leo'd been in town. It was exactly what Tom had needed.

Tom had loved Leo more than he'd ever loved anyone, with the exception of Megs. The fact that he'd had to lose them both in one fell swoop was the cruelest of fates.

But today, right now, Tom was going to love himself enough to create his own anarchy.

"Let's golf, motherfuckers!" he cried to the mild alarm of his father and bottomless amusement of his brother. When Brody offered his flask, Tom drained it. *Let the games begin*, he thought.

"I hope this crass enthusiasm means last night's client dinner went well," John said, narrowing his eyes at the flask.

"Oh yeah. The client dinner was amazing. And did I tell you how super-pumped Megs is to move to the Midwest? We've been talking about it nonstop."

Although obviously annoyed at Tom's caustic flippancy, John let it go while they paid for the round. Tom vacillated between giddiness and an anxious sort of awe at not questioning what his father would want him to do before making each move.

"Broderick, your stance is too wide," John hollered on the first hole from the shade of the cart.

Tom had nothing in his stomach, so the early-morning alcohol hit his bloodstream like a freight train and he immediately felt punchy. "Criticizing your firstborn?" Tom tossed at his father. He ran to Brody and his flask. "That calls for a drink!"

"You cleaned me out, remember?" Brody shifted his weight and swung.

Without a top-up of booze, the next several holes began boring Tom. A quick glance at his watch told him the restaurant that doubled as a clubhouse would be open and serving alcohol.

"Let's take a break and get some brunch," he suggested.

Brody had been uncharacteristically quiet and readily agreed.

"You two go ahead." John waved them off, pulling his phone from his pocket.

John had never received a phone call this early in any other loop, which meant he was faking it to get out of spending time with his sons. Classic.

Tom and Brody took a table on the patio and ordered greasy food and beers. Their sixty-something server didn't even bat an eye.

"No tablecloths." Brody knocked on the wood. "No wonder Dad didn't want to join us."

"Screw him."

"Wow. Strong words. That's basically patricide coming from you. You nervous or something, Spare Parts?" Brody asked between bites of sausage.

"For tomorrow?" Tom was riding a solid buzz now. "Nah. Why should tomorrow make me nervous?" As far as Tom was concerned, tomorrow didn't exist.

Brody put down his fork and gazed meaningfully at his brother as though he were attempting telepathy. "Marriage, man. It's not what you expect."

Even through the day-drinking buzz, Tom felt a palpitation in his heart that told him not to waste this moment. A Prescott was about to say something real. He could feel it. "What do you mean?"

"I mean dating, even living together, it's all sex and playing house. Something changes when you sign that piece of paper."

"What could possibly change with a signature?"

Brody guzzled the rest of his beer and held the empty pint glass up like an asshole to get the attention of their server. "All the little things, the gripes, the complaints, the stuff you thought was rolling off your back and hers...it's not actually rolling off. It's seeping in."

"What's seeping in?" Tom's buzz was in danger of wearing off. He blamed the ominous turn this conversation had taken, so he drained his glass. And because he was being an asshole today, he wordlessly held it up to her too.

She was definitely going to spit in their next round.

"Emmeline and I are getting divorced."

The hairs on Tom's arms stood on end. He nearly dropped his glass. He knew things weren't great between Brody and Emmeline, but he'd had no idea they'd call it quits. "What? Why? Do Mom and Dad know?"

"What do you mean, what? I said we're getting divorced. We can barely stand to be in the same room. And yes, they know."

"Mom and Dad know and you're *still* their favorite?" Tom's tipsy id had formed that response. He wished he could take it back until he remembered he was in the land of no consequences. Even so, he reached out and put a hand on Brody's arm. "You okay?"

"Yes, I'm fucking okay." Brody snatched his arm away. "I've got more money than most people see in a lifetime, an apartment in a city that will leave me drowning in one-night stands, and parents who like me better than my little brother. Just because my wife can't stand me doesn't mean I'm not okay."

He was deflecting, Tom knew that. But he still hated Brody in that moment, just a little.

They finished up, tossed a hundred-dollar bill on the table, drained their third (or was it fourth?) beers, and headed back to the golf game, swaying as they walked.

It was the somethingth hole. Tom wasn't keeping track anymore. Nor was he even trying to play a good game. Because this was boring. Golf was boring. Almost as boring as law. Oddly enough, he was winning. Or at least, he assumed he was. He wasn't keeping score.

Brody was shifting his weight, readjusting his grip. Ready to swing.

A breeze came up and the trees had the nerve to sway just enough for the sun to get in Tom's eyes. He took Brody's forgotten visor from the golf cart and plopped it on his head as he took a seat. Brody was still waiting to take his shot. John stepped up to physically correct his stance.

Tom wondered if the brunch beers combined with the shit-mix from Brody's flask (which had tasted like every bottle in the hotel minibar combined) were giving him x-ray vision. He swore he could see his dad's insides, all high-pressure valves, jokes about how they had Tom for spare parts, and variations on *You know what you're going to do, son?*

Come to think of it, Tom wasn't even sure he liked law. Or that he'd ever actually wanted to be a lawyer.

Brody pulled his nine-iron back, ready to show off how fucking far the ball would fly, and when he did...time stood still.

Because, why not. It'd already brought Tom back to the same day over and over again.

And while time paused, Tom saw his brother. Truly *saw* him. His crumbling marriage. The lithe yet lethal barbs he and Emmeline launched at each other.

Death by a million paper cuts.

Just as Brody was about to swing, Tom also thought of Leo, of his dad…of Megs. And then Tom screamed, *"Anarchy reigns supreme,"* pushed down on the gas of the golf cart, and blazed out of there like Lewis Hamilton on lap seventy of an F1 Grand Prix.

In the distance he could hear his father yell (politely) and Brody curse because he'd missed his shot. Tom let out a maniacal laugh.

For the amount of time it took a lightning bolt to split the sky, Tom was elated. Free from the trappings of his family, his choices, the loop ensnaring him and Megs.

And then, just as quickly, his sense of freedom evaporated.

This golf cart wasn't cornering like a Ferrari. Tom nearly tipped himself out on the first turn. A group of retirees gaped at him rolling by, so Tom flipped them all the bird and attempted to drive faster. However, the golf cart topped out at fifteen miles an hour, making this bit of anarchy slower and less satisfying than intended.

The cart might have been traveling at a playground-zone speed, but Tom's resentment was flying far and fast.

Brody, golden child, was shaming the family by divorcing his shiny pedigreed wife and Tom was *still* the disappointment.

He ripped off Brody's visor, threw it at an elderly lady on the putting green, and peeled straight for the exit. Tom had a plan.

And it involved driving that cart all the way back to Roche Harbor.

CHAPTER TWENTY-ONE

MEGAN

HOTEL BATHROBES WERE cozy, but they definitely weren't sexy. Her wedding night La Perla lingerie, on the other hand, was *very* sexy. Still, the idea of putting it on today made her feel like she couldn't breathe.

Megan opted for a jewel-toned bra and a matching pair of lace underwear and contemplated the top layer. She felt as though she were wrapping a gift, but the gift was what *she* wanted, and she was giving it to herself.

She clearly needed to sober up a little. She started the coffeemaker—possibly without putting in a filter—then promptly forgot she'd started it and opened the minibar.

The startling price of one bottle of water didn't stop her from chugging the entire thing. The way things were going, she'd never get the bill. She chased it with an energy drink. Then she had to pee.

Her skin tingled with anticipation when she thought of Leo. Wasn't this what she'd wanted late in those nights while Tom slept and her shadow self emerged? Wasn't this what she'd imagined every time she'd gotten angry about having her post-college life mapped out for her? When she'd thought about every opportunity she'd either given up or not even reached for because her role had always been to contort herself into the shapes others wanted to see?

She'd done a lot for Tom and his family. She'd done so much for her own family. Now she was going to do something for herself.

And she refused to feel even a smidgen of guilt about it, even if the guilt was peering through the curtains of her conscience.

She threw her jersey dress over her carefully selected underwear, sprayed her hair with dry shampoo, and applied blush, mascara, and a light sheen of lip gloss.

And then the guilt stared her down, so she gave herself a pep talk.

After a quick call to the lobby to find out which room she needed (normally they didn't give out that information, but she was staying in the bridal suite and they apparently made exceptions for brides), she walked the length of the hallway to the elevator and pressed the down button.

A little light-headed from gin, caffeine, and a tiny dose of panic, Megan slowed her breathing and asked herself if this was what she wanted. And then she got off the elevator and knocked on the door of Leo's hotel room.

He opened it; his face registered surprise, followed quickly by longing.

"Hi," she said. It was cliché in its breathlessness, but it was real. "Can I come in?"

Instead of answering, he pulled her into a hug so warm and strong, she thought she could live there. Have food delivered to that hug. Sleep in that hug. Never leave.

She thought again about the fraying connection she had to Tom, measured it against the pull she felt to Leo. How had she never realized how powerfully they were linked despite time and geographical distance?

"I wasn't sure if you were going to avoid me, but I want to talk to you." He pulled her into the room and closed the door.

With his hands gently on her shoulders, he pushed her away just far enough to drink her in with his eyes. "I thought about calling, about writing, and I know my timing—"

Megan shook her head and he stopped talking. A slow smile crawled across her face, growing wider by the second. "Your timing is perfect."

Not knowing how to communicate what she had planned, she started by placing her hand on his chest, enjoying the feel of his muscles under her palms.

Today was about what *she* wanted.

She knew what Leo wanted already, but she still checked in with him, raising her eyes to his as she let her fingers trail achingly slowly down the muscles of his abdomen to the waist of his worn jeans. He nodded and reached one hand around to the small of her back, the other behind her head. His fingers tangled in her hair and he pulled her closer until their parted mouths met and they melted into each other.

Their tongues, warm and slick, teased as their bodies pressed together harder. She heaved her chest just to feel more of him against her. She could live in his hug, but she could die in this kiss.

Greedily, Megan fiddled with the button fly of his jeans. While she did so, he whipped his shirt off, revealing a torso that was familiar and yet firmer, his shoulders broader.

His pants dropped to the floor and she dug her fingers into the light dusting of chest hair that had grown in the years since she'd last taken off his shirt. She wanted to lick, nip, feel every part of him, but she was still far too clothed.

Leo reached for the hem of her dress, ready to pull it over her head, and paused, a question in his eyes. The look was so tender it nearly undid her.

"Are you sure?" he asked. "Should we talk first?"

"Yes to being sure, no to the talking." She whipped her dress off herself, nearly swooning from the lust in his eyes as he took in her body.

She was enjoying teasing him too much, letting his anticipation build, to remove her bra and underwear just yet. She gave him a playful push toward the bed, and he walked backward as she angled herself against him, biting at his bottom lip.

"I've thought about this, about you, so many times since—" he managed to get out.

"So have I." The way he wanted her made Megan feel powerful. Desire ached deep within her.

Leo rolled her over until she lay on her back, the hotel covers tangling beneath them. Starting at her jaw, he kissed his way to her mouth, marking a path over her. She hadn't seen anyone naked other than Tom in years. Not since, well, Leo.

But Megan didn't want to think about Tom. Not even as the gin wore off and her nerves knocked politely at her subconscious. She muted those nerves by encouraging Leo to move faster to the main event.

Eight years had passed and yet it felt like that same morning, the day of her graduation, when they'd first succumbed to their mutual attraction.

Their bodies gave into those years of anticipation and Megan decided it was most assuredly worth the wait.

CHAPTER TWENTY-TWO

TOM

AS THE GOLF cart rumbled over the gravelly shoulder, cars whipping by and honking at Tom, he couldn't stop thinking about Brody and Emmeline. About how Brody's upward trajectory always seemed so effortless and how, over brunch, Brody had instantly dispelled a lifetime of myths.

Brody had been miserable. For years. Maybe forever.

And now Tom was miserable.

If trying to walk the path John wanted for him was futile and stumbling after his brother was riddled with misery, Tom had to find a new path. It should start with something he'd never done before. Because today was about being the anti-Tom. No more chasing validation. No more obsessing about keeping things smooth and civil. He'd done all that and it'd led him into a damn time loop.

He'd tried to keep Megs happy and his parents happy and Megs's family happy and his coworkers happy and now he was going to do the one thing he'd never thought he'd do.

But first, he needed a shower.

Once he reached Roche Harbor, he jogged up the steps to the hotel's gift and clothing shop, chose the least dorky chinos and pastel golf shirt he could find (complete with Roche Harbor insignia), bought a beach towel, and headed for the public showers at the marina. Unfortunately, the gift shop didn't sell underwear, and Tom's suitcase was presumably at the bottom of the ocean, so once he showered, he was going commando.

Smelling of eucalyptus and whatever else was provided in the soap dispenser, Tom wiped the steamed mirror with a paper towel, finger-combed his hair, and took his wallet and a packet of breath mints out of his suit pants before ditching them in the garbage can. He might be wearing clothes from the gift shop, but he hoped his boy-next-door looks and a little charisma could make up for that.

Because, after twelve years of dedication to one woman, he was about to experience something new. *Someone* new. He was going to do the first 100 percent selfishly motivated act of his entire existence.

Tom was about to figure out how Megan felt when she'd cheated on him.

At the hotel restaurant, the hostess offered him a table with a view. He waved her off, heading for the bar. He took a seat at the same stool he'd occupied that second day and waited for Casey to appear.

When she did, she did not disappoint. This time he took the opportunity to register how she reacted to him. Despite his pastel-and-khaki motif—or perhaps because of it, who knew—she appeared to light up, drink him in. He gave her his best impression of Brody's smile, the one that somehow balanced wolfishness and disarming sheepishness.

"Hi," he said with an ease he wasn't sure he felt.

This was delicate. Coming on to women might be second nature for Leo, but Tom was out of practice. In fact, Tom had never really practiced at all. Sure, he'd had a few girlfriends in high school, prom dates and casual teen flings. But he'd never had to pursue Megs. They'd clicked right away. Their chemistry had been effortless.

For some reason, every move he was about to make with Casey seemed smarmy. He didn't want smarmy; he wanted hot. Unattached. Other people did unattached, so why couldn't he?

"Hey there, sailor." He wondered how many times she'd used that line on customers. Eyes gleaming with sass and a smirk Tom instantly wanted to kiss, she leaned on the bar. "I see you've visited our gift shop."

Her voice was as sultry as he'd remembered. He wanted to twist her long ponytail with its blue raspberry ends around his fingers. He looked down at his outfit and let out a self-deprecating laugh. "Yeah. I had a bit of an emergency."

"What happened?" Her eyes were wide, amusement dancing in them.

"You wouldn't believe me if I told you."

"Try me."

If he was in a day of no consequences and zero fucks, why not tell her the truth? He leaned in conspiratorially. "I seem to have ripped a bit of a hole in the space-time continuum."

Her eyebrows lifted. "Well…that doesn't totally explain the gift-shop ensemble, but I agree that's quite a story. How'd you manage to do that?"

"I haven't figured that part out yet."

"Did you piss off some Time Lords or something?"

He laughed, catching her *Doctor Who* reference. "I guess I must've."

"Just when I think I've heard everything at this bar," she called over to a coworker. "This guy walks in." She turned back to Tom. "You're an intriguing man…"

"Tom," he filled in for her.

She tapped her name tag with a zebra-patterned fingernail. "Casey. What can I get you, Tom?"

Now what? How did one move from small talk to something more? He supposed he could use some of the natural rapport he'd already experienced with Casey. She wouldn't remember and he could go from there.

"I think I'm in the mood for some liquid sunshine." Tom could feel his growing confidence beaming out of him like a spotlight.

She laughed. "Then you're in the wrong place. You know alcohol is a depressant, right?"

He'd known she would say that but enjoyed it nonetheless. He liked the sound of her laugh and wanted to keep things light.

"Technically, yes." Putting both arms on the bar, he leaned forward. Megs had always told him she loved his arms. "So why does it make me so happy?"

"I should start ordering whatever *you* get," she said, cocking an eyebrow. "What's your drink?"

She was back to business. He needed to keep her engaged before he lost her to another customer. The way she smiled at him flirtatiously encouraged Tom. He rubbed his hands together, making a great show of turning her question over in his mind. "I don't know."

"Well, what are you in the mood for?" She leaned forward and wiped at the already clean bar with a towel. She was stalling. That was a good sign.

Now for his secret weapon. A phrase he knew would get her attention because, quite frankly, it had come from her.

"Why don't you surprise me? I'm looking to chase the great unknown," he said, keeping his gaze focused on her to gauge her reaction.

She froze and blinked. "I *always* say that."

"Say what?" He played innocent.

"Say I'm chasing the great unknown." She was leaning close now, her voice losing its polite-to-customers timbre and sliding into something more intimate.

She was intrigued, he could tell, by the way this meeting felt fated. She didn't have to know fate was really just a glitch in the universe.

"Have you found it yet?" he asked. His cheeks were beginning to ache. He couldn't stop smiling at her. What had begun as a strategy was becoming real for him too.

"Have I found the great unknown?" she asked, biting her plump bottom lip.

"Because I've been wondering if the great unknown was a place or a feeling...or a person." He swallowed, a boyish gesture belying the confidence he was trying to exude. She saw it, the indicator of his nerves, and instead of laughing, she seemed to light up.

"You're kind of adorable, you know." She stage-whispered, "You're new at this, aren't you?"

Tom nodded, almost imperceptibly. "I am."

"Then you could use some help." She shrugged coyly. "I thought I saw something unknown next to the shed behind the pool."

"I guess I should go check, then." He patted the bar twice, maintaining eye contact, looking for clues they were on the same page. He'd never been this brash before and was afraid he was misreading the entire situation. But she winked at him.

"I'll meet you there in five," she tossed lightly over her shoulder before refilling some sodas at the other end of the bar.

He kept his cool until he was at the bottom of the steps and then his jaunty, confident stroll broke into a run.

The shed behind the pool.

He scanned the area, looking for the quickest and most discreet route. He must've calculated wrong, because by the time he got to a copse of trees looming over the shed, she was already there. Leaning against the wood siding. Looking even hotter than before.

His physiological reaction made it clear his body was ready. Now he just had to convince his wavering mind that this was a good idea.

Tom was about to kiss another woman. He wanted to high-five himself and maybe take an aspirin.

"You took your sweet time," she teased.

"You have freckles," Tom replied, noticing the faint speckles across her nose and cheeks for the first time in the natural light.

"I do." Her laughter trilled as she leaned farther back, her body so close to Tom all he had to do was take a breath and they'd connect. More than anything, he wanted to connect with someone right now.

"They're really cute," he whispered, afraid this would all go away—that she would go away and leave him with his thoughts. He knew he had plenty forming and suspected none of them were good.

"*You're* really cute." In a flash, her fingers were on his face, pulling his lips to hers. Tom pressed against her, grazing one hand under her thigh to hitch up her leg. She moaned into his mouth.

Their kiss deepened as he rocked against her, driving them both insane. She took the hand that wasn't on her thigh and brought it to her breast. Tom became dizzy, wanting this to go on forever— and they were both still clothed. He couldn't imagine how much fun he could have with Casey if they were naked.

As though reading his mind, she tucked her hands under his shirt, scratching at his back with her painted nails, until her phone unexpectedly started chirping.

"Should you get that?" he asked as her teeth grazed his neck.

"Nah, it's probably my boyfriend."

The knee-jerk conscience he'd been trying to smother all day pulled him back. "Boyfriend?"

"Relax, we have an open relationship. Not that I normally make out with customers..." She went back to kissing his neck and he felt her smile into his flesh. "But you were an exception. Intriguing under those preppy clothes."

He took a breath, trying to recapture the fracturing mood they'd created.

She laughed softly. "Besides, he's kind of scrawny. You could totally take him."

Regardless of the tacit approval, the magic had withered. He heard the squeals of small children from the pool, and the spell between him and Casey was officially broken. He took a half step back.

"I should..." His attempt to extricate himself fell flat between them.

"Oh, should you?" she asked, a mischievous glint in her eye. "You should probably also start thinking of baseball or your mother because this is a family-friendly resort and that"—she pointed to the front of his pants—"ain't family-friendly."

The pheromone high washed off Tom much faster than it had arrived. He suddenly felt absurd, leaning against a shed with a woman who was beautiful but a stranger. He missed Megs with such ferocity, his knees buckled beneath him.

"I think I hate myself," he said to the ground, forgetting Casey was still with him.

He heard her scoff and looked up.

"Poor little rich boy." All the flirtation had dissipated from her demeanor and been replaced with a note of disgust. He wondered just how many wealthy yet secretly miserable hotel guests she'd been with. She pulled out her phone and checked her texts as she walked away.

Whatever she did was her business. Tom respected her un-abashed pursuit of pleasure. But the feeling of being some guy whose name she wouldn't remember, a face among a sea of faces, left him with an aftertaste of self-loathing. Tom and Megs had had sex hundreds of times. Probably thousands. Sex with Megs came in a myriad of different colors and flavors, each with varying degrees of intensity. They almost never kept their shirts on and they'd definitely never *fucked*. But that was exactly what almost hooking up with Casey had felt like. A precursor to fucking.

He wondered if this was how Megs had felt after sleeping with Leo. Or was it different because he'd meant something to her?

A hollow sense of loneliness was rising like seawater. And he didn't want to drown.

Wherever she was, whatever point in this day they were in, had her heart shattered when Tom touched Casey? Tom could have sworn he felt it happen.

Or maybe that was his own heart breaking all over again.

He slumped to the ground, head pounding, an ache in his chest. He remembered one night, maybe three years ago, maybe five. When you spent so many years together, the memories didn't always stay chronological; they scattered and shuffled like cards. But that night he and Megs had been fooling around on the couch, their television playing some show from the Bachelor franchise.

"If this goes any further, we'll have to get a condom, Mr. Prescott," Megs had said to him mock sternly.

"Or we could just make a baby," he'd replied, only half joking.

They proceeded to come up with the worst baby names they could think of ("What about Alexander Graham Bellhop?" "No, no, I much prefer Camembert Von Gouda") and laugh until they were in tears.

"I just hope I don't end up like my mother." Megs wiped at her eyes, her tone losing its mirth.

Without even thinking about it, he'd let a long-covered memory tumble out.

"Me neither. One time I asked my mom to take me to the park and she said she had a meeting. So the nanny took me. We came back early because I stayed on some spinning contraption too long and made myself sick. I found my mom wearing a faux fur coat, parked in front of the television, eating processed snacks and watching *Days of Our Lives*. She was crying."

Tom had never told anyone that before. There was a way he could've delivered the anecdote that would've made it comical.

Something they could laugh about. But the way it came out made him sound tragic. Megs pulled him into her arms and told him she loved him.

Then, when Tom was starting to feel embarrassed about making a big deal over something that had happened so long ago, Megs kissed his nose and said, "I promise to never choose daytime television over you."

The mood had lifted and they'd spent the next several minutes coming up with the worst names they could think of for soap opera characters.

Tom hit the back of his head against the shed once in an attempt to pull himself together. Prescotts weren't criers. Crying didn't solve problems; crying showed weakness, which was probably why his mother hadn't taken him to the park that day—so she could do it quietly, without witnesses.

He raked his fingers through his sensible hair ("Didn't you know? Sensible is the new sexy," Megs often told him). He tugged at the ends until he felt a pull. And then Tom pulled harder, making his eyes water.

That morning he'd wanted to wake up to a new day. Now he wanted a do-over.

As it turned out, there was nothing supreme about anarchy.

CHAPTER TWENTY-THREE

MEGAN

THE LIGHT HAD shifted outside, constellations becoming visible through the hotel window. Megan and Leo had been in bed for hours. They'd done very little talking.

Curled up in the nook under his arm, his fingers tracing lazy circles over every inch of her skin he could reach, Megan couldn't believe she'd thought *yesterday's* today was the right version. Clearly this was what she was meant to be doing. The universe hadn't been pushing her and Tom together—it had been doing its best to rip them apart.

Leo's tracing fingers froze. She sat up and leaned on her elbow to get a better look at him. "What's wrong?"

"It's a little late to be bringing this up, but you're on some sort of pill or ring or cup, right?"

She snorted. "Cup? Did the makers of red Solo put out a birth-control *cup* I haven't heard about?"

Amusement couldn't penetrate Leo's rising panic. "No, you know. Like a diaphragm or an IUD or something."

"You think those are *cups?*" Megan's laughter bubbled up and over. For all Leo's experience with women, he was still naive about certain details.

"Megan! I'm serious."

His seriousness only made her laugh harder. She was imagining what would happen if she did get pregnant in this day that repeated forever. Would she go back to not being pregnant every morning? Or would her body protect the baby from this time-loop catastrophe and one day she'd show up at her and Tom's rehearsal dinner forty weeks pregnant? Oh, how she would love to see Donna and Carol then. John's head might actually explode.

That could be worth it.

Perhaps she should try getting a tattoo or shaving her head to see if her body was immune to the loop.

"You're smiling," Leo pointed out. "Does that mean we're all good? Nothing to worry about?"

"Nothing to worry about." Megan kissed the tip of his nose. He wrapped his arms around her, rolled her over onto her back, and brushed her hair away so he could get a better look at her face.

"Hi," he said, his voice low, tender.

"Hi."

He kissed her, tenderness turning into passion. Lust. But the mention of pregnancy was messing with her head. Unwillingly, she began thinking of the time she and Tom had come up with ridiculous baby names. The thought buffeted her with nostalgia for their lost intimacy. From the beginning, pleasure had been only a small component of being with Tom. She'd had plenty of that during her high-school hookups. She and Tom shared a connection, yes. But above everything else, the power of having sex with Tom stemmed from their willingness to be completely vulnerable to each other.

For Megan, that vulnerability was in the details, in the way she'd let him take in what gravity did to her large-ish breasts, which she'd always kind of hated; in the way he let her see his body convulse when he climaxed; in the way they would be open with each other about what felt good and what didn't.

It was the place they were most honest, something they'd obviously had trouble with everywhere else.

Leo pulled away ever so slightly. "Where'd your mind go, Givens?"

She took in his flickering eyes, the way the sun darkened his skin and lightened his hair. They had known each other forever, but achieving the intimacy she craved would take time. It wasn't fair to compare where she was with Leo to where she'd been with Tom. It was easier to be vulnerable when you started at the age of eighteen.

"If my red Solo cup birth control failed and I accidentally got knocked up, what would you want to name the baby?" When Leo's brow furrowed, she understood he wasn't in on the gag. She opened the door for the inside joke a little wider. "I mean, you do a lot of traveling, so maybe you'd want to name it United Airlines Flight 7421."

"I love how secretly weird you are," Leo said, cracking a smile. "But I'm not having kids. Not even hypothetical ones."

"Oh." It'd been assumed for so long that Megan would be a mother, planned by Tom's parents, pushed by Donna, that Megan realized she wasn't actually sure how she felt about having kids.

"It just seems irresponsible to bring a kid into the world only to inherit the environmental crisis and a sociopolitical hellscape."

It was an opinion held by a lot of people Megan knew. She didn't disagree. Selfishly, though, she'd always wondered what it'd be like to have a child in her arms. Her own child. A little one to love and nurture the way Paulina had with her. "I mean, you're not wrong." Kids weren't a deal-breaker for Megan, she decided. Leo made some compelling points.

"Is that...okay?"

The fear in his voice tapped on her chest. She took his face in her hands and kissed away the worried lines between his eyebrows. "Of course it's okay. I'm not going anywhere, Leo."

He held her tightly, their bodies cocooned in the tornado of sheets. The gurgling of his stomach broke their mood and they both dissolved into laughter.

"Hungry?"

"Famished," Leo admitted. "You want to get some dinner? We could order room service."

But Megan couldn't respond. Her brain hitched at the word *dinner*. She rolled over to look at the clock: 7:25 p.m. She was almost half an hour late for her rehearsal dinner. Anxiety rippled through her, but before it could burst, she remembered she didn't have to go.

She didn't have to go.

"Dinner. Yes," she said. "Then what?"

Leo made a great production of stretching out his arms, his biceps flexing as he linked his hands behind his head. Megan marveled that she found even his little tufts of armpit hair sexy. Everything about Leo was alluring.

"I have to go to Belize on Sunday to do a quality-control check on the tours down there. You want to come?"

Megan tried to wrap her head around the idea of giving every obligation she had the middle finger and *literally* running away with Leo. Assuming, of course, time started moving again.

She could do that. She could run away with the one who'd gotten away.

It felt as though someone had just taken a sledgehammer to the shackles she'd been wearing for years. "Dinner, then Belize."

The shock registered on his face. "You mean it? You'll come?"

Megan grabbed her dress from where it had pooled on the floor and held it up to her chest. "I absolutely mean it. Belize with you sounds perfect. I'll just run to my room and get the rest of my stuff."

On the off chance tomorrow decided to make an appearance, she couldn't let this escape pod fly away without her. She wanted to head for a new life as quickly as possible.

Before she left, Leo reached out, his fingers grazing along her arm until his hand found hers. "We're doing this."

The sides of her mouth curved up. "We're doing this."

CHAPTER TWENTY-FOUR

TOM

MEGS WASN'T AT the rehearsal dinner—Tom had peeked through the windows and checked. Not knowing where else to look, he paced their hotel room, still wearing the clothes from the gift shop. He'd spent the past several hours trying to formulate what he wanted to say to Megs, but the words were still jumbled in his mind, syllables thrown into a popcorn maker, spinning and bursting when they got too hot.

The faint beep of the key card startled him. He waited what felt like hours for the doorknob to turn and then there she was. Flushed, her hair wild, wearing a wrinkled dress.

And Tom thought *he'd* had an erratic day.

"Hey." It was the first hot syllable that popped out of his mouth.

"Hey." There was surprise in her voice. She hadn't expected to see him here.

Making conversation was hard when you couldn't work out how you felt about the other person. Two years ago, when he'd proposed, he knew. A week ago, when they'd lain in bed talking about what to pack for their honeymoon, he knew. For the past twelve years, with every fiber of his being, he *knew*...but this time-loop thing was telling him over and over again that, actually, he knew nothing.

"I guess you're playing hooky from the dinner too." Not the coolest start.

"I didn't really see the point," she replied flatly.

"Yeah." He adjusted his collar, which was scratching at his neck.

"What are you wearing?" she asked, scrutinizing his chinos and pastel Roche Harbor golf shirt at the same moment he said, "Should we talk?"

Their feet seemed rooted to the spot, neither sure whose question should be responded to first.

"I threw my luggage into the ocean," Tom reminded her.

"I don't really have time to talk right now, but if things keep going the way they've been going, never fear. We'll have eternity."

This wasn't a new concept to Tom. He didn't know what he thought about the afterlife, but deep down he'd always figured he'd be with Megs for eternity. It was part of the reason why, as their relationship matured, they'd stopped marking holidays like Valentine's Day and their anniversaries. And they never could decide which anniversary deserved the most attention. Was it the day they first sat together in Natural Disasters? Their first date? Their first kiss? The day they officially moved in together?

They compensated by scooping all these events under one umbrella and surprising each other randomly with an anniversary gift or dinner. One time Megs borrowed a karaoke machine from work and changed the lyrics to the Cure's "Mint Car" to include highlights from their relationship. Another time Tom made a terrible scrapbook composed of ticket stubs, the receipts from take-out orders they'd shared, podcast recommendations she'd written down for Tom's commute to work, and that one pair of her underwear that had torn when they'd had sex up against the kitchen cupboards and it'd gotten snagged on the handle of a drawer.

Looking at her now, mascara flaked under her eyes, clothing askew, he felt a warmth for her spreading through his chest. He not only wanted to forgive her for cheating on him—he knew he could.

"Have you checked your phone?" Megs asked, breaking the heavy silence.

"Not in a while. Why?" He pulled out his phone. An almost never-ending scroll of messages flashed on his lock screen. If this were a real day and he believed in the future, his anxiety would be spiking. Instead, he laughed, partially because it *was* funny, this idea of crucial things (keeping their families content, making sure the events of the weekend went smoothly) suddenly becoming meaningless. His laugh was also an attempt to break the tension between them. Because there was something different about Megs's behavior right now. This morning she had been angry. Now she was angry with a *purpose* and he didn't know what that purpose was.

"I'm assuming yours is blowing up too. Guess this is what happens when you bail on your own wedding." She grabbed her suitcase out of the closet and began throwing in clothes and toiletries seemingly at random.

A chill spread through him.

She was about to leave him.

That was what was driving her. A need to leave. Now.

Panic bubbled inside him. He wasn't ready to go through this alone, to endure this loop with a Megs-shaped hole in him. There were things that still needed to be said. "Wait—" He strode the length of the room and took her hand. "Can we talk?"

"What's there to talk about?" She spun on him, shaking him off. "Nothing's fixed here, Tom. I think we got it wrong. Hasn't it occurred to you that this whole loop is about us being *apart*, not us being together?"

Her sudden anger pushed him back. "What are you talking about?"

"I slept with Leo."

Were they on the same loop? He knew they'd fought at the docks that morning, but surely she wasn't so full of disdain she

couldn't have a conversation with him. And why was she presenting this like it was new information?

"I know you did."

"No. Tom. *I slept with Leo.*"

The realization came in slow motion. Suddenly her appearance
made sense.

His naïveté gripped him, embarrassed him. Of course she had.
Because they'd both decided to let anarchy reign supreme today,
so she'd run to the person who'd coined the phrase. The person
she'd probably wanted all along.

The one she didn't see as a coward.

There was no forgiveness to be had here. No resolution, no
divine intervention. If she was going to blow up the world they'd
created, then so was he. Still, he couldn't help trying to get one
last barb in to cover his humiliation. His defeat.

"Great. Congratulations." He threw up his hands. "Because I
screwed a bartender."

Not exactly true, but…

"Excellent. I hope you enjoyed it." She grabbed the door handle
and pulled, her suitcase half zipped, clothes spilling out. "Have a
nice life."

"Yeah. Enjoy fucking Leo."

She slammed the door behind her and he waited until he could
no longer hear her footsteps in the hall before he collapsed on
the bed.

They never talked about it, but he and Megs had nearly broken up
once, back when they were twenty-five. He was a first-year associate
and, on a whim, she'd applied for a position at *GQ* in London, thinking it'd be fun to live abroad and be closer to Paulina and Hamza.

"Come with me," she'd said to Tom from across their kitchen
table, which had a small pad of Post-its under one leg to keep
it level. Even so, the table tilted slightly anytime either of them
rested an elbow on it.

He'd encouraged her to apply, not thinking through what would happen if she got the position. She frequently applied for jobs in far-off places as a method of blowing off steam. It seemed like an adorably quirky coping mechanism, not something that could actually alter their lives. But now the offer had come in, and so had the threat to the life they shared.

"I can't come with you," he'd replied. It'd taken years for him to get to where he was. Now he was mere months away from making a paycheck he could be proud of. Hopping on a plane and leaving it all behind seemed scary. Unreasonably scary.

He leaned forward, searching for a sign she didn't really mean it, wasn't really interested in dropping everything she'd worked for too. The table tilted.

"Can't you?" she'd asked. Pleaded. "It would be amazing. You know it would. Just you and me and occasionally Paulina and Hamza. Why not?"

But they'd already made plans. They were living their plans. Harvard, grad school for her, law school for him, then New York. They'd done this together. Where was the Megs who loved checking off items on her to-do list?

I can't come with you and *Can't you?* swirled between them. He was still waiting for that sign that she didn't mean all this. Didn't really want to leave.

"Do you want me to go without you?" she said finally.

When the words stretched between them, he felt like the table was the only thing holding him up. Dust particles that were usually invisible danced around them as the sun came through the kitchen window.

The pain in her eyes as she waited for him to answer was agonizing, and soon they were both crying. He reached for her and she reached back. They moved from the kitchen to the couch, where they held each other. In the end, the conversation didn't go any further and Megs never left. He'd never felt quite as close to tragedy.

Though, as far as disasters went, Tom would now classify it as only about a two on his own personal Saffir-Simpson hurricane scale.

Today he was hitting a five.

He'd been close...*so* close to actually being able to forgive her. And all she wanted to do was get the hell away from him. His eyes prickled. A lump formed in his throat.

This time was no near miss; she was truly leaving him. And she'd slept with his best friend. *Again.* Megs had been everything to him and he really had just been...a placeholder.

He wanted to punch a wall; he wanted to cry. They'd ended things more than once on this never-ending day. But there was something about watching her pack her bags, presumably to run off with Leo, that made it all seem final. She'd made her choice.

He peeled off his chinos and pastel golf shirt and climbed into the hotel bed naked. The adrenaline from their sudden fight and the punctuation of the slamming door waned. If the universe would let him, Tom would sleep forever.

DAY

5

CHAPTER TWENTY-FIVE

MEGAN

DESPITE FALLING ASLEEP wrapped in Leo, Megan awoke to Donna bursting into her room.

Bleary-eyed, Megan squinted and sarcastically saluted Donna. She passed by her to loudly pee with the door open.

"What are you..." Donna covered her eyes, scandalized. "Maybe you and Tom have this kind of relationship, but that's not the way to keep a man."

A thousand comebacks flashed through Megan's mind. Instead of speaking, she grabbed her hotel robe and threw it on over her skimpy pajamas. Tuning out her mother's monologue, she walked out of the room.

Her hair resembled an otter's den, she was sure her cheeks were creased from her pillowcase, and her morning breath was so potent she could taste it. Still, Megan trudged down the hallway, got in the elevator, got out in the lobby, and slumped in a wingback chair.

She was approached by the desk clerk, the same one ready to check in all the guests she couldn't seem to get rid of for the wedding she couldn't seem to stop. "Can I get you something, miss?" he asked, so polite it bordered on aggression.

"Nope." Megan squinted at him, her eyes still adjusting to the new-old day. "I'm waiting for someone."

"Perhaps you might be more comfortable—"

Megan let her head flop back so she could get a better look at this poor hotel employee. He was clearly ill-equipped to deal with the creature that time forgot in his lobby.

"I'm the bride," she told him through gritted teeth.

Evidently, those were the three magic words, because he scuttled off to use the front desk as a shield.

Megan had no idea what Tom was going to be up to today. She'd already decided that if he walked by, she'd high-five him and tell him to keep walking. She wasn't in the mood for another screaming match or an insincere heart-to-heart.

Given all the talking they'd done on this day from hell, one would think they'd be getting closer. Instead, she'd never felt so distant from him.

While she waited, she doodled on the pad of paper next to the lobby telephone, trying to beat herself at tic-tac-toe. She drew swirls that went on for as long as the page allowed, imagining herself falling through the inked eye of the tornado, trying to decide what was on the other end. Trying to decide why this was happening to her.

Problem-solving was so ingrained in Megan, she imagined it had its very own gene. Though she definitely hadn't gotten that gene from her mother.

Her body begged for coffee, for sustenance. She was experiencing a perverse pleasure in denying herself these basic needs. Megan was not going to make one more move until she took care of item one on today's to-do list.

Finally, bathed in sunlight and the accompanying breeze when she opened the door, Paulina appeared. She was holding her stomach, complaining the baby had the hiccups and that its bouncing made her look like the host of some alien species. Hamza laughed, rubbed her belly gently, and stage-whispered to the baby to stop torturing its mother.

Megan watched them as though she were removed, an audience to their play. She wanted their easy love so much, her eyes pricked with tears. If soul mates existed, she was looking at a pair of them right now. With the sleeves of the hotel robe, she wiped the tears away, taking a deep breath to steady herself. The motion caught Paulina's attention.

"Megan!" Paulina threw her purse into Hamza's arms and rushed over as quickly as her body would allow. "You're going to have to stand up to get this hug I have locked and loaded, because if I so much as bend over, I'm a goner. My center of gravity is not what it used to be."

Megan laughed through her growing tears. Yes, she'd seen her aunt in every other day. But today of all days, Megan really needed Paulina.

"What's going on, baby girl?" Paulina said into Megan's hair as she held her tight. "Not that I don't love the hotel-hobo look, but you're a bit of a train wreck."

"It's off, everything's off."

When Megan was little, getting in trouble at school was devastating. If she was scolded by a teacher, she'd push every sob and wail deep, deep down so as not to embarrass herself further in front of her classmates and then, when the bell rang, she'd run as fast as her legs could carry her to Paulina's house. As soon as Paulina opened the door, the dam would burst, and Megan would cry in her aunt's arms until she'd let every miserable shuddering sob out.

Standing in the hotel lobby, her aunt squeezing her tight, her pregnant belly wedged comfortably between them, Megan felt like that little girl who'd gotten into trouble at school.

Only this problem was considerably more convoluted.

"Hamza," Paulina called over Megan's trembling head. "Are we checked in? Do you have the keys?"

"Got 'em," Megan heard Hamza say.

"Okay, baby girl. Let's take this conversation somewhere a little less public, hmm?"

They walked to Paulina and Hamza's room together, Megan assisting with the luggage, Hamza sweetly distracting her by talking about her aunt's baffling mood swings and desire to eat only dairy.

"I came home and she was pouring chocolate syrup directly into the jug of milk," Hamza said with a bewildered smile.

"Yeah, don't let him regale you with the tales of the pregnancy flatulence that followed," Paulina added wryly.

"We like to blame Lina's current inability to behave herself in polite society on the baby." Hamza patted Paulina's belly. "*The baby* is a gassy little thing."

Hamza used the key card to let them into the room, pushing the door open so Paulina and Megan could go first. And then, because he truly was one of the greatest men to walk the earth, he offered to leave.

"I'll go get us some coffees, shall I?"

"And some scones." Paulina pointed at Megan. "I'm allowed to have a certain amount of milligrams of caffeine a day and you better believe I consume every one."

"Yes, I could definitely use some coffee. Thanks, Hamza," Megan said, then sat down on the edge of the bed while Paulina sprawled back against the headboard, taking off her shoes as though it were a religious experience.

As soon as Hamza opened the door to leave, Gran and Granddad poked their heads in.

"There's my Paulina," Gran said, patting Hamza on the cheek affectionately before pushing her way in. "Are you ready for brunch?"

Granddad followed her, gave Hamza a hug, and immediately tried to cover Paulina's toes with a blanket. It was a warm, muggy day, but he always assumed people were chilly. Blankets were Granddad's love language.

Paulina cast a glance at Megan, who silently pleaded with her aunt not to leave her alone in her distress.

"Mom and Dad, you are sights for jet-lagged eyes," Paulina said, still stretched out on the bed. She reached a hand out for each of them. "But I am so, so knackered from the flight. Can we skip brunch and just go for our little sail around the harbor afterward?"

"I've been excited to get on that boat of yours for weeks," Hamza added charitably.

"We'll let you get some rest." Gran patted Paulina's leg and turned to Megan. "And how's the bride-to-be? Any pre-wedding jitters? Because there's still time for you to haul your tush out of here."

"Our Meggy doesn't need to run away." Granddad's light blue eyes twinkled. "Tom's such a nice young man."

Not knowing how to respond, Megan smiled blankly. "Yep. All good here."

"Well, try not to wander around the hotel in your bathrobe." Gran gave her the once-over. "Makes you look like a floozy."

With that, Hamza ushered Gran and Granddad out the door, asking if they'd like to walk down to the market with him.

"I'm sorry I'm ruining your brunch plans," Megan said when they were alone again.

Paulina blew out a breath. "Please. I'm not too keen on going to a restaurant right now. As long as we take a spin on *Happy Accident* later, both Mom and Hamza will be appeased."

Megan wanted to stay in this moment of feeling normal, of just being with her aunt, pretending the world was still spinning as it should. "How are you feeling?"

"Pregnant," Paulina said sardonically. "Did you know Hamza's shaving my legs for me now? I can't even see my knees and the angle's too awkward, but I hate the feel of hairy legs."

"He's one of the good ones." Megan crawled up to the top of the bed and rested her cheek on the pillow next to her aunt. She let her head fall onto Paulina's shoulder and tried not to cry.

"So what's off? What's over?" Paulina asked kindly.

"The wedding." Megan thought she could fall asleep right here, stay unconscious for the next several incarnations of this day. But she wasn't sure she could ever sleep enough to overcome this exhaustion.

"Are you sure?" Paulina wasn't an alarmist. She'd stayed calm when Brianna was a toddler and had choked on one of Alistair's Legos; she'd deftly flipped her over and performed the Heimlich. Likewise, she remained serene through all of Donna's tantrums, even the ones in which her sister threw whatever breakable objects were within reach.

"I'm sure." Megan swallowed, fighting fresh tears. "I hate to put this on you, but can you let everyone know? Take care of the nasty details?"

"Nasty details? You mean like Donna?"

A choked laugh burst out of Megan. "Don't forget Tom's parents."

Paulina sat up, adjusted a pillow behind her lower back. "Megan, honey, you know I will do absolutely anything in the world for you—within reason. That includes calling off your wedding while you hide from the aftershocks."

"Thank you."

"*However*, I will do it only if you're sure." Paulina waited for Megan to look at her before continuing. "You remember my best friend from high school, Joanie?"

Megan nodded. "She drove a blue Chevette and owned more tube tops than all the other people in Montana combined."

"That's Joanie." Paulina smiled at the memory. "A couple of years ago she flew out to London to visit us. She told me she was getting a divorce."

"Doesn't she have a dozen kids?"

"Five, but once you get past three it must feel like a dozen. Anyway, when she told me, she had this light in her eyes. She exuded this sense of calm, of relief."

"Good for her."

"Exactly. Good for her. It turned out to be the best decision for both Joanie and her husband—not to mention the kids. My point is, if calling off the wedding is going to bring you peace, I will absolutely take care of it for you." Paulina tucked some hair that had fallen in front of Megan's eyes behind her ear. "But you two have been together for—what? Ten years? What's changed?"

"Twelve." Megan's stomach was churning, her chin trembling. "But I've been on this path for so long, kicking away all the stones that trip me up—like how Tom lets his family run our lives and the way I've given up what I always wanted to do."

Megan thought back to the job in London she'd nearly taken five years ago. The one that would've brought her closer to her favorite aunt and uncle. Then she thought about the one Tom had taken in Missouri.

"Paulina, he accepted a job in a different state without even telling me. I can't believe it. Like I'm some accessory he can pack up, not a person who should get a say." She blew out a breath. "I knew his family came with baggage—everyone's family does. I just didn't know it ran this deep. That he'd let what they want take priority over what I want…forever. Now I keep imagining the rest of my life and it's all dictated by John and Carol."

Paulina gingerly sat up and turned toward Megan. "Hold on. He unilaterally decided to uproot you two without talking to you first? That doesn't sound like Tom."

"I know. It's like his need to defer to his parents is getting worse." Paulina rubbed Megan's back as she leaned forward, into her fears. "I don't want to spend my entire life feeling like I'm not good enough. Like I don't get a vote. I want to commit myself to a partner, not a family of passive-aggressive tyrants."

"I'm so sorry you've been feeling this way."

"I want what you and Hamza have." The words came out choked.

Paulina laughed. "What Hamza and I have is great, yes. But do you really think our relationship hatched fully grown? Oh, honey. When we first moved in together, I freaked out. He freaked out. I blamed him for the struggles I had making friends and finding a job in London; he resented me for blaming him...it was a mess. But guess what—people are messy. Relationships are messy."

Megan had never looked at Paulina and Hamza as messy. Their relationship was so solid. "So what did you do? How did you make things better?"

Paulina shrugged. "We started being honest with each other, with ourselves. We stopped defaulting to blame and went to therapy. Through all of it, we realized we loved each other so much, we were willing to be messy together."

"I had no idea." Megan's mind wandered to an interview she'd sat in on at *GQ* with famed actor Kenneth Birch. She'd always remembered what he'd said about fights, that couples have the same one over and over again. He should know. He had one of the longest marriages in the movie business. She wondered what Paulina and Hamza's root fight was.

"Oh yeah." Paulina smiled gently. "This relationship of ours is amazing. We laugh a lot, we love each other more than anything else in the world, but you better believe we work at it. Some days it's easy. Other days we have to choose each other, choose to be compassionate, to be patient."

Megan couldn't explain to her aunt that she understood a relationship needed work, she just suspected she'd been working on it with the wrong person. Searching for a way to phrase the question she most needed to ask without giving away that she'd slept with Leo or that she was stuck in this loop, she settled on "How do I know what will make me happy, though? Because it's become abundantly clear it isn't Tom."

To Megan's surprise, Paulina threw her head back and laughed.

"Do you know a lot of Europeans think the American idea of happiness is ridiculous? Europeans see happiness as something fleeting, like frustration or fatigue—regular-person fatigue, not pregnant-lady fatigue. That shit's real and it is inescapable." Paulina must've registered the fear in Megan's eyes, because she reached out and cupped Megan's cheek in her hand. Just as she had dozens of times when she was talking Megan through a fight with Brianna or drama with Donna. "Hey. You know I love Tom. But you need to do what's right for you. Follow that heart and that head of yours. They're both pretty smart."

That was exactly what Megan needed. Her heart was being loud and clear right now.

Hamza came in holding a tray of coffee and a bag that Megan prayed contained several one-thousand-calorie pastries.

As they had breakfast in the room, looking out the window and reminiscing about summers spent on the docks trying to catch whatever fish they could, Megan pictured her life with Tom and held that life up against the promises Leo was making her. She thought about how being in bed with Leo all afternoon had made her feel. How he understood her anger at Tom and his family in a way she wasn't sure Tom ever would.

Her relationship with Tom had a lot of good, but it had also become so cumbersome, swollen with countless hurts and resentments. She just wasn't sure she could carry it anymore.

She sipped her coffee, half listening to Hamza tell a story about when Paulina had tried to teach him how to fish and he'd yelled apologies in advance to the fish every time he cast off. She smiled and laughed in all the right places, pretending a storm of fears and uncertainties and excitement and possibilities wasn't raging inside her.

As soon as she finished her breakfast, she kissed them both on the cheek and made her exit.

It was time to listen to the thunder from that loud heart of hers.

* * *

In the space between breakfast and Leo's arrival, Megan showered, packed, and made peace with her decision. This was the right one. This was what the universe had been trying to tell her.

She'd needed a push of this magnitude to find the courage to pursue things with Leo.

For years, Megan had made concessions to be with Tom. She'd done it because she loved him. Being with him made sense. But little by little, each accommodation had chipped away at who Megan really was, at what she wanted. And now, with Leo, she had the chance to get it all back. To get all of *herself* back. To travel to distant places and take up filmmaking again. To be with someone who knew her inside and out and whose family might finally be the one she'd always dreamed of.

It was as terrifying as it was thrilling, this new beginning.

Having been through this day four times already, she knew the instant Leo would walk through the lobby doors, and she was waiting. The yearning, the lust, she felt from him when he laid eyes on her made her shiver.

It didn't matter who saw. She dropped her purse and ran to him, surprising him with the force of her embrace. It didn't take long for him to wrap his arms around her and squeeze her back just as tightly.

"Givens." His breath tickled the back of her neck. "What…"

She released him just enough so they could search each other's faces. "I've been waiting for you to get here." She bit her bottom lip to stop herself from grinning with free-flowing delight. No need to scare him off. She would ease into this…after all, Leo had some catching up to do.

"I'm happy to see you." He let his hands slide down the length of her arms. "It's been too long."

"Agreed. So let's get out of here."

He let go of her and reached for his bag. "Yeah, we can go for a walk. Just let me check in and get rid of my luggage."

"No, *Leo*." She got up on her tiptoes, and her lips grazed his earlobe as she said, "The wedding's off. You and I are getting out of here."

There was a pause long enough for Megan to worry that something had changed in this incarnation of the day. Something might have shifted enough for Leo not to want to run away with her.

And then his face broke into a grin. He grabbed her hand and said, "Anarchy reigns supreme, baby."

CHAPTER TWENTY-SIX

TOM

I'M SORRY," THE sympathetic older woman working the airline kiosk told him. "No luck yet. This flight's full too. You're welcome to keep checking back."

"Thanks." Tom, ticket in hand, wandered away. He hadn't been able to purchase a seat on a New York flight and was trying his best to get on standby. Having never flown standby before, Tom wondered if it was always this difficult.

Of course he'd woken up on the ferry next to Henry Winkler again. But as soon as they'd docked and he saw Megs wasn't even there to meet him, Tom turned around and got right back on the ferry. In Seattle, he shuffled onto the first airport shuttle he saw.

As far as he was concerned, today was about avoiding the island altogether and getting back to New York. That was where his life made sense. Time moved forward in New York. People were who you thought they were in New York. It wasn't magical and serene; it was fast and crowded and exactly where he needed to be.

However, the universe seemed to have other plans. Because the universe was an even bigger asshole than he'd thought.

Tom bided his time, looking in every shop, wandering through Seattle-Tacoma International Airport's food court. There was some sort of event going on; every corridor seemed to have a different singer performing. Tom took out his wallet and dropped bills in every hat, every guitar case. Why not?

When he became sluggish from hunger and the need for coffee, he decided to forgo the food court for a restaurant resembling a log cabin. The sign out front instructed him to seat himself, so he chose a stool at the bar, wondering if he could get his coffee spiked.

Two seats down, a large man shifted. Tom looked over; the familiarity of the man's posture struck him immediately. He was trying to place him when the man turned, raised his coffee mug in a kind of salute, and smiled.

It was Kenneth Birch. Tom couldn't believe it.

"Top of the morning." Kenneth's gravelly voice carried the gravitas of his years in Hollywood, his collected wisdom. And maybe his millions of dollars too.

"Morning." Tom wasn't quite sure how to play this, but the actor's appearance didn't seem coincidental. As someone who hadn't believed in signs a week ago, he was sure desperate to believe in this guardian angel now.

"Can I…" Tom wasn't sure how to start.

"What do you need? Autograph? Selfie?" Kenneth said *selfie* as if it were a foreign word he was trying out for the first time. Luckily, his demeanor was friendly. He didn't seem bothered by Tom. Rather, he seemed to welcome the company. Tom scrambled to a closer seat.

Unsure where to begin, he gave the actor a feeble "I'm a big fan."

"Thanks. Any particular movie? I can usually guess based on age and general appearance."

Blanking under pressure, Tom tried to think of a title as a pack of rowdy twenty-somethings walked past the restaurant, pointed at Kenneth, and yelled, "Duuuuuuude! It's Beau from *Money City Cha-Cha!*"

Good-naturedly, Kenneth waved a peace sign at the crew. When the ruckus subsided, Kenneth turned back to Tom. "You were saying something, weren't you? Or you were about to?"

"Yeah, I wanted to ask you...to talk to you about..." Tom took a breath, decided to get straight to the point. "You said something a few years ago that resonated with me."

"A line?" The actor shifted in his seat, clearly intrigued. He winked. "I'm guessing it wasn't from *Money City Cha-Cha*."

"Actually, it was something you said in an interview with *GQ*. My girlfriend was there." Tom paused, wanting to get the wording right. "She told me you said couples that are together a long time always have the same fight, it just comes out in different ways."

The actor's face broke into a grin, dimples faintly visible beneath his scruffy salt-and-pepper beard. "Ah, yes. I've said that a lot. Apparently, not only do couples always have the same fight, but old dogs like me always give the same interview."

Tom chuckled appreciatively.

"My wife and I have been together for, oh, I think it's going on forty-two years now. Before you get all congratulatory," he said, waving off the congratulations Tom really was about to offer, "you should know that she and I had a rocky start. But it made me appreciate her more, I think. The difficult things are sometimes the best things, you know?"

Tom nodded. *Did* he know?

"You still with that girlfriend? Having the same fight?" The man was a well-respected actor, but Tom could instinctively tell he was being sincere.

"I'm supposed to marry her tomorrow." He tried to toss it off as though it weren't a big deal, as though the universe weren't conspiring to keep that day from ever arriving.

"I'd offer you my felicitations, but you qualified that with a *supposed to*." He scratched absentmindedly at his chest, looking up at Tom from under bushy eyebrows. "Getting cold feet, son? That's normal."

Running a hand over his face, Tom gathered his thoughts, wondering just how much to reveal. He couldn't very well tell

Kenneth Birch he was caught in a time loop. He dug deep until he hit on what he really wanted to know.

No matter what happened in these loops, he kept going back to Megs. And he wanted to make sure it wasn't out of habit. He wanted to know that what they had was real and worth fighting for. A difficult thing that was also the best thing, as Kenneth had said.

"How do I know if this is right? If I should be with this person or not? Up until recently, it seemed like my whole life had come with an instruction manual. I knew where I was supposed to go, what I was supposed to do. But suddenly it feels like it was the manual for someone else's life."

The actor ripped open a sugar packet and dumped it into his coffee, contemplating. "No one's life has an instruction manual. That's the best damn thing about it. I choose and you choose and everyone makes choices that have these butterfly effects on everything else—the results are either this exquisite ballet or an avant-garde multimedia melee."

"Sounds terrifying."

"I think it sounds beautiful, my friend."

Tom was, quite literally, on the edge of his seat. He was close to an answer. He knew he was. "So what you're saying is that committing to someone for the remainder of your existence is either a ballet or chaos?"

"Yes and no." After shaking salt onto his eggs, Kenneth paused. "The key to a relationship, to a partnership for life, is really quite simple."

"Oh yeah?" There was no way this could be true. Nothing was simple. That was the one thing Tom knew for sure.

A baritone laugh erupted from the actor's belly. "Sure it is. All you gotta do is find someone who makes you better and then you've got to make *her* better too. When she tells you something, you evaluate it. 'Is what she's saying true? Am I stubborn or flippant or casually cruel?'"

Or a coward, Tom thought.

"And then you try to be better. And when you tell her, 'You're being selfish' or 'You hurt my feelings' or 'You're prioritizing another relationship and it's negatively affecting me,' then *she* tries to do better. Pretty soon, you get to be my age and the relationship is a hell of a lot easier. Because you've done the work."

Tom ordered a coffee and some toast from the bartender, mulling it all over.

"Mind you," Kenneth continued, interrupting his thoughts, "if it's too much work from the beginning, that's a bad sign. But if things are mostly great, you laugh a lot together, you love a lot together, you genuinely want to spend time together, then the work becomes part of it."

For the first time in days, Tom's mind was beginning to clear. He thought about the times he'd assumed he was keeping the peace by outwardly agreeing with his dad when he hated what John was saying. About the dinners with surprise dates his parents orchestrated for him in college. About sticking with law, agreeing to move...every moment he thought he was supposed to maintain these important relationships, even if he suspected it was hurting Megs. And then he tried to imagine what his life would've looked like if that trajectory hadn't existed—or if he'd resisted it.

Would he be a lawyer? Would he still be in New York? Would he sit through unbearable family dinners, buttoned up so tightly he'd forget to breathe?

Of all the things he'd experienced since this loop began, the realization that he'd never been his own person and never would be if he didn't stand up to his family felt the most important.

Because *not* making any choices had been a choice all its own.

Even if things were truly over between him and Megs, she'd given him a parting gift—a way he could be better. Braver.

"Thank you," Tom told Kenneth Birch, meaning it with his whole heart, and he and the actor finished their breakfasts in companionable silence.

CHAPTER TWENTY-SEVEN

MEGAN

GOING FOR LUNCH in Friday Harbor was risky. Even though consequences didn't seem to be a thing anymore, Megan didn't want to run into Tom. She didn't want to put Leo through it. However, they had to get out of Roche in order to avoid everyone else, so she'd chosen a small, sexy Mexican restaurant tucked away off the main street.

It wasn't until they arrived that she made the connection to that Mexican restaurant in Cambridge she and Tom had gone to the night they'd had their first kiss. But maybe the parallel was okay. A way to rewind and press Play on a new story.

In addition to being discreet, the restaurant had the added benefit of meeting both of Leo's requirements: no franchises, no tourist traps.

Sitting across from each other, they kept grinning broadly, almost laughing, both clearly thinking, *I can't believe we're here together*. She was on a date. With Leo. After twelve years of dating only Tom.

But Megan didn't want to think about Tom. Not when this beautiful, sun-kissed man was sitting before her.

Their wooden table was one of only a few on an outdoor

patio overlooking an alley. If they craned their necks, they could see the marina. A bright umbrella kept the sun from their eyes, which stayed fixed on each other. The setting was romantic in an unexpected way, which was a pretty good metaphor for their whole relationship, Megan thought.

"Tell me more about what's happening in Belize," she said once they'd settled in.

"You wanna know what you're signing up for?" he teased.

"I want to know more about *you*," she clarified. "Your life in the present."

His face lit up as he spoke. Leo wasn't one to boast and yet it was clear he was proud of how far he'd come. "This whole tours thing started out with me and one other guy—someone I'd met backpacking through Thailand. We started small, just one tour, and now we have a dozen different tours through four different countries."

"Leo!" Of course, she already knew all this from Tom and her covert late-night googling. Still, it was much more fun hearing it firsthand. "That's amazing!"

Because it was. Here, sitting across from her, was a shining example of someone who'd decided he didn't like what his life was looking like and turned it into something entirely new.

"You aren't doing the actual tours anymore, then?" Her question was innocent on the surface. She wanted to dig a little, to figure out what her life would look like with Leo. As proud as she was of him, Megan worried she might wind up spending days hanging back while he led packs of beautiful twenty-somethings through exotic locations.

His fingers interlaced with hers. "I'm mostly on the business and logistics side right now. But I'm willing to make an exception if there's somewhere you'd like to see."

Her stomach fluttered. "I want to see it all," she answered truthfully.

"You got it." He took a sip of water and laughed a little into his glass. "Wait, are you still afraid of lizards? Because there's this water monitor lizard in Thailand that's, like, six feet long."

"It's not weird to be scared of lizards!" Megan fell easily into the conversation they'd had often, what felt like a million lifetimes ago. "They all look invincible with their scaly armor. And like they're a hundred years old! I don't mess with anything that won't die."

"Hey, hey." Leo released her fingers to put up his hands, relenting. "We're all entitled to our irrational fears."

"I just explained why that fear *isn't* irrational," she said defensively before breaking into laughter.

Their server came by with complimentary chips and salsa. Megan was both ravenous and too overwhelmed—in the best way—to eat. They put in their orders and waited for their server to go inside before turning back to each other, goofy smiles on their faces. Megan's foot found Leo's leg and she savored the thrill of being able to touch him whenever she wanted.

"So." She shrugged and tried not to let her voice get too high or waver with too much excitement. "What happens *after* Belize?"

He cocked his head; his easy smile still played on his lips. "What do you mean, *after* Belize?"

"Come on, Leo. I know you love to fly by the seat of your pants, but indulge the planner in me. What happens after we run away to Belize and confirm your tours are going well?"

Possibilities fanned out between them. Megan couldn't remember the last time she'd had endless days stretched out before her, days not filled by work or obligations or the daily grind. Probably never.

"What do you mean?" he asked again, linking his fingers through hers once more. His hands were rough, scarred by his misadventures. They felt nothing like Tom's hands. She shook that thought away. "We go to Belize and then...go from there."

The breeze picked up and they both moved to steady their

umbrella, which teetered precariously. A staff member from the restaurant rushed out to adjust and secure it.

When they were alone again, Leo found Megan's leg with *his* toes. The tease of contact emboldened her. She wanted to splash in the waves of this new life she was getting. She wanted to plan out their entire future *right now*.

"Yeah, about that 'go from there' business," she said cheekily, trying to get Leo to give her a more concrete answer. "When we get back from Belize, I'll obviously need to move out of my apartment…"

"Obviously," he agreed.

"…and I was wondering where I should put my stuff."

"Your stuff?"

She shifted in her chair, which tilted on the uneven patio. Spelling it out wasn't ideal; however, Megan was done with dancing around what she wanted. She didn't have to skirt issues or play games. This was *Leo*. *Her* Leo. "From my apartment. Do I put it in storage or send it directly to your place? Do you still have that apartment in Boston?"

His smile wavered and his eyes widened before he recovered. It happened so quickly, she wondered if she'd imagined it.

"Yeah. Of course," Leo assured her. "You can definitely send your stuff to my apartment. We'll…I'll make space. Obviously."

The confidence he'd been exuding had just faltered. She was sure she hadn't imagined it.

No, that was ridiculous. He came to the island for *her*. Megan was overthinking things. Leo wanted her to move in with him. He wouldn't be sitting across from her now if he didn't.

The entrées arrived and they both dug in; the conversation halted while they ate. Between bites, they flirted like teenagers— he'd raise his eyebrow at her, she'd wrinkle her nose at him. And Megan tried very hard to determine the difference between the excitement and the nerves growing within her.

Once Leo had polished off his first taco, he winked. "Hey, Givens. About this whole Boston thing. You know you'll have to go easy on me, right? I haven't lived with anyone in years."

She caught his calf in the crook of her foot under the table. "I promise I'll be the best roommate you ever had."

Suddenly, their light banter dipped with the weight of what they *hadn't* been saying. The weight of that one person they hadn't been talking about.

Tom had been Leo's last roommate. Leo knew it. Megan knew it.

A pause stretched out between them. It was probably only a few seconds at most but it felt like a whole other time loop could've squeezed in and out of it. Megan grew more and more eager to change the subject. She just couldn't think of a safe one right now.

Which was ridiculous. They had so much to talk about, to get caught up on. Why couldn't she figure out what those unspoken words were?

Seconds bundled together to become minutes, minutes that felt like hours. Apart from taking her hand in his to kiss her knuckles and say, "I can't believe we're doing this," Leo was suddenly being quiet. Or perhaps Megan was.

It was a relief when their server showed up to refill their water glasses, giving them something to focus on. Megan fought to regain the levity they'd started lunch with. And she knew just the right approach. They had years of fond memories to wade through and were finally free to do so without any guilt.

She found his leg with her foot again. "Remember when I convinced you to take that class about museums with me? Thinking we'd be learning about all these different galleries and collections?"

Leo laughed. "But it ended up being about docents and curators and how museums actually operate. Tom made those flashcards for us so we'd pass the—"

He stopped himself. They'd once again invoked the name that they'd been avoiding all morning.

It wouldn't always be this hard, Megan told herself. She wondered if Leo was telling himself the same thing. Just because their history had baggage didn't change all the good stuff between them. They simply had to learn to move past it. And maybe one day they really could reminisce without being haunted by Tom's ghost. She quietly searched for a safe topic to broach in the meantime. Leo beat her to it.

"Well, Givens. You've heard all about me and my business. Tell me about *you*. What's been going on in the highfalutin world of men's magazines?"

"*Highfalutin?*" She laughed at his choice of adjective. This was a safe topic. A *great* topic. Because there was a lot Megan had accomplished over the past few years that she hadn't been able to share directly with Leo, even though she'd been dying to. "Did I tell you I was promoted to senior visuals editor at *GQ* last year?"

"Of course you were." Leo rubbed his thumb over her knuckles and stared at her adoringly. "It's awesome—even though that stuff doesn't matter anymore."

"What do you mean?"

"I mean, because you're saved."

"Saved?" She smiled quizzically at him.

"Yeah. You don't have to work for that corporate empire anymore."

She'd somehow forgotten about that detail. About how running off with Leo meant leaving a lot more than Tom and the Prescotts behind. *Of course* she knew it meant quitting her job. She just hadn't thought about it in such a definitive way until now. She sat uncomfortably with the realization.

Why was she feeling uncomfortable? This was what she wanted. "I…"

"I can't wait to see what stories you tell when you get away from all that. You always wanted to be a filmmaker, right?" Leo pressed. "Wasn't that the plan ever since undergrad?"

"Since before undergrad." And here was the opportunity to chase that dream again. Funny how ready she'd been to charge ahead as a kid, and now...she didn't even know where to start. Pursuing a new career at thirty. People did that all the time. Megan could do it too, right?

"Getting back to the thing you love, that's gotta feel good," Leo said.

Megan nodded, suddenly needing to clear her throat. "Yeah, I just have to figure out *how* to get back to it."

"Hey." He took her face gently in his hand, cold from the condensation on his water glass, and tilted her chin up. "You don't have to figure that out alone. We're in this together, Givens. You and me."

Megan imagined herself buying new (or, more likely, used) equipment. Waiting in the emptiness she'd always felt before a new idea revealed itself. That could be exciting. And she loved the way Leo said *you and me*.

"I'll need funding—once I get the idea," Megan said, almost to herself.

"You of all people must have some savings," Leo said. "You were always the responsible one."

The comment was true, though Tom-adjacent, making it edge the danger zone. Leo was the adventurer, Megan was the responsible one, and Tom had been the optimist, the life preserver when the other two started to drown.

"I live in New York," Megan reminded him. "The city that eats savings for breakfast."

"So you'll figure it out." Leo waved her concerns off with the ease of someone who'd never met a DON'T WORRY, BE HAPPY bumper sticker he didn't like.

"Yeah, I'll figure it out," Megan agreed, tiny fears gathering and rising.

"The important thing is that you've got your life back. You get to do what *you* want to do. To help people. Make an impact. Change the world by changing people's minds."

"Yeah..." She nibbled at her bottom lip.

"You can finally jump off that corporate ladder you've been chained to." His tone was teasing, but his words still nagged and she couldn't figure out why.

He wasn't wrong. This was what Megan had wanted to do for ages—be adventurous and a little reckless. Say goodbye to all the compromises and concessions she'd made and do what *she* wanted.

But each turn Megan's life had taken had come with new opportunities and unexpected highs too. Faced with the possibility of actually quitting, she started thinking through all the things she loved about her job at *GQ*: her coworkers, the surprising ways she got to be creative. And there was definitely something to be said for a regular paycheck.

"I'm still proud of how quickly I worked my way up that so-called corporate ladder." Megan tried to keep her tone light, free of those tiny fears rising inside her.

"You're one of the smartest people I know. You're hyper-capable. Of course you worked your way up quickly. But just because you're good at something doesn't mean you should do it." Leo brushed the hair out of his eyes, gazing off into the middle distance. "If you're not doing what you love, what's the point? If you aren't making a difference to someone or a lot of someones, why do it? I've watched you bending over backward for everyone else for years. This is *your time*, Givens."

She nodded, willing herself to agree with what sounded like a true statement, but something kept tripping up her affirmation of what he was saying. "I mean, I *have* been able to make a difference at *GQ*."

"Yeah, I'm sure they love you there." The response was a

throwaway. Dismissive. It made Megan bristle. "But do *you* love it there?"

"I…there are things I think I love there." She smiled at him to soften the blow of her sudden backpedaling. "I'm spearheading this new program to recruit interns—interns we'll *pay*—from marginalized communities to help them break into media, because the expense of living in New York prevents a lot of talented people from even applying to the industry. I compiled a list of positions best suited for remote work and now we're in the process of—"

Leo laughed softly. "There's that Givens passion."

She barely heard him. She was remembering how excited she'd been starting this project and how much she'd wanted to go through the applications and meet the prospective interns, even if only over a video chat.

Giving up something so concrete to possibly make a documentary on a topic she hadn't even dreamed up seemed…frivolous. Self-indulgent.

Although wasn't that the point of finally being with Leo? To be a little self-indulgent?

She flitted her eyes over the expansive margarita menu. "Is it too early for tequila?"

"It's never too early for tequila."

What she needed was more information to understand all the reasons why this was exciting and right. And tequila.

Anxious energy spilled through her stomach. That was normal, to feel anxious about such a big leap. And they were really doing this. Maybe the nerves would turn to excitement if she could get a clearer picture of what she was saying yes to. "Tell me what a day in the life of Leo looks like."

A small child toddled by the restaurant in pursuit of a seagull, her parents rushing after her. Megan looked to Leo to share an amused grin, but he was gazing out toward the ocean.

"That's the best thing about a life with me," he said.

"What's the best thing?"

"Every day looks different. A lot of the time, my job is flexible—"

"So I can recruit you to be a film-crew member?" she teased, imagining his biceps as he held the boom mic overhead.

He chuckled. "Sure, I can crew sometimes. And sometimes you can help me too—bookkeeping, readying tour itineraries and stuff."

"Sounds like our lives will be pretty intertwined." It was odd to imagine blurring all those lines of home and relationship and work and play. *Not odd—exciting. It's exciting.* Megan felt knots forming in her neck and shoulders, even though everything Leo said was appealing. Every day she rode the subway to work, she'd fantasized about not going into the office. About waking up in the morning and making her own schedule. Or not having a schedule at all. Leo could give her all that. Lazy Sundays and Mondays and Tuesdays, staying in bed until they both felt ready to dive into their unorthodox work, their unorthodox life.

The ideas were foreign to Megan, who'd always been the responsible one. But there were ways to be responsible and still carve out these freedoms. There had to be.

"What are you thinking about?" he asked.

"Change," she answered honestly.

"You're free, Givens." Leo gave her a lazy grin and dipped a chip in salsa. "Throw caution to the wind and let yourself be free."

And yet, suddenly quitting, losing not only the new intern project but also the growing creative freedom she'd been awarded over time…her concerns collected and multiplied. The more she pictured drowning her old life in a flash flood and starting over from scratch, the more protective she grew of that old life.

She searched again for the part of her that agreed with him. "I definitely won't miss the brutal hours and juggling a million different elements for one perfect shot. Dealing with the talent alone could drive a gal to drink."

"Well, you don't have to compromise what you want anymore."
Leo winked as he flagged down their server and before she knew
what was happening, their awkward conversational stumbling was
replaced with margaritas and *actual* stumbling down into the
alley below.

The tequila was making her head spin just enough to be fun
again. Like she was on an amusement-park ride. She pushed Leo
against the nearest wall and let her body do the rest of the talking.
Yes. Leo was like a very hot amusement-park ride.

Since hangovers didn't seem to exist anymore, maybe she'd
spend the rest of her days getting drunk and naked with this man.
A lifetime of—maybe not talking, that part hadn't gone so well
today, but a lifetime of alcohol and sex. Wasn't that what most
people dreamed of?

That didn't sound quite right. What was she chasing again? A
way to find herself. To be herself. That was it.

Leo had said she didn't need to compromise anymore. Something that sounded so appealing…or did it? She thought about it
as she kissed Leo in the alley.

There were always compromises to be made in life. And that
wasn't always a bad thing. Living a self-indulgent existence, thinking only of herself, doing what *she* wanted…didn't that just make
her another Alistair? And who wanted to be Alistair?

What was wrong with her? Was this a grass-is-greener complex
on steroids? Or was she broken, unable to imagine any scenario in
which she could be happy?

Paulina had said happiness was fleeting, Megan reminded herself. All this time she'd been viewing it as a destination, an
achievement, thinking that if she could only diagnose what was
wrong with her life, she'd have it instantly.

But Paulina had also talked about making decisions that brought
a sense of calm into her life. Relief. And Megan wasn't feeling any
of those things.

It was the middle of the afternoon. Leo had offered her exactly what she thought she wanted, and yet she was growing defensive about the life she'd already created. She had to admit, juggling those millions of details for one perfect shot was kind of a rush. And her hours were brutal mostly because she had a tendency toward workaholism and because, in addition to her full-time job, she'd been full-time planning a wedding.

"Hey, where'd you go?" Leo nuzzled her neck.

"I don't know," she whispered, mourning all the things she was sacrificing for what she thought she wanted.

While Megan had been vilifying all the worst parts of what she'd built since college, she'd forgotten to fully appreciate all the best parts too. No, working at *GQ* hadn't been the original plan, but plans were meant to morph and change. Futures were meant to expand and contract as opportunities came and went and people grew. She *didn't* want to give it all up. There was too much she loved.

And as she realized all this, Leo murmured into her ear that he wanted to give her everything.

Her body went cold. Under the late-afternoon sun, pushed against a brick building, Megan suddenly felt nothing.

No all-consuming love, no answers to questions deep within. Even her hormones had jumped ship. With her hands on his chest, she pulled back to look at him. "I don't know if running away right now is very smart."

"What are you talking about? Of course it is. In fact, I'm pretty sure it was your idea as much as mine."

She searched his face, willing herself to feel calm. Sober.

"Come to Belize with me," he begged. "We can leave tomorrow. Tonight. Now. Whenever you want. I know you need this. This is your escape hatch, your path *out*, Givens."

She swallowed, the world tipping from the tequila. "No, what I mean is, I don't know if running away is what I want."

Leo's chest rose and fell. Two times. Three times. "You still want *me*, though, right?"

Drunkenness came in stages: happy, randy, confused, melancholy. Megan had just hit the last one.

"What if I don't know what I want anymore? What if I can't see it?" she whispered, her eyes filling with tears.

"Maybe day-drinking doesn't agree with you, Givens." His words were playful, but his face was growing stony.

"Am I what *you* want?" She reached out, touched his chest. "You didn't seem fully stoked about me moving in with you."

He flinched from her touch. "You know I want you. And yeah, maybe the idea of shacking up right away caught me off guard, but this is all happening pretty fast."

"*Pretty fast?*" She raised her eyebrows. "You were the one who came here to bust up my wedding."

"And you're the one who said yes."

The air between them stilled; there was silence apart from the cawing of a few seagulls in the distance.

"Are you going to jerk me around again?" His voice was quiet. Hurt, not accusatory.

She froze, her heart grasping for a lifeline. "Jerk you around again? What are you talking about?"

"What am I—" He took a few steps away from her before spinning back, pointing accusingly. "Graduation morning when you're all over me, making me promises, and then running off to the Prescotts again."

Could that have been right? Had she made him promises? "I didn't—"

How could this have gone sideways too? Every choice she made in every single day seemed to be the wrong one. How could she try on life after life and still have nothing fit?

Leo watched her, his face a mixture of pain and pride. Megan had to look away.

"You know what I am to you?" he said.

"What?" If he understood this better than she did, Megan was desperate for enlightenment.

"I'm your fantasy. Your little escape. Whenever your life gets too predictable or stifling, you make out with me, get it out of your system, then ditch me."

Heat flushed her face, her body. She wanted the world to stop tilting. She wanted to undrink those margaritas. "You make it sound like this is a pattern. It's happened twice, Leo."

For a man of his stature, he crumbled easily. The pride he'd exuded moments ago gone, he asked, "Is it me, Megan? Am I really what you want? If I am, let's get out of here. Let's go to Belize. Let's be together."

Her lips parted. She willed the words to come. She wanted to escape.

Escape.

Leo was right. That's what he'd been to her. Every thought that had traveled to him, the day she'd spent in his bed, the make-out in the alley…it was an escape. It wasn't a life.

A cloud passed over the sun, blocking it long enough for goose bumps to rise on her arms. She hugged herself.

It seemed Leo wasn't what the universe wanted for her. More important, he wasn't what *she* wanted. Suddenly all the nights she'd spent looking for traces of him online, picturing the life they could've had together, felt immature. Shameful.

"Givens." Leo pinched the bridge of his nose. "I can't spend another decade wanting you, wondering if I have a shot. Please. Just…give me an answer."

The weight of the sky descended on her as she willed herself to have the courage to meet his eyes. When their gazes connected, she knew what the answer was.

She shook her head.

No.

He raised his face to the cloudy sky and she watched his Adam's apple go up and down as he tried to compose himself. When his eyes met hers again, they were filled with pain.

And then she let him walk away.

Back at the hotel, her arms full of bundles of underwear and socks, Megan was trying not to think about how each item she was taking from the hotel closet and drawers had been carefully curated, intended for her honeymoon.

In two days, presuming time was linear and not the Slinky of Satan's spawn, she and Tom were supposed to be heading to the Amalfi coast, where they'd drink wine in a little bubble away from the rest of the world and promise not to look at their phones.

Work had been so busy for them both (busier for Tom, it'd seemed, and now she understood why) that they hadn't even had the chance to plan an itinerary. Not long ago, the prospect of unscheduled time had been so seductive.

Megan threw everything haphazardly into her suitcase, slammed it shut, and zipped it up roughly as though it could contain her eviscerated life. She still wasn't sure where she was going. She just knew that she had to get out of this hotel. Off this island.

She closed her eyes and asked herself if she'd made a mistake breaking things off with Leo in the alley. But her resolve had only strengthened. It seemed the farther away she got from Leo, the more clearly she saw her fixation on him for what it was.

Going to Belize with him would have been just swapping out one problem, one man's prescribed path for her, for another.

What Megan had to do was get away from all this and find the space to really think things through. A fast decision wasn't necessarily a good one, and she needed the time to shake off all the impulsive things she'd done in the past few days, to chart a new course of action.

A jolt of inspiration hit and she knew just where to go.

She'd take the ferry over to Seattle, head straight to the airport, and fly to Montana.

She missed the mountains and big skies of her home state. And since everyone who normally drove her crazy there was actually *here*, she'd be able to return to her roots alone. To think. It wasn't an answer, but maybe it was a place where she could *find* answers. Saying goodbye to both Tom and Leo might have broken the loop, or maybe a change in geography would do the trick, but she had a feeling that getting on that plane was what she needed to do to move forward.

Luggage in hand, looking back at the hotel room to make sure she wasn't forgetting anything, she thought better of the garment bag containing her wedding dress slung over her shoulder. With one last vision of the day she'd tried it on in front of Paulina, Gran, Donna, and Brianna, she tossed it onto the bed. A symbol of a different life. One she no longer needed to live.

CHAPTER TWENTY-EIGHT

TOM

EVENING WAS FALLING. Tom could see it through the expansive windows of the airport. He'd been wandering the terminal for hours, checking with airline kiosks, desperate for a standby ticket to New York, or even somewhere in the general vicinity of New York. He was getting less picky as the day went on.

His feet ached; a migraine pulsed behind his eyes. There was a feeling in his chest that he'd decided was a slow-burn heart attack. And he was no closer to a flight, had nothing to show for any of these symptoms.

Although, if there really was a lifetime of this same day ahead of him, one day wasted didn't matter.

Wasted, that is, apart from his breakfast with Hollywood royalty.

He kept turning the words of the old actor over in his mind, thinking of ways he could build the life he wanted, be the person he wanted to be.

Sitting down in a quiet corner near a dim gate where the lights overhead buzzed gently, he promised himself something: Tomorrow he wouldn't be a coward. Because while he'd been walking between gates A through N, occasionally taking the shuttle for a change of scenery, he figured out everything he'd do differently the day of his rehearsal dinner.

Not that it mattered. If Brody and Emmeline's relationship had been taken down by a series of persistent nudges, Tom and Megan's had been exploded by dynamite. Bit by bit, Tom was learning to accept his new reality. But to get there, he had to get over what he'd lost.

Grief was a mercurial beast. Just when you thought numbness had settled in, a fresh wave of pain coursed through your body like fire.

He'd never hold Megs again, never spoon against her warm body while her cold toes iced his legs. Never kiss her again or slow dance with her in their SoHo apartment. He no longer had anyone to help him ditch New Year's Eve parties.

No one to watch him cook.

So many inside jokes and silly songs were suddenly and irrevocably irrelevant.

It was miraculous how twelve years of shared memories and future plans could evaporate. How their wedding could simply cease to exist.

Although his parents had insisted on a traditional ceremony, Tom and Megs had secretly promised to write their own vows. They'd share the vows only with each other and only when they'd gotten through the weekend.

Megs, he'd planned to say once they were on their honeymoon. *You and I connected over a shared taste in music, in humor. Those things seemed so important when we were eighteen. But that wasn't what carried us through the next twelve years. It was the little things—the way you'd wolf-whistle when I cooked for you, the way I'd kiss your forehead when you had a bad day. We did these things because we wanted to make each other smile.*

But it was the big things that carried us through too—the way you made me feel accepted and loved and chosen just the way I was. The way I've tried to make you feel adored and loved and chosen just the way you are.

I chose you the day we met, twelve years ago, in an undergrad science class designed for people with very little interest in science. I chose you again when you told me you thought the way I cried at happy endings was sexy and I told you I thought the snort that escapes whenever you laugh too hard was sexy. I kept choosing you as I discovered just how clever you were, how you could see through people instantly and how, when you looked at me, you saw someone worthy of your time. Your care. Your heart.

As he was reciting the vows in his head, he could practically see her swatting him, accusing him of being cheesy, and then wiping away tears. The vows were perfect for Megs, just as she was perfect for him.

Or as they'd once believed they were perfect for each other. *He'd* believed.

Now he wondered if he'd been holding her back all this time. When they moved through adulthood, becoming more settled, more entwined, he'd thought it was because they were choosing each other. But he hadn't always given her a choice. His life had been mapped out, rigidly planned, and so she'd been the one to do all the compromising. He'd said no to London years ago and she'd stuck by his side. It was all a mess. He didn't want Missouri *or* New York if it meant not having her.

Light rain pattered against the windows. With no one else around, he stretched out his legs at gate B32. Across the way, at gate B33, passengers were boarding a flight to Helena. The thought of Montana made Tom's chest constrict so severely, he had to sit up. When he straightened, he caught sight of a familiar silhouette standing in line, preparing to board.

How had she gotten here? Was she a miracle he'd somehow conjured? When and why was she getting on that plane?

He willed her to turn around, hoping for answers.

In an instant, she did.

Tom's eyes connected with Megan's. She lifted her hand, clutching a boarding pass, and tapped the side of her nose twice. Their secret code that could mean a million things.

I see you.

It's really over.

I'm leaving.

With a heaviness he thought might never lift, Tom tapped the side of his nose in reply.

I love you.

I'm sorry.

Goodbye.

DAY

6

CHAPTER TWENTY-NINE

MEGAN

WHEN MEGAN WOKE up, she didn't check to see what she was wearing or whether she'd washed off her mascara. She didn't get annoyed when her mother beeped into the room and fluttered around in a panic that evolved into anger at her daughter for just lying there. Ignoring her.

Megan was in an emotional vegetative state. Staying in bed for the rest of the day wasn't a plan—it was all she could do.

She'd tried to leave the island last night and there was Tom, looking crumpled with his hair mussed from however many hours he'd been hiding in that airport. His familiarity intertwined with the ache she now felt whenever she saw him. They'd spent the first loops trying to be together and the last loops apart trying to hurt each other.

And none of their actions seemed to bring them any relief.

Even so, seeing him sitting at that gate, alone, had made her unbelievably sad. After their bittersweet moment, a tap to the nose that said everything and nothing, she'd boarded her flight. Stowed her luggage. Fastened her seat belt. Looked out the window at the lights on the runway. She sat for a long time. The pilot's garbled voice came on to alert passengers they needed to stay on the tarmac while some technical glitch was looked at.

They sat for hours until babies cried, claustrophobia took hold, and passengers started to revolt in small if polite ways: taking off their seat belts and wandering the cabin, passive-aggressively bellowing about their hunger and thirst until the flight attendants tossed them packages of pretzels and water bottles.

Eventually the airline gave them all hotel vouchers and Megan ended her night crawling into the sheets of a bed in a nearby Marriott.

She was trapped not only in this day but also in the Pacific Northwest.

Donna started ripping Megan's covers off, yelling as loudly as she dared in a nice hotel. Megan ignored her and stared at the ceiling as though in a trance. For how long, she didn't know. But when she finally sat up, Donna was furiously texting on her phone, mumbling about her daughter's selfishness.

Megan's breathing sped up. She felt herself reviving, coming back to life—perhaps only to murder her needy mother—when another figure appeared at the doorway.

"Hey, Donna. Mind if I have some time alone with my fiancée?" In Tom's hands was a tray with two large coffees and a pastry bag. He had his luggage with him.

Was Tom not in the loop with her anymore? He'd called her his fiancée and brought her breakfast. That wasn't what they did. Not now. Not anymore.

Donna delicately touched her hair and carefully put it all back in place before giving Tom the once-over. "Breakfast in bed? That's Husband Number One behavior. Good for you."

She swept out of the room. It wasn't until the door clicked shut that Megan sat up. "Please tell me you're on day six too and you can't take it anymore and you're seriously thinking about putting rocks in your pockets and wading into the sea."

"We could do that, definitely." Tom handed her a coffee, which she gratefully accepted. "There's raw sugar and a splash of almond milk in there."

"Thanks." She took a sip. Perfectly prepared. Why was Tom being so nice?

"But instead of walking into the ocean with rocks in our pockets, why not make the most of today?"

Megan groaned. "It's the return of Optimist Tom."

Optimist Tom was the nickname she'd given him in college when he'd take her by the shoulders before an exam and say things like "You're going to nail this. You're the academic assassinator. Feel those good grades buzzing!" It made her laugh and relaxed her, which usually resulted in a good grade. He continued doing it occasionally after they'd graduated, like when she was up for a promotion ("Hear that sound? I think it was something cracking. You're about to shatter the glass ceiling!") and when her mother started seeing someone new ("This guy's actually going to be nice to her. I can feel his good nature all the way across four states and two Great Lakes!").

Tom tried a bite of blackberry Danish, set it down, and took her by the shoulders. "Today we're going to experience a different day. Yes, it'll technically be the same day, but we're going to *make* it different and therefore better."

"We're spending the day together?" Megan asked, her voice thick with doubt.

It was particularly cruel that her only ally in this never-ending loop was also the person with whom she shared the most baggage. Baggage she was not keen on carrying around all day.

"As *friends*," Tom clarified. "I don't know about you, but the only thing I want to do today is shake it up. Screw golf and the salon and the rehearsal dinner. The hell with our families."

Megan raised her coffee cup in a *cheers* motion. "The hell with our families."

"Let's avoid it all today. Try to actually experience a bit of joy."

"Mmm...that word sounds familiar."

It wasn't a terrible idea. She wasn't sure she wanted to spend the day with Tom, but it was better than shopping with Donna and Brianna again. And there was no way she was even *considering* walking into that rehearsal dinner.

She eyed the man who had been her best friend for over a decade. Certainly she could tolerate one day with him. "All right," she conceded. "As long as we can get off this damn island."

"Deal." Tom's smile was too wide at her acquiescence. She was suspicious of that smile.

"What are we doing, Optimist Tom? Where are we going?"

He stood up, put his breakfast on the nightstand, and began unbuttoning his shirt.

"Whoa, whoa, whoa." Megan raised her hands. "I think you might be feeling a little *too* optimistic. That is not on the table."

"Relax." He slipped his shirt off, and despite herself, she admired the familiar grooves beneath his white undershirt. "I'm just going to get in the shower while you figure out what'll make you happy today."

Once the water was running, Megan took a final gulp of coffee and got out of bed. This morning she chose a different outfit: high-waisted shorts and a fitted top she'd bought for their honeymoon. She put on a little mascara, to define her eyes, and a swipe of bold lipstick. She shook out her hair and finger-combed the dry shampoo through, opting for wild humidity-induced waves.

The shower turned off just as she was picking out some accessories. Her fingers grazed the filigree chain and heart pendant. But she left it on the dresser.

What did she want today? In an instant she knew.

"I want to go on a boat today," she called to Tom through the bathroom door. She grabbed them both sweaters since it could get chilly out on the water.

"We can do whatever you want," he called back before opening the door a crack. "But can I request please no more ferries?"

"Deal. I've got a better idea."

There was the destructive anarchy she'd succumbed to on day four of this mess and then there was gentler mischief. And that gentle mischief was precisely where her heart was landing today.

Tom came out of the bathroom, hair wet and curling endearingly around his ears. He looked so comfortable, so sweet, in his shorts and white V-necked T-shirt. For the briefest of moments, he looked exactly like the boy she'd fallen for at eighteen.

Just as quickly, the list of ways he'd hurt her and she'd hurt him replaced that vision. Megan resolved to have fun today—without falling into old habits or letting her veneer crack. "Grab your passport, you're going to need it."

"Where are we going?" he asked, sitting down to put on his shoes.

Megan winked. "Where they keep the boats. To the docks."

"How much do you remember from that sailing course we took a couple of summers ago?" Megan was unhooking the electrical and water lines from *Happy Accident*, invigorated with the anticipation of setting out on the water. Sure, it'd been a while since she'd docked solo. Gran and Granddad's sailboat might not have bow thrusters, but it was only a twenty-five-footer, which helped.

"I remember some charting stuff. Not a lot of the knots." Tom was beginning to look panicked. "Aren't your grandparents going to be upset when they come back from brunch with Paulina and find their boat gone?"

"You're right." Megan pulled out her phone and shot a text off to Paulina. Tell Gran and Granddad we're taking their boat for a spin!

She'd never actually taken *Happy Accident* out by herself before and knew this would make her grandparents nervous. And of course, there wouldn't be an afternoon sail with Paulina and Hamza.

But Megan's guilt was tamped down by the knowledge that

none of her actions mattered. She might as well indulge this small act of rebellion.

When the three dots indicating Paulina was responding appeared, blinking as though the response were a lengthy one, Megan flashed the screen to Tom. "Think this is a bad sign?"

Their eyes connected, reminding Megan of the times they'd broken into buildings on their college campus as students and spontaneously ditched stiff parties as adults. On a whim, she tossed the phone over her shoulder and smiled when she heard the ensuing—not to mention satisfying—splash.

"That is a *great* idea." Tom pulled out his phone and tossed it over his shoulder. Instead of landing in the water, it plonked onto the dock. They burst out laughing at the same time before catching themselves.

Megan wasn't sure she wanted to laugh with Tom right now. She just wanted to feel something less complicated than the turmoil she'd been feeling over the past week.

More than a week, when she thought of it. She hadn't really been happy for a long time. That was a thought to be folded and tucked away for later. For now, she had a boat to hijack.

"Unwrap the stern line and hand it to me," she directed Tom while starting up the engine. "Then take the bowline, push us off from the dock just a little, and hop on."

"Aye, aye." Tom saluted her.

The marina at Roche was a moderate size, making their escape manageable. Had the boat been docked at the sprawling slips in Friday Harbor, she might not have been such a confident captain.

They charted their course, decided that trying to put up the sails was pushing their luck, and found an easy pace to motor. It'd take a few hours to get to their destination, but Megan was already feeling better than she had in days.

It reminded her of the last time she'd been on the island with

Tom, three years ago, when he'd reluctantly agreed to take that sailing course. They'd studied together for the tests, rewarding each other's right answers by removing articles of clothing and penalizing wrong answers by making each other eat the sourest candies they could find at the corner store.

Out on the water, they'd navigated the stresses of passing their night-sailing course by doing what they did best: Tom was the optimist and Megan kept their spirits up with pep talks.

It was, to date, one of her favorite memories.

Despite her unruly wants and emotions, she was more than a little excited about getting back on a boat with him.

Today was definitely going to be different. And different was good.

CHAPTER THIRTY

TOM

PERCHED ON THE edge of the boat, Tom was able to watch Megs unabashedly while she talked on the customs phone at the dock, alerting the Canadian authorities of their invasion. He had to remain visible to the customs camera as she relayed their passport information to the agent, but he would've stayed out there in the sun regardless.

The marina in Sidney, British Columbia, was one of the prettiest he'd ever seen, with a cobblestone path along the seawall, stout buildings lining the main street, and an amphitheater shaped like a shell visible from the docks.

If he ever broke out of this day, maybe he should consider packing his bags and moving to Canada.

The thought came with two others that caused pangs in his chest. The first was the thought of leaving Prescott and Prescott altogether, an intimidating yet not completely unappealing idea. The second hurt more. It was the reality of a life without Megs.

Funny how just a few days ago he was having doubts about them, regretting all the women he hadn't had an opportunity to date. And now, with freedom potentially on the horizon, all he wanted to do was forgive her. And have her forgive him.

At the very least, he had this day. And he was going to make the most of it.

"All set." Megs had hung up the phone and was climbing back onto the boat. "By the way, Sidney Marina assigned us a slip on E dock for tonight, so we're going to have to turn around."

Tom could feel himself blanch. Knowing they were living a life without real consequences didn't make the prospect of damaging other people's expensive boats less daunting.

"Hey." Megs gave him a playful pat on the cheek. "Where's Optimist Tom? I'm going to need him on the bowline."

Tom swallowed his fears and saluted his captain.

Docking ended up being less precarious thanks to some nearby boaters who jumped in to catch their lines. There were two kinds of boat people, Tom had learned—the kind who wanted to watch rookies for entertainment and the kind who were eager to help.

Through it all, Megs kept a look of determination on her face. She was one of the most capable people he'd ever met, a quality he realized he'd been taking for granted. Somewhere along the way, he'd stopped checking in with her and assumed she was fine. A fresh wave of guilt rolled over him.

As they walked up to Sidney's main street, on a whim, he reached for her hand.

"This isn't that kind of day," she said quietly. He released it.

"I'm sorry."

"It's okay." She gave him a thin smile, looking up at him under her lashes. "I get it. Force of habit. Just think of us as two people stuck in a never-ending cyclone together, making the best of it."

Tom stopped walking, sure that if he let this moment pass without making her understand, it would be a bigger regret than all the others combined. Realizing he was no longer in stride with her, she stopped and turned around.

"No—I'm sorry for holding your hand, but I'm also sorry for

assuming that because you're good at taking care of everything and everyone, you always would."

A cloud passed in front of the sun, flickering a shadow over them. When they were bathed in light again, he continued. "Your job is every bit as stressful as mine and I don't think I ever acknowledged that. I was too busy racing my brother to these meaningless milestones and trying to get my parents' approval."

He watched her chest rise and fall, though she continued to say nothing. It was too soon to have a heady talk. He'd save the rest of his words for later. After his discussion with Kenneth Birch and a day alone in the airport, there was suddenly a lot he had to say to her. For now, he decided to lighten the mood. He looked around for inspiration and saw just what they needed. "I'm also sorry that we're only a block and a half away from a bakery and I'm standing in the middle of the sidewalk talking about my feelings."

She laughed. A sound that made him feel like he had a jet pack strapped to his back.

"I know we already had pastries for breakfast, but they have the *best* cinnamon rolls," she said. She put her hands on her hips, mischief returning to her eyes. "Race you there."

They took off running, dodging senior citizens walking their dogs and boaters out for a stroll. When they reached the bakery, they were out of breath and grinning.

It was the first time in days Tom felt as though he was finally doing something right.

The field by the amphitheater was peppered with multicolored Adirondack chairs. Tom and Megs settled into two facing the ocean and dug into their very sticky cinnamon buns.

Megs moaned. "Wedding's back on, but instead I'm marrying *this* thing."

Tom chuckled and tried not to think X-rated thoughts about the sounds Megs was making.

She wasn't wearing the necklace, he noted. Over the past six days he'd been watching with vague interest, clocking the days she wore it and the days she didn't. He could still clearly recall the afternoon he'd bought it for her. It was a week before Valentine's Day. Falling in love with Megs wasn't something he could pinpoint with a date or a word or a kiss. It was more of an inevitability. Something he was destined to do, to feel. But he hadn't been ready to tell her yet. He'd had a lifetime of what'd felt like rejection, mostly from his parents, and he didn't think he could take rejection from her. And so he'd promised himself he'd bide his time and wait to tell her when he felt ready. (As it turned out, she beat him to the L-word punch months later over ice cream.) Still, he'd never experienced a Valentine's Day with a girlfriend—definitely not someone he felt this strongly about. There had to be some way to commemorate it. To tell her how he felt without actually telling her.

He went to a jewelry store and was subsequently talked into the necklace by a salesman who assured him it was the height of fashion and romance. Megs had gushed and worn it every day despite its on-the-nose pendant. Now he was so well acquainted with her taste, he could go into a jewelry store and easily pick out something she'd love. But he was still proud of that necklace, of what it represented.

He hoped she'd wear it again. Another day. Another loop.

Megs had grown quiet. It was time to perk her up.

"Remember in college when you said you couldn't wait until you could read for fun again?"

She threw her head back and groaned. "That was when I'd accidentally signed up for that advanced mythology course and spent an entire semester reading Homer and Virgil and other verbose white dudes."

"When's the last time you read something for fun? Not for work or for some book club my mom pressured you into joining?"

She squinted at the sun and wrinkled her nose. "I can't remember."

"I saw at least three bookstores in this town." Tom wiped his hands on a napkin and stood up. "If we're stuck in this day forever, we might as well catch up on our reading."

"Excellent plan." Megs licked a dab of icing off her lips, sending a current through Tom.

They strolled up Beacon Street, window-shopping and admiring the bronze statues artfully positioned along the way.

"I love this place," Megs gushed. "I could spend a few repeating days in this town."

"Me too."

They found an indie bookshop on the corner of a lazy intersection and popped in. The store sprawled, warm and inviting, with an array of merchandise and lots of kindly staff.

"I'm going to become polyamorous," Megs announced. "I'm going to marry that cinnamon roll *and* this bookstore."

It'd been years since Tom had seen her so unencumbered. The woman he fell in love with was shining through. It made him ache with a desire to stay in *this* day.

She wandered around the shelves, picking up the occasional book and reading the back. He took a different route, keeping an eye out for her, enjoying seeing her be Megs again.

They stayed in there for as long as they pleased, exciting the staff when they approached the register with their arms full of everything from commercial thrillers to feminist poetry and local-interest coffee-table books.

"Best day ever," he whispered to her as they watched their total hit the hundreds.

She eyed him with an expression that was a cross between suspicion and total agreement. The combination was enough for now.

CHAPTER THIRTY-ONE

MEGAN

SWAP VANCOUVER ISLAND for the Amalfi coast and the day was going similarly to how Megan had envisioned their honeymoon. When she let everything go, all her thoughts of real life and the days before and beyond this one, she felt an easy clarity. But then she'd snap back to reality and find herself confused all over again.

Even so, she couldn't help but compare this day to how she'd felt when she'd chosen Leo. *Really* chosen him. There'd been no easy clarity, no answers, no peace. Just questions that expanded and multiplied.

Megan shouldn't have been surprised. Her relationship with Tom was at its strongest when it was the two of them against the world. And so, as they carried their bookstore loot back to the park and stretched out in the shade, flipping through their newly purchased books—sharing photos and passages with each other—*of course* she could delude herself into thinking that if this day had never looped and she and Tom hadn't fought, maybe they could've had a good life together.

However, she and Tom weren't the only factors in the equation. There would always be interfering parents and high-maintenance siblings and Leo and Midwest states. Which meant what Megan had to fix was herself. She might not have gotten the solitude in Montana she'd wanted to figure this all out, but spending a day on the water and in a charming seaside town, away from the wedding bedlam at Roche, was almost as good.

Megan was pleasantly astonished to find having Tom around was a welcome comfort. Since the whole time loop started, he was the one person she didn't have to wear a mask for. There was something to be said for that.

She could be as messy as she wanted with him. As together as she wanted. Being able to just *be* relaxed her in a way she hadn't experienced in years. From behind the wisps of her hair blowing around in the breeze, she snuck peeks of his profile: the strong jaw she'd always adored, the slope of his nose, his eyebrows that got so bushy, every few weeks he'd put his head in her lap so she could trim and tweeze them into submission. The custom usually devolved into them laughing as she threatened to tweeze her initials into his eyebrows.

Megan tried to reconcile that image of easy companionship with what had obviously been brewing underneath.

She put down a book of West Coast photography and stretched out her legs. "Who do you think we'd be if we'd grown up in stable, loving households?"

Tom looked up from a book of poetry by Amanda Lovelace. "Do such households exist?"

"I don't know. I'm just trying to figure out who I'd be if I hadn't spent my childhood forging signatures on field-trip forms for Brianna while my mom was cruising for guys at the bar. If I'd had parents like Paulina and Hamza." Her eyes became hot with tears. Tom reached out to rub her calf, his face full of empathy. "I think that was part of what I loved about our time at Harvard," she went on. "I was so far away from everyone else, it was like I got to take up space for the first time. To make mistakes and…"

She was veering too close to Leo territory and Tom's hand stilled. Even if they had a million more versions of this day, she wasn't sure if they'd ever truly forgive each other.

"I'm sorry," Tom said.

His apology—and the timing of it—was unexpected. She kept her tone light. "For what?"

"For all the times I made it harder for you to take up space."

She took those words from him. Held them in her hands to feel the weight, the depth. And then made herself a promise: she was going to stop measuring herself against her childhood and people like John and Carol.

"That said..." Tom put his book down, folded his hands in his lap. "I think who you are at your core is who you'd be regardless."

She sniffed derisively, wondering if Tom still knew her better than anyone. "Oh yeah? And who's that?"

"The most capable, efficient, bravest, and warmest person I know."

The compliment hit its mark. She resisted reaching out to him, though the instinct was there. Instead, Megan settled into the reassuring feeling of finally being in a place where she and Tom could perhaps be friends again.

Because she didn't have to lose everything to this never-ending day. And she was starting to see what she wanted to keep.

Megan might not be able to control how every day in this loop began, but she could certainly control how each ended, and she knew exactly what she wanted to do right now.

CHAPTER THIRTY-TWO

TOM

COME ON." MEGS held her hand out.

"Where are we going? What about all these books we bought?"

She shrugged. "Let other people come by and read them. The sun's setting soon."

"You want to head back?" The last thing Tom was keen on doing right now was manning the bowline while Megan took them out of the slip. They were docked next to a very expensive-looking yacht. However, she was holding out her hand to him, and it felt like forever since she'd done that. Tom was willing to do almost anything if it meant holding Megs's hand. "We can head back, if that's what you really want."

"Never." Megs pointed to the man-made break in the water. "I want to climb that."

Unsure about how much better lumbering up and over a wall of giant boulders was than potentially running *Happy Accident* into a cranky billionaire's boat, he let her help him to his feet. Sadly, she let go of his hand as soon as he was standing. She took off and Tom followed along behind, thinking about the conversation they'd just had.

It was a seemingly small moment of honesty. Something they'd once had in truckloads. He had scores of memories of them lying on the lumpy mattress in their first New York apartment, the light of the moon streaming through the tablecloth they'd hung as a makeshift curtain, sharing secrets like they were kids at a sleepover.

Over the past few years, their secrets had gone unshared and their conversations had become about trivial daily things, not fears or epiphanies or lofty thoughts about their future. It was part of growing up, Tom told himself as he and Megs climbed over the fence and went down the hill to the rock breaker made entirely of grayscale boulders that separated the marina from the open ocean. You stopped thinking in expansive ways and started dealing with the day-to-day.

But he wasn't sure that was true or that he wanted it to be. He just knew he wanted to stop thinking about Megs and Leo anytime he heard her say the word *mistake*. In any context.

"Are you sure we're allowed to do this?" Tom asked as Megs started her precarious ascent up the first boulder.

"Oh, we're definitely not allowed to do this." She cast a backward glance at him. "But we're doing it anyway."

He wiped perspiration from the back of his neck and climbed up after her. Once at the top, they walked along as though on a slightly uneven balance beam.

"Have you done this before?" He was trying to keep the worry from his voice, although what was the point? Megs of all people knew he was a chicken when it came to heights. He tried not to look at the thrashing ocean below. This wasn't like falling into the water in Hawaii; the sea here was cold enough to induce hypothermia. Probably within minutes. Plus, odds were he'd crack his skull on the jagged rocks on the way down. He swallowed hard and kept taking gingerly steps.

"Brianna, Alistair, and I did this when we were teenagers. Gran and Granddad took us here for Canada Day a couple of times.

These were the best seats for the fireworks. I suspect they'll be the best seats for the sunset."

When she finally stopped walking and crouched down, Tom nearly wept with relief. He was quite a ways behind, but she waited patiently until he sat next to her.

Once seated, his center of gravity nice and low, he allowed himself to look up and out rather than down. "Wow."

The marina was quiet, despite nearly every slip being filled by a sailboat or yacht. Behind them, the ocean crested. Ahead, on the other side of the breaker, the water in the marina looked like glass, like a mirror. He was amazed at how different the ocean could be on either side of the wall.

"Yeah. Not a bad view, huh?" She gave him a crooked smile. "God, I love it out here. Forgive me, New York, but West Coast, best coast."

He laughed. "Traitor."

On the open-ocean side of the wall, the horizon line seemed forever away. A handful of boats moved so slowly across the water, they might as well have been still. As the sky lit up in pinks and oranges and colors that reminded Tom of a candy shop, he decided sharing secrets definitely wasn't just for kids at a sleepover. Or something you ever grew out of. Light-years away, a single brave star emerged before night fell completely.

"When you called me a coward..." The memory snagged, creating a layer of emotion in his throat.

"I'm sorry about that," Megs immediately replied, her shoulders dropping.

"No, no, you were right. I think that's why it hit me so hard." A rock beneath him wobbled and he splayed his fingers on either side to steady himself.

"You're okay," Megs murmured. "This thing is steadier than you and I combined."

Tom could see the regret pass over her face as soon as she said it.

He let the moment roll off and away before continuing. "I let my dad make all my choices for me."

She nodded.

"Like I was too scared to make any choices for myself." He smiled sadly. "You being the exception."

"We chose each other," she confirmed so softly he felt his heart breaking all over again.

"Yeah. We did. As it turns out, I'm pretty good at making my own decisions—when it happens."

"You think so?"

He knew she was referring to the absolute war zone their relationship had exploded into, but he still stood by their discussion in Natural Disasters and the necklace and the ice cream and all the New Year's Eve parties and the proposal and everything else in between.

"Yeah, I think so." He wanted to take her hand so badly. To hold it as long as he could this time, not just in a fleeting moment of rising to his feet. "I'm sorry about asking you to make concessions for my career goals—goals that weren't even mine. I did that even before I took that job in Missouri."

She shrugged, and he knew they were both thinking about New York, about London, about all the things that could have been. "It doesn't matter now."

"Yes, it does." Carefully, so as not to plunge to a watery grave, he turned to face her. "It was a cowardly, dick move. Every time. And I regret it so much."

"I can't really hold it over your head when I have one or two regrets of my own." She bit her lower lip and he cursed the image of her and Leo that flashed in his mind.

"Speaking of that particular regret..." Tom cleared his throat. "I'm also really sorry I lied to you about that note. The one you thought I left on your windshield in college."

"Tom, I—" Megs tried to wave off his words.

"No, I mean it. And I want you to know why I did it."

The sky was getting darker, but the moon was big enough to illuminate them. He could see her eyes as clearly as if a spotlight shone above her.

"How I felt about you…it was bigger than I knew how to say. I could kiss you and cook for you and buy you a cheesy necklace…"

Tom watched her instinctively reach for the pendant that wasn't there.

"But I didn't always know how to tell you. Words were much scarier. And so when you were upset that night and really opened up to me, and Leo wrote you that note…" Tom wanted to cry, to let every painful memory be exorcised through his tear ducts. "I saw that his note was exactly what you'd needed. I wanted to be the person who'd made you feel the way his words had. And so I let you believe the note was mine."

She nodded slowly, deliberately. The air was growing colder. She rubbed at the goose bumps on her legs.

"Can I…" More stars were appearing, each one giving Tom courage to ask for the answers he knew could hurt him the most. "Can I ask? Why *Leo?*"

She stiffened beside him, obviously not expecting him to try and traverse this particular road. Her silence was thoughtful, and he let her take all the time she needed. When she finally spoke, it came out steady. Strong. "He loved me. The real me, the *true* me—whatever you wanted to call it. And when I was with him, I didn't feel like I had to try so hard for his approval."

"Do I make you feel that way?" Tom couldn't patch the break in his voice before it emerged. "Like you have to try and be someone you're not?"

She shook her head. "No, not you, but…"

"My family." It wasn't a question.

"Yeah. Although I think *my* family makes me feel that way too.

And I make myself feel that way, which is really irritating." She smirked, giving him a sidelong glance. "I don't think I've been doing myself any favors there."

Tom wanted to feel better and he didn't. Not yet. He tried to banish those pervasive thoughts of what Megs must've looked like making love to his adventurous best friend. He tried to focus on what really mattered. "If I didn't make you feel that way, was Leo a way of punishing me? For not standing up to my family?"

She bit her bottom lip. "I think being with Leo was about a life I thought I wanted but was afraid of. You know I've always had to be steady, responsible. To hold everything and everyone together because when Paulina and Gran weren't around, I was the only one left to do it. Do you know what my mom said the first time she met Leo?"

He wasn't sure he wanted to know, but still asked. "What?"

"'Oh, he's the best kind of trouble, isn't he?'" Megs did her Donna impression, which was pretty good. Her face fell. "I loved Leo and was afraid to be with him because I thought choosing him was reckless. It was the Donna thing to do."

He swallowed the growing lump in his throat. "So being with me was a way not to turn into your mother?" That prospect was almost as bad as being a placeholder.

"No." Megs turned to him fiercely. "*No.* I chose you because I loved *you.* Leo was just this…this alternate reality that was appealing until I realized it wasn't what I wanted. It was a make-believe life that didn't actually fit me or make me feel safe like I thought it would. I'm so sorry I hurt you, Tom. Not just the first time, years ago. If the second time I chose Leo hurt, I'm sorry for that too."

He nodded, trying to maintain control of his emotions. There was a lot to process in what Megs had just said. On the one hand, she'd said she loved him. Past tense. On the other hand, she'd just admitted Leo wasn't what she wanted. Tom could work with that.

They continued to watch the stars speckle the sky as the dark curtain fell on the day.

"Do you want to head back to the boat?" Megs eventually asked.

They were ending the day together. He clung to hope just as he was clinging to this rock wall. "Sure."

"I'll make up the bed in the galley for you," Megan continued.

Of course she was taking the V-berth bed for herself.

Sleeping on the bench of the boat's kitchen was only slightly more comfortable than spending the night in the rental car. Still, there were hatches overhead offering him a view of the stars, and knowing Megs was a few feet away gave him comfort.

As he replayed the loops they'd shared, he thought back to his apologies. To the times she'd said sorry about what had happened with Leo eight years ago. To her insistence that it was a mistake that hadn't been repeated.

To the fact that she'd repeated it so recently, as they'd tumbled through this day that wouldn't end.

He thought about how she wasn't with Leo now; she'd willingly spent the day with Tom instead. And it had been one hell of a day. The best in a long time.

Even so, they were in separate beds tonight. One perfect day speckled with a series of belated conversations didn't mean they would sleep side by side tonight. Or maybe ever again.

Tom just knew that he finally and unequivocally really, *really* wanted to.

DAY
7

CHAPTER THIRTY-THREE

MEGAN

WITH THE MORNING sun came no surprise or anger. No emotional vegetative state. Just a feeling of deep and weighted bereavement as Megan realized she was back in the hotel room. She'd gotten as far as another country and yet here she was again. The same pajamas. The same bed. Donna minutes away from bursting into the room.

Despite all her efforts, good and bad, Megan had lost her future. Not just the one with Tom that had been erased that first night. She'd lost *any* future. With anyone. Or no one. It was as complex and disorienting as looking through a prism; all she could see was the same refracted day over and over again. No consequences, sure, but also no rewards.

Last night, after she'd turned the bench seat in the boat's galley into a bed for Tom and given him a pillow and a sleeping bag, she gazed at him with fondness, thinking about the way they could have fun together, how easy it was to laugh and open up. To sit in comfortable silences. In a lot of ways, he remained her best friend, and so it was a consolation knowing they wouldn't hate each other forever.

Talking about their regrets and worries in Sidney had felt

so good. Saying some of their apologies out loud had been a baptism.

Not enough to save them. Just enough to heal them a little.

She was surprised at how candidly they'd been able to broach the topic of Leo, which wasn't easy for her and definitely couldn't have been easy for Tom. And yet once she'd said all those things out loud, she'd been able to better process her fixation on Leo. Lying in the V-berth of *Happy Accident*, waiting for sleep to come, she'd thought it all over and found herself feeling surprisingly angry at him for what he'd done to Tom, leaving the note on her windshield knowing how Tom had felt about her. Showing up to the wedding as Tom's best man and yet fully ready to break up the marriage if he could.

Who did that to his best friend?

Of course, Megan wasn't sure she'd treated Tom any better. The thought sat low in her stomach.

Any lingering feelings she'd had for Leo were officially and unambiguously extinguished, making it time to repaint her future all over again.

What she wanted from her life, should she ever be able to reclaim it, was on the tip of her tongue. During lunch with Leo, she'd discovered she still wanted her job at *GQ*—or something like it. As for all those other holes in the hypothetical days ahead…perhaps if she held very still, the answers would come.

Her epiphanies were undermined by a darker truth: Even if she caught the wants, the words, the magical recipe to concoct a better life, did it matter? Her life wasn't her own.

Megan pulled the covers up to her chin. Mourning what she'd lost—what she was *actively losing*—wasn't going to make this repeated day any better. She needed answers. As though on cue, her phone rang. Tom's name lit up the screen.

"Hello?"

"Megs." Her name came out rushed, full of excitement.

"Remember when you said we needed to do things right? To get out of this?"

"Yeah." She wriggled her toes, trying to warm them up and shake out her darker thoughts.

"I think we got it wrong."

She snorted. "You think?"

He ignored her sarcasm. "Yeah. Experiment with me?"

"I'm not interested in a threesome, Tom. Unless the third person is Idris Elba, and I don't think he's on the island."

She could practically hear the smile in his voice when he said, "Let's try to be our best selves today. Take everything we've said to each other—even the stuff that hurt, the stuff that seemed like bullshit—and be better."

She let out a sigh that could've extinguished a forest fire. Hadn't they tried that already?

She sat with his proposal, the soft sounds of his presence in her ear. Perhaps this suggestion wasn't about trying to get *out* of the loop.

There was a nucleus in that thought. She just needed to get to it.

Without waiting for her answer he added, "See you at the rehearsal dinner."

The line went dead.

Even though the call was over, Megan kept staring at her phone. People were able to carry around the collective knowledge of the ages in their pockets and yet nothing could give her a concrete answer on how she, Megan Givens, could be her best self.

Because, ultimately, being her best self really was what the "doing everything right" day had been about. She'd tried placating her mother with encouragement and support and agreed to house her younger sister, even though Brianna despised Megan 50 percent of the time. She'd kicked Leo to the curb repeatedly and attempted to make nice with Tom. She'd folded and contorted herself to fit in the spaces everyone else had formed around her.

But.

In all the incarnations of this bastard of a day, the only thing that had felt like the incontrovertibly right thing to do was when she identified Carol's issue (or at least *one* of her issues; you could construct the New York City skyline from Carol's issues) and had a separate plate made up to help her feel more comfortable.

And in all the incarnations, the only time she'd felt as though she'd found the eye of the storm was when she and Tom were being honest and swapping secrets in Sidney.

Megan pulled the covers over her head and kicked her feet in frustration like a child.

"*Oh!* Am I interrupting something?"

Megan flipped the white duvet back, folded it across her stomach. Her mother seemed horrified at the thought that Megan wasn't alone.

"Good morning, Mom." Megan got out of bed. She strode to the bathroom and closed the door to pee and give herself more time to think. When she emerged, wrapped in the hotel robe, she found her mother staring out the window, her fingers grazing the curtains.

"You can see Gran and Granddad's boat from here."

"I know." She stood by her mother, willing herself to feel affection for the woman who never did *her* best.

Maybe because she didn't know how.

Donna's mood shifted and she tossed her hair; her eyes were brimming with tears and locked on the ceiling. "I need something to wear to the rehearsal dinner tonight."

And there.

Megan saw it.

Megan had spent a lifetime trying to appease her mother and it'd only reinforced her behavior. But what if this *wasn't* about her mother trying to make the day about her, so the solution to this problem wasn't fixing Donna's ensemble? "Why do you need a new dress?" Megan asked.

The simplicity of the question, the desire Megan was showing for a real answer, clearly caught Donna off guard. Odds were she'd rehearsed this production in the elevator—the lines she'd say to Megan, the blocking to illustrate this grand offense by Gran.

Donna should know by now she couldn't change the way Gran behaved or what she said. The only thing she could control was how she reacted to Gran.

"Your grandmother—" Donna began. Megan cut her off with a wave. She took her by the hand and sat her down on the edge of the bed.

"Mom. Listen to me. If you have a problem with Brianna, you need to talk to her, not whisper into my ear about it. If you have a problem with me, you need to talk to me about it, not gossip with Brianna. And if Gran's hurting your feelings—"

"This isn't about Gran!" Donna shouted.

"Then what's it about?" Megan sensed her mom was on the cusp of a breakthrough, so she needed to tread carefully. "Because I've got a hunch it's not about the dress."

"It is." Donna's commitment to stubbornness outshone every commitment she'd ever made to a man.

"Mom…" Megan gently squeezed Donna's hand. "Please. Just be honest with me. Are you maybe feeling a bit insecure right now? Do you think that's what this is about?"

It was as though Megan was a kid playing Jenga and she'd finally removed the block that made her mom's facade tumble. With an exasperated sob, Donna said, "Fine. You want to know what this is about? This is about me needing to feel my best during a very stressful weekend when I'm being judged and I'm alone and I don't have anyone to put his arm around me and tell me I'm beautiful. You have that every single day. I've had to *fight* for it."

An overwhelming sense of pity washed over Megan as she took in her mother. Donna *was* a ridiculous person. Megan had a life-time of stories to support that theory. But she was starting to see that Donna's bid to split her daughters' affection so it might shine more brightly on her was rooted in her unbearable insecurity. She'd searched for this validation in every father figure she'd paraded through her kids' lives.

Maybe Donna had even pretended to go to all those job interviews because she didn't think she was good enough to ever get the job.

Meanwhile, Megan had spent half her life being the mother in the house and the other half clinging to Tom because he was stable. He represented commitment and roots and everything her mother hadn't.

She'd chosen Tom in opposition to her mother as much as she'd chosen him because she loved him.

And yet one didn't negate the other. Maybe part of her attraction to Tom was based on his stability, but that wasn't what had carried them through twelve years. What had carried them were all the little things, their shared memories and senses of humor, as well as all the big things, like Tom's good heart and Megan's desire to see him happy. They'd lost their way when they'd tried too hard to please everyone instead of just being honest with each other. With themselves.

Megan was flooded with a new comprehension of what being her *best self* meant. She didn't need to contort herself to fit in the spaces the people in her life left for her. She had to create space for herself. That was the key. That was how she'd get out of this day. Or at least, it was worth a shot.

Once again, Megan allowed her mother to be the child, knowing she had to indulge her one last time in order to establish necessary boundaries.

"I love you, Mom. And you are beautiful no matter what you wear. That said, I need you—Brianna and probably Alistair too— we all need you to try harder." Her hands still clasped over Donna's, Megan squeezed. "I will support you if you need help writing a résumé, looking for a job. I will support you as you look for love if that's what you really want. But I'm not going to try to solve your problems for you anymore and I'm not going to enable you to define your self-worth through a man."

Donna was rendered speechless. Megan gave her mother a hug and ushered her out the door.

The day Megan had confessed to her mother that she'd secretly applied to Harvard with Paulina's help and gotten in, Donna had clucked her tongue and said, "Well, you aren't actually going, are you?" When Megan replied that she was, Donna stopped speaking to her. The morning Megan had packed Paulina's old Nissan, ready to drive across the country, only Brianna had stood on the doorstep to wave her off. Donna had remained at the breakfast table, sipping instant coffee, pretending to read the newspaper.

Change did not come to Donna easily. She might complain about her life, but she was comfortable in it, and any ripples rattled her, made her revert to adolescent tactics of punishment.

So, while Megan hoped her talk with her mother might spur an evolution, she was staying realistic. Megan could change herself and she could recalibrate her expectations of other people, but she couldn't make others change. And that realization was oddly freeing.

CHAPTER THIRTY-FOUR

TOM

FOR THE FIRST time in a long time, Tom was fired up. Trying to remain calm and complacent had gotten him nowhere.

He'd called Megs from the ferry, serendipitously hitting a sweet spot where he got cell service for long enough to make his case. He could picture her so clearly as he convinced her to participate in today's experiment: creases on her cheek from the pillowcase, snuggling into the covers like a linen nest, desperately trying to warm her freezing feet.

Once he hung up, he made a mental list of what he needed to do. Number one scared him in the best possible way. This rev inside him was so satisfying, he wished Henry Winkler a very good morning and then walked around the ferry, unable—not wanting—to sit still.

At the bow, two men with graying hair were reenacting the famous "king of the world" scene from *Titanic*. There was an innocence in their joy, despite their age. An undercurrent of love that must have made everything in their periphery fade at the edges.

Sea air whipped at his suit jacket and collar, ruffling Tom's hair. Staying inside would've been more comfortable, controlled, but Tom didn't want comfort today. He wanted the shrillness of the wind in his ears, his eyes tearing, as he contemplated his life. Not the path that had gotten him here, that had already been trudged, but whether or not he was satisfied with where he was going.

It'd been assumed since Tom's birth that he'd attend Harvard. He was a legacy, after all. There were family photos displayed in crystal frames of baby Tom dressed in a Harvard V-necked sweater.

He didn't regret Harvard. Not for a second. Not when it'd given him what he'd had with Megs. Even with Leo. His best friends had taught him to shake off stress and cackle at the absurd.

Megan and Leo had been there to absorb his love, something his immediate family had always refused with a discomfort that bordered on embarrassment. For that alone, he couldn't regret Megs. Especially after the day they'd had in Sidney. The flap of the butterfly wing that knocked everything into place.

Surprising even himself, Tom realized he didn't regret law school either. The nightly pile of reading that seemed to reproduce when his back was turned had exhausted him and required an increase in his glasses prescription, but his law homework hadn't been all bad. It'd taught him to see things from multiple angles. Plus, he'd made some friends in law school. Friends he missed and kept meaning to catch up with. If he ever got out of this day, reconnecting with them would be toward the top of his to-do list.

He didn't hate law, didn't hate the work. He hated the type of law he practiced at Prescott and Prescott.

Or maybe he *did* hate law. Maybe he wished he'd become a history professor or a librarian.

If he was ever going to figure out what he wanted, he needed to start forging that path for himself. Today. And the next day and the next.

Tom was officially done being a coward.

Once the ferry had docked, Tom caught a cab to the golf course, leaving the rental car at the hotel in case Megs needed it.

"It's about damn time, Spare Parts," Brody called to him upon his arrival. "You didn't bother changing? Showering? I can smell you from here."

One would've thought that being raised by withholding parents would've brought Tom and Brody together, but their closeness was superficial. Tom couldn't help but note that Brody's confession about his divorce had occurred in only one of the loops.

But Brody could wait. The fire in Tom was burning. He had to find his father.

He marched into the clubhouse that wasn't shiny enough to impress John, wryly noting the symbolism. Tom would probably never be good enough to impress John either.

Upon seeing Tom, John pointedly looked at his watch and wordlessly made his way out to the tee, Tom marching after him.

If John had taken note of Tom's mood, he didn't acknowledge it as he carefully placed his clubs in the back of a cart and slid behind the wheel.

"I need to talk to you, Dad."

"Is it about last night's dinner? You aren't getting cold feet about Missouri, are you? Look, if Megan's having trouble adjusting to the idea of moving, you just have to—"

"This isn't about the merger or the dinner. That all went well, no worries there." Of course that was all his father cared about. "I need to talk to you about something else."

"Fine." John tugged on his gloves, presumably so his flesh didn't have to touch the scuffed steering wheel. "We'll talk on the first hole. Tell Broderick to hustle."

Instead of waiting for his sons to climb in the cart, he pulled a U-turn and drove off, assuming they'd follow. Brody walked out, squinting in the sun despite his visor. "Have I told you about my favorite new drinking game?"

"Two planes and a ferry," Tom muttered, sliding into the driver's seat of another cart.

"Exactly. Wait—when did I tell you about it? And what are you doing on the course wearing work clothes? And you know you need golf clubs to *golf*, right?" Brody took a sip from his flask. "You just gave me an idea for a *new* game: I'm going to take a drink every time you do something stupid today."

On any other day, Tom would've silently seethed, pushing down his resentments at his brother's constant jabs.

On any *other* day.

He'd spent his entire life thinking of himself as a peacekeeper, not a coward, and now he was seeing his willingness to be silent in a different light. It was like Kenneth Birch said—he'd listened to Megs and was trying to do better. To *be* better.

"Hey, Brody." He rested one arm on the back of the seat and turned his attention to his brother. "I'm sorry your marriage is falling apart and I'm sorry you don't seem to have the capacity to deal with it. But get into couples counseling or get into therapy or both, because I can't be your punching bag anymore."

Brody was so stunned he quite literally stumbled. By the time he was righting himself, Tom was already lead-footing the cart in the direction of his father. But then he stopped.

He needed to be the *best* version of himself.

He turned to look back at Brody and added, "If you ever need someone to talk to—not punch, *talk* to—I'm here for you."

At the first hole, John was placing his ball on the tee. Tom watched his father examine his clubs, eventually slip one out of the bag, and readjust his grip.

He's a sad old man, Tom thought. *A sad old man who clings to work because he doesn't know how to connect with his own family.*

Tom had never really known his paternal grandfather, as he was quite ill by the time Tom was born. When Tom turned four, his grandfather passed. Tom had fuzzy memories of sitting in a church pew while a man droned on, quoting Scripture Tom didn't understand, as Tom's grandmother touched a cloth handkerchief to her eyes. He'd been too young to comprehend the rare example of Prescott vulnerability he was witnessing.

His paternal grandmother, however, had been a formidable presence in his life. They spent most major holidays at her Connecticut home. Her voice, though now frail, would echo through the halls as she barked orders to her staff and castigated her family. He'd always been terrified of her and suspected John had too. The question of who'd raised John to be cold and calculating wasn't a question at all. But his father never spoke of his upbringing or his past, preferring to focus on the things he could control: work, the firm, his wife, and his sons.

Even though Tom was softer than his father, there was still a scenario in which he could continue this cold spiral, train himself to ignore the people he loved because he didn't have the capacity to deal with them. He thought about how many nights he'd wasted stressing about work when he'd had Megs right in front of him. How he hadn't made the space for her that she needed.

Understanding took time. And the universe had granted it to him.

"*John.*" Tom didn't consciously choose to use his father's given name instead of "Dad," but here they were.

Nothing startled John. He slowly relaxed his grip and turned toward Tom, waiting for his second-born to speak, which for once Tom was more than happy to do.

"You've been comparing me to Brody my entire life, bombarding me with examples of how I keep coming up short. Maybe you thought it'd push me to work harder, but all it did was push a wedge between Brody and me, and now his life's shit, my life's shit, and you don't even care. You don't care." Tom's voice was on the rise. It felt so good to finally yell at his dad. "Because for you, it's all about how we reflect the Prescott name. How many zeroes are in our bank accounts, how attractive and demure our wives are."

John wasn't a man to interrupt or make excuses. Tom barreled on, ignoring the swift flicker of pain in his dad's eyes.

"I know you disapprove of Megan's family, but, quite frankly, I've been disappointed in you. And me. And the way you've dictated the entire scope of my life without ever once considering that I may want something different."

"Do you?"

Tom was breathless, hopped up on adrenaline. His mind was working faster than his mouth. "Do I what?"

"Do you want something different?"

John's look wasn't one of cold calculation; it was genuine curiosity. Tom wasn't sure what reaction he'd expected, but a seemingly authentic interest in what Tom wanted from his life wouldn't even have made his top ten guesses.

So this was it. The moment. The opportunity to choose something else.

"Yeah. I think I do want something different. Totally different. In fact, I quit."

"You *quit?*" The surprise in John's voice was palpable.

Tom checked in with himself to make sure he wasn't doing anything he regretted. A warmth vibrated through him as he saw an unknown future. One he could choose himself. He threw his arms out and declared, with a note of glee, "I. Quit."

And then he spun on his heel and whistled as he sauntered off the golf course.

CHAPTER THIRTY-FIVE

MEGAN

WHEN MEGAN SHOWED up for her salon appointment, the receptionist informed her Donna had canceled it. Canceled everyone's. She'd told the receptionist there'd been a family emergency.

Vacillating between calling her mother to check on her and leaving her be, Megan finally settled on making the best of a situation that wasn't actually terrible. In fact, getting ready for the rehearsal dinner with Paulina and Brianna in Paulina's room ended up being much more fun.

Megan was pretending this was her first time through this, and the fantasy was blissful.

It was a small act of doing exactly what she wanted. Not as dramatic as running away with a college crush or hijacking her grandparents' boat, but still, it was a victory. That life she wanted, the picture of it, was becoming less fuzzy.

Paulina, Brianna, and Megan reminisced about summers spent on the island—the times they'd rented scooters and had slow races up winding roads framed by endless forests; the game they'd played where they'd buy the grossest candies they could find and eat them blindfolded, trying to guess the flavors.

Megan almost never saw Brianna without Donna lurking in the shadows, but now they were remembering that they actually enjoyed each other's company. That, in addition to sharing a mother, they also shared a sense of humor and so many good memories.

"Should I check on Mom?" Brianna asked in a rare show of selflessness.

"I texted her and invited her to join us, but she said she needed some time to herself. Just leave her be, Bree." Paulina finished applying a second coat of mascara to her lashes and turned around. "Now. Please lie to me and tell me I look radiant, because my sciatic nerve is acting up and I have hemorrhoids the size of baby chicks."

Megan laughed and grabbed Brianna's hand, and together they hugged her, making a Paulina sandwich.

"You're gorgeous," Megan assured her.

"A true yummy mummy," Brianna chimed in.

This rare alliance with Brianna reminded Megan of their childhood. When the winter temperatures would plummet and blizzards would descend, they'd tiptoe into the basement and hang an old sheet over the nook under the stairs using thumbtacks, and Megan would read to her little sister. Their favorite book was *Matilda*. After every chapter, they'd put a small object on the floor in front of them and try to move it with their minds.

It was funny how the years had made Megan forget how much she used to genuinely enjoy being with Brianna. It was helpful that, in this version of the day, Brianna hadn't even mentioned her move to New York yet, though Megs knew it would eventually come up.

But before she could deal with her sister, she had another flame to extinguish. One she'd let burn for far too long.

She inspected her makeup one last time, had Brianna zip up her dress, and blew them both kisses. "I have to go check on a few details," she lied.

"Of course you do." Brianna rolled her eyes. "Megan Givens, first of her name, keeper of to-do lists and master of efficiency."

"I'll take that title."

"Good luck." Paulina blew her a kiss. "Let us know if there's anything we can help you with."

A kaleidoscope of butterflies hatched in Megan's stomach as she walked out of the hotel. She planned to catch Leo on his way to the restaurant, so she lurked in the shadows of the trees, taking up residence at a table outside the hotel's miniature market. It offered a good view of both the hotel lobby and the restaurant's entrance.

She shouldn't be nervous. She'd seen Leo so many times in so many ways over the past few days. But since she'd successfully avoided him during this incarnation, this would be his first time seeing *her*.

She'd spent the morning on one of her favorite trails on the island. After wrestling with what she wanted and what moving forward *could* look like, she'd gained the insight she needed.

Now all she had to do was communicate this to Leo and hope he'd understand.

She recognized his lazily confident gait, smiling at his familiar gesture of running his hands over his hair, an indication, she now understood, that he was nervous. She waved at him, leaning forward until the lights from the market bathed her face.

As he drew nearer, his smile grew. "I've been looking for you all day."

"I know."

"You know?" His smile faltered just a little. "Have you been avoiding me, Givens? Because that'd be par for the course, considering the past ten years."

"Eight," she corrected him. There was a tug in her chest.

The one thing she couldn't get used to as she relived this day was how she had to wait for him to catch up, listen to him address her as though for the first time.

Saying goodbye to him wouldn't be easy, but she was ready. That tug in her chest wasn't one of longing or regret. It was a response to knowing she could move on from him. Finally.

"You were my biggest what-if," she told him once he'd taken a seat. He scooted his chair closer and they both winced as its legs scraped against the cobblestone.

"I'm nervous," he admitted. "Because you've been my biggest what-if too. And if we pause this conversation right here, I can live in a world where you feel the same way I do. But if this conversation continues, I'm afraid you're going to say something that'll break my heart."

"I don't want to break your heart, Leo," she offered truthfully. "But I realized something very recently—you and I have been using the memory of what happened between us as an escape. As long as we didn't pursue anything further, this relationship of ours could be the perfect fantasy. But that's just what it is. A fantasy."

His eyes shone in the twilight. "How do you know it's just a fantasy? I know I could make you happy. More than anything, Givens, I want to see you happy."

"Happiness is fleeting. And there are already a lot of incredible and wonderful things in my life," she said. "I don't have any regrets right now, Leo, even though you think I do. In another life, you and I could be really great friends. But it's too late for that. Too much has happened. And as far as a relationship goes, we don't want the same things. You think you know me, but you only see the qualities that align with you. And I know that even if we let anything happen between us, it wouldn't last."

She let eight years of tension ease out of her body, relieved to have told him the truth. To have told herself the truth. "We aren't each other's endgame, Leo."

He shook his head, reaching for her hand. "How can you be so sure? Aren't we just going to walk away from tonight wondering *What if* again?"

Megan gave his hand a squeeze before releasing it. "Not this time, we won't."

"But…"

The morning she'd graduated, after they'd had sex on the roof, there'd been a moment between realizing what time it was and rushing off so she wouldn't be late to meet Tom and his parents. A moment when time seemed to take a breath. She'd often thought back to that moment, to what she could have said or should have done. Some nights she imagined she'd grabbed his hand and they'd hopped in her Nissan and driven off wherever the highway took them. Other nights she'd envisioned telling him it was a mistake and that he should never contact her or Tom again.

But that moment had been all it needed to be. A breath. And sometimes it was hard to remember to breathe.

It was nearing seven o'clock. Megan stood up from the table, indicating he should too. That it was the end. "Goodbye, Leo. I hope you find a lot of happiness out there."

Without a backward glance, Megan walked away, feeling lighter than she ever had.

It was okay not to have all the answers right now. Because at least she finally saw what she needed to hold on to and what she was ready to let go.

CHAPTER THIRTY-SIX

TOM

TOM GOT READY alone in the suite he was still technically sharing with Megs. Whether it was to allay his nerves or because he'd really do anything to be his best self, he'd taken extra care showering, shaving, and dressing for the occasion.

The adrenaline spike of telling off his dad and quitting (God, he'd really quit the firm) had settled, leaving him with a sense of ease he hadn't experienced…maybe ever. He'd spent the remainder of his afternoon on a rented scooter, seeing the island, carefree. Letting his mind wander to the great unknown, Tom had indulged the history major still kicking within, signing up to tour the island's best-known historical attraction.

He listened intently to the costumed actor pretending to be a nineteenth-century soldier who told him how a war had raged between two camps, the American and the English. How the English camp had thrown parties with women and a surplus of food while American soldiers had faced isolation, supply shortages, and mind-numbing boredom.

How they'd never actually engaged in battle. And how a war that had stretched for fourteen years had been started, unbelievably, by the death of a pig.

Tom kept thinking about all the times he and Megan had opted not to fight, like two separate camps, two sides of the same island.

As he wound his way through the forests, he kept trying to envision what he'd do with his life if he ever got a true tomorrow. Switch to a more fulfilling type of law? Go to culinary school? Get a PhD in history? Run away to New Zealand and become a hermit? The possibilities were, quite literally, endless. They were also terrifying. Terrifying in the greatest possible way.

He was free. From expectation, from self-delusion and doubt and loathing. Today he was a man he himself could be proud of; something, he'd learned, that was more important than his father's approval.

Tom wondered benignly if his father would show up to the dinner tonight.

Of course he would. John lived for appearances. And there was no way Carol would agree to sit at the table alone with the Givenses.

It was too early to leave, but Tom didn't want to wait in the hotel doing nothing. He decided to take a stroll around the grounds to pass the time. It was a warm night, the end of summer, a full moon reflecting off the ocean. Soft folk music rolled lazily through the air as guests for the wedding on the front lawn found their seats. Tom sat down on the stub rock wall to watch from a safe distance.

If time had continued as it was supposed to and he and Megs had never fought, that would've eventually been them on that front lawn with their guests. He thought he'd feel regret watching the brides walk down the aisle together. But instead, he felt an enormous sense of gratitude. He and Megs had uncovered so many layers between them, aspects of their personalities, their wants and desires, their grudges and vexations; layers they'd been actively ignoring and burying for years.

They would've been saying "I do" in a state of denial. Disingenuously.

With a deep heaviness in his chest, resolute, Tom understood that if he could turn back the clocks and take control of time, he wouldn't. Even if it meant missing the hell out of the woman he loved so much.

"Tom." Leo ambled toward him, looking as though his usual confidence had been steamrolled.

Tom stood, nearly giving his oldest and dearest friend a hug out of sheer habit.

"Hey."

"I'm glad I found you." Leo quickly recovered from Tom's aloof greeting. "I…I don't know how much I should tell you, but I'm sorry, man. I can't stay for your wedding."

Tom nodded. He didn't need to yell or punch Leo again. He didn't need to let Leo off the hook either. He wasn't sure when or if he'd be ready to forgive the brother he'd chosen, but now was definitely not the time.

Clearly uncomfortable with the lack of follow-up questions, Leo rambled on. "Again, sorry to leave you in the best-man lurch, buddy."

"You're not the best man."

"I…what?" Leo chuckled nervously.

"You're not the best man," Tom repeated. "Not for me, and obviously not for her."

Tom didn't need to say which *her* he was referring to. Leo slumped, all bravado slipping.

An uneasy silence plunged between them. Tom made no move to speak. He had nothing else to say.

"For what it's worth," Leo began, raking his fingers through his hair before gaining the courage to look Tom in the eye. "I'm sorry."

"I don't think you are, Leo. And that's okay. I can't blame you for falling for someone I fell for too. But considering everything that's happened and everything you've kept from me, I'm not sure I can ever see you again." The words no longer stung quite so acutely; they felt right.

Without another word, Leo left. Tom didn't stay to watch him go. After all, he had a rehearsal dinner to get to.

Tonight Tom was going to absorb every detail. Everything he'd missed all the other times.

The first thing he noticed was the music. It was a song he'd put on a playlist for Megs in college, one they'd argued about the meaning of over bagels and cream cheese. Every time they heard the song afterward, Megs lovingly referred to it as "The Great Debate-Over-Bagels Song, or: How I Learned to Love Tom Despite How Wrong He Can Be."

The second detail he noted was also song-related: a sign at the entrance of their private room that said BETTER TOGETHER. He remembered strumming the Jack Johnson song on his ukulele and singing it to Megs. Before he could get too choked up, he turned his attention to all the guests who'd traveled here to wish the two of them well. He wandered through the tables, greeting relatives and friends, lingering a little longer at Paulina's and Hamza's seats so he could tell them just how much he'd appreciated their support and sanity over the years. Tell them that London, to this day, had been one of the best trips of his life.

When Paulina pulled him in for a hug, the baby hiccupped between them, a small comical miracle.

"I'm so nervous to be a dad," Hamza confessed. "But people keep saying kids are hilarious—sometimes by accident, sometimes on purpose—and that's getting me through."

An ache in Tom's chest pulsed, a mourning call for the kids he thought he'd one day have with Megs. The little one growing inside Paulina would've been his own child's playmate. Someone to make mischief with at family gatherings.

At the center of each table was a picture frame featuring a carefully selected photo of Tom and Megan: the two of them posing with the lion statues in Trafalgar Square; Megs, on the day they took possession of their SoHo apartment, trying to carry a large box that, on close inspection, revealed a folded-up Tom (only partially blurred by their laughing neighbor's fingers); Megs and Tom kissing on a Boston duck boat sightseeing tour; the outtakes from their engagement photo session that scandalously depicted Megs grabbing Tom's ass (that photo was placed at her grandparents' table, which made Tom laugh).

When had she had the time to go through twelve years of pictures? A prickle of guilt rippled up his spine. Because he knew he hadn't just abandoned her in the wedding planning; he'd abandoned her in a hundred different pocket-size ways.

His eyes were drawn to Megs as soon as she entered. She looked fresh, beautiful. Calm in a way she hadn't in ages. But he knew her so well, he could see the telltale signs that she'd cried before reapplying her makeup. Her nose always turned bright pink.

For a millisecond, before guests swarmed her, a thread connected them. Like those telephones made from tin cans and string. Time slowed as they each sent a message along.

We made it, it said. *Survived another day.*

If this was indeed a day to be their best, then this was going to be the rehearsal dinner *they'd* wanted, not the result of a million compromises.

Tom took his seat beside his mother. "Is Dad coming?"

"He's talking to your aunt Florence. Is this dinner really being served family-style?" When Tom nodded, the tiniest of shudders rippled through Carol.

"I've asked the kitchen to make you up a separate plate." Megan sat down on the other side of Tom.

Carol wasn't one to show emotion, but a small approving nod told Tom she appreciated Megs's thoughtfulness.

They'd never discussed his mom's debilitating germaphobia. Megs had obviously seen it on her own. It was a very Megs thing to do.

When he'd called off the wedding the first time, he hadn't actually sat down to make a ledger of all the things he'd miss about her. The list had formed on its own and now it seemed infinite.

"Ah, Tom. You're here." John loomed over the table, waiting to belittle his second son before sitting down. "I wondered if you were quitting *everything* today."

Before Tom could formulate a response or give Megs a reassuring look, Brody and Emmeline appeared. Tom stood to kiss Emmeline's cheek and give Brody a hug. "You okay?" he asked. Not because he was trying to do things right, but because he was seeing his brother for what he was: a facade of success covering a man who didn't know who he was.

"Fine, Spare Parts. Why? You wondering if I'll be needing any of your organs anytime soon?" Brody replied a little too loudly. Then he stage-whispered, "Has Mom said 'two planes and a ferry' yet?"

Megs stood to greet a very somber-looking Donna.

"I suppose if anyone's allowed to be late for the rehearsal dinner, it is the mother of the bride," Carol trilled.

"She isn't late, she's right on time." Megan delivered the polite but clipped response through a tight smile.

Had this been two days ago, Tom would've been sweating, worrying about juggling the many unpredictable personalities throughout the dinner. Tonight, Tom knew he was at a table of adults and he couldn't be responsible for arranging an armistice among them all.

But he could still stand up for what he believed.

"Ease up, Mom." Tom was keeping his voice low, though he felt Megs shift beside him.

"Watch your tone with your mother," John said, also keeping his volume low so as not to cause a scene.

"For years I've listened to you criticize my fiancée and her family." Tom's voice was steady. Grave. "That ends now. You'll treat them all with respect or you'll stop seeing us."

Tom heard Megs inhale sharply beside him and risked a glance at Donna, whose cheeks were flushed, eyes glassy with emotion. Brianna gave him a thumbs-up and mumbled something about glass houses.

Brody, meanwhile, gave him a small wink and appeared to be smiling behind his drink.

His parents said nothing.

As people found their seats, and salads began circulating, Tom stood, tapping a fork against his glass. The room hushed.

"We'd like to thank everyone for coming this weekend. Travel days, like relationships, are rarely smooth, and so we want to acknowledge the efforts you've made to get here."

"Two planes and a ferry!" Brody bellowed, raising his glass, clearly deciding he no longer had to wait for Carol before he could drink.

Tom raised his own glass good-naturedly to his brother. He scanned the room of family and friends before landing on the most important person. "Most of all, I'd like to thank Megs. There are a thousand details in this room that are a testament to her capabilities, her dedication to those who are lucky enough to be loved by her."

He smiled sadly at his once bride-to-be and saw the gratitude in the quirk of her mouth, the soft blush in her cheeks.

"Whatever happens, whatever else the universe has in store for me, I am grateful now for the journey I've taken to get here. For the many ways my partner of the past twelve years has taught me to be a better person, even if I didn't always listen."

A murmur of soft laughter rippled through the crowd and they applauded.

Tom took his seat just as John stood.

He felt his fingers grip his seat, his body on high alert, ready to interrupt or attack.

"My second son," John began, his impressive baritone carrying through the restaurant—this was a man who needed no utensil to get the crowd's attention—"has never been what I expected. Always trailing behind his older brother, Broderick, never making his own decisions—until he met Megan Givens, a young woman from a town in Montana who made him happier than we'd ever seen him."

In his peripheral vision, Tom saw Megs blush.

"I've given my son everything. Tonight I planned to announce I was even going to give him a house in Kirkwood, Missouri." There was a tittering among the crowd. "But then he stomped onto the golf course this morning and quit his job." He held a hand to the side of his mouth as though he were telling the crowd a secret. "I hear his boss is a real hard-ass."

The crowd laughed nervously.

"I will say, despite the audacity of his tone and the surprise I feel about Thomas leaving Prescott and Prescott, I'm proud of him. Because he is clearly determined to pave his own path. And he couldn't have a better woman at his side as he does it."

John raised his glass and the guests joined him, applauding.

He'd done it. Tom had finally gotten his dad's approval. He tried settling into the victory of the moment and was struck with a surprising epiphany: He didn't actually feel any relief. And perhaps this was the greatest gift his father could have given him today.

"Well, that was some speech." Brianna, who'd scurried off to lurk at Paulina's table, retook her seat. "A tad heteronormative at the end, but nice."

"Agreed," Megs said to her sister before raising an eyebrow at Tom. He was about to respond when Alistair walked in.

"It's sure quiet in here for a party! What'd I miss?"

Donna bolted to his side, weeping and calling him her baby.

Apparently whatever had happened to her over the course of the day had left her more emotionally unstable than usual.

Remembering Megs's accusation that he'd left her alone to deal with their families, Tom crossed the room to greet Alistair. Clasping his right hand firmly and sneakily guiding his shoulders with the left, he led Alistair and Donna to the table.

"You have no freaking idea what it took to get here," Alistair said, indicating his story of intrigue and terrible decisions was to follow.

"We don't, Al. But we're sure glad you're here. Let me get a plate started for you." Tom heaped food onto a dish, knowing that if Alistair's mouth was full, he'd be less likely to embarrass Megs.

She squeezed Tom's hand under the table.

Once again he got the strange feeling that even though they might have unlimited hours in this day, there wasn't enough time to fix everything that needed fixing, to say everything they needed to say.

But this day wasn't over yet.

CHAPTER THIRTY-SEVEN

MEGAN

THERE WAS NO perfect rehearsal dinner. If there was one thing Megan had learned over the course of this repetitive hell, that was it. And yet tonight had been the best version she could've hoped for. Every now and then, particularly when she caught her grandparents holding hands under the table, she let herself imagine the dinner as the beginning to her own happy ending. That one day she'd be holding the hand of someone she'd spent a lifetime with.

It occurred to Megan that *Begin as you mean to go on* wasn't the catch-all mantra she'd thought it was. Because beginning as you meant to go on was setting yourself up for stasis. Complacency. Her new mantra was *Do your best and fuck the rest*. Not as poetic, perhaps, though it had so far proven efficient.

Guests lingered over their desserts, mingling, discussing the wedding they anticipated the next day. A raw melancholy tugged at Megan's chest. Even if tomorrow arrived as it should, she knew there could be no wedding. The Tom and Megan who had agreed to pledge themselves to each other were not the same people who sat here now.

She made her way around the room, chatting with family

members, sharing jokes and anecdotes, all the while stealing glances at Tom.

Why did he have to look so devastating in that midnight-blue suit? She kept imagining running her fingertips along the collar of his dress shirt, nuzzling against his chest and smelling his familiar aftershave.

Between the day they'd shared in Sidney and the bold choices he'd made today, there was a newness to him. He was still the steady, sweet man she'd fallen for, but now there was an air of adventure, of unpredictability.

A 1990s R&B song came on that Megan and Brianna used to dance to in Donna's kitchen, using whisks and spatulas in place of microphones, and she caught her sister's eye.

"You never let me take the high harmony," Brianna teased.

"I know. Controlling little thing, wasn't I?"

"The mother I never had," she said with faux wistfulness. "You're still a controlling little thing, just with bigger boobs and a steady paycheck."

The fondness for Brianna that Megan had been rediscovering that afternoon blossomed. Her life might be riddled with unhealthy relationships, but that didn't mean she had to accept them as they were. And that's why she turned to her sister and said, "Want to take a walk?" and held her breath until Brianna said yes.

They took off their heels and made their way down to the docks to where *Happy Accident* was moored, correcting each other's reminiscences of summers past and laughing at who they'd been. They listened quietly to the trumpet music from the colors ceremony, sharing looks as they recalled the many nights they'd heard this same evening tradition as kids. She'd somehow missed it every other night.

"Do you think if Mom had been less of a lunatic, we'd be closer?" Megan asked her sister after the cannon shot boomed through the harbor, signaling the end.

"Maybe." Brianna climbed aboard the old sailboat, took a seat behind the helm. "But if Mom's a lunatic, that means you think I'm a lunatic too."

"What are you talking about?" Megan's surprise was genuine.

"Come on." Brianna gave Megan a light shove to the shoulder. "All those comments you make when you're trying to keep up with my dating life. You think I'm exactly like her."

"No, I don't." The words didn't feel right coming out of Megan's mouth, something Brianna picked up on.

"Yeah, okay. I'm sorry I couldn't be mature and self-possessed like you."

Megan didn't want to fight with her sister. Not tonight. Not perpetually. Without thinking about it she replied, "I'm sorry I came out of the womb a middle-aged woman."

Brianna laughed, breaking the tension. "You did."

"Someone had to be the mom in our house."

They grew quiet, likely reflecting on the same highs and lows. Yes, Megan and her sister had a lot of happy memories from their childhood. They also had plenty of memories that bordered on trauma.

"Whenever Mom cornered me to gossip about some horrid thing you'd done, I jumped right into that 'Isn't Megan So Up-tight' cesspool with her." Brianna rested her feet against the helm, pretending to steer with her toes. "I hate that I did that."

"You weren't the only one who fell for Mom's little gossip traps. But don't you think we were just so desperate for her attention, we took what we could get?" Megan turned to her sister. "We were kids, Bree. I'm actually pretty impressed with how we turned out considering what we had to work with."

Brianna laughed again, a little bitterly this time. "Yeah. Speak for yourself. I don't know if you've noticed, but my entire adult life has been a train wreck. And let's not even get started on my teens."

Megan thought about all the things Brianna had started only to quit them. The money she'd poured down the drain in an attempt to find a vocation she could stick with. Megan had been judging her sister rather than trying to help her find the root cause. To look after her.

"I don't know if Tom and I will be in that SoHo apartment for long," Megan said after a pause. "But I'd like to get you set up there, no matter where I end up. And if you need help with money..."

In the distance, yacht rock carried over, punctuated with far-away laughter and whooping. A group of weekend boaters were drunk and having a great time.

"I'm okay," Brianna eventually replied. "I don't know that I really want to be a filmmaker so much as I wanted..."

When she didn't continue, Megan gently prodded, "What?"

"God, this is so embarrassing." Brianna cast her eyes upward. They were glistening with tears. "I wanted to be less like Mom and more like you."

An incredulous bark of a laugh escaped Megan's lips. *"Really?"* Megan was touched. She never knew her sister had been turning to her, looking up to her, the same way Megan had looked up to Paulina.

Brianna shook her head. "We were raised in the same dys-functional house and yet somehow—I don't mean *somehow*, I know you worked hard—you wound up at an Ivy League school with a well-adjusted boyfriend who loves you. And then you got this cool artsy job at *GQ* and this apartment I've always wanted to move straight into. It just...I feel like a walking hot mess. Like you got all the shit-together genes and I ended up with the ones that made me a full-on disaster."

"I think it's obvious those disaster genes mostly went to Alistair."

The sisters laughed, full-bellied and free.

"You got to be the opposite of Mom," Brianna said, her voice thickening with emotion. "Leaving me to be like her."

"Hey." Megan put her arm around Brianna, overwhelmed by a sudden feeling of protectiveness. She could be Brianna's Paulina. She'd be honored. Their heads tilted toward each other. "What if you and I stop defining ourselves in relation to Donna Givens altogether and actually just try to be ourselves?"

"Not to be all emo"—Brianna blew her bangs out of her eyes—"but I'm not totally sure who that person is."

Megan's heart ached for her sister. "You're one of the funniest people I know. I wish I had your courage and sass. And whatever you decide to do, I've got your back."

Brianna sank into the hug before pulling away. "All right, all right, future Mrs. Givens-Prescott. That's enough nauseating honesty. Let's get you back to your party."

The first thing she saw when she finally arrived at the hotel suite was Tom looking more relaxed than he'd appeared in days. Perhaps even years.

He was seated at the table by the window, his sleeves rolled up to his elbows, sexy-sensible hair in place, carefully taking off his watch.

Looking at him, Megan imagined a world in which their lives hadn't imploded, this day hadn't repeated. A world in which they would've proceeded with the wedding as planned.

There would've been love and happy memories. But one day, they'd find themselves sitting wordlessly side by side at the dinner table, realizing they'd allowed themselves to become another John and Carol or Brody and Emmeline or Donna and Whoever, their lives full of what-ifs.

She knew then that, as excruciating as reliving this day had been, the repetition had saved them from something much graver. Mistakes they wouldn't ever have been able to correct.

It was time to say goodbye to Tom, time to truly let go of the life they'd imagined together.

"How was your day?" he asked her, still fiddling with the strap of his watch.

"Oh, you know." She shrugged, dropped her shoes in the front entrance, and joined him at the table. "I told my mother she needed to start solving her own problems and stop relying on men for validation. I bonded with Paulina, went for a hike, then made up with my estranged sister."

"Sounds eventful." He smiled at her, not bothering to cover the sadness in his eyes.

"What about you? A tall and litigious bird told me you quit your job."

"I did. That happened *after* I yelled at Brody to fix his marriage and stop being a dick to me and *while* I was yelling at my dad on the golf course for treating me like a citizen in his dictatorship."

She resisted the temptation to reach for his hand. Instead, she settled on the words "That must've been hard." *And long overdue*, she thought.

"I also said goodbye to Leo."

"What a coincidence, so did I." Suddenly nervous, she wished *she* had something to fiddle with. She reached for the heart pendant around her neck, remembering only when her fingers grazed her skin that she hadn't put it on. She continued. "This morning, when you said we should be the best versions of ourselves...I thought about that a lot. I don't think I've let myself be my best with you." Her words stung him; she could see that in the set of his jaw. But she needed him to understand.

"There was this ease with us, and yet the more we let the outside world in, let our families in, the more I let that outside world shape who I was. I was making decisions based on either this bottomless fear of turning into my mother or what your family wanted. I told myself you couldn't ever understand but I also didn't let you try. I hate that I couldn't just say, 'Donna messed me up and now I'm afraid to do anything even remotely spontaneous' or 'Hey, I'm feeling pushed out of all the decisions that actually affect our life together.'"

Letting go of everything, even briefly, to imagine a life with Leo had taught Megan that letting go wasn't necessarily what she wanted; that to get what she wanted, she had to face her fear of speaking up. Of allowing the messiness of life to gather and show.

"I get it," Tom replied. "I thought if I could be the peacekeeper, it would make things easier for everyone, but all I actually accomplished was making you feel like you weren't supported. And the whole thing was this misguided pursuit to get my father's approval. A man who said he was proud of me only *after* I yelled at him and quit his firm. It's pretty messed up."

They locked eyes. He stopped fiddling with his watch and set it on the table.

There was one question that had been burning within Megan all afternoon on her hike. She had to ask. "What if we had known this all along? What if, that first day I sat next to you in Natural Disasters, we'd been able to just be ourselves? Wholly and honestly?"

He leaned his elbows on his knees, drew a hand over his face. "I don't know."

Megan knew. She and Tom could've had something spectacular. In fact, they *had*, in a lot of ways.

But the damage was done and it was *also* spectacular.

She shook those thoughts free. She couldn't get caught on any more what-ifs.

"What are your plans for tomorrow should the actual tomorrow not arrive?" Tom asked.

Even if the repetition didn't stop, Megan had decided on her hike today that she would try to have some semblance of a life, one that began in the hotel bed but always continued away from the wedding that would never happen. "I think I'm done jumping through these rehearsal hoops, regardless of what day it is when I wake up."

"I figured. Me too."

She only wished this knowledge they'd fought for, that had come at such a price, wasn't for nothing. Because chances were, everything they'd done today wouldn't matter.

She walked over to the minibar, pulled out a tiny bottle of champagne, and poured it into two disposable cups. When she offered one to Tom, he raised it with her. "To not repeating our mistakes tomorrow," she said.

"Cheers."

CHAPTER THIRTY-EIGHT

TOM

DROPLETS OF RAIN broke free of the clouds to patter at the bay window. Tom and Megs sipped their champagne, the accompanying silence uncomfortable. Thinking through the mistakes he'd made over the years was like opening the flaps on the world's worst Advent calendar.

Still, every other time he and Megs had been in this room, they'd been arguing. To be able to sit with her and just be, even in an impossible situation, was its own salvation. He couldn't let the moment pass without saying something he still owed her. Sure, they'd covered a lot of ground while watching the sunset on that rock wall in Sidney. There was still one thing he needed her to know.

He turned pretty words over in his mouth but finally let the simplest combination fall out. "I'm sorry, Megs. I'm a bottomless pit of sorry."

It was an apology that required no qualifier, a shapeshifting thing that could be as small as she wanted it to be or as vast as she needed.

"I'm sorry too." A sweet sort of anguish touched her eyes as they finally reached an understanding.

There had been a lot of apologies between them in a lot of different loops, most notably yesterday, yet this one tasted different.

The *sorrys* they exchanged tonight weren't about airing grievances or confessing sins. They were about marking a path forward.

Or at least Tom's was.

The wind picked up and rain pelted the windows, offering cover; white noise to shield them from the outside world. He hadn't remembered it raining this hard on any other night. Maybe a sprinkle? This was a deluge.

"Oh no!" Megs suddenly exclaimed, getting up to look out the window. "The brides who are outside. Their wedding!"

"The ones who danced to 'And I Love Her'?" Tom asked.

Megs nodded.

"Great song."

"Great song," she agreed, just as she had in an earlier loop, though this time the exchange was warmer. "I see them…it looks like they're not letting this downpour ruin things—the whole wedding party's dancing around in it."

She let the curtains drop and sat back down at the table.

"Hey." Tom drained the rest of his warmish champagne and lightly tapped her hand on the table with his pinkie as he put the cup down. It was the smallest of gestures, an inkling of contact, and it only made him miss her…despite having her across from him. "Since there's no wedding tomorrow, can you tell me what song *we* were supposed to dance to?"

Their intention was to plan the wedding together save for a few details. Megs let Tom pick the destination of their honeymoon; he'd been Optimist Tom when he'd eyed the Amalfi coast, imagining them several time zones removed from work and family pressures. Tom let Megs choose the song they would dance to for the first time as a married couple. She'd insisted on total secrecy.

Of course, they hadn't actually done any wedding planning together.

"You would've been happy with my song choice," Megs said coyly.

"If you don't tell me what it is, I'll never find out." It was meant to be a playful comment.

Megs finished her champagne and slid her empty cup into his before tossing them into the recycling bin. She worried her bottom lip, sorrow in her eyes, although a pull at her mouth indicated she'd been pretty pleased with herself when she'd made the selection.

"I went with your favorite Cure song," she said, waiting until the end of the confession to meet his eyes. When she did, something in his chest exploded.

How could he let go of this woman forever? Tom knew it was time. He owed it to them both to take a risk. To bet on himself. On them.

Those private vows he'd written months ago—he still meant them; even more, they'd evolved and grown over the past several reincarnations of this day. The vows he'd say to her now would mean more. Because they knew each other better than they ever had.

"Seems a shame to let that blatant act of diplomacy go to waste." Tom got up, found "Pictures of You" on his phone, and turned up the volume.

The familiar dreamy guitar riff played, muffled slightly by the storm outside. He reached out to her, the bursting in his chest flickering like fireworks when she put her fingers in his palm.

He placed one hand on the small of her back, and they swayed, their bodies moving closer together in blissful habit, an attraction so familiar he hoped they'd still feel that pull when they were ninety. He wanted to feel it forever. He wanted *her* forever.

"Thanks for this," he murmured into her ear.

"Don't get too excited. The only reason I didn't go with *my* favorite is that the beat of 'Just Like Heaven' is too quick for a slow dance."

He chuckled softly; her head nuzzled into his in response.

The storm clouds outside obscured the stars. If Tom could, he'd move those clouds so Megs could have her starry sky. He'd stick plastic constellations onto every ceiling so she'd always have them above her head.

Whether it was Tom who made the first move or Megs, he didn't know; they seemed to make the decision together. Touching each other desperately yet with care because they knew they needed to one last time. To remember what it was to have the intimacy that was uniquely, spectacularly *theirs*.

Grazing a finger across her cheek because he was tired of not grazing a finger across her cheek. Pulling him closer because she was tired of not pulling him closer. It seemed to happen in a choreographed dance; first through their fingers, then arms, then bodies. Just as they had years ago at his beach house. He said, "Please, may I?" and she said, "What are you waiting for?" and then his fingers delicately unzipped her dress while hers slipped each button through its eye. As their touches became familiar, muscle memory they'd built up over so many years, their lips came together, hungrily.

When a clap of thunder startled them, they laughed softly— smiling as they continued to kiss, refusing to let go, to release this connection.

Being with Megs had never been just one color, one shade. It was heat, it was humor; sweetness and depth.

Clothes slid to the floor and his fingers raked through her silky hair. He promised himself he'd remember this, memorize every caress and feeling. The softness of her skin, the push of her kiss. The way her body opened to his, accepting him, wanting him, relishing him. He held her tighter and she gripped him in kind.

He couldn't imagine doing this with anyone else.

They came together, their climaxes shaking the earth. They rolled through the aftershocks together, her tears dipping into their kiss. Or perhaps those were his.

As the storm raged on outside their room, it was the perfect conclusion to a most imperfect journey.

DAY

8

CHAPTER THIRTY-NINE

MEGAN

MORNING TIPTOED SOFTLY in with the sun, as though someone were slowly turning up the dimmer switch. They'd forgotten to close the curtains last night. Megan rolled over, her feet cold, wrapping more blankets around her.

As she tugged at the sheets, there was an answering tug back from the other side of the bed. She opened one eye. And then the other.

Incredulity covered her like a mist, altogether startling and refreshing.

"Good morning." Tom stretched luxuriously and then froze, catching up to what Megan had already realized.

"We did it," she whispered.

"How can we be sure?" he whispered back as though their voices might crack this delicate discovery.

They both reached for their phones, showing each other the new day on their calendars.

"But how can we be sure?" Tom asked again, still whispering.

"Well, if it is the same day, then Donna's at least an hour late bursting in here and pitching a fit about her rehearsal-dinner dress."

They gave each other mini-high-fives before glee yielded to the gravity of a looming wedding. Despite how hard Megan had wished for the day of the rehearsal dinner to end, she hadn't quite worked out just what she'd do if her wedding day actually arrived.

Taking a deep breath, she leaned back onto her pillow. Tom mirrored her actions. Whenever Megan had a seemingly unsolvable problem rise up at work, she'd breathe, clear her mind, and wait for the brainstorm to come.

But instead of answers, all she saw were the dollar signs of their families' travel and event expenses, cash that might be a drop in the bucket for the Prescotts but for the Givenses side *were* the bucket.

She thought of the friends who'd taken time off work to come to the other side of the country, used portions of their hard-earned paychecks to buy wedding gifts.

She imagined the shocked faces that would fall, giving way to anger or tears or I-told-you-sos. Every messy imminent exchange, not to mention all the gossip.

"What do we do?" Tom asked, obviously full of the same questions.

"I don't know."

"Should we start telling everyone the wedding's off?" There was a small crack in his voice. She might have missed it if she hadn't been so close to him. If she didn't know him as well as she did.

Megan rolled to her side and took in his familiar profile, the cut of his jaw, the line of his forehead, the angle of his nose. She'd stared at this face for countless minutes over the years, never stopping to appreciate that one day she might not have his face to stare at. She searched his expression now for answers. Indicators.

"Yeah," she agreed, her own voice threatening to break. "I guess we should."

"Then we should probably get started. We've got a lot to do."

Tom swung his legs around and off the bed with great effort. He retrieved clean clothes from his suitcase, pulled on his briefs, his slacks. Slipped his arms through his shirt, taking care as he buttoned it closed.

Megan followed suit, because it seemed to be the thing to do. Get dressed. Close this chapter.

They brushed their teeth, avoiding each other's gaze in the mirror. When he left to give her a moment of privacy, she tried to feel anything but bottomless grief. She washed and dried her hands. Opened the bathroom door. And took a moment to stare at her former fiancé—the man she'd loved her whole adult life—seated at the table where they'd sipped champagne the night before so he could put on his socks and shoes and walk out of her life. Forever.

Life was a series of actions and consequences, coincidences and happy accidents (to borrow a phrase from her grandparents' sailboat). Over and over again, the past seven days had taught her what she was willing to let go of and what she wanted to keep.

What she wanted to *keep*.

A fondness for Tom broke through her until she was flooded with nothing but how much she loved him. Not based on nostalgia or the devil she knew. It was a feeling of seeing him in the light of a new day. It made her knees buckle.

Over the course of their relationship, she'd tried to be a good partner to him. Over the course of the last few days, she'd tried to be true to herself. Could there be a way to do both? To have both?

Because Megan suddenly knew that if she let him walk out now, she'd never forgive herself.

"Hey," she said softly, leaning against the door frame.

"Hey." He spared her a quick glance before returning to his shoes with extreme focus.

She wondered if he were trying very hard not to cry.

She took a seat beside him and rested her chin on her hands, willing him to look at her. "For a class called Natural Disasters, this lecture is pretty dull. Disaster-free, even."

He froze, only the smallest of smiles indicating he knew just what she was doing. He locked onto her with his gaze. "Have you ever noticed our professor looks like a nerdy version of the lead singer from the Cure?"

"I have." She nodded, then reached out, an invisible thread reaching out too, winding around their connected hands. "Megan, by the way."

"Hi, Megan By-the-Way. I'm Tom."

She snorted at his ridiculous joke, watching the flicker of familiar amusement dance in his eyes at the snort. "So, Tom. What's your favorite song by the Cure?"

He appeared to consider this. "Good question. I'm going to have to think on this. I mean, I'm partial to 'Pictures of You'... but I'm also willing to admit that 'Just Like Heaven' has its merits."

Megan leaned across him, her arms grazing his chest, and grabbed the notepad and pen on the side table where the phone lay. She scrawled some of the lyrics to "Just Like Heaven" onto the paper followed by something just as important. She ripped the top page off, folded it, and gave it to him.

"What's this?" A catch in his voice gave her all the hope she needed.

"It's my phone number, Tom." She swallowed, tamping down the emotion in her own voice so the next thing she said to him would be clear. "I'd really like to see you again."

He unfolded the paper, eyes gleaming with happiness as he read the lyrics and her number. He folded it back up, put it in his pocket, and looked up at her. "Well, now I know exactly what I want to do with this day."

Her heart beat against the pendant she'd been sure to put on that morning. "Yeah? And what's that?"

"I want to go wherever you're going."

ACKNOWLEDGMENTS

I've felt compelled to write for as long as I've been able to write. For years this was a solitary act. What a delight it was when I began pursuing this career in earnest to learn that writing doesn't have to be solitary at all. I am surrounded by some of the smartest and kindest people in the industry, which makes this dream-come-true all the sweeter.

Thank you to my editors, Helen O'Hare and Kimberley Atkins. Your enthusiasm and vision for this story from the very beginning made the process of revising it so painless. Working with you both has brought me such joy and I'm endlessly proud of how this book turned out. Thank you for believing in me and these characters.

I'm so grateful to the teams at Little, Brown and Hodder and Stoughton for championing this book and making my experience memorable, exciting, and everything I'd hoped it would be.

To the team at Alloy Entertainment: Les Morgenstein, Josh Bank, Sara Shandler, Joelle Hobeika, and Viana Siniscalchi...I will forever be grateful for your support and enamored with your creative minds. Viana and Joelle, you two have truly been my literary soul mates on this project and beyond.

Jess Dallow, my brilliant agent and friend, I am a better writer because of you. Thank you for your notes on this book and others, for being in my corner, for the care you take with my career...and for enthusiastically texting with me about television shows.

My coven: Sonia Hartl, Kelsey Rodkey, Andrea Contos, Auriane Desombre, Susan Lee, and Rachel Lynn Solomon—I love your books, your humor, your support, and all of you in general. I got lucky when I found you.

Two of my favorite writers and dear friends caught both me and this book early on when we were falling: Doctor Professor Author Jenny Howe and Jen "Gator Whisperer" DeLuca. Your words inspire me; your friendship nourishes me.

I'm fortunate enough to have writer friends and CPs who are as talented as they are wise and funny. Much love and gratitude to Roselle Lim (my life coach), Suzanne Park (my hoodie twin), J. R. Yates (my Monday writing buddy), and Milo Mowery (my fellow Aggie). Thank you to Jody Honywood, who may not be a writer but still held my hand through so much of this process.

Team Dallow, I appreciate the group celebrating and commiserating that has occurred through our ups and downs. You are all wonderful.

Much love to my Pitch Wars family, particularly the table-flippers of 2016. Thank you for the writing sprints and shenanigans. I sure like you weirdos.

My friends and family have provided so much support as I pursued this uncertain career path. There are too many to name, but I'm blowing kisses your way.

To my parents, Ray and Sally Pyne, who encouraged my lofty goals and gave me my quirky sense of humor: I love you both. Aren't you glad I didn't actually become an accountant? I'm terrible at math.

Paula Smith, I'm sorry your name isn't in thirty-two-point bold font here, but it is in my heart. Thanks for your continued encouragement. There's no one I'd rather eat pickles and cheese with.

My darling kids, G and A: I really hit the jackpot with you two. Being your mom has been one of the greatest pleasures of my life. Thanks for cheering me on and making me laugh (and for naming at least half of my characters).

And, of course, to that handsome man I married: I love you *and* I like you. I'm grateful to have you by my side through this and every journey.

Dear Reader,

I am delighted to share my debut novel, *The Rehearsals*, with you. It's a book that pairs perfectly with summer—as well as the conflicting emotions we're collectively experiencing as we try to figure out what life looks like now. I hope you find it a cathartic and entertaining read.

The seed of this story was nourished by my love of the West Coast (the beautiful San Juan Islands, specifically), my fascination with *Groundhog Day* (not to mention my childhood crush on Bill Murray), and my love of the "bottle episode" trope, in which a cast of characters is somehow trapped together, forced to face everything about themselves—good and bad—while they wait to escape. But above all, I was inspired by a thought that has followed me my entire life: How do you know which relationships are worth saving and which ones you should walk away from? Megan and Tom, the main characters in *The Rehearsals*, have to answer this question while the worst day of their lives—the disastrous day before their wedding—repeats over and over again. Hoping to escape this time loop, they make different choices each time, choices that force them to confront the dreams and desires of their pasts, and a few doubts about their future. Ultimately, these choices lead them to know themselves better, and to decide what they want the next chapter of their lives to look like.

I hope this book brings you comfort, makes you laugh, makes you feel, and maybe even makes you reflect on the choices that have rippled through your own life.

Sincerely,
Annette Christie

QUESTIONS AND TOPICS
FOR DISCUSSION

1. Megan and Tom met when they were freshmen in college. How do you think the course of their relationship, leading up to their wedding, might have been different if they'd met later? Or earlier?

2. The novel asks the question "Which relationships are worth saving and which need to be broken?" Which relationships were you really rooting for? Which relationships did you want to sever?

3. What role did the island setting play vis-à-vis the time-loop device?

4. Discuss the love triangle involving Megan, Tom, and Leo. How does it illustrate the inner turmoil Megan experienced about marrying Tom? In the end, did Megan choose the right partner? Was her cheating forgivable? Who would you have chosen?

5. Were you surprised by the trajectory of Tom's character arc, particularly with regard to his career? Why or why not?

6. The novel alternates between both Megan and Tom's perspectives. How did reading these two narrative strands

affect the way you understood their relationship? Did you relate more to one character or the other? How would the novel be different if it presented only one side to the story?

7. Where do you see Megan and Tom in five days? In five years?

8. Megan and Tom both had fraught relationships with their families. How did their struggles compare? How important do you think family background is to marriage?

9. Is there such a thing as the perfect wedding? Was there a way in which things could have worked out for Megan and Tom the first time around?

10. Megan and Tom didn't really fight or argue for the duration of their relationship—until the night of the rehearsal dinner. Do you think it's possible to have a healthy relationship without conflict?

11. If you were trapped in a time loop, how many "loops" would it take for you to throw caution to the wind and experience your own "anarchy reigns supreme" day, like Megan and Tom on Day 4? Do any of their approaches feel closer to your own choices than others?

12. Did you find the ending satisfying? If not, how would you have liked the book to end?

13. What do Megan's and Tom's favorite songs by the Cure reveal about their characters?

ABOUT THE AUTHOR

Annette Christie has a BFA in theater and a history of very odd jobs. The back of her head is featured prominently in the film *Mean Girls*. She currently resides in Phoenix with her husband and two children.

Keep reading for an excerpt from Christie's next novel, *For Twice in My Life*.

CHAPTER ONE

THERE IS A perverse pleasure in being able to pinpoint exactly where you've gone wrong in life. To take each failed moment and place it on your memory's mantel, only to be examined in your darkest hours: on Sunday afternoons, when the rain is coming down like sheets and you can't stop listening to Frank Sinatra singing "In the Wee Small Hours of the Morning"; or in the middle of the night when insomnia is your only friend and, quite frankly, he's a bit of a dick. Or, perhaps, when you are on the verge of making another grave mistake and you aren't sure you can stop yourself.

At least, that was Layla Rockford's experience. And right now her apartment was one big reminder of everything she'd lost. Of *him*. She dreaded being there as potently as she craved its hidey-hole comforts. And yet that was where she was headed. Because these days, when work was over, there weren't a lot of other options. She couldn't bear the thought of being at a restaurant surrounded by couples. Or being at a bar surrounded by couples. Even Sunday dinner at her parents' house meant being surrounded by *couples*, which was why she'd been opting out for the past two weeks.

She sped up, the wool pants she'd chosen for work that morning itching her legs. In their original glory, they'd had a satin lining. She'd seen the remnants of the shimmery pink fabric when she bought them at her go-to vintage store in Belltown and vowed to repair them. It hadn't happened yet. She silently promised her itchy legs she'd tear those pants off and throw them to the back of her closet as soon as she made it home.

Layla dodged a teenage couple making out under the awning of a coffee shop, and her heart hiccupped.

Thinking about Ian was like pressing on a bruise. A dull, familiar pain washed over her.

She sidestepped as a man in a suit traveled by on a Segway, his ponytail flapping. Ian had been keeping track of their Segway Man sightings. If he were here, he would've turned to her, a twinkle in his eye, and mouthed *twelve*. She could picture it: his single, playful dimple flickering as he smiled, his blond hair ruffling in the coastal breeze. Layla would've then reminded Ian that when they got to twenty, they'd agreed to go on one of those Seattle Segway tours, and Ian, laughing, would've protested that he'd never agreed to those terms, and she'd have reached for his hand...

She didn't know why she was still counting. The number didn't matter anymore.

Layla arrived at her apartment building, fifteen stories of brick stacked up to the overcast sky. She sighed, using her key card to buzz through the main entrance (and rode the elevator that made just a little *too much* noise but not quite enough to try to track down the super) up to the eighth floor, avoiding her own eyes in the mirrored door. She got off, unlocked her studio apartment, and heaved an even greater sigh.

It was a space her best friend from work, Pearl Kaes, had referred to as The Museum—back when Layla had dusted and vacuumed regularly. Not just because it was clean, but because everything inside had been carefully curated and placed just so. Ian had helped Layla make sure of that.

To give the impression that there was some separation between her bedroom and her living room and her kitchen, Layla had put up lovely antique dividers that Ian had gamely helped her carry home from a flea market—dividers that were currently closed and leaning against the far wall so Layla could more easily watch TV from her bed. Ian had also encouraged her to hang her large mirror with the art deco frame by the stub-wall galley kitchen, to create the illusion of space where, quite frankly, there was none. It'd also caught the light from the lone kitchen window. It'd been a great idea.

These days, the mirror was covered in multicolored Post-it notes proclaiming self-affirmations. And The Museum looked as if it'd been looted: clothes were strewn over every piece of furniture; her mail had become a small mountain, overtaking the entry table once carefully placed by the door; the coffee table was currently host to a peanut butter jar with a spoon sticking out of it *and* a Nutella jar with a spoon sticking out of it (and a jar of raspberry jam, for which, regrettably, she'd had to move on to the forks).

Layla pulled her vinyl copy of Ella Fitzgerald's greatest hits out of its sleeve and was about to put the needle down on the record when her phone rang. Seeing *Mom* on the caller ID, she felt a familiar wash of conflicting emotions. Layla swiveled the record player's needle back to its resting place and put the call on speaker. She flung her purse—and then herself, facedown—onto her bed, trying to shimmy out of the offending pants despite the awkward position.

"Hey." Layla turned her head to the side so her voice wouldn't be muffled by her unmade sheets and attempted to sound perkier than she felt.

"There's my girl!" No matter how often Layla spoke to her mom, Rena always greeted her as though they had just been reunited after years of being separated by some godless tragedy. It was one of the best things about her mom. But today her mom's enthusiasm was sounding forced, which engaged Layla's familiar guilt complex.

Meanwhile, Layla's orange tabby cat, Deano Martini Rockford, hopped on the bed, purring, and parked himself on her butt. Perfect. The pants she'd been trying to shimmy off stayed on. She'd adopted Deano after moving out of her parents' place (for the second time, because living by herself had been surprisingly lonely). And when she'd seen him on the website for the local shelter, he'd looked surprisingly lonely, too. How could she have known that behind his big, soulful eyes lurked a manipulative misanthrope who demanded love on unpredictable terms?

"How was your day?" Layla asked, still lying down. "You mentoring the next Jerry Lee Lewis yet?"

Rena was a part-time piano teacher, a saint of a woman who could listen to the atonal plunkings of children all day and still put her arm around their little shoulders to tell them they were really coming along. She'd tried to teach Layla, but Layla had never had the patience to practice. Instead, she'd preferred to tap-dance around the piano, making up lyrics while her mom played the tune.

"I hope not," Rena said. "You know as well as I do that Jerry Lee Lewis was a pervert."

Layla let out a surprised laugh, a bit strangled by the now-constant tightness in her throat. Deano, irritated by this disruption, let out a disgruntled meow and hopped off Layla. Somehow, despite never being more than ten feet from his water bowl, he still managed to sound like a lifelong smoker whenever he was displeased.

"You okay, honey?" The concern in her mother's voice, so familiar to her—and so upsetting *because* it was so familiar— sharpened the ache in Layla's chest.

With Deano gone, Layla successfully removed her wool pants and grabbed a pair of nearby sweats with her toe, bending her knee to fling them onto the bed, where she could better reach them with her hands. She slid them on.

"Mm-hmm," Layla replied, not trusting her mouth to open without letting out an embarrassing sob. Desperate to change the subject, to not have to discuss the Ian-shaped hole in her heart with her mom, she said, "That guy came into the theater again."

"Which guy?"

"The one who goes to the bar next door every day—"

"But sometimes chooses the wrong door?" Rena supplied. "Oh dear. What did he walk into?"

Layla worked for Northwest End, a sleeper theater company in downtown Seattle that had been around for ages. Northwest had been chugging along with a small but loyal following, one killer review away from really breaking into Seattle's bustling art scene. Or one *bad* review away from shutting off the lights, although no one wanted to think about that. Layla's job title was technically office administrator, but most days she thought of herself as the human fire extinguisher. Usually the fires were figurative—the exception being at that cast party last year when an actor had decided to show everyone just how flammable powdered coffee creamer was. The answer: *very*. Powdered coffee creamer was *very* flammable. Luckily, Layla was in charge of getting the theater's *actual* fire extinguishers checked every year and knew exactly where they were.

"We were striking a set, so all the furniture and fake walls were being dismantled," Layla went on. "He couldn't stop yelling, *'What the hell happened to the bar?'*"

Rena chuckled softly. Appreciating that her mom really was her best—and right now, only—audience, Layla sat up and continued. "It took me ten minutes to convince him to head next door."

"I'm sure he was relieved when he made it."

"Yeah." Layla's smile faltered.

As though Rena could hear it happen, she asked, "How are

you *really?* You've missed the last two family dinners—and I know the theater's been keeping you busy, but I know things have been tough since—"

The lump in Layla's throat caught between her words when she lied. "I'm sorry. There's just been so much going on."

The truth was, she couldn't go to Sunday dinner with her family. Not when that meant being squashed at the same table as her four siblings and their four partners. Not when that meant fielding their insensitive questions about why Ian had ended things (she didn't *know* why). And not when that meant letting her parents see how miserable she was, which would make them worry about her, about her future, about her behavior, all over again.

So Layla had opted to avoid the whole thing. She'd opted to stay home, drink something called Chardon-*yay!* straight from the bottle, and hang out with her grumpy cat.

"Well, do you need help with anything?" Rena persisted. "We miss you. Can I volunteer at your theater and ease things that way? Or maybe you need some help paying bills?"

Shame blazed Layla's cheeks. Her mother's automatic assumption that she was in financial trouble was a ghost that would forever haunt her. She sat straight up, insulted.

But also. In relation to the Sunday Chardon-*yay!*, she had indeed done a *teensy* bit of online shopping.

"I'm fine," she insisted, kicking two boxes of recently purchased go-go boots and a hatbox containing a 1940s fascinator under her bed and out of her own view. "Work's fine, finances are fine, it's all fine."

There was a pause. Uncomfortable, yet totally reasonable considering Layla had just snapped. But she did not have the bandwidth to keep pretending when every moment was punctuated with missing Ian.

"I should go feed Deano." Layla closed, then opened her eyes to look at her cat, who yowled in reply. He barely knew his own name, but the darn creature was more than well acquainted with the words "food," "feed," and, more bafflingly, "frangipane" (this one thanks to Layla's addiction to *The Great British Baking Show*). If he didn't get some kibble within seconds of hearing any one of those f-words, he'd riot.

"You'll be at Sunday dinner, right? You're not going to miss three weeks in a row, are you?"

"I'll be there," Layla said, already flipping through a series of reasonable excuses she could use to get out of it once the time came.

There was an audible sigh of relief from her mom. "I'm so glad. Have a good week, honey. We'll talk soon."

"Yep. You too." Layla summoned enough energy to return to the record player and start Ella's crooning, then meandered the short distance to the kitchen. She filled Deano's bowl and began opening drawers at random, pretending to decide what to make herself for dinner, knowing that she was definitely going to resort to one of the frozen pizzas with Paul Newman's smug face on the box. Even on cardboard the man knew he'd always have his soul mate, his beautiful Joanne.

On her way to the fridge, she tripped over Deano *and* a teal-green velvet slingback shoe he'd apparently pulled out of her closet and was now batting around on the kitchen floor.

And, just like that, she stumbled off the curb of missing Ian, and into the black hole of the night they'd met.

Layla had first laid eyes on Ian Barnett at Winston & Tux, a chic rooftop bar overlooking South Lake Union. After pointing out Ian—tall, blond, handsome, smiling Ian—Pearl had dared Layla to pick him up without saying a single word. But Layla had only just moved back out of her parents' house in Bellevue, had finally downgraded her financial situation—from the high-concept horror of having enormous credit card debt on top of her college debt to the more low-key horror of *just* having college debt—and her heart was only starting to feel like it might have room for something romantic. She was about to remind Pearl she wasn't looking when two guys, dangerously close to the balcony's edge, started to give each other little shoves, punctuated with syllables that didn't sound much more sophisticated than "Bro," "S'up," and a high-pitched, "You want this? A piece of this?"

"Maybe we should get out of here," Pearl had suggested. She was bored by even the scent of toxic alpha conflict. Layla wasn't interested in witnessing any barbarianism either and, under different circumstances, she would've paid her tab in a rush and bolted.

But in that moment, her feet, which were housed in the 1960s teal-green velvet slingbacks she loved so much, were stuck to the spot. She couldn't look away from the tall stranger who had stepped in to gently push the bros apart.

She saw in the globe string lights scalloped overhead that his carefully parted hair was more of a sandy blond than a *blond* blond. She saw that his sculpted jaw must've been formed in the palm of Zeus himself.

She was struck, beyond his Instagram good looks, by his demeanor; the way he took control and spoke with authority, until the bros looked sufficiently chastised. And then one had wiped at his eyes and pulled in the other, who mere seconds ago had been his mortal enemy, for a whiskey-scented hug.

The tall man had clapped the bros on the back as though to congratulate them for choosing *not* to be Neanderthals, and then, turning away, locked eyes directly with Layla. Her debt, her worries, her fresh start—none of it mattered. Layla knew this was fate.

"Go get him," Pearl whispered.

As though in a trance, Layla grabbed a semi-soggy cardboard coaster off the table and scrawled, "Thanks for saving us all, hero," followed by her phone number. She'd strode toward him, as sexy and smooth as she'd ever been in her entire (back then) twenty-eight years of existence, slipped the coaster into his hands with one gentle squeeze, then turned around and walked away.

It felt as though the room had stilled, the rowdy crowd parting to let her return to her table with grace and ease. Reaching Pearl, Layla released the breath she'd been holding, letting her smile fall just enough to whisper, "Let's go before I pee my pants from nerves." Pearl had laughed, delighted and proud, and grabbed their purses.

Ian had called the following day and asked her to go to Bite of Seattle, the summer food festival. If she'd been intrigued by him at the bar, she was fully smitten at the festival. It had been overwhelmingly crowded, and he'd offered to hold her hand so they didn't lose each other. Her palm tingled where her skin met his. He was everything all her exes hadn't been: considerate, attentive, kind. She'd felt safe with him. *He's the type of guy you call in a crisis*, she remembered thinking as they visited booth after booth, eating until she was sure she'd pop. *The guy who would drive you to the airport at five in the morning.* Here was a guy who would hold her heart in his hands carefully, who she could trust to not chuck it and run.

But in the end, he'd done just that. And she still didn't understand why.

They'd had almost two precious years together, years that were easy and sweet. But then two weeks ago it had all come screeching to a halt. They'd gone to a tiny Italian bistro to have dessert for dinner. Layla should have known there was something wrong because Ian was barely touching the tiramisu and kept only dabbing his spoon toward the bowl of gelato. Normally he'd be checking his work email when there was a lull in the conversation or a quiet moment between them—he worked in finance, and his clients were relentless—but he wasn't even looking at his phone. He didn't seem to be looking at anything at all. *He's having an off night*, she remembered reasoning with herself. *Who doesn't have off nights?*

But when they'd pulled up to his building, and she'd parked in one of the guest spots in his tree-shaded lot, he'd turned to her, grave. Instead of grinning, asking her to come up as on any other night, he'd simply said, *"I love you, Layla. I've loved being with you. But we've been trying for so long to make our schedules work and we still barely see each other. My hours are endless, and yours are sporadic. Doesn't it feel like we're trying too hard? That it shouldn't be this hard?"*

She was embarrassed, now, to remember how her chin had trembled, at least a three on the Richter scale, when she'd replied, *"You're breaking up with me because you don't see me enough? So now you don't want to see me at all? That doesn't make any sense."*

He'd apologized, he'd agreed, but he hadn't changed his mind as he climbed out of her car, settling the seat belt carefully before closing the door. She'd become breathless and speechless, and here she was, two weeks later, still both.

Layla picked up the green slingback. She considered throwing it out the window. She considered lovingly wrapping it in tissue and donating the pair to a secondhand shop. In the end, she carefully put it back in her closet.